ZADDIK

DAVID ROSENBAUM

THE MYSTERIOUS PRESS

Published by Warner Books

A Time Warner Company

For Sarah
"Hot a Yid a vaybeleh
Hot a vayb a Yideleh . . ."

MYSTERIOUS PRESS EDITION

Copyright © 1993 by David Rosenbaum
All rights reserved.

Cover design by Tom Tafuri
Cover illustration by Dru Blair

The Mysterious Press name and logo are registered trademarks of Warner Books, Inc.

 Mysterious Press books are published by
Warner Books, Inc.
1271 Avenue of the Americas
New York, NY 10020.

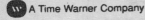 A Time Warner Company

Printed in the United States of America

Originally published in hardcover by The Mysterious Press.
First Printing in Paperback: August, 1994

10 9 8 7 6 5 4 3

Acknowledgments

I WOULD LIKE TO ACKNOWLEDGE THE FOLLOWING BOOKS AS sources for *Zaddik*: Martin Buber's *Tales of the Hasidim*, both volumes; Solomon Poll's *The Hasidic Community of Williamsburg*; Mark Zborowski and Elizabeth Herzog's *Life Is with People*.

Hebrew prayers in the text are taken from the *Ha-Siddur Ha-Shalem*, translated by Philip Birnbaum. Citations of Jewish law are from the *Kitzur Shulhan Arukh*, by Rabbi Solomon Ganzfried, translated by Hyman E. Goldin. Yiddish orthography is from the *Transliterated English-Yiddish Yiddish-English Dictionary*, by D. M. Harduf.

For their knowledge and support, I would like to thank Gary Callahan, Fred Feldmesser, Stacey Fredericks, Sergeant Margot Hill, Andy Irving, Wayne Kabak, Larry Katz, David Maisel, Bill Malloy, J. B. Nayduch, Carl Oglesby, Helen Rees, and Cantor Ellen Stettner.

No, he hasn't come in to work on Friday. Was that un-

Prologue
Brooklyn, 1954

EVERY SUNDAY, WHEN HE WAS FIVE YEARS OLD, DOV TAYlor's grandmother Rebecca would take him on the subway to visit his *tante* Lecha, who was very old and very lonely. They would ride the elevated from Borough Park to Williamsburg, and Dov would sit next to Rebecca, a large, soft woman, at that time sixty-three. One Sunday, as the train clattered along the rails, Rebecca told Dov a story.

Rebecca and her husband, Dov's grandfather Sam, were crossing the border into Rumania from Bessarabia, fleeing the Bolsheviks. Sam, who at first had helped the Bolsheviks by visiting Jewish towns to urge the people to give food and lodging to the Red Army, had decided that the Communists were as anti-Semitic as the tsar. He had decided that he and his young bride could have no future in Russia.

It was dark as Sam and Rebecca crossed the frozen earth of a potato field, but they could see a lone figure approaching. There was no place to hide, and there was no turning back, so they continued walking until the figure raised a rifle, pointed it at them, and told them they were under arrest.

The young soldier marched them through the night for an hour or so until they came to a small shed in the woods.

Outside, another young soldier crouched over a small fire, heating a pan of water for tea.

"I have two people here," the first soldier said. "Put them in the shed and guard them while I get the major."

The second soldier stood up and motioned Rebecca and Sam into the shed while the first soldier went off.

The shed was a simple, windowless structure with an earthen floor, no more than six feet square. It was just a rude shelter for the soldiers. There was no place to sit, so Sam and Rebecca stood with their arms around each other, shivering from the cold, frightened that at best they would be beaten, robbed, and sent back. At worst they would be killed.

They did not speak. Rebecca felt protective of Sam, who was a small, slender young man. He had a grave manner and the smallest, whitest feet she had ever seen. She remembered how on her wedding night she had peeked under the sheets while Sam slept and seen how her own feet looked enormous next to Sam's. Their marriage had, of course, been a *shidukh*, arranged, but at that moment she had begun to love him.

Now Rebecca called out to the soldier: "It is cold in here, sir, and for a cup of tea we would be most thankful. We have some money, and we would pay anything."

"How much money do you have?" asked the young soldier—who was really no more than a boy—pressing his cheek against the shed's wooden door.

"I have a diamond," said Rebecca. "It belonged to my mother. It's very beautiful and very valuable."

Sam was furious. "He will just come and take all our jewels," he whispered.

Before leaving Russia, Sam had turned most of their money into diamonds, which were easy to carry, easy to hide, and far more negotiable than scraps of paper bearing the tsar's picture. "You stupid woman," Sam hissed. "Maybe we could have bribed this major to let us go. Now we are lost."

The door swung open. "Give me the diamond," the young soldier said to Rebecca, "and I will give you some tea. But if you tell anyone about this, I will kill you."

"Of course," said Rebecca. "Thank you, kind sir. I have it right here."

And then she threw herself at the soldier, her weight driving him hard against the shed's wall. She put her hands around his throat and squeezed. The soldier tried to lift his rifle, but Rebecca's body pinned his gun arm against the wall. With his free hand he punched Rebecca's shoulders, but her heavy coat absorbed the blows. He struck the back of her head, but she didn't feel it. All she could feel was the soldier's Adam's apple beneath her thumbs.

Rebecca squeezed harder as the soldier dropped his rifle and tried to pull her hands away from his throat. She squeezed harder still as his body bucked against the wall. He let himself slide to the floor, and Rebecca fell on top of him, still squeezing as she watched his eyes grow wide and the spit fly from his lips as he tried to curse her. She brought her elbows close to her body to get her weight behind her hands, trying to crack that little walnut of an Adam's apple.

The soldier shook his head from side to side, and his body heaved up and down. Rebecca began to hum, as she did when she sewed or when she massaged one of her patients, for, indeed, in Russia she had been a nurse. And the thought entered her mind that it was a blessing from God that she had such strong hands.

The soldier's eyes were popping out of his head, his face a dark purple. Rebecca could no longer feel his breath against her cheek. Then the walnut cracked and blood belched out of the young soldier's mouth and ran from his eyes down his cheeks. Rebecca straightened her arms and then she jerked back, lifting the soldier's head and smashing it back down on the frozen earth. She did this two, three times until she felt his neck muscles go loose. She imagined that his flesh would begin to ooze through her fingers like dough.

After a little while, Rebecca's hands began to cramp. She let go of the soldier's throat and stood up. "Let's go before the other murderer comes back," she said to Sam, who was staring at his young bride in astonishment.

They stayed in the forest that night, hugging each other for warmth, and they stayed there throughout the next day. When the sun went down, they slipped across the border to Rumania.

"So, your grandmother killed a soldier with these hands," Rebecca told Dov Taylor, who would grow up to be a policeman, a homicide detective.

As the train pulled into the East Third Street station, Rebecca said, "God will punish me. You hear me, Dov? God will punish me. But if I didn't do it, there would be no Dov because your mother would never be born.

"Come, let's go. Remember to kiss your *tante* Lecha. She loves you."

They walked down the iron stairs from the elevated train to the street, and Dov thought he would not kiss Tante Lecha, who was old and ugly. She was skinny, not like Rebecca, and her hands were like a chicken's feet. Worst of all, she had one eye that was all white. It had no eyeball because, as Rebecca had once told him, when the Nazis took her away in the train, a cinder from the tracks had flown up and stuck in her eye, and she had rubbed it and her eye had died.

Rebecca and Dov walked up the stairs to Lecha's apartment. Dov watched his feet leave marks in the soot. It was so dirty here, he began to cry.

"Why do you always cry when we visit Lecha?" Rebecca asked angrily, tugging at Dov's hand, dragging him up the stairs. "It hurts her, and she is an old woman who will die soon and just wants a kiss."

"I hate her," said Dov.

"You murderer," said Rebecca. "You Gypsy. Where did your mother find you?"

They stopped in front of Lecha's door, and Rebecca fumbled inside her black velvet purse for the key. Around her shoulders she wore a fur wrap with the head of a small animal with red marbles for eyes and pointy white teeth. "Tomorrow," whispered Rebecca, "we'll go to Coney Island. But only if you give Lecha a kiss."

Rebecca opened the door. Lecha sat by the window. She turned her milky eye to Dov.

"Rivkah," she said. "Doveleh. Give your aunt a kiss."

Dov crossed the room slowly and grudgingly kissed Lecha on her yellow cheek, his lips brushing the sharp black hairs that grew from a mole above her lips.

"That's a kiss?" Rebecca scolded lightly. She sat down, and she and Lecha began talking in Yiddish. Dov sat down on a big purple chair. A train roared by, and dust blew through the open window.

He felt guilty and angry. Maybe someday he would kill all the Nazis in the world, and then God would forgive him for finding Tante Leche disgusting. My grandmother is a murderer, Dov Taylor thought. Maybe someday I'll be a murderer, too.

BOOK
ONE

1

Forty-seventh Street, Manhattan
Friday, September 3
The Present

THE CUTTER EMERGED FROM THE SUBWAY ON FORTY-
seventh Street and Sixth Avenue. Like many of the men
coming out of the ground with him that autumn afternoon, he
wore the *bord un payes*, the beard and sidelocks, that marked
the ultra-observant Hasidic Jew.

But he was not a Hasid.

Like the men around him, he was headed for a small office
in the largest diamond market in the world.

But his business was quite different from theirs.

In his right pocket, instead of a little parcel of sparkling
stones, a diamond loupe, or a prayer book, was the knife that
he had spent the long night sharpening. And during that long
night, he had pondered the question: Could good come from
evil?

Didn't the Holy One drown the Egyptian hosts in the Red
Sea? Didn't He smite their firstborn? Didn't Jael cave in
Sisera the Canaanite's head with a hammer? And didn't all
Israel call her a heroine?

So didn't God Himself use evil to achieve His ends?

When the Cutter was a child in the camps, didn't the old
rabbi tell him that God was testing His people? That the death
all around him was a prelude to the coming of the Messiah?

As a member of the Irgun in 1947, fighting for the unborn state of Israel, wasn't the dynamite holy that the Cutter used to blow up the King David Hotel? Didn't Menachem Begin himself, then a terrorist, later the prime minister, tell the Cutter, then barely in his teens, that those English soldiers who had died in the blast were small potatoes, of no consequence? That the Cutter had struck a blow for the land of Israel?

And all those throats he had cut for Branch 40 of the Mossad, the Israeli secret service's covert operations arm, wasn't that blood shed to keep His children safe?

And wasn't his current errand like those? Weren't these Hasidim a cancer on the body of Israel?

The Cutter felt himself floating above his body. He watched himself—a tall, pale, hollow-cheeked figure—glide past the Merchant's Bank of New York, past the shops with the signs in their windows: "Discount Solitaires," "We Buy Old Silver and Diamonds," "Diamond and Jewelry Appraisal." He passed Coopers & Jacobs, Sideman's, Freeman's, and Katz's Jewelry. He saw himself moving through the crowded, narrow street, surrounded by bearded men in black coats who looked like ghosts from some nineteenth-century ghetto. They were Orthodox Jews and Hasidic Jews, Forty-seventh Street's diamond dealers, diamond buyers, diamond brokers, diamond cutters, diamond polishers, and diamond setters. They pushed their way down the street, their heads down, the little black leather purses they carried containing hundreds of thousands of dollars' worth of gems. They huddled in twos and threes, meeting old friends and making new ones. Gossiping. Doing business. Buying and selling. Keeping the stones—"the goods," as they called them—moving. Making profits both large and small. It was called *hondeling*, bargaining.

But the Cutter had not come to Forty-seventh Street this morning either to buy or to sell. He had not come to bargain. He was as implacable as the Angel of Death.

See me move, the Cutter thought to himself. Weightlessly. Unnoticed. This is because I am a dead man, a *golem*.

Now the Cutter remembered the voice of his old friend,

the man he thought of as the Magician, speaking to him out of the darkness, speaking in a soft, cultured voice with just a trace of Poland: "You have killed many times, my friend. You have killed for your God. You have killed for your people. You have killed for your country. Now you will kill for me, and this killing will redeem you.

"You are my *golem* now," the voice said. "My soul shall dwell in you. My will shall be your will. Your eyes shall be my eyes. Your hands shall be my hands. And together we will save you."

The Cutter paused before the glass door at 52 West Forty-seventh Street. On the side of the entrance was a brass plate engraved with the names of the merchants: Alvarez Jewels, Midtown Jewelers, Union Diamonds, Gottleib Gem Stones. The plate listed scores of dealers big and small, most in tiny, grubby offices containing thousands of sparkling stones in every color of the rainbow. An unassuming building filled with riches.

The Cutter checked his left pocket. There was the rope. His right hand touched the knife. His thumb caressed the cool blade. He imagined how it would gleam when he took it out. It will shine, he thought, like the full moon in the desert sky. It will glitter, he thought, like fresh blood in the moonlight.

I will do this, thought the Cutter, so that good cannot help but come from it. I will do this so that the court in heaven will find me as innocent as the lamb. I will do this like my father, the *shoykhet*, the ritual slaughterer. This killing, he promised himself, I will do *kosher*.

The Cutter entered the building.

2

Forty-seventh Street, Manhattan
Friday, September 3

The last day of Zalman Gottleib's life began as he took the elevator down to the vault beneath 52 West Forty-seventh. In the safe-deposit box in his compartment of the vault was five thousand dollars in hundreds—the day's working capital—and scores of little glassine envelopes containing the hundreds of stones that made up his current inventory. There was also one small locked box.

A short, round, balding Hasid in his early seventies, a widower with an unkempt, wiry gray beard, Gottleib specialized in side stones, the small diamonds of unusual cut that were used to set off bigger, more significant stones in rings and bracelets and necklaces. Today, among his other business, Gottleib was expecting a visit from a dealer with a seven-carat D flawless square-cut diamond. If the stone was what the dealer said it was—which Gottleib doubted both out of habit and because he had never before met or done business with this man, who had come recommended by a diamond setter Gottleib knew slightly—it would be worth about $7,500 a carat. The dealer had told Gottleib over the phone yesterday that he wanted to turn his gem into a ring, and he would need two side stones, either half-moons or trillions, triangles.

Gottleib loaded his goods into the black leather purse that was once his father's and slipped the small locked box into his pocket. But on his way up to his fourteenth-floor office, Gottleib yielded to a sudden impulse and punched the button for the ninth floor.

Ariel Levin's office was no larger than a closet, and it contained Levin—a short, muscular young Israeli with curly hair and a colorful knitted *kippa*, or *yarmulke*, who for the past two years had turned many of Gottleib's stones into gold and platinum rings—a desk, and a large safe. After being buzzed in (most of the offices in the diamond district were secured by double-locked doors), Gottleib greeted Levin and thrust the small locked box into his hands. "I don't want to hold this today," he said in English. Levin, like most young Israelis, spoke no Yiddish, and Gottleib would never discuss secular matters in Hebrew, the holy tongue. "Just a feeling. For me, keep it this weekend, okay?"

"Sure, Zally," said Levin, putting it into his safe.

"You want to know what is it?" Gottleib asked.

"If you want to tell me," said Levin.

"I'll pick it up Monday," Gottleib said.

Feeling somewhat relieved, Gottleib got off on the fourteenth floor and walked down the hall to the office he shared with Morris Schumach.

Sometimes Gottleib went partners with Schumach when one or the other came across an expensive stone on which they thought they could turn a profit, but mainly they went their separate ways and split the exorbitant $5,000-a-month rent typical of the diamond district. They also shared a buxom, red-haired secretary, Shirley Stein, whose main job, it seemed to Gottleib, was to read magazines.

"Good morning, Shirley," said Gottleib, not looking at her because, once again, the combination of her large breasts and her tight sweater, not to mention the fact that she was divorced and lived alone, offended Gottleib's sense of propriety.

I should fire her, he thought, not for the first time. But how can I? She was the sister of the daughter-in-law of Reb Oppen of Crown Heights. And even though, in Gottleib's view, Reb Oppen was far too liberal and careless about *halakhah*, Jewish law, he was still a friend of Reb Klein, whose sister was the Satmarer *rebbetzin*, the wife of Rebbe Joel Teitel, the Satmarer *rebbe*, may his light shine.

Gottleib glanced up at the picture of Rebbe Teitel framed on the bookshelf. Rebbe Teitel was no mere rabbi. He was *the rebbe*, the spiritual leader of thousands of God-fearing

Satmarer Hasids. He was a miracle worker who knew the secret names of the Lord. He was that and much, much more. He was a *zaddik*.

No, firing Shirley Stein was, Gottleib thought, again not for the first time, an impossibility.

"Hello, Zally," said Shirley. "Going to do good business today?"

"The Lord willing," Gottleib muttered more to himself than to Shirley, who was used to her boss's gruffness and took it as a compliment on her figure, of which she was rather vain.

Gottleib turned on the fluorescent desk lamp and opened his large office safe, leaving its door open. Then he put some of his goods in the safe and began spilling out the rest on the desk's white blotter. He wanted to get a head start on choosing a likely pair of stones for his buyer.

"Morris won't be in until later this afternoon," Shirley called out from her post by the door. "He said he had a seller he was going to visit in Queens."

Gottleib grunted as he picked over the stones with his long tweezers. These were commercial goods, grade F and lower, some brighter than others, few more than a carat in weight, and few more than $2,000 a carat. With his practiced eye, he didn't need a millimeter gauge to tell if two stones were nearly identical. And for this preliminary sorting, he didn't need his diamond scale to weigh the stones or his loupe to search for flaws or dark carbon spots within the diamonds. But the work would have gone a lot faster, he would have already had at least three pairs for the buyer to choose from, if he wasn't preoccupied with that other stone, the one now sitting in Ari Levin's office safe. The big stone. The biggest one, in fact, that he had ever seen. Not to mention the most beautiful.

Gottleib took off his glasses, rubbed his eyes, and thought back to when he was ten years old and had started working for his father, may he rest in peace, sweeping up behind the small booth his father rented at 4 West Forty-seventh on the Diamond Exchange floor.

Things were better then, thought Gottleib. His father knew

all the customers, and the customers knew him. And everyone knew stones. They knew cost, but more important, they knew quality. Now, Gottleib thought, the people on the street were more like Schumach: a good man, but one who felt nothing for a beautiful stone. All he cared about was his profit.

Schumach would salivate over the big stone, but he wouldn't understand, wouldn't feel in his *kishkes*, in his guts, how beautiful it was. In his sixty-plus years in the business, Zalman Gottleib had never seen a stone like it.

It was D flawless with a sapphire tint.

An oval cut with sixty-six blinding facets.

Flawless.

Its table, the stone's flat top surface, was a still, unblemished pool above the shifting and flashing fires below.

Its girdle, its widest point, was nearly three inches in diameter.

It was seventy-two incredible carats or, as Gottleib reminded himself, twenty-eight carats more than the Hope diamond.

What was it worth? Who knew? Anything would be a guess. Six million? More. Sixty million? Why not? One hundred million? Whatever.

Why had he never heard of it? Why had he never read about it? A stone like that would have to have a history. Where did it come from? South Africa? Brazil? Perhaps India, a long, long time ago. But when the Satmarer *rebbe*, Joel Teitel, may his light shine, handed it to him, all he said was, "Keep this safe, my friend. I will tell you later what I want you to do with it. It will be my daughter Esther's dowry. It will be her crown."

Gottleib was honored, of course, that his *rebbe* had chosen him to keep the stone, but it also made him incredibly nervous. It was that nervousness that led him to drop it off with Ari Levin, thinking that would purchase him a few days of peace. Actually, he thought, checking the clock on the wall, all it had bought him was a few minutes.

I shouldn't have left it with Levin, he thought. What if something should happen to it? But what, he asked himself, could happen? Still, Gottleib would feel better when the marriage came off and he could be relieved of the stone and the responsibility.

He knew, as the whole Hasidic world knew, that a *shidukh*, an arranged match, had been made for his *rebbe*'s daughter and the Lubavitcher *rebbe*'s adopted son. Most of the people in his community, the Satmarer Hasidim, were scandalized. They regarded the Lubavitchers as the enemy, as fanatics, even atheists. The Lubavitchers proselytized, seeking out assimilated Jews to swell their numbers, and as a result, the Satmarers suspected that the Lubavitchers were less than rigorous in enforcing Jewish law. No good Satmarer would ever eat at a Lubavitcher restaurant (and vice versa), no matter how many signs swore that the food there was *Glatt kosher*, the highest level. Since it was a Lubavitcher rabbi doing the swearing, who knew?

In the diamond district, Lubavitchers and Satmarers did business together, often working side by side cutting stones on the wheel, but they rarely socialized and often fought. Most often they fought over the respective merits of their two leaders, their *rebbes*. Every Satmarer knew that Rebbe Joel Teitel was the world's greatest man, while every Lubavitcher swore that that title belonged to their grand *rebbe*, Menachem Seligson.

To the *goyishe*, non-Hasidic world, the Satmarers and Lubavitchers looked the same. Indeed, to outsiders, Jews and non-Jews alike, all the scores of different Hasidic sects and clans seemed identically fanatical—Jewish fundamentalists who swore by the magical powers of their respective *rebbes*, their spiritual leaders. But to the Hasids themselves, the differences between them were of earth-and-heaven-shaking import. And anyway, who cared what the ignorant *goyim* (and to a Hasid, anyone who wasn't a Hasid, Jewish or not, was an ignorant *goy*) thought?

But Gottleib would never question Reb Teitel's wisdom. The man, after all, was a *zaddik*, a saint, a prince of Israel, one of the Holy One's chosen servants. If he was binding his dynasty to those crazy Lubavitchers, then it was the right thing to do.

Gottleib went back to his little stones. Where was that dealer? He looked at the clock on the wall. It was past noon. He glanced up at the closed-circuit television screen that showed him Shirley behind the bulletproof glass and the office's outer door. In another minute, Gottleib thought, I'm going to lunch. And if I miss this dealer with his so-called seven-carat stone, well, he'll be back. Zally Gottleib had the best side stones on the street. Everyone in the business knew that.

Just then the outer door buzzed. On the screen, Gottleib saw a tall, pale, skinny Hasid enter. Over the intercom, he heard the man tell Shirley that he was sent for Zalman Gottleib.

This man looks like he could use a good meal, Gottleib thought. Maybe if we do a *mazl un brukha*, the luck and blessing that accompanied the handshake that closed every deal on the street, we'll share some cheese blintzes, the best in New York, across the street at the Diamond Dairy Luncheonette.

"Send him in, Shirley," said Gottleib.

3

Williamsburg, Brooklyn, and Flushing, Queens Friday, September 3

It was still dark when Morris Schumach awoke. For a moment he lay quietly, listening to his wife's breathing, to the clock ticking, coming back to himself after his night's dreams. Then, thanking God for returning his soul to him, he lit the table lamp and slipped out of bed, careful not to disturb his Elizabeth, sleeping soundly by his side.

Walking softly to the nightstand, holding the water pitcher in his left hand, pouring the water over his right, he recited the blessing for washing:

Blessed art Thou, our Lord our God, King of the Universe, who has sanctified us with His commandments, and commanded us to wash our hands.

Then he switched hands, washing his left. He repeated this three times. This was *halakhah*, the law, and Schumach knew that with the fulfillment of the commandment, the *mitzvah*, his soul should soar up to God. But instead he thought of his father's oft repeated, bitter joke. "In America," his father would say, "even the water is not *kosher*."

Maybe not, thought Schumach. But wasn't it, he silently asked his father—now dead a year, the little *yahrzeit* candle flickering in the kitchen marking the anniversary—wasn't it better to have this un*kosher* American water than the holy water of Hungary, the water the *goyim* used for a thousand years to wash their hands after murdering Jews?

Schumach could never understand his father's hatred for all things American. But then again, as his father always made sure to remind him, Morris was a blockhead. He was fit for nothing but buying and selling those silly stones that would decorate the hands and throats of foolish, impious women. His father, on the other hand, was known throughout the neighborhood as a *sheyner Yid*, a beautiful Jew, a respected man who often led the congregation in prayer.

Of course, thought Schumach, the neighbors didn't have to live with his father's sarcasm, his drinking, the drunken curses.

After the ritual washing, Schumach moved his bowels (another *mitzvah* because it further purified his body for his morning prayers), showered, dried his full black beard, lately streaked with gray although he was still a young man of forty, and put on his *tallis katan*, his fringed undershirt with the knotted threads, the *tzitzis*, dangling off the four corners. He put on his white shirt and laid out the black kaftan overcoat he would take off as soon as he got to the office he shared with Zally Gottleib on Forty-seventh Street.

But first I have to drive to Queens, Schumach reminded himself. It was odd. The woman on the phone said she'd gotten Schumach's number from a rabbi Schumach had never heard of. She said her husband had died recently and she had to sell her jewelry. When Schumach suggested that she come to the office, the woman refused, saying she was still in mourning.

So, if she was in mourning, thought Schumach, why is she doing business? *Ach*, who knows? Must be she needs the money. A terrible thing to be a widow.

Finally Schumach completed his morning ritual by putting on his *tallis*, his prayer shawl, and then his *tefillin*, the two small boxes—one tied to his left bicep with leather straps, one tied to his forehead—containing four passages of Torah, including the one that said, "And you shall bind them as a sign upon your hand, and they shall serve as a symbol between your eyes."

As he recited his morning prayers from memory, thanking God for not making him a *goy*, a slave, or a woman, Schumach's thoughts flickered back to the widow in Queens, and he felt ashamed. *Ach*, I'm no scholar, and I don't study enough, he scolded himself, putting away his *tallis* and his *tefillin* in their velvet pouches. But, God be praised, he thought as he left his house on Lee Avenue—for Schumach, unlike his father, was not a brooder—I may not be as pious as my father, may he rest in peace, but I am something better: a happy man.

Schumach steered his big blue Buick through the streets of Williamsburg and onto the Brooklyn-Queens Expressway. As soon as he got on the highway, he put on a tape of Rebbe Teitel's lecture on the great *mitzvah* of *tevilah*, immersion.

The *rebbe* believed that men should visit the *mikvah*, the ritual bathhouse, more often that they did, more often, indeed, than the law required. Before a child is born, the *rebbe* said, he knows everything—all the Torah, the teachings—by heart. When the child is born, an angel slaps him to make him forget everything so that he can praise the Holy One, blessed is He, by relearning His laws. But when we are immersed, the *rebbe* said, we are like an unborn child in the womb and we know everything.

I can follow that, I understand that, Schumach thought proudly. The *rebbe*'s talks frequently left Schumach's brain spinning, but now he vowed to visit the *mikvah* that very night, and he promised himself to contribute some more money to the fund to fix up the drafty old bathhouse on Williamsburg Street. If it were a nicer place, thought Schumach, maybe people would go more often, and that would be another blessing.

When he got to the address in Queens Schumach found, to his distress, a much younger woman than he had expected, in her late twenties at most. She was very tall, taller than Schumach, powerfully built, with a mountain of gold hair done up in a bun.

She was wearing a black dress that Schumach found extremely immodest. It stopped just above her knees, bared her arms, and hugged her breasts. Some widow, thought Schumach. Sure, a merry widow. She introduced herself as Maria Rudenstein. She spoke English in an accent Schumach thought was Polish.

There had been a brand-new *mezuzah* on the doorframe, but Schumach doubted that this woman was Jewish. Maybe her husband, God rest his soul, was Jewish, although obviously not pious. I'll get this over quickly, thought Schumach, who felt acutely uncomfortable in the presence of women, especially unmarried women, especially young, unmarried, non-Jewish women.

But Rudenstein insisted upon going on and on about her husband, who, she said, had died in an auto accident. There were no children. Then she kept offering Schumach food that, this obviously not being a *kosher* home, he could not possibly eat. Not wanting to offend her, he did accept a glass of water. Even that took time to produce.

After what seemed to Schumach to be at least an hour, the woman produced the jewelry. One glance told Schumach that he had wasted his time. Most of it was costume jewelry. All of it was cheap stuff, garbage. Only one ring had a decent diamond solitaire, a little yellow, maybe three carats, and the band was rose gold.

"I'm sorry, lady," said Schumach, dismissing the rings and bracelets and earrings spread out on the coffee table. "I can't help you. This kind of jewelry is not my business. But this one," he said, looking at the solitaire through his loupe, "is not bad. It's not the stone; that's cut all wrong. But I can tell this is an old ring. By the setting. Nobody makes them like this anymore. See how high the stone is set. I don't know if I can sell it, but I like it. Okay. I'll give you three thousand dollars."

"Three thousand?" the woman said, apparently shocked. "This was my husband's mother's engagement ring. My father-in-law bought it for her in Warsaw before the war. She gave it to her son to give to me when we got engaged. If I had had a son, I would have given it to him for his wife when he got engaged." The woman paused as if overcome. Her wide-set, dark brown eyes seemed to grow moist. Schumach felt pity well up in him, and he stared at the floor.

Schumach sighed. "Your father-in-law had good taste. It's a nice ring. But I'm not a collector. My advice to you is to go down to the Diamond Exchange and take it around to the booths. Maybe you'll find someone to give you what you think it's worth." Schumach had wasted enough time and had no intention of *hondeling* with this *shiksa* widow.

"Mr. Schumach," she said, leaning toward him, "how about six thousand dollars for the ring and you can take all the rest?"

Schumach, who was acutely aware of her body, particularly her breasts swelling out of her dress, could feel his cheeks burning in embarrassment. "Listen, lady," he said, looking away. "I feel sorry for you your husband died. A terrible thing. But three thousand dollars is my price." He shrugged.

"Please, Mr. Schumach," said Mrs. Rudenstein. "Let me make a phone call. I have to ask somebody about this. Just a few minutes."

She left the room, and Schumach looked at his watch. It was past noon, and his stomach was growling. At this rate, by the time he got to the office it would be two o'clock, he'd have missed his afternoon prayers and his lunch. And since it was Friday, he had to be home by four to get ready for the Sabbath. Maybe he should forget about going to the office altogether.

Schumach sat there ten, fifteen, twenty minutes, squirming. Then the woman came back with a new offer: $5,000 for everything.

Maybe I could sell the ring for $5,000, thought Schumach. Rose gold is popular these days. I could sell the rest for another $500. All this for a $500 profit? Well, as Zally said over and over, you could drive from here to Chicago and not find $50. A profit is a profit.

He looked at his watch again. Nearly one o'clock. It would be crazy to go to the office now.

"Maybe I could go to four thousand dollars," said Schumach. "But now I have to make a call. Could I use your phone?"

"Of course," said the woman, leading him to a small, spare bedroom. It looked to Schumach like nobody, least of all a young married couple, had ever slept in it. Painful memories, thought Schumach. She's already cleared the room of any trace of her husband. The phone was on a table next to the bed.

Schumach dialed the office. He let it ring twelve times before hanging up. Strange, he thought. Zally and Shirley never took lunch at the same time. Could Zally have closed up for *Shabbos*? So early?

Schumach shrugged and went back into the living room to close the deal with the young widow.

4

Forty-seventh Street, Manhattan
Friday, September 3

When the Cutter was buzzed into Zalman Gottleib's office, he stepped swiftly behind Shirley Stein, grabbed her red hair in his left hand, pulled her head back, and severed her jugular vein and carotid artery in one stroke. She felt little but the unpleasant sensation of her hair being pulled. Blood spouted from her throat, spattering the bulletproof glass as her body instantly went into shock. The Cutter tossed her away from him, turning his back as the body shuddered and jerked on the carpet.

The Cutter walked swiftly to Gottleib's desk, noting that the door to the safe was open. That would make it easier. Gottleib, who after telling Shirley to let in the Cutter had returned his gaze to the little stones spread out on his blotter, had neither heard nor seen his secretary's murder. He stood up to meet his customer.

Gottleib was surprised when the man stepped quickly around the desk; he was surprised when the man reached out, ignoring Gottleib's hand extended in greeting, and, pulling him by his collar, threw him down painfully across the arms of his chair. Then Gottleib saw the glittering knife.

"The stone," said the Cutter.

"What stone?" asked Gottleib, his voice quaking. "I have lots of stones. Take. Take what you want."

"The Seer's stone," said the Cutter.

"I don't know what you're talking about," said Gottleib.

"Then die," said the Cutter.

"Wait," said Gottleib. "I gave a stone to a setter, Ari Levin, on the ninth floor."

"Good," said the Cutter. "Now I will let you say the *Shema*."

Zalman Gottleib knew he was dead. Really, he had known it from the moment he had felt the Cutter's hands upon him. All right, he thought. I'm ready. And to his surprise, Gottleib knew that to be the truth. He had been ready ever since his wife, his Sarah, had died five years ago. So, calmly, he began reciting the *Shema*, the first prayer he had learned as a child, the last utterance of Jewish martyrs for centuries:

Shema Yisroel, Adonoy eloyheinu, Adonoy ekhud.

"Hear O Israel, the Lord is our God, the Lord is One."

The Cutter held back his hand. But when Gottleib began speaking the prayer's second verse, "Blessed is the Name of . . ." the Cutter's patience ran out, and as he had cut Shirley Stein's throat, he cut Zalman Gottleib's.

The Cutter stepped back quickly to avoid being splattered by Gottleib's blood. He watched Gottleib trying to finish the

Shema, his trachea severed, his lips moving soundlessly, the only noise in the office the Cutter's breathing.

For a moment the Cutter thought of heading right down to this Ari Levin and taking the Seer's stone. But the Cutter had survived by never deviating from a plan, never improvising, unless his very life was threatened. He would not start now. Levin, and the stone, would have to wait for a new plan from the Magician.

When Gottlieb lay still, the arterial blood pumping out of him like an ocean tide, the Cutter climbed up on his desk and knocked out a soundproof square of the dropped ceiling, revealing the metal struts above. Then he stepped down, took the rope out of his pocket, and bound Gottlieb's ankles. He lifted Gottlieb's body onto the desk, tossed the end of the rope over a strut, and pulled until Gottlieb hung upside down.

The Cutter tore off Gottlieb's blood-soaked shirt, then pulled his *tallis katan* over his head. As the Cutter had seen his father do so many times, he examined the knife and saw that it had suffered no knicks and was therefore still valid for *shekhita*, ritual slaughter. Not that anyone would ever know if it wasn't, thought the Cutter as he inserted the point of the knife just below Gottlieb's sternum, but I observe the ritual as closely as I can in order to please myself. And, of course, my father.

He jerked the knife upward, slicing Gottlieb open, watching as his intestines spilled out onto the desk. Then, prying open the rib cage, he examined the lungs. Not a smoker, the Cutter thought. Gottlieb's lungs were a healthy pink. This man is *Glatt kosher*, the highest level of *kashrus*, the Cutter thought, chuckling to himself.

The Cutter began removing cardboard boxes filled with little envelopes of diamonds from Gottlieb's safe. He ripped them open, spilling the sparkling stones on the carpet, setting the scene for the police. It was a hailstorm of wealth and beauty.

The Cutter looked around the room, admiring his work. Zalman Gottlieb's body revolved slowly at the end of the rope. The blood dripping from his throat made circular patterns on the white desk blotter and splashed drop by drop onto the diamonds—the trillions and half-moons, the stars and baguettes—scattered on the desk. It's magic, thought the Cutter. It's alchemy. I've turned those diamonds into rubies.

For a second it occurred to him to gather up some of the diamonds and take them with him. An unworthy thought, he scolded himself. How can good come from this if I act like a *gonef*, a thief? I have never taken anything that did not belong to me. Never. I will not start now.

He placed the knife on the desk. Let them find it, he thought. Let them try to find me.

He examined himself. His hands were bloody. He would have to keep them in his pockets as he left the office until he could go to the washroom at the end of the hall. His black coat and pants did not show the blood, but he could feel where they were wet with it. Well, they could be disposed of easily.

He glanced at Shirley Stein's body lying on the blood-soaked carpet. Another unworthy thought flashed through his mind, but this one he gave in to. Turning her over with his foot, he bent and ripped open her sweater, pulling up her brassiere. Freed, her breasts flopped to the left and right. The Cutter stared and felt nothing.

Yes, I am truly a *golem*, he thought as he left the office, glancing left and right down the hallway, closing the door behind him, hearing the lock click into place.

I am a *golem*, and I am not responsible.

The Magician will have to decide what to do next.

A phone in the office began to ring. It rang twelve times.

5

The Lower East Side, Manhattan
Saturday, September 4

Ladislaw Czartoryski—who in Poland was known as Vladimir Cartovksy, and whose old comrades-in-arms often called him the Magician—sat on the edge of a plastic chair in a dark room in an apartment on East Fourth Street between Avenues B and C. He was waiting for the Cutter.

The room stank of ammonia and rat droppings. Roaches skittered over the linoleum floors. Throughout the building and up and down the street, junkies stuck needles into their arms and legs, injecting weak heroin cut dozens of times with milk sugar, quinine, and baby powder. Then they'd pass the needle to a friend and along with it hepatitis or AIDS.

Sometimes the junkies would get lucky, and their $25 waxed-paper bag of heroin, stamped with the dealer's ironic logo—King Kong, Midnight Express, Make My Day— would be purer, stronger. Then they'd feel the heat swell through their veins, making their eyelids heavy, bringing the sweat to their foreheads. And sometimes they'd close their eyes in bliss and die.

Czartoryski supplied some of that dope. The opium paste came from his friends in Cambodia. It was smuggled by his Palestinian friends to factories where it was refined in Turkey, Algeria, and Morocco and then distributed to his German and Scandinavian friends, who brought it to New York concealed in diplomatic pouches, BMWs and Porsches, briefcases, handbags, and sometimes vaginas and assholes. It was, thought Czartoryski, a beautiful example of the interconnect-edness of the modern global economy. And after paying off the Italians for the privilege of operating in their city, Czartor-yski deposited his profits in a numbered Swiss bank account.

It was a good business, but not interesting. No, what inter-ested Ladislaw Czartoryski was diamonds, and one diamond in particular: the Seer's stone, or what the Magician always thought of as the Czartoryski diamond.

Czartoryski imagined himself an aristocrat, a man of the world, an entrepreneur. He was nearing his seventy-first birth-day but looked younger, a healthy sixty-five. He was short, trim, and he still had a sufficiency of silver hair combed sleekly against his skull. Once a member in good standing in the youth brigade of the Polish National Socialist party, then a member, in similar good standing, in the Polish Communist party, and now a rosy-cheeked elder statesman of the ''new''

Poland, Czartoryski believed in making new friends but keeping the old. The Cambodians were new friends. The Palestinians, whom he helped and who helped him, were somewhat older.

His oldest friends were the men of the Odessa, the secret society of SS veterans that had facilitated Czartoryski's escape from Poland after the war. Many members of the Odessa, such as Klaus Barbie, had ended up in the American intelligence community; others had been placed in the Soviet; and still others, such as the founder of the Odessa, General Reinhard Gehlen, had helped create NATO's intelligence service.

Some had drifted, famously, to South America, to Argentina, Brazil, Bolivia, Colombia, and Paraguay. There, they had hired themselves out as free-lance Cold War "security consultants." The Death Squads had benefited from their expertise. Later, so did the paramilitary arm of the Medellin cocaine cartel.

The Magician, who had seen little action in the war and bitterly regretted its end, had volunteered for an active theater of operations and so had ended up in the Middle East.

Indeed, it was during the Zionist takeover of Palestine in 1947 that Czartoryski—who, according to the Odessa's program, was resting up in Beirut, waiting for the memory of his Nazi past to fade from the minds of Poland's new Communist rulers—had met the Cutter.

Czartoryski checked his watch and shifted on the unlovely plastic chair, the only article of furniture in this hole that he felt fairly sure was free of lice. His old friend should be here soon.

Czartoryski remembered precisely what he had thought when he'd met the tall, cadaverously thin, teenage Zionist with the blue numbers tattooed on the inside of his forearm: "I wonder if he was at Belzec? Some of them made it out of that camp. I wonder if he recognizes me?"

It would be many years before Czartoryski stopped worrying about meeting survivors of the Belzec work camp near Lublin, many years before he had transformed himself from the muscular, feral thug of his youth to the distinguished diplomat wearing English tweeds he appeared to be today.

Czartoryski had known that the Cutter was mad as soon as he'd laid eyes upon him. Most of them were, the survivors. Especially those like the Cutter, the *sonderkommandos*, the Jews who survived by hustling their fathers and mothers and brothers and sisters in and out of the gas chambers, who stripped them of their clothing and jewelry, who tore the gold out of their dead mouths, and who buried their bodies, first dousing them with lye. Czartoryski had pried all this out of the Cutter after buying the starving boy a meal and a bottle of cheap Greek wine.

"What's your name?" Czartoryski had asked the teenager when he had eaten and drunk his fill.

"I don't have a name anymore," the boy had said. "My father was a slaughterer in Poland, before the war. You can call me the Cutter."

My old friend, thought Czartoryski. How easy it had been to convince this boy that he, too, had hated the Nazis. That he had been a nationalist in the Polish Resistance. That he had helped Jews escape. And after letting the boy stay with him, finding him a woman, and giving him money, Czartoryski had helped smuggle him past the British lines into Palestine, where the Cutter could join the other killers creating the Zionist state. And by playing on his guilt, his hate, and his sentimentality, the Magician had made the Cutter his creature, and he had remained so during the long years, working, in essence, for the Odessa even as he worked for the Mossad, the Israeli secret service. Czartoryski smiled at the thought of the old *sonderkommando*, the man with the blue numbers tattooed on his forearm, still working for the SS after all these years.

Of course, that was the way of the world. Czartoryski himself had had some unusual employers. As had many members of the Odessa. In the world of espionage, old enemies could become new friends at any moment. What did the Arabs say? "The enemy of my enemy is my friend." How true.

Indeed, even now, didn't the Israelis think that the Magician was running their errand, doing their dirty work? Wasn't it the Israelis who had told him that the stone—his stone— was in the possession of the Satmarers? They imagined that he would turn over the stone to them—for a price, of course—and they would use it to get back at De Beers, the diamond syndicate. They wanted to destroy a man named Alfred Berg, a member of the De Beers board of directors, but they didn't want to shed Jewish blood. They were too delicate.

Well, thought the Magician, let them think what they want.

Just then the bell rang in the apartment—one long, one short, one long. The Cutter. Czartoryski got up to buzz him in, opened the police lock on the door, opened the curtains behind his chair, and sat back down. Moments later the Cutter entered.

The beard was gone, exposing the Cutter's hollow, blue-gray cheeks. The kaftan was gone. The Cutter wore blue jeans, sneakers, and an Italian leather sport jacket. Czartoryski thought he looked sick.

The Cutter closed the door behind him and paused, squinting in the bright light coming from the dirty window behind Czartoryski.

"You have the stone?" the Magician asked.

"No," said the Cutter.

Czartoryski's hand tightened on the 9-mm Beretta concealed in his lap. The Cutter was his, true, but a diamond such as this one would be a great temptation to any man, even one as mad as the Cutter.

"Why not?"

"The Hasid gave it to a setter in the same building. I know who, but I did not want to be hasty."

"That was wise," said Czartoryski, relaxing. "I am disappointed, of course, but I do not despair. All good things come to those who wait, is that not what they say? And how did you dispose of the diamond merchant?"

"As I said. *Kosher.*"

"Good. Excellent. Very amusing, really. So. We will just have to remain here a little longer, and what's wrong with that? Such an exciting city."

"Well, if we are going to stay here," said Maria Radziwell, who had been the widow Rudenstein, emerging from the kitchen, "can we find a better place? This is—how do you say?—a real shithole."

6

Forty-seventh Street, Manhattan
Monday, September 6

Morris Schumach arrived at work Monday morning, rested and revived from the Sabbath. He unlocked his office door and discovered the bodies of Zalman Gottleib and Shirley Stein. He phoned the police and looked for somewhere to sit down to wait for them. Not finding a place that didn't look bloody, he left the office and sat down on the floor in the hallway, which is where Officer Mike Gallagher of the Eighteenth Precinct found him.

Moments after Gallagher went into the office, saw the bodies, and radioed homicide, Forty-seventh Street between Fifth and Sixth avenues was sealed off. Patrol cars blocked the intersection, diverting traffic. Uniformed officers stretched sawhorses across the sidewalk; men going to work and customers going to shop were informed that the street was temporarily off limits.

By the time the homicide team led by Sergeant Detective Frank Hill arrived, two uniforms were posted outside the entrance to 52 West Forty-seventh. Frank Hill nodded to the officers, and he and Detectives Art Jahnke and Harry White rode the elevator up to the fourteenth floor.

ID—photographers and forensics—waited outside, along with the medical examiner, while Hill, Jahnke, and White looked around the office, pulling on the surgical gloves from their evidence collection kits.

"Always makes me feel like the fucking Playtex lady," said Hill, struggling with the gloves.

One look at Shirley Stein told them that she had been dead for a while, and the state of Zalman Gottleib's body confirmed it. He had gone through rigor mortis and was turning soft. He smelled. The flesh around the rope binding his ankles was decomposing. Fly larvae were clearly visible in his nostrils, his mouth, and his eyes. The detectives returned to the outer office, silently impressed by the mute afterimages of the violence that had taken place here.

Harry White began sketching the crime scene in his pad, and Hill pointed to Stein's breasts. "Sex crime?" he asked. "Somebody very fucking crazy had a hell of a party here."

"Panties still on," said Jahnke.

"So?" Hill said.

"Nothing," said Jahnke.

"Dead at least a couple of days," White said.

"I know," said Hill. "So our perp is probably in Bangladesh by now."

"Probably," White agreed, looking up from his pad. "Or at least New Jersey."

"Stinks in here," said Hill. "Open a window."

"Lookee here," Jahnke said from the inner office. He pointed to the knife on the desk. "Guess he wanted us to find it. Either he wore gloves or his prints won't mean anything to us or he's so crazy he doesn't give a shit."

"More than one killer," said Hill.

"Probably. Yeah, maybe two, three," said Jahnke.

"Or one guy, very fucking strong."

"Very fucking strong," Jahnke agreed.

"Not a robbery," said White, who had joined them, pointing at the diamonds scattered on the desk and the floor.

"Wanna bet?" said Jahnke. "Maybe robbery wasn't the main idea, but something's been taken. Something's always taken. And something's always left."

"Yeah, the knife," said Hill. "Rocks. Prints. Maybe the killer's name and address and an autographed eight-by-ten glossy. My bet is none of it's gonna do us any fucking good at all."

"Maybe the guy's a friend of his." Hill jerked a thumb at Zalman Gottleib's still-dangling corpse. "Pissed off. Maybe he fucked someone in a deal. These guys are always fucking some poor dumb *goy*."

"Must have fucked him pretty good to do all this," said White.

The three detectives examined Gottleib's and Stein's hands and fingernails, looking for signs of a struggle. They looked for anything odd in a crime scene as odd as any they'd ever seen. Slowly they fell silent and stopped walking around. Each one turned in on himself, checking to see how much damage this newest example of human savagery had done to his own soul. It was always bad, thought Hill, but this one was worse. He shook himself.

"You finished sketching, Harry?" he asked. At White's nod Hill said, "Okay, let's let the ID guys in. I'm gonna talk to the guy outside, what's his name? Shoemaker? Then we'll split up the floors, and then we'll hit the streets, talk to everybody."

"You know you'll never get a straight answer in the diamond district," Jahnke said. "They hate cops."

"You're just a fucking anti-Semite, Art," said Hill, who was Irish. "*Achtung!*" he said, giving Jahnke, whom Hill loved to tease about his German ancestry, the straight-armed Hitler salute.

Morris Schumach wanted to help this policeman in the brown suit, but how could he? No, he didn't know Gottleib well. No, really. They weren't partners; they just split the rent and shared a secretary, poor, poor Miss Stein.

No, Zally had no wife, she died. Children? Probably, but he never talked about them, and there were no pictures. Brothers, sisters, cousins? Who knew? Enemies? Of course not. He was a pious man.

No, he really didn't know much about Miss Stein either, except she was divorced. Zally had hired her. Her ex-husband? Who knew?

No, it wouldn't do any good to look at Zally's safe to see what was missing. Why should he know Zally's inventory? They weren't partners.

The diamonds, Schumach said, go to the Diamond Club. They'd take care of them; they'd know what to do.

How should he know who could have done such a thing? It was crazy, horrible, a holocaust. Must have been a crazy man, an anti-Semite, a Nazi.

No, he hadn't come in to work on Friday. Was that unusual? A little. Did he tell Zally? No, he had tried, but he couldn't reach him.

"My God," said Morris Schumach, clapping his hand to his forehead. "Do you think, could it be that they were already, like this, when I called from Queens?"

Schumach gave the detective the name and address of the widow in Queens. Yes, he bought some jewelry from her, nothing special. Yes, he could give it to the police if they wanted. A receipt? No. He paid cash. No, that was not unusual.

No, he didn't think anyone would have missed Zalman this weekend except maybe his friends in his synagogue. Sure, he could tell the detective which one, but he belonged to a different synagogue. Maybe he knew some people in Zalman's congregation, maybe not. Of course he would give the officer his name and address.

And anything he could do, anything at all.

For the next three hours, the detectives interviewed everyone in the building. No, no one had seen anything unusual that Friday. Only an Ariel Levin had even seen Gottleib that morning. He had seemed normal to Levin. He had just dropped by to say hello.

The custodians? No, they never entered the offices unless invited.

Art Jahnke interviewed the Puerto Rican security guard who had been on duty that Friday. Yeah, sure, Zalman Gottleib's last visitor had signed the book in the lobby at 1:05 P.M. Here's the signature. I can't make it out either. He may have been a Hasid. Tall, short, fat, thin, who knew? They all looked the same.

No, the guard had never seen Gottleib that day, either coming or going. He had seen Shirley Stein, the one with the big boobs. How did she look? She looked fine.

A shitload of evidence, Frank Hill told his captain back at the station house late that afternoon, but no witnesses and a lot of time had passed. Hill could smell a difficult case, and this one smelled real bad.

The medical examiner, he told the captain, confirmed that the bodies had been there over the weekend. The male victim's partner said that he had called shortly after one and gotten no answer. We're fixing the time of death around then until we hear from the medical examiner.

We're running down both victims' known relations and associates, said Hill. The woman had not been molested, although her tits were hanging out.

The male victim's partner said he didn't come into the office that day. Said he went to an address in Queens and then went home. We're checking at both ends. There was nobody at the house in Queens. Odd about that. The neighbors had thought the place was empty. We're looking for the landlord.

Forensics, Hill went on, says the knife we found is the murder weapon in both killings. Yes, there were prints all over the place, but that made Hill think the killer's prints were not on file, otherwise he'd have been more careful.

Motive? He was going with robbery right now, but he didn't like it. If theft was the point, why gut the guy like that? Why string him up? Why not string up the girl? It smelled like payback to Hill, a revenge killing. Sure, something was probably taken, some stones, but who knows what or how much? These people keep their records in their heads.

Hill and the captain stared at each other. "You were here for the Pinchos Jaroslawicz killing in '77, weren't you, Captain?" asked Hill. "Diamond dealer, right? Found in his office? Shot?"

The captain nodded.

"And . . . ?" asked Hill.

"It was a fucking nightmare," the captain said. "These fucking people," he said, shaking his head. "A goddamn nightmare."

7

Sullivan Street, between Prince and Spring,
SoHo, Manhattan
Tuesday, September 7

Dov Taylor, son of Hank and Luba, formerly Private First Class Taylor of the Eighteenth Artillery Division, I-Corp, formerly Sergeant Detective Taylor of the New York City Police Department, attached to homicide, now just plain Dov Taylor, security guard at the First Bank of Williamsburg, in Brooklyn, climbed out of bed shortly after dawn. An hour later he was still fumbling with his brand-new *tefillin*, trying to remember how he was supposed to wrap the leather thong around his left hand, when Naomi sat up in bed and looked at her new boyfriend.

"That's the strangest-looking thing I've ever seen," she said.

"It only looks strange because you're not used to it," said Taylor. "Just let me finish."

"Oh, no," said Naomi, a tall, thin, auburn-haired young woman who was a teller in the bank, and whom Taylor had been seeing for a month and sleeping with since last weekend. "It's really normal to tie a little black box to your head."

"You got a thing for normal?"

"Obviously not," said Naomi, coyly allowing the sheet to fall from her high, smallish breasts.

"This is not working," said Taylor, getting up. "I'm going to go into the bathroom to finish."

"Am I distracting you?" she asked, smiling.

"Yes," he answered, not smiling.

In the bathroom, with the door closed, Taylor looked at himself in the mirror. It *did* look weird—the *tefillin* on his forehead and on his arm. What am I doing? he asked the mirror. Trying out for the road show of *Fiddler on the Roof*?

He stroked his month-old beard, still, to his surprise, more black than gray. I look like my great-grandfather, he thought, an old man, a ghost out of the nineteenth century, an antique Jew in a dusty photo album. Boo! he said to his face in the mirror. Or rather, he thought, *Oy*, boo!

Christ, I'm only forty. I've still got my strength. I feel good. And if I feel good after all the booze and Percodan I've done, I'm doing pretty good. Then why am I doing so shitty? Why am I sitting in my bathroom putting on these ridiculous things?

Obviously, he told himself, you drowned a few too many brain cells, and now you're paying for it.

"Dov," Naomi called from the bedroom. "Do you think God really cares if you put a box on your head every morning? Do you think God is inside the box?"

Knock, knock, thought Taylor, tapping the box on his forehead. Anybody home? You in there, God?

A little more than two years ago, Dov Taylor had a house in Eastchester, a blond wife, a degree in criminology, a law degree, and a blossoming career in the department. His colleagues respected him; they called him Super-Jew, and he liked it. Women followed him with their eyes, and he liked that, too. He was a leanly muscular six feet two. Blue-black hair still covered his head, hair the color of Superman's in the comic strips. His eyes were sea green with flecks of ocher. His most distinctive feature was a vein that protruded slightly above his temple. It throbbed when he got angry. He called it his Tarzan vein.

The only fly in the ointment was a little trouble with booze and drugs. Not trouble, exactly. He just drank a little more than most people, and maybe most people didn't eat twelve to fifteen Percodan a day. But he could stop if he wanted to. He had stopped for almost a year after he got back from Vietnam. He just didn't want to. And, anyway, it was all manageable.

Sure.

That was just twenty-four months ago, thought Taylor. What happened?

The house? Gone. Traded in for a one-bedroom apartment in a basement on Sullivan Street in what used to be an Italian enclave and was now, to Taylor's distress, SoHo's hipster central.

Carol, his wife? Gone. Traded, it now seemed, for a succession of increasingly younger women whom he tired of with ever-increasing rapidity.

His career? Also gone.

His life? Well, that was better. He was sober. There was, he reminded himself, nothing, absolutely nothing, more important than that.

At least that's what his Alcoholics Anonymous sponsor said.

Sometimes he even believed it.

But sometimes he didn't. Maybe that was why, between daily AA meetings, he had been going two nights a week to a class for *baalei teshuvah*, literally "ones who have returned," at the Mathew Rosenthal Lubavitcher Yeshiva on Eastern Parkway in Crown Heights. His teacher, Rabbi Jacob Kalman, thought that it was funny to have an ex-cop in the class along with all the earnest college boys and, on the other side of a curtain dividing the men from the women in the room, divorced matrons looking for meaning in their lives.

"They think He is going to save them," Rabbi Kalman once told Taylor after class. "They think the Holy One, blessed is He, is a friendly, kindly old man whose heart is brimming with love and forgiveness. He is, of course, full of love, but He is also King of the Universe, and you approach Him with fear and trembling in your *kishkes*. It is hard to serve Him. This"—he snorted—"they don't like."

But Taylor wanted it to be hard. He remembered telling Alex, his sponsor, a criminal lawyer in a downtown firm and a former assistant district attorney, that that was what had appealed to him. All his life he had been taught that the Hasids were weird, smelly fanatics. That their brand of Judaism was too hard for the modern world. But fuck the modern world, Taylor had said. It almost killed me.

"And doesn't the Big Book say to trust in your Higher Power?" Taylor had asked Alex. "Well, maybe my Higher Power doesn't know from the Lord's Prayer. Maybe my Higher Power might like it if I could talk to Him in His own language, which—excuse me, Alex, I know you're a good Catholic, eat fish on Friday, got a million kids, and all that—but my Higher Power, whoever He is, probably does not speak Latin, which, believe me, I probably know better than Hebrew from hanging around cops all my life."

Alex, of course, had said what he always said: Take it easy. Keep it simple. Don't drink. Keep going to meetings.

Taylor studied his face in the mirror. On second thought, there was gray in the beard, and more than before on top of his head. Another signpost on the road to death.

That's a pretty thought, Dov, he told himself. That's the anxiety you used to treat with booze and drugs, the anxiety you've got to learn to live with sober. Not a lot of fun, but being an addict wasn't much fun, either. Six of one, half dozen of the other. Not true, he reminded himself. The booze didn't kill the anxiety, it just masked it and at the same time fed it and encouraged it to grow bigger, stronger.

I'll shave the beard, he thought. Rabbi Kalman will be disappointed, but the hell with it. After all, you're not becoming a Hasid. You told Kalman that right off the bat. You're just finding out about your roots, right? Like every other fucked-up middle-aged divorcé in New York.

Am I a divorcé? he wondered. Can men be divorcés, or only women?

Wait a second. Christ, thought Taylor. I'm not supposed to be wearing my *tallis* and *tefillin* in the bathroom. That's a sin.

He left the bathroom and saw Naomi sitting up in bed. That's a sin, too, he thought. Two sins, actually. The little sin is that I shouldn't be saying prayers in the presence of a naked woman, not to mention one who isn't my wife. The big sin is that I'm sleeping with someone I don't care about, let alone love. I'm not even hot for her, he realized.

This *tefillin* stuff isn't working, he thought. I'm too old to learn how to do it. Too old and too fucked up.

"Are you finished?" Naomi asked.

"Sure," said Taylor, thinking that maybe he'd bag the *baalei teshuvah* classes entirely. Who are you trying to kid, Dov? he asked himself.

A few hours later he was alone in his efficiency kitchen. He had shaved off the beard, made the bed, washed last night's dishes, dried them, and stacked them just so in his cupboard. Then he arranged the magazines on his coffee table. Over his third cup of coffee, he decided not to go to work. Partly he didn't want to see Naomi, and partly he just enjoyed the feeling of having a day to himself, being free.

He turned to a sketchy *New York Newsday* story about the murder of a Forty-seventh Street diamond dealer and his secretary. Thank God, thought Dov Taylor, or my Higher Power, or whatever—I'm done with all that.

8

Forty-seventh Street, Manhattan
Tuesday, September 7

A day after the murders of Zalman Gottleib and Shirley Stein had been discovered, rumors were still flashing through the diamond district's offices and exchanges, the prayer rooms and luncheonettes.

Zalman Gottleib had been shot, stabbed, poisoned, beheaded. His secretary, Shirley Stein, had been tortured, raped, mutilated beyond recognition.

Thousands of dollars' worth of diamonds had been stolen. Hundreds of thousands. Millions.

It was the Russians, the Arabs, the Colombians, the Israelis, the Mafia.

Gottleib was a cheat, a saint, a spy. He had been having an affair with his secretary.

"What!?" shouted Sidney Metzer outside the elevator in 30 West Forty-seventh, the home of the Diamond Dealers

Club on the ninth and tenth floors. "The man was in his seventies, for God's sake."

"So?" asked William Goldberg as the men pressed into the crowded elevator. "A seventy-year-old man can't fool around?" Goldberg was sixty-five.

"He was a Hasid," said Metzer, who, although he lived in Crown Heights, attended the Lubavitcher synagogue, and was observant, was not.

"So? Take off the beard and *payes* and what have you got? Aren't the Hasidim men like you and me?"

Before Metzer could answer, the elevator doors opened onto a tiny, crowded anteroom. Men pressed their faces against a small bulletproof window so that the man behind the desk could recognize them and open the double-locked doors to the Diamond Club floor.

Once through the doors, the club members—men who had been nominated and screened by two committees, whose bank records had been examined and applications approved by the club's two thousand members—charged back and forth across a ballroom-size room with high ceilings, fluorescent lights, and a slippery, stained linoleum floor. Undistinguished wooden tables, some with desk lamps, lined the walls by the high windows.

Men sat at these tables with diamond loupes held up to their eyes, picking through glittering mountains of diamonds. Their deft fingers wrapped and unwrapped parcels of gems in double-sheeted paper—the outside sheet white, waxy, and strong; the inside sheet a pale blue tissue.

Visiting dealers with name tags affixed to their lapels bargained, rushing from table to table. Diamonds bought by one man were sold five minutes later to another for a profit of 1 or 2 percent, then sold again and again. Loudspeakers called the names of dealers in English, Hebrew, and Yiddish, summoning them to telephones or to the foyer for meetings. It was bedlam.

But today, although the club was as noisy as ever, and as crowded as ever—maybe even a little more so—there was less business being done. Instead there was more talk. About what happened to Zalman Gottleib. About what it meant to the street, to the business. The small prayer room off the main floor was more crowded than usual, with men reciting their afternoon prayers or talking to each other in hushed tones.

Many of the Satmarer Hasidim in the prayer room had been at Gottleib's funeral that morning and had said the mourner's *kaddish* over the grave. The funeral had been arranged by the Satmarer burial society, which had supplied the handfuls of soil from Israel that the mourners sprinkled on Gottleib's simple wooden coffin.

Because Gottleib had been murdered, he was buried, as a sign of wrath, in the clothes he had been wearing when his life left him.

As the mourners left, each plucked a few blades of grass and threw them over their shoulders, saying, "He remembereth that we are dust."

Upstairs, on the tenth floor, behind the closed doors of the club's boardroom, thirty-six men sat and stood around a polished wooden table. These were the club's board of overseers. Some were clean-shaven, impeccably dressed in gray and olive Armani suits, Charvet shirts, and Hermès ties. Others had *bord un payes* and wore black kaftans and *yarmulkes*. Still others wore frayed white shirts, ancient khaki pants, colorfully knitted *yarmulkes*, and sneakers. Few wore jewelry.

Several of these men were sight holders. That meant they dealt directly with the De Beer's diamond syndicate, whose Diamond Trading Company handled 95 percent of the world's total production of diamonds and through whose Central Selling Organization passed 85 percent of the world's uncut stones. These sight holders traveled to London, to Syndicate headquarters at 17 Charterhouse Street, ten times a year, on every fifth Monday, to pick up and pay for the stones they had requested.

All these men were globe trotters, regularly visiting the capitals of the diamond world: London, for the sights; Antwerp, where some of the best stones in the world were cut on the Pelikanstraat; Amsterdam, where the diamond dealers had their banks and where smuggling, or "submarining," was the order of the day; Tel Aviv, where the Israeli govern-

ment built the twin twenty-eight-story skyscrapers of Ramat
Gan for the cutters and traders and where dealers who couldn't
get syndicate sights could buy small rough stones. Some
dealers got invited to Moscow: there the Russians only sold;
they did not buy. And there, rather uniquely in the diamond
world, there were no Jews involved. Some traveled to Johannesburg, South Africa, the home of De Beers's Consolidated
Mines, Ltd., which was a world, and a law, unto itself.

And all these men, no matter how they dressed or appeared
or comported themselves, were wealthy beyond most people's
dreams.

Today, for once, they sat quietly, listening to the club's
director, Fred Feldman, report on his conversation with the
police captain.

While downstairs rumor held sway, here, upstairs in the
boardroom, the information was of higher quality. But the
facts were bad enough.

When Feldman finished, the debate began.

"First Jaroslawicz," said Sherman Teicher, who had inherited his club membership from his father, "then Peretsky.
Then Gupta. Now Gottleib. I don't know about you, gentle-
men, but I am taking my business elsewhere."

"Oh, so you'll move to Israel," said William Goldberg,
recently elected to a director's two-year term with no pay,
"and get blown up by some Arab *meshuggener*."

"The point is," said Robert Katz, a man in a beautifully
cut fawn-colored suit, a sight holder who dealt exclusively
with the diamond palaces—Van Cleef & Arpels, Tiffany's,
and Harry Winston's—"we have become targets here. Any
shmuck can come to the street, hit someone over the head,
and walk off with a fortune. We need protection, and we need
better protection than the police seem to be able to give us."

"We got more cops on the street than ever before," said
a Hasid.

"Exactly my point," Katz said.

"I told the captain we would cooperate fully," said Feldman, whose father had also been a club director and who was
trying vainly to convince the members that they should move

the club to a larger, newer, cleaner, and more expensive location on Fifth Avenue.

"Of course," said an elderly Hasid leaning against the wall, staring at the ceiling as he spoke. "Let us cooperate fully. Let us all open our safes to these Irisher policemen. Let us show them our goods," he said with heavy sarcasm. "Let us explain how we do our business here. Let us explain *mazl un brukha*. Maybe we should invite the IRS, too? And after that, let us welcome them all into our homes to question our wives and daughters. Or perhaps, Mr. Director, we should take them to the police station ourselves? Maybe they'll find a nice Irish boy, or a *shvartzer* maybe, to bring home."

"This is not the Gestapo we're talking about, Mendel," said Feldman.

"No?"

"Look," said an Israeli dealer who had moved to New York two years ago, "the police are fine, but we should do something ourselves. It is *our* business, *our* lives."

"What can we do except cooperate with the police? It's their job to find killers."

"We should do both," said Sidney Metzer. "We should cooperate with the police—as much as we can—*and* do something ourselves. I have an idea, if we are willing to pay. I have heard of a man who was once a policeman, a detective, studying at the Lubavitcher yeshiva. A rabbi I know, a Lubavitcher who teaches there, Rabbi Kalman, mentioned him to me. Shall I speak to Reb Kalman?"

And after much debate, it was agreed.

Fred Feldman went back to the director's office. He had a phone message. An Ariel Levin wished to see him.

Well, thought Feldman, that could wait.

9

The Mathew Rosenthal Lubavitcher Yeshiva Crown Heights, Brooklyn Wednesday, September 8

"I thought you understood," said Dov Taylor. "The last thing I need right now is to go around knocking on doors, asking people about a dead man."

"You know," said Rabbi Jacob Kalman, the *yeshiva*'s director and the *gabbai*, or personal secretary, to Reb Mena-chem Mendel Seligson, the Lubavitcher *rebbe*, "I've been looking through those old family papers you gave me. Very interesting."

Rabbi Kalman's habit of never speaking to the point, never answering directly, usually amused Taylor. Today, however, it was simply annoying.

"Forget that," said Taylor. "The point is, I can't believe you would ask me to get involved, I don't care who was killed. You're just upset because I'm not going to come to class anymore. But believe me, it has nothing to do with you. I'd still like to be able to come here and *shmooze*."

"Did you know that your great-great-grandfather was Rabbi Hirsh Leib, the *Zaddik* of Orlik?"

"Also, there's nothing I can do to catch this guy that the police can't do. We'd be wasting your money, my time, and, and, it would be a waste of time," Taylor concluded lamely, seeing that Kalman, like the Ancient Mariner, had fixed him with a glittering eye and was poised to plow ahead.

"Do you know," asked Rabbi Kalman, "who was Rabbi Hirsh Leib?"

Taylor looked around the rabbi's cozy book-lined office off the main study room of the *yeshiva*. Among the countless Jewish texts and portraits of Rabbi Seligson were candlelabras, menorahs, and photographs of Rabbi Kalman with his children and grandchildren. Taylor felt comfortable here, a fact that never ceased to surprise him, considering that he rarely felt comfortable anywhere these days except in AA meetings.

"Yes," said Taylor. "My grandmother always told me it was a big deal, something to be proud of."

"Do you know why it was a big deal?"

"No way you're not going to tell me, right?"

"I think it's important that you know that you carry the spark of a great and holy man, yes," said Rabbi Kalman, wriggling onto his leather chair to get comfortable and gazing at the ceiling, summoning the story. "It means that you have a kind of *yikhus*, merit, that we call *zekhus avos*, the merit of your forefathers."

Taylor felt a sudden wave of frustration sweep over him. Why was Kalman pushing him to do something he didn't want to do? It wasn't fair. He looked down at his hands and forced them to unclench. Relax, he told himself. Easy does it. Keep it simple. No power on earth is going to stop him from telling you a story, so just relax. Then you can say no, and go.

"First," began Rabbi Kalman, "you must understand that for Jews things had reached a terrible pass.

"I am speaking of the beginning of the eighteenth century, not so long ago. Many people were still mourning the disaster of the false messiah, Sabbatai Tzvi. You know about him?"

"He proclaimed himself the Messiah."

"And converted to Islam when he was arrested by the Turkish sultan. He had the spark of holiness in him, but he was ensnared by pride. Many thousands of Jews left their homes to follow him. When he betrayed them, they returned home in despair, only to be slaughtered in pogroms, may their blood be avenged.

"The Russian and Polish and Hungarian lords made laws forbidding Jews to own land, forbidding them to trade with Christians. The peasants were encouraged to go into Jewish towns, burn our books, our *shuls*, kill men, women, children. We weep for these martyrs.

"So," said Rabbi Kalman, "that's the way it was. Then, at the beginning of the eighteenth century, was born in Podolia, in the Ukraine, a child who would become Rabbi Israel ben Eliezer, the Baal Shem Tov, the Master of the Good Name, may his memory protect us.

"Now, throughout history, there had been many *baalei shem*, men who knew one or more of the many names of God. And knowing a name or two, they could perform miracles. But the Baal Shem Tov knew the one, true name, and the miracle he performed every day of his life was to bind man to God.

"We call him the Besht.

"It is said that when all the souls of all the men to come were gathered in Adam's soul, and Adam went to eat the apple, the Besht's soul walked away and would not eat.

"The Besht became a *melamed*, a teacher of children, got married, worked as a slaughterer, and then began to wander through Podolia, living in the mountains, fasting and meditating. There is a story told that once he was so deep in meditation that he stepped off a mountain and would have fallen had not another mountain jumped over and put itself under his foot."

Kalman paused. "Why are you smiling?" he asked Taylor.

"Was I smiling?"

"I said something funny?"

"No. It's very pretty."

"You don't think a mountain can move? You think this is a, a, children's story?"

"I think it's a metaphor."

"Is that a fancy word for nonsense?"

"Come on, Rabbi. Do you think mountains can jump around?"

"I think there is no limit to what the Creator can do. And if you think logically, my friend, you will have to agree with me."

And this, thought Taylor, was why the idea of his becoming a Hasid was so ridiculous. Put on *tefillin*? It only made sense if you believed that every word in the Bible was dictated by God and was therefore meant to be taken absolutely literally.

If you believed that, then mountains jumped, the sun stood still, and God cared if you tied a box to your forehead.

"May I continue?" asked Rabbi Kalman.

"Please. But I'm not changing my mind."

"Soon," said Rabbi Kalman, clearing his throat and staring again at the ceiling, "Jews all over had heard of this man. The Besht. They came to him to be healed, and they stayed to gaze in wonder at his face, which had the sign of God upon it.

"It is said that when the Baal Shem prayed, people saw the terrible fear of God grip his limbs and they themselves felt fear. It is said that the fear of God was so great in him that when he prayed, everyone in the room could hear the beating of his heart. 'I am surprised, body,' the Besht once said, 'that you have not crumbled to bits for fear of your Maker.'

"It is said that when the Baal Shem sang the morning prayer, his voice was so loud that it woke up all the Jews in the world."

Kalman paused. "That," he said, "is a metaphor."

Taylor smiled.

"The Besht performed many miracles," Kalman continued, "but his greatest miracle was reawakening hope in the people. The moment their eyes fell upon the Baal Shem Tov, they began again to love God. These were the first Hasidim.

"Of course," he said, "the Besht had many disciples. And many of these disciples became themselves *zaddikim*, the righteous, and went off and founded their own schools with their own Hasidim.

"One of the greatest of these disciples of the disciples of the Besht was Rabbi Jacob Yitzhak, the Seer of Lublin.

"He was called 'the Seer,' " said Rabbi Kalman, "because when he met a man he could see on his forehead all the lives the man's soul had lived, right back to Cain and Abel, and saw all the soul's sins and virtues.

"Each year, Rabbi Yitzhak was confident that the Messiah would come. And each year when he did not, the rabbi did not, like other men, blame the people for their sinfulness; he blamed the wise men because they could not achieve humility.

"It is said that the Seer's very clothes whispered constantly of his greatness."

Kalman stared a challenge at Taylor. Taylor felt a wise-crack coming on and then thought better of it. Why stretch this out?

"Now your great-great-grandfather," said Rabbi Kalman, "Rabbi Hirsh Leib of Orlik, was a disciple of the Seer. It was said that he was a very strong man, physically, like you, and a great horseman, too. It was said that he knew the language of horses, that he could speak to them. Do you like horses?"

Taylor's answer was abrupt. "Hate 'em."

"You hate them? How can you hate an animal? People, I understand. But a poor animal?"

"Can't stand them. Every time I've been on one, they do what they want. Maybe Hirsh Leib could talk to them, but I can't."

"I'm surprised," said Rabbi Kalman. "Such things are usually passed on. But, of course, it's been such a long time. Anyway," he continued, "it is said that once, when Rabbi Zusya of Hanipol took to his sickbed to suffer for the Jews, the Seer and Rabbi Hirsh Leib went to visit him. When they came to his bed, Hirsh Leib told the Seer to give Rabbi Zusya his hand so he could rise. The Seer burst into tears. And Rabbi Hirsh Leib asked him, 'Why do you weep? Do you think he is sick because it is his destiny? He has taken suffering upon himself of his own free will, and if he wanted to rise, he would not need the hand of a stranger to do so.' "

Rabbi Kalman stopped and fell silent, and Dov Taylor started as if Rabbi Kalman had shouted.

"That's it?" asked Taylor. "You tell me all this for one little story about my great-great-grandfather? What else do you know about him?"

"You can find out for yourself," said Rabbi Kalman. "What are you, lazy? Is that your problem? You're a lazy person."

"What are you talking about?" asked Taylor, feeling confused, a trifle guilty, and angry at the rabbi for making him feel that way. Today, again, he had called in sick at work.

"You want me to do everything for you?" Rabbi Kalman asked accusingly.

"All right, all right. I'll find out about this Hirsh Leib."

"That's not what I'm talking about. I'm talking about why you won't help us find this murderer."

"I told you," Dov Taylor said heatedly, the vein in his forehead beginning to swell. "I was a cop for fifteen years. It almost killed me. I drank. I passed out drunk every night for five years. Every night. I took drugs. I was stoned every day.

"I killed a little boy. He was twelve years old. I told you that. I've told you all of this."

"And you have shame for this?"

"Yes. Of course. For God's sake, you know I do."

"And you have taken to your sickbed, eh? Like Rabbi Zusya? You suffer for all the little children who live in this terrible world you think you know so well. You know what Hirsh Leib would tell you? He would say, 'Dov, my son, it is time you got up off your sickbed. If you wish to be healthy, you must stop acting like a sick one.' And you know you cannot do this by yourself. You go to your meetings, yes, and the people there help you with this drinking sickness, but you suffer from another sickness, a sickness of the heart, of the soul, and there are others who can help you with these. I do what I can, but Hirsh Leib could also help you."

"You're talking about my great-great-grandfather? My dead great-great-grandfather?"

"You think this is impossible? Don't answer. Of course you do. So don't think about that. Think about getting off your sickbed and doing something with your life. Think about helping us.

"Besides," said Rabbi Kalman, "the *rebbe* has seen this. It is your destiny."

"No," said Dov Taylor.

"It is good that you fight for yourself," Rabbi Kalman said. "That is a good beginning. Next, you will fight for someone you love, and then you will learn that there is no difference between the one and the two. And that will be your salvation."

10

Forty-seventh Street, Manhattan
Wednesday, September 8

When Ariel Levin heard about Zalman Gottleib's murder, the first thing he did was open his safe and pop the little locked box Gottleib had given him to hold. When Levin saw the stone, he called Fred Feldman at the Diamond Dealers Club.

All this he did without thinking.

Now he was thinking.

This amazing stone—and Levin had never seen one remotely like it—could not have belonged to Gottleib. One- and two-carat stones were Gottleib's business. Half carats and quarter carats. Side stones. Commercial-grade stones. Not this.

Levin popped the stone into his vacuum scale. My God! Seventy-two carats.

He looked at it through his loupe.

Flawless.

What the hell was Gottleib doing with a treasure like this?

Maybe Gottleib was a good friend of Elizabeth Taylor's, Levin thought, chuckling at the image that popped into his mind of the famous star and little Zalman Gottleib sharing a bowl of borscht with sour cream and potatoes at the Diamond Dairy Luncheonette.

Then he thought of them in bed. Elizabeth Taylor lying on her back while Gottleib humped her, his *yarmulke* flying off his head, his *tzitzis* whipping her huge, milky-white breasts. *Give it to me, Zally!* he imagined her crying out. *Give me your big Yiddish salami!*

Levin forced himself to focus. Who had this diamond really belonged to?

Now, a day after his call to Feldman—which that big-shot

son of a bitch had yet to return—Levin wondered if he had been acting smart.

Was it smart not to have told the cops about the locked box? Was it smart not to have told them about the Israeli—the diamond cutter, what was his name?—who had called him asking for a reference to Gottleib early last week?

Well, screw the cops. Every time you got involved with cops it meant trouble. It meant them poking around in his affairs. And one of the last things Ariel Levin—who did pretty well selling smuggled stones for his friends back home in Israel—needed was cops snooping around.

What if Feldman told him to go to the police now? Would he get in trouble with them for holding out? Would they hold that against him? Sure they would.

What if Feldman asked for the stone? Should he just hand it over like a *shmuck*? But how could he refuse?

Well, thought Levin, I certainly can't sell it. Who the hell do I know who could buy it? And even if I walked into Cartier or Harry Winston's, they'd want to know where I got it. What could I say?

More likely, he thought, they'd throw me out and call the cops.

Levin stared at the stone, his mind doing fast circles, figuring, figuring.

What if I tried to take it to Israel? Who do I know who could sell a stone like this?

No one.

Levin had a high regard for his own intelligence. Hadn't he been smart enough to have emigrated from Israel, leaving a dull, dead-end job in Ramat Gan, cutting stones for big-shot New York dealers while he lived in a tiny cinderblock apartment complex in Tel Aviv? Hadn't he been sharp enough to avoid getting trapped by the military career his father, a lifelong Israeli Defense Force bureaucrat, had decreed for him? Shit, thought Levin, I'd probably be a fried egg in some goddamn tank right now. And most of all, hadn't he been shrewd enough to divorce Betsy Moskowitz, who nagged and nagged and wanted to tie him down with babies and more babies?

So why should I hand this fortune over to Feldman, this big shot who doesn't know me or want to know me?

On the other hand, whoever killed Gottleib probably killed him for this stone. Which is now my stone. Which could make me a target if anybody knew about it.

So what are you doing? Levin asked himself. Making sure Feldman knows about it. And who will he tell? The killer?

Look, Levin told himself, you need more time to think. Gottleib probably didn't tell anyone about the stone. Probably no one knows you have it. Maybe there's an angle here. Maybe whoever owns it would pay to get it back. Pay a lot. Maybe you should make some discreet inquiries, talk to some of Gottleib's pals, whoever they were. Schumach, for one. And if and when Feldman calls back, well, just tell him you wanted to join the club. Fat chance of that, Levin thought, but he'll believe it.

Just then Levin's phone rang. A woman named Mary Rubel, a widow who'd gotten his name from an Israeli acquaintance of his, wished to see him about a ring she wanted reset. It was her engagement ring. Perhaps she could come to his office this afternoon. Around four o'clock, say?

She sounds young, thought Levin. Sounds Polish. A nice, young, Polish widow.

"Fine," said Levin. "When you come to the door, I'll buzz you in. Tell me," he asked, wanting to know just how much he should anticipate meeting this woman, "how will I recognize you?"

"I am tall," the woman said, "and blond."

Better and better, thought Levin, hanging up. Like many short men, he liked his women tall; like many swarthy men, he liked them fair. Better and better, he thought, congratulating himself on his shrewdness.

Levin congratulated himself again several hours later when Mary Rubel walked through his door. His feelings at that moment were quite different from Morris Schumach's, who was leaning against the marble wall in the lobby nine stories below, fighting to catch his breath. If the woman he had just seen entering the building had not been that disturbing widow from Queens, thought Schumach, then it was her twin sister, God preserve him.

11

Lambs Club Basement
Forty-third Street, Manhattan
Wednesday, September 8

After listening to Rabbi Kalman's story Dov Taylor felt agitated, and it annoyed him that his great-great-grandfather was good with horses and he wasn't. It was dumb, he knew, but it had always bothered him that he felt so uncomfortable on a horse. He had always felt that he should enjoy riding, that he should be able to master a horse. The fact that he could not made him feel less than competent. And that, he knew, was one of the feelings he drank over. The wounded ego. What had he heard one old-timer say in a meeting? "Poor me; poor me; pour me a drink."

Time to go to a meeting, Dov, he told himself. Checking his book, he saw that there was one at four P.M. in the basement of the Lambs Club.

Taylor had not been to this meeting before, but all meetings were pretty much the same. There were the same men and women, young and old, guzzling gallons of bad coffee, smoking like fiends. There was the same banner in the front of the room proclaiming Alcoholics Anonymous's famous Twelve Steps. There were the same idiotic, simpleminded, yet profoundly useful slogans: Keep It Simple. First Things First. Easy Does It. Indeed, the predictability of the meetings was one of the things Taylor liked about them.

Because the Lambs Club was in the theater district, and right next to the slime pit of Forty-second Street, the meeting this afternoon was rather more diverse than Taylor's home meeting on Prince Street. A glamorous old woman with short white hair and buckets of costume jewelry sat at one of the Formica tables, addressing dozens of formal invitations with a fountain pen in purple ink. An ancient rummy, his brain half-gone from the booze, shuffled back and forth from the coffee urn to his folding chair, coughing, wheezing, and greeting almost everyone. A young man dressed in army fatigues studied a script.

And how do I fit in? thought Taylor.

Real well, he answered himself.

This afternoon's guest speaker was a lawyer in his late thirties named John, who had slipped after seven years of sobriety.

"I shouldn't even be qualifying," John said. "I mean, I only have ninety days. I had seven years and now I only have ninety days. Because what they tell you is true. When you pick up, it doesn't matter how long you've been sober. You're right back where you started. Seven years. I threw it away. Why? Oh, I had a million reasons. The job. The pressure. Real estate. But, you know, none of it means anything. You know. I picked up because I have a progressive and fatal illness, alcoholism, and drinking is what I do.

"So there I was, sitting in my house in Bridgehampton at nine in the morning, a glass of Scotch in my hand. My wife had gone back to the city with my two kids. She was leaving me.

"These kids, they were gifts of sobriety. I'm forty-eight. They're six and four. So I'm sitting there, and, thanks to my Higher Power—it sure wasn't me—I put down that glass and drove myself to a meeting in Amagansett. And now, like I said, I've got ninety days.

"It's embarrassing as hell, and it's no fun talking about it. But my sponsor said I should speak about it, maybe help someone else, remind myself about what a *shmuck* I am. So what I can tell you is this: If you pick up, you'll be back where you started. Fast. Maybe it took you ten, twenty years of drinking to get where you were when you entered the program, but if you pick up, it won't take that long. You'll be right back where you left off in a few days, I guarantee it. Actually, you'll be right back where you left off the minute you pick up.

"I guess that's it. Thanks for listening."

Everybody took turns commenting on or adding to John's story. When it was Taylor's turn, he fought back his inclination to pass. Better, he thought, to talk, to tell the story he had told fifty, a hundred times before at meetings all over the city.

"I was glad to hear John's story," Taylor began, "because I think about picking up all the time. I mean, my wife is gone, I lost my job, why not? Why not? But I know that's the booze talking.

"I was a cop. I killed a kid. My partner had gone into an apartment and I was in the hallway. It was dark and I was scared. And drunk and stoned. As usual. By that time, that was normal. Scary, huh? You'd be amazed how many cops are out there messed up out of their minds. Or maybe you wouldn't be amazed.

"Anyway, someone came running at me with what I knew was a gun. I saw a flash. I shot him. It was a twelve-year-old. It was a toy, a battery-operated laser gun. Cops talk about it, talk about some other guy who fucked up. Well, this time it was me.

"So they took away my gun, suspended me, and that gave me more time for you know what. It also gave me more reasons. Not, like John said, that I needed any. I drank because I drank; I took twelve, fourteen Percodans a day just to feel normal. I took half a dozen Valiums just to fall asleep. On top of the booze. Every morning I'd vomit, do a few Percs to kill the hangover, wash them down with a few beers to settle the stomach. That was breakfast. Then I was ready to start my day.

"Of course, like most cops, I had a lot of guns around, and one day, a few months later, I must have been in a blackout, I found myself in a bar with my piece shoved down a guy's throat, screaming shit like I was going to blow him away. I still don't know what it was all about. Can you believe it? I haven't got a clue. Well, of course you believe it. I just wanted to hurt somebody. I hated myself and I wanted to take it out on somebody.

"My life had become, as they say, unmanageable. And then a cop I knew dragged me into the program, and after a few months I met my sponsor, and together with the program and my sponsor, here I am.

"See, I know that if I pick up, I'll kill someone. I know that. So I stay sober, a day at a time. And, a day at a time, things get a little better. And even if they don't, at least I've got the program.

"Right now, someone is asking me to do something that scares the shit out of me. My sponsor says 'Easy does it.' He's right, I know, but I'm starting to think I need to get more involved. It's something I got to work out.

"So, again, thanks, John."

The meeting ended a few minutes later. After the Lord's Prayer, everyone joined hands and chanted: "It works if you work it, so work it. Keep coming back."

Taylor left quickly, feeling, he had to admit, calmer. Tomorrow he would call Rabbi Kalman and tell him that he would make a few calls.

Sure. That's not a big commitment. That's easy.

That's putting first things first, he told himself.

That's keeping it simple.

12

The Satmarer Rebbe's House
Williamsburg, Brooklyn
Thursday, September 9

When Dov Taylor called Rabbi Kalman to tell him that he was going to take the day off to make a few calls and ask around before deciding whether or not he could be of use,

Rabbi Kalman insisted that he first see the Satmarer *rebbe*, Joel Teitel.

"The murdered man was a Hasid," Rabbi Kalman said, "and a follower of the Satmarer *rebbe*. Am I right in thinking that if you're going to find out who murdered this man, you're going to have to understand him first?"

"If I were going to try to do that, Rabbi," said Taylor, "and that's a big 'if,' then, yes, I would try to get to understand him."

"Well," said Rabbi Kalman, "to understand a Hasid, you must understand his *zaddik*. Not," he added, "that that will be easy. The Satmarer *rebbe* is a holy man, a learned man, but he is, God forgive me for saying it, a hard man, an intolerant man. He does not reach out to the world; he speaks only to his Hasids."

"Sounds like a peach," said Taylor.

"Yes," said Rabbi Kalman, "as you say, a peach. He's nothing like Rabbi Seligson, may he live long and happily. Reb Seligson tries to bring different people together; Reb Teitel broods on their differences. In a way, I hate to send you to him.

"But if he doesn't give you his blessing, you will not be able to talk to any of his followers. So this is something you must do. Also"—and Rabbi Kalman's voice dropped—"I hear rumors that the Satmarers are blaming us for the murders."

"The Lubavitchers?"

"Yes," said Kalman. "There is much bitterness between Satmar and Lubavitch."

"But what about the wedding?"

"Yes, the wedding is a good thing. So it would be good if the Satmarers see someone sent by us, see that we are trying to help them."

"What should I do, call him?" asked Taylor.

"I will arrange it. And when you go see him, wear your *yarmulke*, a simple black one so you won't look like a *Bar Mitzvah* boy or an Israeli cabdriver."

An hour later Taylor's phone rang. It was the Satmarer *rebbe*'s *gabbai*, his personal secretary, telling Taylor to present himself at the *rebbe*'s house at eight that evening. And a few minutes before eight, an uneasy Dov Taylor—a black *yarmulke* perched precariously if, thought Taylor, rakishly on the back of his head—found himself standing in the dying autumn light, looking up at the *rebbe*'s unassuming brownstone on South Ninth Street in Williamsburg.

Looking over his shoulder, Taylor noted a parked car—in its studied drabness, obviously an unmarked police unit. For the past several years, ever since confrontations between the Hasidim and Williamsburg's mostly West Indian blacks had started to become violent, the city had been providing twenty-four-hour security in front of the *rebbe*'s home.

To Taylor, the whole neighborhood seemed to be in a state of psychological siege. Everywhere he looked, he saw the signs. Forget the squad car. What about those two stocky Hasids standing guard on either side of the *rebbe*'s door? They were staring at Taylor with flat, expressionless eyes—stone killer eyes—and Taylor could see the guns bulging beneath their kaftans.

Staring was big in Williamsburg, thought Taylor. First they stared, then they looked away in contempt. Right now men were staring at him, wondering why this *goyishe Yid* was standing in front of their *rebbe*'s home. Women, pushing baby carriages, stared, too. It made Taylor angry. Who did they think they were, these Hasids? So arrogant, so sure that they were better than everyone else.

It occurred to Taylor that what Jews like him thought about Hasids, the *goys* thought about Jews.

More women passed by, giving him a wide berth as he stood in front of the *rebbe*'s house. To Taylor it seemed that every woman he saw in Williamsburg and in Crown Heights was either pregnant, pushing a baby carriage, or pulling a small gang of children in her wake. He remembered that he had once read that the average Hasidic household boasted six or seven children. The Hasidim took God's injunction to be fruitful and multiply very seriously and regarded using birth control as defying God's commandment. They were also intent, Rabbi Kalman had said, upon replacing the six million murdered in the Holocaust, most of whom had been Hasids.

Indeed, before the war, Hasids had made up much of the world's Jews.

Taylor stared at the *rebbe*'s house, at the heavy wooden door. Why am I nervous? he asked himself. Walking over from the subway, he had expected the hostility of the Hasids for an assimilated Jew like himself. *Goyishe Yidn*, the Hasids called them scornfully. But Taylor had been in hostile situations before. In fact, until two years ago they had been his life.

Of course, thought Taylor, that's it. I'm nervous because I'm on a cop's errand.

And also because I've never before met a Hasidic *rebbe* in the flesh.

No Hasid, Taylor remembered Rabbi Kalman telling him, would dream of marrying, buying a house, choosing a career, or going into a business without consulting his *rebbe*. And no Hasid would dream of ignoring his *rebbe*'s advice. This relationship with his *rebbe* was what defined the Hasid and separated him from all other Jews.

In his own community, the *rebbe* was as powerful as any medieval king. And, like a medieval king, the *rebbe* inherited his throne. The Satmarer *reb*, the Lubavitcher *reb*, the Belzer *reb*, the Gerer *reb*, the Lelover *reb*, the Talner *reb*—all named for the city in Poland or Russia or, in the case of the Satmarer *rebbe*, in Hungary, where they originally held court—could all trace their lines back to the Baal Shem Tov or to one of his disciples.

The *rebbe*'s power was absolute. His every word, his every gesture, was considered by his followers to have profound religious and cosmic significance. Indeed, many Satmarer Hasidim did not wear watches, Rabbi Kalman once mentioned, simply because the Satmarer *reb* did not wear one.

And why not? Taylor asked. Who knows? said Rabbi Kalman. The point is, because their *zaddik* does not wear a watch, they believe that there is something holy about not wearing one. A Hasid believes that his *zaddik* is perfect, and that how he lives his life is the way the Holy One wants all men to live.

Taylor felt uneasy as he began moving up the walk to the

rebbe's door, but he smiled broadly at the two Hasids guarding the entrance as he reached for the bell. From behind, one of the Hasids grabbed his arms and pulled them down to his side, pinning them. The other Hasid put his hand on his chest.

"Tell him to let me go," Taylor said calmly. He had been expecting something like this and began calculating whether it would be better to grab the man's balls and squeeze or to bring his foot down into the man's instep.

"Easy," said the Hasid. "No trouble. We know who you are. But this we must do. You understand."

"Sure," said Taylor. "Nobody wants any trouble. But tell him to let go of me right now. Right now."

The Hasid looked into Taylor's eyes and then said something in Yiddish. Taylor felt his arms released.

"Okay," said Taylor, lifting his hands. "No trouble."

The Hasid ran his hand lightly over Taylor's torso, under his arms, down his legs, and up into his groin. A good, professional frisk, thought Taylor.

"What have you got there, under your coat?" he asked the Hasid.

The Hasid closed his eyes and leaned back against the *rebbe*'s brownstone, elaborately bored.

"I mean, what kind of gun?" Taylor asked.

The Hasid unbuttoned his kaftan and allowed Taylor a peek at the eight-and-three-quarter-inch-long barrel of the .44-caliber Smith & Wesson Model 29 sticking out from an oily, low-slung, brown leather shoulder holster. It was a cannon for cutting people in half. The Hasid closed his coat.

"Just like Dirty Harry," Taylor said.

"What is Dirty Harry?" asked the Hasid.

"Forget it," said Taylor. Different worlds, he thought.

The Hasid shrugged and, folding his arms over his chest, resumed his watch, dismissing Taylor from his mind, from his world.

Taylor rang the Satmarer *rebbe*'s doorbell.

The door swung open. A young, pretty, stylishly dressed woman wearing a curly red *sheitel*, or wig (married Hasidic women cut their hair short and covered it with wigs as an act of modesty), said, "Come," and ushered Taylor inside. They turned off a short hallway and entered a large parlor filled with about twenty people. The shades were drawn, and every chair was occupied by a fidgeting Hasid waiting for either an audience with the *rebbe* or a chance to submit to him a question or request on a piece of paper. As the woman led Taylor through the room, he could feel their eyes upon him. Who was this *goyishe Yid*, he imagined them thinking, being treated like someone important? Nervously he touched his *yarmulke* to make sure it was still on his head.

The woman led Taylor to a broad, polished wooden staircase lined with gaudily framed oil paintings of Israel and Jerusalem and one full-length portrait of a rabbi wearing a white silk robe. To his left, Taylor saw a door opened to a large dining room dominated by a long mahogany table surrounded by leather-backed chairs and, beyond that, a gleaming white kitchen, one of four in the house: one for milk, one for meat, one for the Sabbath, and one for Passover.

"Go up," the woman said, and Taylor saw a small bearded figure standing at the top of the stairs waiting for him.

When Taylor reached the landing, the man extended a moist, limp hand. "Dov Taylor?" he asked. Taylor nodded.

"Nice guys you got down there, guarding the door," said Taylor.

"Yes, very good, very pious. So. I'm Pinchus Mayer, the *rebbe*'s *gabbai*. I spoke with you, yes? Tell me, you speak some Yiddish?"

"No."

"No? How sad. Well, Rabbi Kalman tells me that you're the great-great-grandson of Rabbi Hirsh Leib. That's good, yes? The *rebbe* was very pleased to hear it. A blessing. We are honored. Tell me, what was your mother's name?

"Silberstein. Luba Silberstein."

"From where?

"Rumania. Bucharest."

"And what was her mother's name?"

"Rebecca."

"Rebecca what?"

"Rebecca Silberstein."

"No, her mother's name."

"You know," said Taylor, "I don't know. I never thought about it."

"You should find out, yes?" said Mayer.

"Excuse me," Taylor said, "I don't mean to be rude, but why are you asking me about my mother and grandmother?"

"You are offended?" the *gabbai* asked.

"No, it's not that," said Taylor. "I just don't understand."

"That's all right," Mayer said casually, as if to say that as there were so many things Taylor didn't understand, one more would hardly make a difference. "Now come with me to meet the *rebbe*."

"Is there anything I should know?" asked Taylor, irritated by Mayer's condescending attitude. "I mean, what should I call him? Your Holiness? Your Rabbiness?"

"His name is Joel Teitel," Mayer said mildly, ignoring Taylor's sarcasm. "He is the son-in-law of the *alter rebbe*, Menachem Isaac, may his memory preserve us. You may call him *Rebbe*. Come.

"Oh, yes. Do not attempt to shake his hand. It is not done."

Mayer opened a door beyond the landing and led Taylor into a large, smoky, dusty office. The shades were drawn against the dying September light. The Satmarer *rebbe* sat on a leather chair that rose a foot above his head. His desk was a vast, teak altar piled high with books and papers. Behind him, and on all four walls, were floor-to-ceiling bookshelves crammed with books and scrolls, gold and silver *kiddush* cups, and polished brass menorahs. Taylor saw at least a dozen Torah scrolls, their tattered and worn velvet coverings contrasting with the silver medallions draped over them.

Flanking the *rebbe*'s desk, two young men sat at two small, battered New York City public school desks. They did not look up from their books as Taylor entered, nor did they look up now as he stood in front of the *rebbe*.

In his black silk kaftan and large, dark brown fur hat, his *shtreimel*, Rebbe Joel Teitel had plenty of *malkhus*, imperial sternness. His long, wiry, untrimmed white beard reached to his waist. His eyebrows were gray, thick, and bushy, and his eyes were small and bloodshot. Dark bags hung beneath them.

Mayer left Taylor and walked around the desk to whisper in the *rebbe*'s left ear as the *rebbe* stared at Taylor, looking, it seemed to him, at a spot on his forehead. The *rebbe* nodded several times and then addressed a few words of Yiddish to the two young scholars. They stood up simultaneously and, their eyes cast down, left the room by a door set into the bookshelves that Taylor had not before noted. As they went through the door, Taylor caught a glimpse of another, smaller office containing several typewriters, steel filing cabinets, and a video terminal.

They never looked at me, thought Taylor. Not once. If I murdered their *rebbe* right now, they could never describe me.

Mayer followed the two young men out of the room without looking back, without saying good-bye. Taylor suddenly felt abandoned and berated himself for being so unsure of himself. Alcoholic thinking, he told himself. Poor me. Next thing you know, you'll be wanting to "pour" yourself a drink.

The *rebbe* gestured for Taylor to seat himself on an old leather library chair directly opposite the *rebbe*'s throne.

Taylor sat, and still the *rebbe* stared at his forehead, saying nothing. In the silence, Taylor imagined that he could feel a hole being bored in his head. This is an old cop's trick, he thought suddenly. Wait out the suspect. Well, I'm not going to play.

He coughed. "*Rebbe—*"

The *rebbe* immediately held up his hand in a clear signal for Taylor to remain silent. Then the *rebbe* cleared his throat and began speaking in a voice so soft that Taylor had to lean forward to hear him, annoyed that the *rebbe* had won the first point in the war of nerves.

"It is just as I thought. I cannot speak to you, Mr. Policeman," the *rebbe* whispered. "We cannot talk, you and I. It is an impossibility. You are not only ignorant of the language of your own people, you are a murderer. You have the mark of Cain on your forehead. It is there for anyone to see. You can see it yourself. The blood of assassins flows in your veins. Right now, you have blood on your hands. I can smell it, you know."

Taylor felt his face grow hot; the vein on his forehead began to throb. He felt anger and shame fill his stomach. He wanted to punch this old man in the mouth, and at the same time he wanted to fall on his knees and beg for forgiveness. So, instead, he stood up to leave.

"Sit!" the *rebbe* thundered in a voice as loud as it had just been soft. "Be quiet! There are matters here far more important than your feelings."

Taylor found himself sitting back down.

Now the *rebbe*'s voice again grew soft, softer even than before. "You know, Mr. Policeman, that I am right. How can you and I talk? Can you understand me? Of course not. And I have no interest in trying to understand you.

"But, Mr. Policeman, it is *zeyer* important, very, very important, that I be able to tell you something."

"So tell me," said Taylor, his composure regained, now wondering if this *rebbe* were mad.

"But I have just told you I cannot. It is a problem. You are the problem, Mr. Policeman."

"So write me a letter," said Taylor.

"You see? You are making a joke. I am telling you something is important, and you are making a joke. You are joking about something you do not understand because you are a fool."

"Listen, Reb Teitel—"

"Shah. *Shtil*. Be quiet. Fortunately, with the help of the Holy One, Blessed is He, I arrived at a solution this afternoon. I was in the study house, and a holy voice spoke to me. Do you know whose voice it was?"

I am sitting here, swallowing insults, listening to this nonsense, for Rabbi Kalman's sake, Dov Taylor told himself. But when this is finished, I'm going to tell him I can't help. These people are lunatics. And they hate my guts.

The *rebbe* rapped on his desk as if calling Taylor to attention. Then he looked up at the ceiling.

"It was the voice of the *Zaddik* of Orlik, my comrade Hirsh Leib. You carry his holy spark, and it is to him I must speak."

The Satmarer *rebbe* paused, then began: "My friend, my brother—"

"Wait a minute," said Dov Taylor. "You're going to talk to Hirsh Leib while I just sit here?"

"Please, Mr. Policeman. Permit me to continue."

"I mean, if you're going to talk to Hirsh Leib, why not speak Yiddish? I'll just take a snooze."

"Again a joke. Unfortunately, Mr. Policeman, your great-great-grandfather can only help me through you, using you as his vessel, unworthy though you are. So if Rabbi Leib is to help me, and help you, you must listen and understand."

"By the way, Rabbi, I'm not a policeman anymore, and Mr. Policeman is not my name," Dov Taylor said.

"Enough!" shouted the Satmarer *rebbe*. "Just listen."

"My name is Dov Taylor."

"My friend, my brother, my teacher, Hirsh Leib, wise man of Orlik and Lublin, I have a problem," Teitel began in a strong, clear, conversational tone. "My daughter Esther was to be married to the son of the Lubavitcher *rebbe*, may God show him the error of his ways. Her dowry was to be a diamond, a diamond you remember, my old friend. It was the jewel once possessed, and lost, by our teacher, the holy Rebbe Jacob Yitzhak, the Seer of Lublin, may his memory be blessed. It was recovered by my father-in-law's father, Rebbe David Isaac, may his memory protect us, and my father-in-law, Rebbe Menachem Isaac of holy memory, who used it to save himself and his Hasidim from the Nazis. Then it was taken back from those murderers and returned to our holy community.

"Now, it has again been lost, stolen. I gave it to a righteous man, a pious man, although not a scholar, Zalman Gottleib, may his blood be avenged, because he knew of diamonds, and I was going to ask him to fashion it into a crown for my Esther. And for this, Reb Leib, he was most horribly slaughtered, and the Seer's stone is again in the hands of the evil ones.

"If it is the Lubavitchers who have done this, seeking to stop this marriage, then they have achieved their evil aim. There will be no wedding, and no peace between us, until the jewel is returned to our community. I declare in your presence this *shidukh* null and void. As it is written in the law, I repeat this three times. Null and void. Null and void. So, it is done.

"If it is the Nazis, or their accursed children, or some others we know not of, I beg you, Reb Leib, in the name of the Holy One, Blessed is He, to help this Dov Taylor, son of Luba, the daughter of Rebecca, this one that carries your spark. Lead him to the Seer's stone. Use him to bring your wrath down upon the evil ones who have murdered and thieved. Help this one to see his destiny, for he is ignorant and foolish and even now he puts himself before his brother Jews. Help him understand that, as it is written, 'Neither shalt thou stand idly by the blood of thy neighbor.' And as our sages tell us, 'He who saves one life in Israel is considered as if he had saved the whole world.' Help him, Reb Leib, *Zaddik* of Orlik, and I will bless your memory ten thousand times."

The Satmarer *rebbe* fell silent. Taylor felt as if the curtain had just fallen on a play. Should he applaud? How much of what he had just heard had any relation to reality? Was it all meant to be taken metaphorically? And what about this diamond? Had he just been told the motive for the killing?

"Do the police know?" Taylor asked.

"Do the police know what?" asked Rebbe Teitel.

"About this diamond."

"Why would they? No one knows of it now but you, me, my daughter, and Hirsh Leib."

"You showed it to your daughter?"

"Of course. It was her dowry."

"Did you tell her you gave it to Gottleib?"

"To make for her a crown."

"So who did she tell?" said Taylor.

"My daughter is a good daughter," said the *rebbe*, "a brilliant girl, and not any such stupid *shiksa* as you may know, Mr. Policeman."

Taylor sighed. Even *rebbes* could be foolish when it came to their children. "Maybe the police already have it," he suggested. "The diamond."

"Impossible."

"Why?"

"If the police had it, I would know."

"How would you know?"

"I would know."

"Do you know what Mr. Gottleib did with it before he was killed?"

"How would I know?"

"Describe the diamond to me."

"What's to describe? A diamond is a diamond. Hirsh Leib has seen it, so you will know it when you see it."

"I'll need to describe it to the police."

"*Takeh*, truly, it is hard to believe."

"What is hard to believe?"

"It is hard to believe," said the Satmarer *rebbe*, his voice growing loud, "that a descendant of Hirsh Leib could have such a *goyishe kop*! Look, Reb Leib! See how far Israel has fallen!

"Try to understand, Mr. Policeman, try to get it through your *kop*, that if I had wanted to tell the police about the Seer's stone, I wouldn't be talking to you, I would be talking to them.

"I forbid you to speak of the Seer's stone with anyone. For the rest, you may speak with my Hasidim and do whatever it is that policemen do. As it is written: 'The things that have been permitted thee, think thereupon; thou hast no business with the things that are secret.' "

"But, *Rebbe*—"

"Our seance is finished, Mr. Policeman. With the help of the Holy One, Blessed is He, and your forefather, Hirsh Leib of Orlik, may we meet again to pronounce the benediction, 'Blessed art Thou, O Lord our God, King of the Universe, who hath wrought a miracle for me in this place.'

"Go in peace, Dov Taylor. May the Holy One protect and preserve you."

"Amen," said Dov Taylor.

"Good!" shouted the Satmarer *rebbe*, clapping his hands. As if by a prearranged signal, the door in the bookshelves swung open and Pinchus Mayer and the two young men emerged. The scholars sat down at their desks and resumed their studies, and the *gabbai* walked over to Taylor, said, "Let's go," and almost lifted him out of his chair.

"Wait," said the *rebbe*. He stood up and walked around his desk, waddling right up to Dov Taylor. He must have been sitting on a telephone book, thought Taylor, who fought an urge to giggle. The *rebbe* barely came up to his chest, and with his long white beard he looked like some sort of Jewish hobbit.

Pinchus Mayer stepped back, and the *rebbe* stuck his index finger into Taylor's sternum. Taylor flinched, and the *rebbe* poked him again, hard. "You know, Mr. Policeman," he said, "your great-great-grandfather is in trouble, too. Like you. These troubles of ours, this *tsuris*, has a long, long history. You could help him. You could help each other. That would truly be a great deed, a *mitzvah*.

"You have no children, is that right?"

"Yes," said Taylor.

"Good for you your great-great-grandfather did, eh?" The *rebbe* winked, nodded, and turned back to his desk. Mayer hustled Taylor out of the office, down the stairs, through the parlor, and out the door.

"It went very well, yes?" Mayer said breathlessly, pausing in the doorway. "He gave you his blessing. He touched you. What an honor. He gave you a task. He's an amazing man, yes?"

"Amazing," agreed Taylor. It's amazing, he thought, that someone hasn't locked him up in a padded cell.

"Of course," said Mayer. "He liked you. I could tell. Amazing," Mayer said, shutting the door in Taylor's face. "Amazing."

Dov Taylor stood for a moment on the *rebbe*'s front steps. The evening darkness was warm, yet something in the air promised colder nights to come. A ditty popped into Taylor's head, and as he walked down the street to the subway he mumbled it under his breath to the tune of the "Swamp Fox Song" from the old "Walt Disney Show": "*Zaddik, zaddik*, beanie on his head / Nobody knows what the *zaddik* said."

13

Trattoria Dell'Arte
Seventh Avenue
Thursday, September 9

Ariel Levin sat at a small table in the back of the chic Trattoria Dell'Arte and gulped his second glass of arak, a Lebanese licorice schnapps of which he was quite fond. Mary Rubel had just excused herself to go to the ladies' room, and Levin was almost drooling as he watched her rear end swivel across the room.

When she had shown up at his office yesterday, Levin couldn't believe his luck. First Gottlieb's diamond, now this.

Mary Rubel was almost six feet tall with golden hair down to her waist. In his office she had worn a tight black dress that stopped way above her knees, revealing smooth, strong, tanned thighs. And her breasts! Levin wanted nothing more from life than a chance to bury his head between those breasts.

Levin had been able to tell immediately that this delectable young widow was attracted to him. When she had handed him the ring she wanted reset, and their hands had touched, she had smiled. When he had told her that he could fix it, no problem, she had thanked him profusely. And when, emboldened, he had asked her out to dinner, she had accepted without hesitation.

And tonight was going wonderfully well. He had expected her to be late, as women invariably were, but she had been waiting for him when he had arrived at the restaurant. When they had been shown to their table, Levin had put his arm around her waist and had felt her lean into him. He had seen the well-groomed heads of artsy young women and their big-shot dates turning to follow them. He could feel the envy of the men, the jealousy of the women. Even the waitress had seemed impressed. And why not? thought Levin. They were, he was sure, a striking couple.

Levin's sense of well-being, so different from his usual state of anxiety and anger, had increased during the meal. Mary Rubel seemed interested, even fascinated, in everything he had to say. When he told her about his exploits in the Israeli army—daring operations behind PLO lines that he dreamed up as he spoke—he saw her brown eyes sparkle. When he talked about his work, she asked intelligent questions that showed she was truly listening. And when his leg bumped hers under the table, she didn't pull away.

Now Levin saw her coming back to the table, and again he felt the urge to pinch himself to see if he were dreaming. Tonight she was wearing a simple white linen sleeveless dress that accentuated her powerful shoulders, her long, golden arms, and her large, full breasts. She wore her hair up, and that drew attention to her graceful neck, her high cheekbones, and her wide-set, almost Oriental eyes. On her feet she wore simple sandals, laced up her muscular calves. To Levin, it seemed as if were it not for the floor, her legs would go on forever.

"Would you like dessert?" asked Levin, who no longer knew nor cared how much this meal was costing him.

"No, thank you," Mary Rubel said.

"Would you like coffee?"

"Actually, I am rather tired."

Levin felt a cold ocean wave of disappointment wash over him. He literally shuddered from the chill, like a dog shaking itself after a bath.

"You would like to come over to my place for some coffee or brandy, Ariel?" Mary Rubel continued after a moment. "I live not far from here, a short walk."

"That would be very nice," said Levin, not trusting himself to say more, not wanting to appear too anxious.

Levin paid the bill, barely giving a thought to the fact that it was over one hundred and fifty dollars. He even included a 15 percent tip instead of his normal 10.

As soon as they entered Rubel's apartment on West Fifty-ninth Street and shut the door behind them, Levin pulled her to him and stood on his toes to kiss her. She kissed back, her tongue meeting his, and they began to undress in the darkened hallway. She led him to her bedroom, trailing clothes in her wake, and allowed him to throw her down on the bed.

Levin was fully erect by the time he took off his black bikini undershorts and threw himself on top of her, his brain spinning at the sight of her—a pornographic dream come true. She took him in her hand and guided him into her, and he was momentarily surprised to find her so wet. But soon he was beyond surprise, and all he knew was that he was going to come. Biting down hard on the inside of his cheek, he tried to hold back, and he thought he was succeeding until she reared up and reached underneath her to squeeze the base of his penis. Levin came instantly, his bliss tainted by a sharp stab of regret and the thought that she would despise him for having such slender control. But even as his orgasm took him, he felt her nails rake his back, and he heard her cry out that she was coming. Her legs locked around his waist and she squeezed so hard that he had to fight the urge to ask her to stop.

Afterward, lying in bed, drinking cognac, Levin told her about the diamonds, rubies, emeralds, and sapphires he had turned into wonderful rings, necklaces, and bracelets. He said that it often pained him to make such elegant jewelry for the fat, ugly old women who shopped in the diamond district. By all rights, he said, his creations should be worn only by women as beautiful as she.

Curled up next to him, her leg thrown over his thighs, she asked him if he would spend the night. He said yes. She asked him if sometime he would show her some of these treasures, and Levin promised that Saturday, when the shops were closed for the Sabbath and the street was quiet and empty, he would take her to the office to show her a diamond that was one of the world's wonders.

Later, with Levin snoring loudly, Maria Radziwell slipped out of bed and made a phone call. She whispered a few words into the receiver, hung up, and went to the bathroom to swallow two sleeping pills. Then she climbed back into bed and curled up as far away from Ariel Levin as possible.

Waiting for the pills to work, her thoughts drifted to the Magician, Ladislaw Czartoryski, who many years ago had promised to take her away from Warsaw's grim streets and make her rich. He would give her a new name, he said, and a new life. He would give her Paris. He would give her the world. All she had to do was sleep with him and sleep with anyone he told her to sleep with.

The Magician told her how he had searched for her, using the Party's files, until he had found her in Madame Rizitzkha's cathouse. He told her how much she resembled the old photographs of her great-grandmother, Catherine, who, he said, had also been a whore and had used her body to marry Wilhelm Radziwell, a Prussian prince, and, after leaving him, had seduced Cecil Rhodes, the great English imperialist, founder of the De Beers diamond syndicate.

Maria was entranced. Magically, she had suddenly acquired the glamorous family history to which she had always believed she was entitled. Of course she had aristocratic blood in her veins. How could someone as tall and strong and beautiful as she, beautiful as any movie star, simply have sprung from the loins of her father, a lowly clerk, or the womb of her mother, a frumpy schoolteacher? Maria had always prayed that the life she knew would turn out to be nothing more than a bad dream, and now this rich, silver-haired man, this important Party official, was shaking her, waking her up to a new life.

Lying in bed, listening to Levin snore, Maria tried to recapture that sense of excitement, that feeling of the future unfolding fresh and new. But it was gone. The Magician had indeed awoken her, and he had delivered on many of his promises. But he had never mentioned the Cutter, who seemed immune to her charms and of whom she felt ever more frightened. Czartoryski had never mentioned smelly Israelis, or murder, or the possibility that she would have to stay in this horrible New York while, she felt sure, the police drew near.

Careful not to wake Levin, Maria Radziwell slipped out of bed to take another two pills and washed them down with a glass of cognac. Then, wrapping herself in a blanket, she curled up on a chair in her living room and fell into the unconsciousness she knew as sleep.

14

SoHo, Manhattan
Friday, September 10

Dov Taylor was standing on a hill, looking down at a castle. Dirt roads ran from the castle into a village of tumble-down wooden houses and shops. Smoke curled up from their chimneys.

His grandmother Rebecca stood by his side, wearing a colorful print dress and her fur wrap with the animal's head and the tiny red marble eyes. A man, a tall bearded Hasid wearing a *shtreimel*, was walking up the hill toward them, waving his hand and calling out to them in Yiddish.

"Who is he?" Taylor asked his grandmother.

"It's Rabbi Hirsh Leib," she answered.

"What is he saying?" Taylor asked.

"He's telling you to answer your phone," said Rebecca. "It's ringing, ringing, ringing . . ."

Dov Taylor awoke and reached for the phone. It was Naomi, the girl from the bank. He had not spoken to her since she had left his apartment Tuesday morning.

"You awake?"

"Just."

"Are you coming in to work today, Dov?"

"No, I don't think so."

"Are you sick?"

"No."

" 'Cause if you're sick, I'd be glad to come over, make you some soup or something."

"No, Naomi. Really, I'm fine. I've been busy."

"Busy? What've you been busy with?"

"Just something."

"You're going to get fired."

"Uh-huh."

"What's the matter, Dov? Is it me? Did I do something wrong?"

"No, no. Look, Naomi, I just woke up. Let me call you back."

"I didn't mean to make fun of your *tefillin*. I kind of think it's neat what you're doing."

"It's not that. Really, everything's fine. I'll call you back."

"When?"

"This afternoon, okay?"

"You want me to come over tonight?"

"Can't. Got to see someone."

"A woman?"

"No, not a woman. A man. A rabbi. I gotta see a rabbi. I'll call you, I promise."

"Call me."

"I said I'd call, I'll call."

"I'm feeling very insecure, Dov. I mean, I'm sorry, I don't want to bother you."

"Don't apologize. You've got nothing to apologize for."

"All right."

"I'll call."

"Please, call."

"Good-bye, Naomi."

Taylor hung up. He opened the drawer by his bed, saw his *tallis* and *tefillin* resting in their blue velvet pouches, and closed the drawer. That's finished, he thought, lying back down. Now what?

He closed his eyes, trying to return to his dream. No, it was gone.

Dreaming of Rebecca usually made him happy, but now the good feeling was overlaid with anxiety. Anxious about what? he asked himself. Then he sat up and dialed Rabbi Kalman's number at the yeshiva.

"I spoke to Teitel yesterday," Taylor told Rabbi Kalman. "Actually, I spoke to him, he spoke to Hirsh Leib. Then, this morning, I had a dream and Hirsh Leib was in it."

"Very interesting," said Rabbi Kalman. "You'll tell me about it later. So, you've decided to help?"

"Yes," said Dov Taylor, who until that moment had not known that he had decided and in fact was still not sure that he had. "I mean, I'll talk to the police. I'll talk to some people. If I can help, sure, I'll help. But I still don't think I can do anything the police can't do."

"Of course you can. Listen. Why don't you come to *shul* tonight to welcome the *Shabbos*. I will meet you out front at, let me see, all right, four o'clock. Afterward, you will be my guest for the first *Shabbos* meal. And after that you can tell me all about your meeting with the Satmarer *rebbe*. And your dream. You will, of course, spend the night at my home."

"That's very kind of you, Rabbi. I'd love to have dinner with your family, but I couldn't possibly sleep over."

"You must."

"No, really, I can't."

"I must insist. In any case, how would you get home to your apartment?"

"I'd call a cab."

"No, my friend. Not from my home. Not on *Shabbos*. There is no telephoning, and there is no riding in automobiles."

"Well, I could take the subway."

"No, you could not. That would mean traveling outside the community, and that would mean transgressing the *t'hum Shabbos*, the Sabbath boundary. So, you see, you must spend the night. You will have my son Moshe's old room. You will be very comfortable. Besides, there is someone I wish you to meet. Someone who will be helpful to you."

"Okay, Rabbi. All right. Thank you. I'll sleep over. But tomorrow morning, I have to go."

"We'll discuss it."

"I'm serious, Rabbi."

"We'll discuss it. Agreed?"

"Agreed."

Taylor rummaged in his desk and came up with a small notebook, the kind he used to carry to crime scenes. A little more digging produced a pen. He set the notebook and pen on his desk and stared at them.

This is something I can do, he thought. I've been trained. I have the skills. It will be pleasurable doing something I know how to do.

You're killing time, he told himself. You're just filling up the emptiness.

Okay, okay. I'll accept that. But isn't that what everyone does? We fill up our time waiting to die. We fill it up with work, with booze, with family.

He opened his address book and found the name he was looking for. Phil Horowitz.

When Taylor was twelve or thirteen, Horowitz had been one of his heroes. A short, stocky teenager, Horowitz wore black leather jackets, bicycle chains, and drove a Harley-Davidson motorcycle. He worked for NBC, picking up film at Idlewild Airport and delivering it at top speed through rush-hour traffic to the NBC studios in Manhattan. He used to tell Taylor stories about smashing the windows of cars that got in his way, and Taylor listened raptly. Here was one tough Jew. Here was a Jew who didn't take any shit from anyone.

Many years later, after Taylor had become a cop, he was walking in the old neighborhood and saw a short, bearded Hasid walking toward him. It was Horowitz.

"Phil, what happened?" Taylor had asked, amazed. If there was an unlikelier candidate for piety than Phil Horowitz, Taylor couldn't imagine one. Was he in disguise for some reason?

But Horowitz told him that he had joined the Lubavitchers, and that now, for the first time in his life, he was happy.

"And what do you do now?" Taylor had asked.

As an answer, Horowitz opened his long, black, Hasidic overcoat and showed Taylor the gun resting in its shoulder holster. "I'm a diamond courier," Horowitz had said proudly, and at that moment Taylor realized that Horowitz was the same thug he had always been, only now, instead of black leather, he wore the black robes of the Hasid.

Taylor dialed the number, and Horowitz answered. Taylor asked him if he had heard about the murder in the diamond district, and Horowitz grunted. "But I don't know anything about it," he said.

"I'd like to talk to you, Phil," Taylor said.

"Sure, Dov. You can talk to me anytime. But I don't know anything about this, and I'm not going to talk about business."

"I'm not a cop anymore, Phil."

"But you're still a nosy prick, right?"

"That's right."

"Okay. Come over. How about tonight? Want to spend the *Shabbos* with us?"

"Can't, Phil. Got a date. How about tomorrow night, after?"

"After eight. Okay. Mom'll be glad to see you."

Taylor hung up and then called the Eighteenth Precinct. He was told that Frank Hill was heading up the investigation into the murders of Zalman Gottleib and Shirley Stein. Sergeant Hill, however, was off today. After some *shmoozing* with the desk sergeant, Taylor got Hill's home phone number and wrote it down.

I should be paid for this, he thought. If I'm going to play detective, I should get paid. I should get paid a lot. How about two hundred a day? Plus expenses. That sounds right.

That's another thing we fill up the emptiness with: money.

Above Frank Hill's number, Taylor wrote CALLS in capital letters. What was Gottleib's partner's name? Do I still have the newspaper article about the killings?

No. I threw it away. I like throwing things away. I like everything neat, clean, and tidy. I am always throwing things out.

Carol never threw anything out. She was a pack rat. Taylor remembered their fight the morning they moved to Eastchester from their apartment in Flatbush. They were waiting for the movers when Taylor began checking the boxes. Secretly, Carol had filled three or four large cardboard boxes with ten-year-old art magazines, her notebooks from junior high school, textbooks from college. It was around eleven A.M., Taylor already had most of a six-pack sloshing around in his gut, and the thought of bringing all that useless stuff to their

new home, *shlepping* it to their new world in the suburbs—
the new world he had bought for them by putting his life on
the line every night on the streets—filled him with righteous
anger. Here he was, trying to start fresh, and there she was,
dragging him down. The injustice of it almost brought tears
to his eyes.

So he left, slamming the door behind him. He climbed into
his car, dry-swallowed three of the Percodans he had stashed
in the glove compartment, and drove to the Windsor Inn for
the drinks he so richly deserved. If she wanted to bring that
crap with them, she could do it without his help. She could
move without his help.

And she did.

What a prince I was, thought Taylor. What a prick.

Let it go, thought Taylor. He'd already done his Eighth
and Ninth steps. He had made "a list of all persons he had
harmed, and become willing to make amends to them all,"
and he had made "direct amends to such people wherever
possible, except when to do so would injure them or others."
God knew how many times he had apologized to Carol, even
admitting to her that he had blamed her for the fact that they
couldn't have children.

And he had done his Fifth Step. He had sat down with
Alex, his sponsor, and had "admitted the exact nature of our
wrongs." In other words, he had told Alex about the boy he
had killed; he had told Alex about cheating on Carol even
while she lay on a hospital bed with the surgeons scraping
the endometriosis out of her tubes; he had confessed to the
raging egoism that often made him feel that everyone in the
world was there for the express purpose of either testing or
entertaining him. According to AA, Taylor had done it all.

So why did he keep thinking about the people he had
harmed? Why did he keep thinking about the boy he had
killed? Why did he keep thinking that his and Carol's child-
lessness was God's punishment for that? Why did he still feel
guilty? When would he be able to forgive himself? Why did
he keep feeling as if he were missing something, that there
was something important he had neglected to do?

And now would he have to make an amend to Naomi?

The list keeps getting longer, he thought. I've stopped drinking and drugging, but I keep on hurting. Myself and others.

Forget it, he told himself. What about the diamond? Should he tell Hill about Rebbe Teitel's diamond, the diamond that supposedly belonged to my great-great-grandfather's pal, what's-his-name?

The Seer of Lublin. Right.

Hill would just love to hear a story about a bunch of two-hundred-year-old rabbis. Sure he would.

But, leaving out the mumbo-jumbo, he should tell him about the diamond; it was material to a murder investigation. And who knew who Gottleib had told? Or the *rebbe*'s daughter?

Maybe the *rebbe* was wrong. Maybe the police already knew about the diamond, or even had it.

But he knew the *rebbe* was right. If Hill had discovered a special diamond, a big diamond, he would have shown it to someone in the business, gotten it appraised. And if he had done that, Taylor was sure the *rebbe* would have gotten wind of it.

All right. That brings me back to the beginning. Will I tell Hill?

Somehow, Taylor felt sure that the Satmarer *rebbe* would know if he did.

What did he say before I left? That I could help my great-great-grandfather Hirsh Leib?

Yeah. Mystic bullshit. Stuff to impress his Hasidim. The old faker. The crank.

Morris Schumach. That was Gottleib's partner's name. It was in the paper.

Now why did I remember that? Taylor asked himself, writing Schumach's name in his notebook.

Maybe Hirsh Leib told me.

Snap out of it, Taylor.

He went into the kitchen to brew a cup of coffee. Back at his desk, he called Frank Hill before he could think of any more people he had harmed or to whom he owed amends.

At first Hill was suspicious, but he had heard of Taylor,

knew he had been a cop, and, eventually, grudgingly, he invited him to come over to his house tomorrow. Oddly enough, Hill lived in Eastchester, and Taylor thought about giving Carol a call, maybe dropping by after he finished with Hill, see how she was doing.

Instead he looked up Morris Schumach in the Yellow Pages and made an appointment to see him for lunch that afternoon.

"I heard about you, Mr. Taylor," said Schumach. "I heard you met the *rebbe*."

"Yes, Mr. Schumach. A great man."

"A *zaddik*," said Schumach, his voice throbbing with awe. "The last one in the world. Look, Mr. Taylor, I got something to tell you, but I don't got much time today. I have to get home for *Shabbos*."

"So do I, Mr. Schumach," said Taylor, and felt good saying it. In fact, for the first time that morning, Taylor felt unburdened. A Sabbath miracle, he thought. My first.

15

Henri Bendel's
Fifth Avenue, Manhattan
Friday, September 10

Ladislaw Czartoryski loved clothes, and he loved Charvet ties. He loved the lustrous brilliance of their colors; he loved the butterlike hand of the woven silk. And he loved the fact that they were expensive, more expensive even than those boring Hermès ties worn by vulgar *arrivistes*. Indeed, the dark, wood-paneled, richly carpeted Charvet shop inside Bendel's was one of his favorite places in New York, and Czartoryski breathed a sigh of contentment. Maria Radziwell, however, did not share his sense of *bien-être*. In fact, she was acutely uncomfortable.

"Can we get out of here?" Radziwell hissed in Czartoryski's ear.

"Just a moment, my dear. Calm yourself," Czartoryski said genially.

"We are not two blocks from Forty-seventh Street," said Radziwell. "I do not want to bump into that Israeli."

"I hardly think your Israeli would be shopping here, my dear," said Czartoryski, waving to one of the sleek, dark-suited salesmen, who approached at a decorous trot, eager solicitude writ in large letters on his face.

"I am looking," said Czartoryski, "for a green-and-black-striped tie I once saw a man wear at the captain's table on the *QE Two*. The green was emerald, at once dark and bright. I do not know for a fact that it was a Charvet, but I presume that it was."

"Let me see, sir," said the salesman, pirouetting to a mahogany table and opening its drawer. "Is this what you're looking for, sir?" he asked, presenting the tie as if it were a *billet doux* on a silver salver.

"The green is correct, yes," said Czartoryski, "but I think this is a very dark blue, not a true black."

"It's sometimes hard to tell in this light, sir," said the salesman. "Shall we go over here?"

The salesman walked over to the store's Fifth Avenue entrance, Czartoryski following. Radziwell bent her head to whisper in his ear. "You have never been on a boat in your life. *QE Two* my ass," she said in Polish.

"And you have such a lovely one, Maria," said Czartoryski, responding in English.

"Excuse me, sir?" said the salesman.

"I said it is a lovely tie, but, as you can see, that is blue," said Czartoryski.

"Mr. Cartovsky is correct," said the salesman. "Well, shall we try again?"

As Maria Radziwell stood off a few paces, watching little Ladislaw Czartoryski and the equally small salesman pore over ties like two conspirators, discussing warp and weave, color and texture, her impatience grew. She knew Czartoryski was prolonging this shopping excursion just to annoy her, even as he refused to speak Polish with her just to annoy her. Ever since his failures in bed had become more frequent than his successes, he had begun to discover little ways to torture her, little meannesses meant to assert the dominance he could no longer achieve sexually.

Christ, she loathed small men. And small men, it seemed, were her lot in life. Why is it, she wondered idly, that so many rich men are small? Big wallets and small hands, big homes and small feet, big cars and small penises. At least, she thought, Ladislaw bathes, unlike that Israeli, Ariel Levin. Christ, the stink.

Oh, shit, thought Radziwell, feeling her body growing tense. I must be getting my period.

"We can go now," said Czartoryski, a small package wedged under his arm. "Where shall we lunch?"

"Did you buy a tie?" Radziwell asked.

"I bought several," said Czartoryski, pushing through Bendel's revolving doors and stepping out onto a sunny Fifth Avenue. He paused for Radziwell to follow and smiled broadly, revealing tiny, even teeth, as she emerged. "And now I'm hungry. These days, Maria, shopping is like sex for me. I buy, and then I am hungry. And after I eat, I will nap."

"Then you do not need me anymore."

"I need you desperately, Maria. Just looking at you makes me feel like a young man. A frustrated young man, true, but a young man nevertheless. And, of course, I need you to bring my diamond back to me.

"So," he said, offering her his arm, "do you like sushi? I have a taste for it. Accompanied by that excellent Japanese beer. There is a charming place not two blocks from here. We shall enjoy the walk."

Radziwell shortened her stride to accommodate Czartoryski's. "We are walking toward Forty-seventh Street," she said. "I don't want this."

"I doubt that your Israeli is a devotee of Japanese cuisine. In my experience, I have found Israelis to have extremely undeveloped, parochial tastes. They like everything overcooked, mashed, and stuffed into pita bread. The food in Tel Aviv is almost as bad as the food in London, and that is the worst in the world. In both cities the only food worth eating is cooked by the Chinese, the Levantines, or the Indians.

"In any case, Maria, it is unlike you to be so negative. Are you getting your period?"

"Fuck you, Ladislaw."

"Ah, you are getting your period. That will present a problem for your Israeli, will it not? Even if he is not Orthodox, the prohibition against intercourse with a menstruating woman is strong in most Jews. They are not, *au fond*, very masculine, the men, do you think? Even though I am sure you have noticed that they are, in general, rather well endowed. Is this Israeli, Levin, well endowed, Maria? The women, of course, are the same. The Jewesses I have known have all had extremely large genitalia. Like you, my dear. In that, you are unusual for a Pole. Perhaps you possess some Jewish blood. I often wonder if I do."

"Not likely."

"No, not likely. Well, I imagine that, if need be, you will have no difficulty in finding an alternative way to satisfy this Levin."

"You are a pig."

"And you are a whore, my dear. But what of it? You are the most beautiful whore I have ever known. You are a regal whore, the image of your great-grandmother. I often wonder how she managed to seduce Rhodes. His tastes, as you may know, were very English and ran to young men. And there was nothing even the slightest bit androgynous about your grandmother.

"Ah, here we are."

Czartoryski led Radziwell into a small restaurant decorated with rice-paper screens bearing Japanese characters. They were seated at a highly lacquered blond wood table for two by a tiny, doll-like woman in a black-and-white kimono who made Radziwell feel huge and ungainly. After being brought two steaming washcloths on a bamboo dish with which they moistened their hands and lips, Czartoryski ordered two Kirin beers and two large orders of *unagi*, broiled eel.

"So, this is quite nice, yes?" said Czartoryski. "What do they say? I love New York? Yes, I love New York. I think it is my favorite city. Is it yours?"

"I hate it," said Radziwell.

"How is that possible?"

"It is filthy."

"That's unworthy of you, Maria," Czartoryski said. "A trite observation. Bombay is filthy. Cairo is filthy. New York is merely dirty. Anyway, you never used to be so boring. But I see nothing I can say will lift your spirits. Shall we discuss your Israeli?"

Maria nodded.

"You will be seeing him this evening?"

"I expect him to call."

"And he will take you to his office tomorrow, Saturday?"

"That is what he said."

"And you do not wish to cut his throat right there and retrieve my diamond."

"No."

"Pity. Well, you must persuade him to bring it to your apartment. There, our old friend the Cutter will pay him a visit. Our friend does not wish to return to the building where he did the job on the diamond dealer, and I cannot blame him for that."

"I do not think he will take the stone out of his office, Ladislaw. What can I say to convince him?"

"Why don't you tell him you want to hold it while he fucks you? Perhaps that's how your great-grandmother stole it from Rhodes. Of course, with Rhodes, I suspect that your great-grandmother offered him her anus. Of course! That is what you shall do. In that way your present condition will not present a problem."

"Stop it."

"Tell him you wish him to suck it out of your ass. I will not mind if my diamond pays a visit to your ass. I will treasure it all the more."

The waitress brought the beer and eels. Czartoryski picked up a sliver of broiled eel and glutinous rice with his chopsticks and popped it into his mouth.

"Delicious," he said, smiling. "This is wonderful, my dear."

Radziwell stared at him, and he read a profound and un-qualified refusal in her eyes. He'd seen that look before in the eyes of Polish prisoners in the camps, a look that said they would rather be shot on the spot than take one more step.

"All right, all right, Maria. If you cannot get the Jew to take the diamond out of his office, tell him you know a rich man who would like to see it. I am sure he has no real idea of its value, and I am sure he knows no one who could buy it. He will jump at the chance."

"But, you will go to him?" asked Radziwell.

"I will go to him."

"But then he will know you."

"But then, Maria, he will be dead and it will not matter."

"Eat your eels."

16

The Diamond Dairy
Forty-seventh Street, Manhattan
Friday, September 10

At the same time Ladislaw Czartoryski and Maria Radziwell were dining on beer and broiled eel, a few blocks away Dov Taylor was perusing the luncheon menu at a Formica table in the Diamond Dairy Kosher Luncheonette of New York.

The Diamond Dairy was on the mezzanine of the Diamond Exchange at 4 West Forty-seventh Street. Through a Plexiglas window, Taylor looked out over a hundred tiny booths—most less than six feet long and four feet deep—stocked with rings, bracelets, necklaces, and earrings. Customers, dealers, brokers, and sightseers wandered up and down the narrow aisles lined with treasure.

Some booths specialized in gold, others in silver. Some booths sold diamonds exclusively, others displayed colored gemstones of every size and hue. Many booths were devoted to watches, both new and vintage.

Behind the counters' glass cases, business was conducted—or gin rummy games played—in spaces that were always too small. For that reason, and because it would have been so easy to pocket a small fortune and walk out with it, these booths were often run as family affairs. Men went partners with their brothers, splitting the always exorbitant rent for booth space; fathers worked next to their sons and sometimes next to their wives. The phones rang constantly.

In the three-foot-wide aisles, suburban women in tight-fitting jeans and high heels sold the detritus of divorce, and businessmen on their lunch hour shopped for baubles for their girlfriends. But the exchange's walk-in business, while huge, was still a small part of what went on. Right in front of the public's eye, but hidden by a veil of language and custom, dealers and brokers bought and sold $10,000, $20,000, and $50,000 stones, negotiating mainly in Yiddish or English, speaking in the shorthand of the diamond trade.

Now, as the unsteady hum of commerce rose up through the windows of the luncheonette, Dov Taylor waited for Morris Schumach and debated between ordering a lox omelet ($6.20) or the blintzes with sour cream ($5.95). He had missed the breakfast special ("two eggs, any style, toast, and coffee"), served from 7:30 to 11:00, and briefly allowed himself to be amazed that it was still possible to eat breakfast in Manhattan for $2.25.

Taylor looked up from the plastic laminated menu with its *kashrus* seal, declaring everything—from the food and the plates and utensils, to the stoves and the cooks—to be *Glatt kosher*. A tall, powerfully built Hasid with twinkly green eyes and a full black beard streaked with gray walked up to stand by his table.

"Dov Taylor?" the man asked.

"Morris Schumach," Taylor said, standing up and extending his hand.

Schumach took Taylor's hand in a strong grip and gave it one, formal shake.

"I was thinking of the cheese blintzes," Taylor said after sitting down.

"The best in the city," said Schumach, his eyes darting

around the luncheonette. "There's better in Brooklyn, of course, but these are good, and the sour cream is first class."

A middle-aged waitress with curly hair dyed blond walked over to take their order. Taylor asked for the blintzes and a cup of tea with lemon; Schumach ordered a bowl of cold borscht with a boiled potato, no cream. The waitress went behind the long counter, where a dozen men, many of them in *kapotes*, sat on stools, hunched over their plates. Morris Schumach pulled a small diamond loupe on a steel chain out of his pocket and began fiddling with it.

"So, what can you tell me about Zalman Gottleib?" Taylor began.

"Not much," Schumach said with a shrug, gazing out over the Diamond Exchange floor. "He was a *frummer Yid*, a pious Jew, may the Holy One bless his memory. He did a good business, he said his prayers, he gave to charity. What more can I say?"

"Did he seem ill at ease the days before he was killed? Did he say anything unusual?"

"No, nothing unusual. I told this to the police."

"I know, Mr. Schumach. I know. What I'm interested in is anything you didn't tell the police. Anything you forgot to tell them. Anything at all."

Schumach shrugged again and leaned back in his chair, staring at the ceiling as the waitress brought their lunch. Why do Hasids so rarely make eye contact? Taylor wondered as he slathered sour cream over four huge golden blintzes. He took a bite. They were sweet and delicious, and the sour cream was the thickest, smoothest, and best Taylor had ever tasted.

"This is wonderful," said Taylor, ignoring the little voice in his head that told him he might as well apply the sour cream directly to his heart.

"Too heavy for me," said Schumach, echoing Taylor's thoughts while bent over his bowl, noisily and rapidly slurping his borscht.

"Look, mister," Schumach said suddenly, his spoon clutched in his big fist, his head still inclined over his bowl. "You know what I think? I think since when is killing Jews some big mystery? I think some *meshuggeneh* anti-Semite bastard did it, and I think the police should get all the Nazis and Arabs and anti-Semites together in Yankee Stadium and beat the hell out of them until the one who did it confesses. But since I know this is not going to happen, I'm not going to hold my breath.''

"We do what we can, Mr. Schumach," said Taylor.

Schumach was silent for a moment, his eyes still on his now empty bowl of borscht. "All right," he said finally, setting down the spoon and, for the first time, looking directly at Dov Taylor. "I'm sorry I got so agitated. But, you know, my wife, she doesn't want me to go to work no more. I tell her, Elizabeth, what else can I do? Up and down the street, people are afraid. In the club, that's all they talk about. So? What's new about Jews being afraid?"

"Can you imagine any reason, any reason at all, why someone would want to kill Mr. Gottleib, other than his being Jewish?" Taylor asked.

"Reason? What reason?"

"Is it possible, Mr. Schumach, that Mr. Gottleib had acquired a diamond, a valuable diamond, that you didn't know about?"

"Sure it's possible. What did I have to do with Zally's business? We shared an office. I bought diamonds from my people, Zally bought from his. I sold to my people, Zally sold to his."

"Can you think of anyone who might know if Mr. Gottleib had received a special stone? Anyone he confided in?"

"If you knew Zally, you wouldn't ask. Zally wasn't a chatterbox. Especially about business. So, what's this about a stone? A diamond?"

"I'm just trying to find a motive, Mr. Schumach. I'm fishing.''

"Fishing? What means fishing?"

"Nothing. Guessing. So, on the day of the murder, you were out of the office?"

"I told this to the police," said Schumach. "You didn't talk to them?"

"Not yet."

"Well, look, Mr. Taylor. The day Zally and Shirley Stein were murdered, I was in Queens doing business. That's right!" Schumach slammed a meaty palm on the Formica table, spilling what was left of Taylor's tea into its saucer. "Sorry," said Schumach. "I get excited. But what a dummy I am. I saw that woman. That's what I wanted to tell you."

"What woman?"

"The woman from Queens. The widow. That's why I wasn't in the office that day. I was in Queens buying jewelry from this woman who said she was a widow, and then yesterday—no, Wednesday—I saw her going into my building."

"Can you describe her?" asked Taylor, pulling out his notebook.

"Sure. A big blond one."

"How big?"

"Tall. Tall like me."

"Six feet tall?"

"Maybe."

"Natural blond or dyed blond?"

"Mister, you think I could tell?"

"Well, was it the same color as the waitress's? That's dyed."

"That's dyed?"

"Yes, that's dyed."

"Imagine that."

"So, was it that color?"

"I don't think so, but I'm not really sure."

"Fat, thin?"

"Not fat, not thin, *zaftig*, you know. Big bubbies."

"How old?"

"Who knows? Maybe twenty-five. Maybe thirty, thirty-five. I'm no good with ages."

"Any scars?"

"Scars? What do you think, she showed me her scars?"

"Hair long or short?"

"I don't know. Who notices these things?"

"Did you notice the color of her eyes?" asked Taylor, wondering how Schumach ever recognized her in the first place.

"She's a blonde, maybe they're blue. Or maybe brown. She didn't wear glasses, I can tell you that. It's strange, isn't it? The day Zally and Shirley get killed, I see this woman in Queens. And then, a few days later, she walks into our building. That's strange, *nu*? I tell you, mister, it almost gave me a heart attack."

"She contacted you to sell you some jewelry?"

"Yes."

"How did she get your name?"

"She said some rabbi gave it to her."

"Do you remember the rabbi's name?"

"No. I never heard of him."

"Did you speak to her when she walked into your building?"

"No. Listen, there's something not right about her."

"What?"

"Something. I don't know. The house, it didn't look like a young couple's home. It didn't look like anybody ever lived there. And the jewelry, it was, if you'll excuse me, crap. But she was dressed nice, if you like that kind of dressing. To me, I got to tell you the truth, she looked like a *nofke*, a hooker. But not cheap. Like she should know the jewelry was crap. Except the ring. The ring was nice. Nothing special, you understand, but nice."

"Did you get her name?"

"Sure. What do you think? It was Rudenstein something. Something Italian. Maria, yes. The name, Rudenstein, I figured was her husband's."

"The dead husband?"

"You know her?"

"No, you just said she was a widow."

"Oh. This is why you're a detective, right?" Schumach looked up at the clock behind the luncheonette's counter; Taylor noticed that he wore no watch, no jewelry but a plain gold wedding band. "I'm sorry, Mr. Taylor, it's late. I got to get home. You too, yes? You observe *Shabbos*?"

"Yes," Taylor lied. "Tell me, Mr. Schumach, did you tell the police all this?"

"About the woman in Queens, yes. About seeing her here, no."

"Did you tell them how you felt about her, how you felt something was wrong?"

"I don't think so," said Schumach, pushing back his chair and standing up. "That was a terrible day. Who knows what I said, who knows what I was thinking? But I really got to go. You got my number you need to ask more questions. *Gut yontif*, Mr. Taylor."

"*Gut yontif*, Mr. Schumach."

17

Forty-seventh Street, Manhattan
Friday, September 10

Ariel Levin wrapped what was left of his half-eaten lunch—tuna fish, lettuce, and tomato in pita bread—in its brown paper bag and shoved it into the top drawer of his desk. He finished his bottle of Orangina and tossed it into a wastepaper basket. Then he removed Zalman Gottleib's locked box from his safe, snapped on his desk lamp, and took out the diamond. Its sixty-six facets caught the light, played with it, and then sent it back into Levin's eyes, making him blink.

Incredible, thought Levin. All week he had been reading the papers, but the stories about the murder had grown smaller and smaller, and none of them had mentioned anything about a special diamond. All week he had been expecting someone to call to claim this astonishing stone, but no one had.

Of course, when Fred Feldman, the director of the Diamond Club's board of overseers, phoned, Levin held his breath. He was half expecting Feldman to denounce him as a thief. But Feldman was just returning Levin's panicked call after discovering the stone in his safe. So he put Feldman off, telling him that he wanted information about applying for guest privileges at the club. Feldman was curt, telling Levin that he should know that there was no such thing; guests had to be invited by members.

Big shot, thought Levin scornfully. He thinks I'm a nothing, but here I am, the owner of one of the world's great gems. I could be Harry Winston. I could be Cartier. If I can sell it, I'm set for life. But how can I sell it? Who can I sell it to?

Could he go partners on the stone with Feldman? Impossible, thought Levin. Feldman would keep the stone and turn me in to the cops. I'd be charged with Gottleib's murder, or at least held as an accessory.

Levin knew he would have to be patient. There was just no way to try to shop the stone now. Even hinting about its existence might be dangerous. The diamond district was still in an uproar over the murders. Levin had heard that Gottleib had been cut open and hung upside down, like a butchered animal. He didn't believe it, but he had peeked into Gottleib's old office yesterday, intending to say hello to Morris Schumach, and through the bulletproof glass he had seen the dark stain on the carpet where Shirley Stein had bled to death. The sight made him turn around and walk out. It had given him the creeps, and he wasn't the only one.

Up and down Forty-seventh Street men walked more quickly than before and looked over their shoulders more often. Dealers carried less cash and left more of their goods in the vaults. Despite the warm, sunny, Indian summer weather, fewer people stopped to *shmooze*. Business was off. Not a lot, but definitely off.

Two days ago, on Wednesday, a young black man running down the street had been tackled in front of the Merchant's Bank by a security officer. In seconds an angry crowd had formed, and a few people had kicked the man while he lay on the ground.

It turned out he had been running to make the Fifth Avenue bus.

Today there was a bunch of blacks marching up and down Fifth Avenue with signs, and some *meshuggeneh* black preacher with gold chains down to his belly button was hollering about the Jews.

Crazy. Almost as crazy, Levin thought, holding the diamond up to the sun coming through his tiny window, as this diamond.

Yesterday, after seeing the bloodstain on the carpet, Levin had gone to a friend's office. His friend had a good collection of gem books, and Levin wanted to see if he could find Gottleib's stone. He couldn't. And that didn't make sense.

How could a stone like this be a secret? It was bigger than the forty-four-carat Hope, which once belonged to Louis XVI and Marie Antoinette, and bigger than the fifty-five-carat Sancy diamond that the Astors owned. Only in weight was it inferior to the one-hundred-seven-carat Tiffany, the only diamond more than one hundred carats known to be, like Gottleib's stone, D flawless.

Levin searched the books but found no seventy-two-carat stones, no blue-whites that looked like his. Of course, there was the 3,106-carat blue-white Cullinan, which in 1907 was cleaved by Joseph Asscher of Amsterdam into nine major gems and ninety-six small ones. The biggest one, 530 carats, named the Great Star of Africa, was set in the imperial scepter and was now in the Tower of London as part of the crown jewels. Other pieces of the Cullinan were set in various royal crowns, necklaces, and brooches.

Could my stone have been cut from the Cullinan? thought Levin.

Oh, sure. Queen Elizabeth gave it to Gottleib to sell because she was a little short of cash.

Levin shook himself. Putting the diamond back in its box, and putting the box back in his safe, he had to admit that as excited as he was, he was also a bit nervous. Don't forget, he reminded himself, that Gottleib was killed, probably over this stone.

Well, that was his bad luck. But for me, he thought, this diamond will mean good luck. Look what it has brought you already. Mary Rubel and her long legs.

Levin decided to call her. Why wait for tomorrow? Tomorrow I'll show her my diamond and fuck her on this desk. Tonight in her bed.

Maria Radziwell was entering her apartment, Ladislaw Czartoryski right behind her, as the phone began to ring. She was not surprised to hear Ariel Levin asking if he could come by this evening, and she immediately said yes.

"That's lovely, Maria," Czartoryski said after she hung up. "You've certainly given this Israeli the scent. What time is he coming over tonight?"

As the sun set, Ariel Levin, carrying a chilled bottle of Moët & Chandon champagne, rang the bell to Mary Rubel's apartment. He did not see the tall, cadaverously thin man in the leather sport jacket standing in a vestibule across the street.

But the Cutter saw him.

18

Agudath Shalom
Kingston Avenue, Crown Heights
Friday, September 10

At the first *baal teshuvah* class Dov Taylor had attended, Rabbi Kalman's subject had been the Sabbath. Kalman had begun with an exegesis of Rabbi Isaac Luria's hymn describing the Sabbath as a bride "adorned in ornaments, jewels, and robes." Her husband, explained Rabbi Kalman, is Israel, who embraces her. It is through this romantic union between Jews and *Shabbos*, said Rabbi Kalman, that all the evil in the world would be destroyed. Therefore, said Kalman, if as a Jew you do nothing else but observe the Sabbath and keep it holy, your name will be written in the Book of Life. "As it is written in the Zohar, the Book of Radiance," said Kalman, "observing the Sabbath properly is equivalent to observing the whole Torah."

On *Shabbos*, Rabbi Kalman continued, every soul and every body is free. No one, no tyrant, can force a Jew to work. Throughout history evil rulers had tried to force Jews to transgress the Sabbath because they hated the idea that on that one day they were no Jew's master. But Israel, said Kalman, has always clung to its bride, its Sabbath queen.

Taylor liked that, and he also liked the idea that by stepping away from the world from sundown Friday to sundown Saturday, you returned the world to God. "When we don't operate machinery, when we don't fish or hunt or sow seeds or pluck fruit, when we don't change darkness into light or turn clay into pots, we are acknowledging that the world is the Holy One's, blessed is He, to do with as He will," Kalman told the class.

Taylor recalled Kalman's lesson as he hurried down Kingston Avenue to meet the rabbi at the *shtibl*, or small storefront synagogue, where Kalman usually welcomed the Sabbath queen. Many Lubavitchers attended these *shtibls* on Fridays instead of going to the big *shul* at 770 Eastern Parkway in order to keep as many synagogues as possible going in the neighborhood.

A few hours before sundown, Crown Heights looked more than ever like a small East European *shtetl*. Earlier that day the women of the community had completed their shopping, and now they had disappeared behind the curtains of their brownstones to finish polishing their silverware, cleaning their houses, setting the table, and cooking not only the enormous Friday night meal, but all the food that would be eaten the next day. Huge coffee urns were placed on low flames so that coffee would be available throughout the next twenty-four hours. The lights that were to stay on were turned on; the toilet paper was pretorn and stacked. The clothes the men and women would wear were checked to make sure that there was no money in any of the pockets, lest someone accidentally break the law by handling or even carrying money on the Sabbath.

Out on the street, as befitted a bridegroom, Lubavitch had donned its finery. The warm, golden September sun was still high in the sky as hundreds of bearded men milled about in front of the synagogues wearing their long silken *bekekhers* instead of their usual *kapotes*. Some men, *balebatisher Yids*, literally house owners or well-off Jews, wore luxurious beaver-trimmed hats, *biber* hats, or *shtreimels*, large hats made of beaver or sable. A few extremely pious ones wore *shikh un zoken*, black patent-leather slippers worn with white knee socks and breeches, an atavism from aristocratic eighteenth-century European dress.

Taylor, with a simple black *yarmulke* on his head and an old blue suit, felt wildly out of place. True, there were other men dressed like him, but they were a definite minority. Here, on Friday afternoon on Kingston Avenue in Brooklyn, it was the assimilated, secular Jew who looked strange, not the Hasid.

Among a small clump of Hasids outside Agudath Shalom, Taylor was relieved to spot Rabbi Kalman, resplendent in his *bekekher* and *biber* hat, in deep conversation with a similarly dressed man. At the same time Taylor noticed Kalman, Kalman broke off to wave Taylor over to his side. The Hasid to whom Kalman had been speaking turned away to engage another man.

"*Shalom*, Dov," said Kalman, shaking his hand.

"*Shalom*, Rabbi," said Taylor, noting that Kalman's handshake seemed firmer than usual and, indeed, his eyes seemed brighter, and he seemed more energetic, more vital, than Taylor had ever seen him before.

"You look great, Rabbi," said Taylor.

"*Ach*, I look like I always look," Kalman said. "A humble *melamed*, a teacher of ignorant children, no offense, Dov. But what you see is my *Shabbos layt*, my Sabbath light. I live from one *Shabbos* to the next. In between, I work, I pray, I exist. But on *Shabbos*, with the help of the Holy One, I live, I shine.

"Come, before services we go to the *mikvah* to purify ourselves for the Sabbath bride."

Kalman took Taylor's elbow and led him around the side of the synagogue into an alley and through a door with a painted tin sign in Hebrew above it. They walked down a narrow flight of metal stairs and through another door into a room off the *shul*'s basement.

Wooden boards were laid over a crumbling white tile floor in a large, gloomy, dank room. On the wall were hooks upon which men hung their clothes before entering the *mikvah*. Four extremely elderly men were undressing as Kalman and Taylor entered.

"What do I do, Rabbi?" Taylor whispered.

"Get undressed and get in the tub," said Kalman. "Go under the water once, twice, three times. It's simple. Make sure to go completely under. And don't talk anymore."

Taylor began to take off his clothes and tried not to stare at the old men. He had never seen people look as naked without their clothes as these men did. Their flesh was fish-belly white, and it hung flaccidly off their arms and legs. Their stomachs drooped over their groins. Their balls hung low between their legs. White hair curled in clumps on their backs. Taylor felt like a visitor from another, healthier planet. Why did being religious entail allowing your body to go to pot? he wondered. It was the Greeks who said a sound mind in a sound body, not the Jews, he answered himself. All the exercise these men got came from pumping Torah, not iron.

Two large, square, stone baths were dug into the basement floor, with three stone steps leading down to them. To Taylor the water looked gray and dirty, and he sniffed, trying to smell it. The old men had already slipped into the tubs, and, closing their eyes, they dunked themselves. Kalman appeared next to Taylor, and Taylor tried to ignore his rabbi's pallid nakedness, his basketball-round pot belly.

"This one's hot, that one's cold," said Kalman. "Come on." And, reading Taylor's mind, he added, "Dirty it's not. Anyway, you're not going to drink it."

Taylor edged cautiously down one wet, slippery step and stuck a toe into the water. It was burning hot, and with a little yelp he pulled out his foot.

Emerging from the bath, one of the old men said something to Taylor in Yiddish. Seeing Taylor's blank look, he said in English, "Hot enough to boil an egg," and grinned at Taylor's distress.

Taylor walked over to the cold tub where Rabbi Kalman was dunking, but its water looked even dirtier. So Taylor went back to the hot tub, thinking, If there are any bugs here, the heat will kill them. He stepped into the water, gasping as it reached his genitals.

The tub was about five feet deep, and when the water came up his armpits Taylor took a deep breath, bent his knees, and submerged, desperate not to swallow any of the dark water. He repeated this two more times and then scrambled out of the bath, looking around for a towel. He saw a small stack of stiff, gray, threadbare old rags by the wall and attempted to dry himself with these. Then, giving it up as a bad job, he threw his clothes back on. He did not feel purified; he did not feel exalted; he felt damp. Rabbi Kalman met him by the door, his hair and beard dripping wet under his *biber* hat. The rabbi checked his watch.

"*Mazel tov*," said Kalman. "We'll be just in time for *Kabbalas Shabbos*, the acceptance of the Sabbath."

Taylor followed Kalman up the stairs and outside. They walked around to the front of the *shul* and joined the crowd of men pushing and shoving to get in and get to their usual seats.

Agudath Shalom was very different from the synagogues Dov Taylor had gone to as a child. It occurred to him that this was not a place where people went once a week or, as was more often the case, two or three times a year, on the High Holy days or for weddings and *Bar Mitzvahs*. This was a place where men came every day to spend the most meaningful hours of their lives. Even to Taylor, a *Yiddishe goy*, it looked cozy; it looked lived in.

Opposite the synagogue's doors was a sink for the men to wash their hands before handling the holy objects: their prayer shawls, their *tefillin*, the Torah. To the left and right of the sink were bookshelves filled with commentaries, the writings of the *zaddikim*, prayer books, and scrolls. Across from the bookshelves, against the wall, were cardboard boxes filled to the brim with *yarmulkes* and *tallisim*, although most of the men brought their own in velvet pouches decorated with silver-embroidered crowns, *Mogen Duvids*, Jewish stars, and Hebrew characters.

Inside, a few small, dirty windows let in a little light.

Plaques filled with lists of names—people who had donated
money to the synagogue or who had money donated in their
names after their deaths—hung on the walls. To Taylor the
shul seemed to be as much a library as a temple. In one
corner there were study tables and bookshelves reaching to the
ceiling, filled with more crumbling books. There were books
stacked on the wooden pews. There were books everywhere.

Taylor pushed and shoved through the milling Hasidim and
took a seat next to Rabbi Kalman. He reached for one of the
prayer books stacked in a wooden box slung over the back of
the pew in front of him. Opening it up, he saw at once that
it was, of course, all in Hebrew, with no English translation.
Taylor closed the *sidur* and put it on his lap.

In front of him was the *Aren Kodesh*, and he knew that
behind its velvet, richly embroidered curtains were the books
of the Torah. To his left, behind another row of pews arranged
at right angles to the *Aren Kodesh* and the *bimah*, the pulpit
at which the Torah was read, was a mirror that ran the length
of the room. Taylor nudged Kalman and pointed to the mirror.

"It's one-way," explained Kalman. "The women sit behind there. They can see and not disturb the men. But most
women do not come to *daven Kabbalas Shabbos*. They are
busy at home."

A man in a white silk robe and a tall, white, brimless hat
that looked like a chef's toque walked up to the *bimah*, and
the service began. At first Kalman would show Taylor where
the congregation was in the *sidur*, pointing to the correct line,
and Taylor tried to follow. But he could not keep up, and soon
they both gave up. Taylor simply stood when the congregation
stood and sat when they sat. At one point everyone turned to
their right, and Taylor turned with them, having no idea what
was going on. Standing, he rocked back and forth, *davening*
like the men around him, and he mumbled wordlessly along
with the singing. He felt both ignorant and conspicuous,
although he knew that no one was paying him the slightest
attention. Yet he felt that what he was doing was right. Even
though it was strange, he felt that, somehow, this was a home.

My grandfather knew all the prayers by heart, Taylor
thought. So, of course, would have Hirsh Leib. They would

have been at home here. Is that why I feel a rightness about it, even though it's strange to me?

The service, like the synagogue itself, was very different from the ones Taylor had attended with his grandfather when he was a boy studying for his *Bar Mitzvah*. Whereas his grandfather had prayed quietly, chanting under his breath—mumbling, actually—the Hasidim, who stressed the importance of fervor, sang at the top of their lungs. They also *davened* vigorously, almost violently, bending their knees, bobbing their heads up and down, rocking back and forth rapidly. It seemed to Taylor that they were competing with each other, trying to see who could pray the loudest and *daven* the most forcefully. Again Taylor felt left out. A home, but not my home, he thought, and he was relieved when the prayers came to an end after about forty-five minutes.

Leaving the *shul*, at least a dozen men shook his hand, wishing him "*Gut Shabbos*." That helped Taylor get over his feeling of alienation, although he mentioned it to Kalman as they walked in the gathering darkness down President Street toward the rabbi's home.

"A terrible thing, yes?" Kalman responded. "Of all the places in the world, a Jew should feel at home in the synagogue." He shook his head. "A terrible thing to feel like a stranger in your own home.

"But the *Shabbos* is not for sad things. Now you will eat like you have never eaten before, Dov Taylor. You will eat until you cry for mercy, but my wife will show you none. Here we are. Home."

Kalman pushed open the unlocked door to the brownstone on President Street and was greeted in the hallway by his wife, Sophie, the *rebbetzin*, a short, trim woman wearing a beige silk blouse and a brown tweed skirt. Her hair was a helmet of tight silver curls, and it looked so natural that Taylor had to remind himself that it was a *sheitl*, a wig. The rabbi and his wife did not kiss, or even touch each other, but her smile was full of welcome.

Sophie led them down the hallway to a large dining room dominated by an elaborately set table with a white linen tablecloth at which half a dozen people were already seated.

Rabbi Kalman made the introductions. There was Kalman's son, Moshe, a short, bearded man with a smaller edition of his father's pot belly. He was also, like his father, a rabbi, and sitting across the table from him was his wife, Channah, who seemed little more than a girl. There was Sophie's elderly mother, Mrs. Bloom, whose lined face and thick, rimless glasses reminded Taylor of his *tante* Lecha, and a quiet, blond, long-haired young man with a wispy beard named Steven whom Taylor recognized from *teshuvah* class. There was another family, a darkly tanned young man, his plump and pregnant wife, and their freckled four-year-old daughter. They were making a pilgrimage from South Africa to see the Lubavitcher *reb* and were staying with the Kalmans. Seeing the pregnant young woman caused Taylor a momentary pang. It made him envious, and he hated that. But the person who claimed Taylor's attention and held it was Sarah, "the person," said Rabbi Kalman, "I wanted you to meet. My daughter."

At first glance Sarah seemed to be in her teens, but in a moment Taylor put her age closer to thirty. She had red hair, down to her waist; her skin was absolutely free of freckles, china white. Her eyes were sea green, and when she stood up to greet him he saw that she was tiny, just a shade over five feet tall. She was also, Taylor noted, quite *zaftig*, a fact her peasant blouse did nothing to disguise. Taylor found himself grinning at her for no reason, and she smiled back.

"My father has told me a great deal about you, Mr. Taylor," Sarah said in a soft, musical voice. "He thinks you're a very powerful man."

"I hope he's right," said Taylor, wondering what Kalman could possibly have meant, and wondering just how much Kalman had told his daughter about him.

"Sit here," called Moshe Kalman, gesturing to the seat to his right, across the table from Sarah. Taylor sensed a certain hostility wafting off Moshe and thought that it was directed at him. He promised himself to chat him up over dinner.

Rabbi Kalman went to the head of the table. He removed his *biber* hat, placed it on an oak sideboard, and touched his head to make sure his *yarmulke* was in place. Then he lifted his hands, palms up, and as everybody stood up, the rabbi began singing "Sholem Aleichem," a song, Taylor remembered being told, that thanked the angels that had accompanied them home from the synagogue. The rabbi beat time on the table and was joined in the song by Moshe, Steve, and the young man from South Africa. Taylor, who did not know the words, hummed along with the tune. None of the women sang.

After the song, the rabbi, still standing, sang a soft tune directly to Sophie, who stood beaming at him. To Taylor it sounded like a love song. He shot a glance at Sarah, who was smiling at her mother and nodding along with the tune. Taylor found himself grinning again and forced himself to look away. He met Moshe's angry eyes. Moshe looked down at his lap.

Kalman filled a silver *kiddush* cup with red wine from a crystal decanter and, resting it on his palm like an offering, recited the blessing *borei piri hagofen*—who created the fruit of the vine—one of the few prayers Taylor knew by heart thanks to a score of repetitions over his grandfather's Passover table. During his drinking days, in various bars around town, Taylor had sometimes mumbled the prayer mockingly over his beer or bourbon. Now, as he heard Kalman chant the familiar words, he grew tense. He knew he wasn't going to drink, but he didn't even want to hold the cup.

Kalman finished the blessing and began to pass the cup to his right, to Moshe. Then he pulled it back.

"Our friend Dov Taylor," said the rabbi, "has pledged himself to abstinence. Wine is injurious to him." Then he passed the cup to Moshe, who took a gulp—ostentatiously, Taylor thought—leaned over Taylor, and passed it on.

When the wine had made a circuit around the table, Sophie and Sarah went into the kitchen and returned with a large blue ceramic bowl and a matching pitcher. They brought it to the rabbi, who poured water over his hands—first the right, then the left, three times—and recited the blessing. Then they carried the bowl and pitcher around the table, and everybody washed.

Rabbi Kalman stood and lifted up two velvet coverlets in front of him, revealing two large loaves of freshly baked *challeh*, the braided holiday bread brushed with egg so it shined. He recited the *motzi*, the blessing for the fruit of the earth, and tore off a piece of *challeh*, dipped it in a small bowl of salt, and ate it as soon as he finished the prayer. Then he tore off pieces for everybody around the table. Everybody dipped the bread in salt, everybody ate. It was delicious. Then the meal began.

Taylor had always thought the Passover meals his grandmother provided defined the word *feast*. But Sophie, Sarah, and Moshe's wife, Channah, never seemed to stop bringing food from the kitchen. First came the gefilte fish, the sweetest Taylor had ever tasted, served cold with a fiery horseradish. Then came a tossed salad with a sweet lemon dressing, followed by a rich, clear chicken soup in which floated perfectly round, perfectly delicate matzoh balls. After the soup came a golden roast chicken, slices of brisket, broccoli, a sweet noodle *kugel* with raisins, and a *tsimmis* of sweet potatoes, pineapple chunks, prunes, and glazed carrots. Taylor watched Kalman and Moshe put it all away, washing the food down with several glasses of Dewar's Scotch from a bottle that stood by the rabbi's right hand. The women drank spritzers, filling their glasses with sweet red wine and topping it off with a splash from a seltzer bottle. Taylor drank apple juice.

As the food arrived at the table, Rabbi Kalman would greet each dish with a song or a *nigun*, a wordless tune composed by one *rebbe* or another. "Dov," urged Kalman, "at least keep time." So Taylor beat his fork against his glass and tapped his foot as the rabbi sang. And several times during the meal, Kalman, Moshe, and the South African got up to do a sort of stomping, shuffling dance around the table as they sang.

During one of these dances, Taylor leaned across the table and asked Sarah what her father had chanted to her mother right after the "Sholem Aleichem."

"It's from the book of Proverbs," said Sarah. "It's traditional for husbands to sing it to their wives on the Sabbath. It says . . . oh, let me see. This will take me a moment."

"It says, 'A woman of valor, who can find? / For her price is above rubies.' Excuse me," said Sophie. "I couldn't help but hear, even though you were speaking softly. Someday, my dear, with the Holy One's help, your husband will sing it for you.''

Later, Taylor asked Sarah why only the men sang, not the women.

"It is believed that a woman's voice is arousing to men," said Sarah, "so we don't sing in front of them.''

"I would like to hear you sing," said Taylor, and Sarah blushed and looked down at her plate. When was the last time I saw a woman blush? thought Taylor. I can't remember.

Several times during the meal Taylor tried to engage Moshe in conversation, only to be answered in grunts and monosyllables. It was clear Moshe did not like him and did not like him being there at the table.

After about three hours the women cleared the table and served coffee, nondairy ice cream, and nips of liqueurs in a straw basket—Drambuie, Kahlúa, Tía Maria, and Cherry Heering. Taylor noticed that the bottle of Dewar's was almost empty, and it seemed to him that almost everyone around the table, including the women, was red in the face and perhaps drunk. It had been quite a while since Taylor had been around so much booze, and it was making him nervous.

"So, Dov Taylor," said Rabbi Kalman, his face flushed and his eyes shining, "did you have enough to eat?"

"More than enough, Rabbi."

"Did you ever eat like this before?"

"No, never. Thank you, Mrs. Kalman."

"You are welcome, Mr. Taylor. But, please, call me Sophie.''

"And you call me Dov."

"Good! We are all using our first names. Very *Amerikanishe*," said Rabbi Kalman. "Now, Dov, tell me, what did you think of the Satmarer *reb*?"

"I think I told you, he seemed angry most of the time. And he didn't really speak to me. He addressed himself mostly to Hirsh Leib."

"And did Hirsh Leib listen?"

"Come on, Rabbi. Please. Anyway, Teitel did say that he

suspected that the Lubavitchers were involved in the murder.''

"What murder?'' Sophie Kalman asked. "Not the murder of that diamond dealer? Lubavitchers involved? How could such a thing be?''

"*Ach,* this is no time to talk about such things,'' said Kalman. "Lubavitch and Satmar have been enemies for many years, for many reasons.''

"They are brutes,'' Sophie said. "Forgive me for saying it, but they are terrible people. They beat up our rabbis, and they cut off their beards. They throw stones at our children. They pray for the defeat of our soldiers in *Eretz Yisroel.*''

"Enough, Sophie. Our guest is not interested in this. Tell me, Dov, tell me about your dream about Hirsh Leib.''

"I am interested. Why do they pray for the defeat of Israel, the Satmarers?'' asked Taylor.

"They believe Israel should not exist until the Messiah comes,'' said Sophie. "*Meshuggeners.* Crazy people.''

"Sophie. Please. This is not important, Dov. Your dream is important. Tell me about it.''

"There's not much to tell,'' said Taylor. "I was standing with my grandmother on a hill overlooking a castle and a village when Hirsh Leib—at least my grandmother said it was Hirsh Leib—came walking up the hill to tell me that my phone was ringing. Then I woke up, and my phone really was ringing.''

"Not much! You say not much!'' said Rabbi Kalman. "That dream is everything. Let me explain it.

"The town with the castle, that's Lublin, of course, that's where Hirsh Leib studied with the Seer, Yakov Yitzhak, may his memory be blessed. It had such a castle, such a hill. That is a town where many miracles happened, let me tell you. And your grandmother is with you because Hirsh Leib cannot speak to you without her. She spoke Yiddish, yes? She was from the old country, she remembered the old ways. You are connected to her. You are bound to her. And Hirsh Leib is telling you your phone is ringing because he wants you to wake up from your dream. He wants you to listen to him. He is going to help you. He was listening when Satmar spoke, and he is going to help. That is what this dream was telling you. As I told you before, you must find out about Hirsh Leib. You must learn about Lublin. That's where you will find the answers to all your questions.

"Such a dream this was! I should have such a dream. And you say it was nothing. This is why you need help. You see? You understand?"

"My husband told me your great-great-grandfather was a *zaddik*. You must be very proud," said Sophie.

"Oh, yes," said Taylor. "Very proud. But, Rabbi, if Satmar and Lubavitch are such enemies, why are you so concerned about the death of this diamond dealer? He was a Satmarer, right? And why would the Satmarer *rebbe* make a wedding for his daughter with the Lubavitcher *rebbe*'s son? I don't understand."

"*Ach*, all this talk about death and fighting. This is not conversation for *Shabbos*," said Kalman. "I'll tell you a proper *Shabbos* story."

As if that were a cue, Moshe stood up from the table and walked into the living room, trailed by his wife and his mother. The young man from South Africa and his wife followed, leaving Taylor at the table with Rabbi Kalman, Sarah, and Sophie's mother, Mrs. Bloom, who was fast asleep and snoring softly on her chair.

"Once," began Rabbi Kalman, ignoring the exodus from the table and speaking directly to Taylor, "Rabbi Barukh of Mezbizh was entertaining a guest from Israel. This man was one of those who are always sad, always mourning for Zion, and cannot forget their sadness for an instant. On the eve of the Sabbath, Rabbi Barukh sang the song 'He who sanctifies the seventh day,' and when he came to the part 'Beloved of the Lord, you who await the rebuilding of Ariel,' he saw his guest sitting there like a lump, gloomy as always. So the rabbi stopped singing and shouted in the man's face, 'Beloved of the Lord, you who await the rebuilding of Ariel, on this holy day of the *Shabbos, be joyful and happy*!' And the man was so stunned, so surprised to be shouted at in this manner, he forgot his sadness and so learned to celebrate the Sabbath properly.

"*Ach*, believe me, Dov," said Kalman, "it's a better story in Yiddish. But this is why we sing and dance on the Sabbath. And this is why such things as we were speaking of before are not to be spoken of."

Rabbi Kalman began to sing another *nigun*. Taylor waited for him to finish, then told him he was growing tired.

"Tired?" said Kalman. "Tired? It's not even one in the morning. So, what do you think of my Saraleh?"

Taylor saw the color rush to Sarah's cheeks as she stood up. "If my father is going to discuss me, it would only be polite for me to leave. I will see you tomorrow morning, Mr. Taylor."

Taylor scrambled to his feet and said, "I hope so," as Sarah left.

"So? *Nu?*" asked Kalman.

"She's very beautiful."

"An old maid. Twenty-eight and never married. I try to make a *shidukh*, a match. She don't want no one. Now she's too old, no one wants her except old men with grandchildren already."

"I can't believe that."

"You think I'm making it up? I'm telling you. You know something else?"

"What?"

"She's a college girl. She went to college, to the Fashion Institute, in Manhattan, to study clothes. Can you imagine? This is a thing you study? Clothes? I told her this is foolishness. I told her, if you go to college, you leave my house. So she does. Imagine. But I'm weak and I take her back. So now she is like a man. She has a business, she sells clothes, and makes money, and no one wants her."

"What's wrong with having a business?"

"*Ach*, there's nothing wrong. Nothing wrong. Except I'll tell you what's wrong. She has no husband, she has no children. So what kind of life is that? Tell me. What kind of life?"

"What's the name of her business?" Taylor asked.

"Some *nareshkayt*, some foolishness. I don't know, I don't care, I don't go there. She makes her mother crazy. She'll be the death of her mother."

"She seems very nice to me."

"To you. To you." Rabbi Kalman poured himself the last of the Scotch and mixed it with a splash of seltzer. "Does it bother you, this Scotch?" he asked Taylor.

"No," Taylor lied. "In AA they teach us that the disease is a personal matter. What you drink, how much you drink, it's not my affair, it's yours."

"A terrible thing, this problem. You'd be surprised how many men in our community have this problem. And drugs, too, would you believe? Terrible. Drugs are a tool of *der Tayvl*, the No-Good-One, to make men forget themselves, to make them despair.

"Anyway, did you eat good?"

"Yes. It was all delicious. Your wife is a wonderful cook."

"She's all right. A good wife. So. So I told my Sarah that you are going to need her help to talk to the friends of that unfortunate man, may his blood be avenged. You will also need help to read the books about Lublin, the Seer, and Hirsh Leib. Unfortunately, there are very few in English, and those are no good. And do you know what?"

"What?"

"She said yes."

"I don't understand."

"What's not to understand? Many people here don't speak English so good. When you talk to them, you will need a translator. And you can't read the books. And so? And so my Sarah will translate."

"I don't think that will be necessary, Rabbi."

"You don't think, you don't think. But I know. Enough of this. We'll sing."

Around two o'clock, while Rabbi Kalman, Moshe, and the South African were in the living room, arguing animatedly in Yiddish about what he assumed to be a point of Torah, Taylor slipped off to what he had been told was Moshe's old bedroom. The walls were bare, and the only furniture was a single bed, a small bed table, an empty bookcase, and a wooden dresser painted yellow. There was a lamp, a bowl of water, a pitcher, and a glass on the bed table. A glass brick filled with clear marbles sat on the windowsill, and a plant grew out of it—mother-in-law's tongue, he thought. Rebecca used to have them in her apartment, he recalled. A small closet was empty, and Taylor hung his suit in it.

He lay down in the boxer shorts he had begun wearing when he'd first started trying to get Carol pregnant. After they'd found out that the odds against them were about a million to one, he had tried to go back to Jockey shorts but discovered that he preferred boxers.

The bed was comfortable and the two feather pillows soft and inviting. He was logy from all the food, and it had been a long day. He thought of Sarah. It wouldn't be hard to get turned on to her, he thought. Good presence. Smart girl. Beautiful hair. Small waist, big breasts. Not his type, but what did they say about variety? Spice of life? And then he remembered that he had forgotten to call Naomi.

Another amend he owed. He'd call her tomorrow to apologize. Might as well break it off, too.

Then he thought of Shumach's mysterious blonde, although he was less impressed with the coincidence than Schumach was. He doubted if Schumach had much experience with women or with tall blondes. Hasids, in general, seemed to be rather short, especially the women. Like Sarah. He'd mention the blonde to Detective Hill tomorrow anyway. It would be something to trade for whatever Hill knew.

As Taylor reached over to turn off the bedside lamp, it blinked out if its own accord. On a timer, he thought. What do they call it? A *Shabbos zeyger*. A Sabbath clock. He checked his watch. So they don't expect to go to sleep until 2:30, Taylor thought. Good. I'll get up early, 5:30, go back to my apartment, have a cup of coffee, then head out to Hill's. I'll make my excuses to the rabbi later.

Is he trying to fix me up with his daughter? Taylor wondered. A *Yiddishe goy* like me? Couldn't be. On the other hand, a translator might come in handy. And she seemed like a nice girl. Very pretty. Beautiful, actually. Incredible hair. Incredible skin.

Taylor slept.

19

West Fifty-ninth Street, Manhattan
Saturday, September 11

A woman walking her cocker spaniel felt a chill as she passed the lobby at 157 West Fifty-ninth. A native New Yorker, she knew enough not to ignore this internal alarm, and she also knew enough not to stop walking. So she glanced furtively into the dark vestibule and saw a tall thin white man in sunglasses and a leather jacket smoking a cigarette. A scary guy, she thought, but not a mugger, not this time, and she hurried on.

The Cutter thought briefly of following her, pulling her into an alley, slitting her throat. It would be easy, he thought. It would be amusing. Then he felt his stomach knot and a bitter fluid flow into his mouth. He spat, but the taste lingered.

The Cutter felt sick, angry, and put upon. He had not planned on being so long in New York, a city he detested, a city of mongrels—*shvartzers* and Puerto Ricans and Chinese. A city that bred the Hasids who were even now overrunning Israel, weakening the state and the army with their old-fashioned religion, refusing to serve, expecting others to do their fighting for them while they screamed about throwing the Arabs out of the Holy Land. He had spent days among them in Williamsburg, weeks, trying to find out to whom the Satmarer *rebbe* would have entrusted the diamond and finally being given a name—Zalman Gottleib—by a fat, foolish, boastful little girl, a friend of the *rebbe*'s silly daughter.

These were Jews like my father, the Cutter thought, Jews who went meekly to the ovens, the *Shema* on their lips. These were the Jews who thought that the Holocaust was God's judgment. Just being among them, just seeing them on the streets with their pasty skin and their black beards, brought back dreams of the camps, dreams of his father standing by as the Nazis came to take his family away. And with the dreams came the fantasies of blood and revenge that made the Cutter's head ache and loosened his bowels.

He spat again. What was he doing here, watching Maria's apartment so early in the morning? The whore and that stupid Israeli would not be up before noon. It was the Magician's fault, he thought, realizing how angry he still was with Czartoryski.

Yesterday afternoon Czartoryski had taken him to pay a courtesy call on the Magician's Italian friend, Joseph della Francesca, in an office in the back of a butcher store near the Brooklyn Navy Yard. The Cutter had not wanted to go, but Czartoryski had insisted.

The Cutter knew that Czartoryski paid the Italians for the right to sell drugs, and he had assumed, correctly, that this della Francesca was a middleman. Czartoryski had told the Cutter that della Francesca was unusually intelligent for an Italian. He told him that the mobster was related to the Renaissance painter Piero della Francesca. But to the Cutter he had seemed to be a typical cowardly mafioso, one of those hoodlums who learned how to act and how to dress from Hollywood movies. He reeked of cologne, and his skin was almost black from sun lamps. To the Cutter, his brown, bovine eyes seemed dumb and frightened. This was a man, the Cutter had thought, who was forever expecting a blow to fall. And that attracted blows. The Cutter's hands twitched.

When they were alone in the office, della Francesca had made a great show of embracing Czartoryski and presenting him with a large salami. Then the Italian had shocked the Cutter. He said that the salami was in honor of the way Czartoryski had disposed of the Jew diamond dealer, and he poured three glasses of brandy. He had smiled at the Cutter as he'd offered him a glass.

The smells coming from the butcher shop out front, the heat, and the idea that this fool knew his business had combined to make the Cutter physically ill. He turned his back on the Italian and walked out of the office. A little later Czartoryski came out, and they took a cab back to Manhattan.

In the taxi Czartoryski had touched the Cutter's knee. "Do not concern yourself about him," Czartoryski said. "He is not as stupid as he seems. And we have done him a great service. The marriage threatened his profits. Now both the Lubavitchers and the Satmarers will continue paying him separately for the *kosher* meat they bring into the city.

"You are not happy, I know," said Czartoryski, studying his old friend and thinking that perhaps the Cutter would soon die. Well, thought Czartoryski, that wouldn't be so bad. It was long past time to recruit a younger assistant. "You wish to return to Tel Aviv," Czartoryski said. "Soon we will be finished here."

But the Cutter had spent another restless night, smoking and staring into the darkness. And when he did doze, his dreams took him back to the camps, and once again he was knee deep in corpses, listening to the guards shout, smelling the rotting flesh combined with the bittersweet aroma of the gas chambers, fishing in black, broken mouths for gold, staring into sightless eyes, trembling on the lip of the mass grave.

Perhaps, thought the Cutter, I will do them both, Levin and Maria. The hell with the Magician, risking our lives in order to curry favor with that comic-book gangster. And as the Cutter contemplated killing Maria Radziwell along with Ariel Levin, he felt his stomach relax and his loins stir. Removing the whore would be a blessing. It would help redeem him.

He made himself a promise: When the time came, he would make her suffer.

20

Eastchester, New York
Saturday, September 11

Detective Frank Hill, wearing a blue-and-red New York Knickerbocker tank top and baggy gray sweat pants that helped conceal his growing gut, greeted Dov Taylor at the door of his split-level home. At first Taylor wondered how Hill could afford such a large house, but as Hill led him into the kitchen Taylor saw that the living room rug was threadbare, the furniture was cheap and battered, the walls and ceilings were cracked and peeling, and the linoleum in the kitchen was stained and chewed up. Every penny he had, thought Taylor, and then a few more, had gone into buying this place. There was nothing left over.

Frank Hill's house depressed him. It smelled of failure. On the other hand, there were toys scattered around the house, so, thought Taylor, he beats me there. He has kids.

"Want a beer?" asked Hill, taking two bottles of Bud out of the refrigerator.

"No, thanks," said Taylor.

"Coffee? It's from breakfast, but it's not bad."

"Sure. Thanks."

Hill poured Taylor a cup from a Mr. Coffee machine.

"You take sugar, cream?"

"Everything," said Taylor.

"Here," said Hill, handing Taylor a sugar bowl and a container of half-and-half. "You make it. Let's go out back."

Hill, beer in hand, led Taylor out through the kitchen door to a small deck with two beach chairs overlooking what seemed to be a field of wheat.

"Like it?" asked Hill. "I haven't cut it for almost two years now. I used to cut it every fucking weekend, or every other fucking weekend, and then one day the guy who lives next door tells me I oughtta mow my lawn more often, I'm making the neighborhood look bad. So I said, You're absolutely right, pal, and I haven't cut it since. I tell everybody it's Japanesy. You know, natural. What do you think?''

''I think it looks good.''

''Yeah? It looks like shit. The neighbors think I'm nuts. They hate me. But so what. The kids can still play in it. They lose a lot of balls, though.''

''How many kids you got?''

''Three. Two boys and a girl.''

''Nice.''

''The two boys are at Little League, and the girl, Jillian, is at her dancing lesson.''

''And your wife?''

''Shopping. You got kids?''

''No.''

''How come?''

''Divorced.''

''You're lucky. I mean, I'm not saying I'd change anything—I love my kids, kids are great—but you, you can do whatever the fuck you please, you know? You're not tied down like me. Not like I had any choice. Bing, bang, bing, you know. Stick it in, nine months later, a kid. Three times. First time we got it on—bang. She was showing at the wedding. Then, right after Jillian, she gets pregnant again. Don't ever let anyone tell you you can't get pregnant while you're nursing. Then I catch a break, talked her into using the diaphragm. Then one day she don't put it in, bing, here come Sean. Then I got smart. Got a vasectomy. Walked around like someone kicked me in the balls for a week, but that's it. Never notice it now.''

Taylor felt his stomach turning over. Why was it that whenever he told anyone he was childless, they always stressed how easy it was for them? How many operations had Carol had? How many doctors had they seen? How much money had they spent? And this asshole has a vasectomy? Fuck him.

''Wish I had two girls, though, instead of two boys,'' Hill continued. ''Girls are better. All the boys want to do is play ball. A little is okay, but they're after you all the fucking time, and I'm not as young as I used to be.''

"None of us are."

"You got that right. Also, girls think the sun rises and sets on Daddy. My little girl, I mean, I come home, she's all over me.''

"Nice."

"Yeah. So, enough about the kids. We're alone. Just us guys. But I'm the only one drinking.''

"Early for me.''

"It's just beer.''

"Still early.''

Hill looked out over his backyard jungle. "So? What can I do you for?''

"You can tell me what you've come up with on the Gottlieb-Stein killing.''

"Nugatz. Shit. Fuck-all. That's what I got. Why?''

"Why what?''

"Why you interested?''

"Well, actually, I haven't been doing much since I retired, and my rabbi asked me to look into it, so I said I would. I told him I couldn't do anything you couldn't do better, but he still asked me, you know, see what I could do,'' said Taylor, hoping to allay Hill's suspicions by stroking his vanity.

"Your rabbi, huh. But you're not one of them. I mean, you ain't got the big beard or nothing.''

"No. But my rabbi does.''

"Uh-huh. So how come you left the force?''

"Just got tired of it. Or it got tired of me.''

"You know,'' said Hill, "I asked around about you.''

"Yeah?''

"Yeah. Heard you were a good cop. Super-Jew, right? Heard you were a big boozer. Guess no more, huh?''

"No more.''

"Okay. Look. You gotta understand. There's a lotta pressure on this case.''

"Pressure from where?''

"From the Jews. Well, you should know. A Jew gets

killed, a religious Jew, and the fucking bells go off all over town. Lotta rabbis calling up the mayor, talking about Nazis. And a Jew in the diamond district is ten times worse. Lotta money floating around there. Lotta money for the mayor come reelection, you know? So my chief, who's a good guy, he's got his balls in an uproar. And therefore my balls are in an uproar, too. So if you know anything you should tell me, tell me."

"I don't know anything about this," said Taylor, who didn't think that Hill, sitting on his deck in Eastchester with a beer in his hand, looked like his balls, or anything else, were in the least bit aroused. "That's why I'm talking to you. And anything I do find out, Frank, well, of course, you got it."

"Okay. So here's what we got."

Hill closed his eyes, and Taylor waited. He knew Hill was both feeling him out, seeing if he could trust him, and playing with him. I know you, Frank, Taylor thought. I've *seen* you, like the Satmarer *rebbe saw* me. Better. I know what your lawn is about. And I know why you offered me that beer. It's all the big *fuck you*, isn't it, Frank? The cop's *fuck you* to the whole world, including yourself. And you're lazy, aren't you, Frank? That's why your house looks like shit. It's not the money. You're lazy, you're getting fat, and pretty soon you're going to be a lousy excuse for a cop, if you're not one already.

Have another beer, my man, thought Taylor. That first one wants company.

"I think I'll have another brew," said Hill, standing up. "Want anything to eat, a doughnut?"

"No, thanks, Frank," said Taylor.

Hill disappeared into the kitchen, came out with a new beer, and sat back down. "Okay," he began. "Gottlieb and Stein died of exsanguination after having their throats cut. The killer didn't do anything to Stein except for cutting her throat. One cut. Ear to ear. Got both carotids. Big fucking butcher's knife. The guy left it.

"Gottlieb was strung up by his ankles. He was gutted, man. Real fucking ugly."

"Cult killing?" asked Taylor.

"I don't know. No messages written in blood, anyway."

"I'd like to look at photos if you don't mind."

"Why should I mind? Stop by the office Monday, I'll show you the whole fucking file."

"Prints?"

"Lots of prints, no makes. A set we figure belongs to the killer. We sent them out—FBI, Interpol, Israel, South Africa, the IDSO—that's the International Diamond Security Organization. They're a bunch of tough monkeys. South Africans. Met one once. Big guy, big boozer. All he could talk about was niggers. Hated them like crazy. Forget what he called them. Funny word. Anyway, nobody's got nothing.

"So, anyway, there were diamonds all over the place. Our killer emptied the safe and threw the diamonds around. No way to tell what was taken."

"Why?"

" 'Cause there's no records, no inventory to match them up against. These fucking people. They keep everything in their heads, and everything's a big fucking secret with them."

"So what happened to Gottleib's diamonds? You holding them?"

"What for? What are they evidence of? No, we took them over to the Diamond Club. A guy named Fred Feldman is the boss. So what happens is guys start showing up at the club with these scraps of paper saying that such-and-such a diamond is theirs, or they loaned Gottleib so many diamonds, and then they pick over the diamonds and take them home. Then we talk to them and they don't know nothing."

"Is Feldman being cooperative?"

"Sure, whatever the fuck good that does. The diamonds nobody claims, he's gonna sell for Gottleib's daughter. And make a good profit for himself, I'm sure.

"The whole fucking business is crazy. I mean, there's thousands of bucks' worth of diamonds, maybe hundreds of thousands, and these guys are just picking them up and taking them home. If I wasn't just a dumb cop, I'd have liberated a few myself. But I'm too stupid, just a dumb mick."

Hill fell silent for a moment, presumably mourning his missed chance. Taylor waited.

"There was about fifteen thousand cash; five in his office safe, ten in his vault," Hill continued. "That went to the Diamond Club, too, and there's more guys with slips of paper saying Gottleib owed them money. And there's also guys saying they owed Gottleib money, and they want to make sure the money gets to his family.

"So we talk to all these guys, and they all say Gottleib was a fucking saint, and probably the Nazis killed him. Try talking to them about their business, it's like asking them how often they fuck their wives. If I was the IRS, I'd arrest them all on general principles. They're all so fucking rich, even though they don't look it, and there's no way they pay taxes."

"What about Gottleib's family?"

"Just the one daughter and some grandchildren. I don't think the daughter's been out of Brooklyn in her life, she don't know nothing about her daddy's business. So the daughter, who don't speak English too good even though she was born here, she says the same thing: Papa was a saint, and the Nazis killed him. What is it with this Nazi business? You'd think they're all still living in Germany, they talk about Nazis so much."

"I don't know," said Taylor. "I guess they made a strong impression. The Nazis." Taylor, his patience running out, decided to shake Hill up a little bit. "You have any luck running down that woman in Queens, the one Gottleib's partner was seeing the day of the murder?" Taylor asked.

Hill made a pained face. "I thought you said you didn't know anything about this."

"I don't. But I did talk to Gottleib's partner."

"Schumach. Tell me about it."

"You know, the woman he saw in Queens. He told me he saw her again."

"When?"

"Last Wednesday. Going into his building."

"His office building?"

"Yeah."

"Fuck."

"So, do you have anything on her?" Taylor asked.

"You know," said Hill, "you should have told me this up

front. I told you to tell me if you knew anything, and I didn't mean when you fucking felt like it. I don't like being jerked around. What else you know?''

"Nothing, Frank. Really.''

"Well, it makes it harder. You were a cop. You should understand. No games, okay?''

"No games.''

"Because, like I said, there's pressure on this one, and it's not going too good. Okay. The guy who owns the house is Korean. Owns a bunch of houses in Flushing, even though he can barely speak English. Fucking Koreans. Yellow Jews, you know? No offense. They make their money in those fruit stores, and then they get into real estate. Anyway, this guy don't know who the hell he rented to, did it all over the phone, dropped the keys off in the mailbox, all he wants to know is where's his money at. He got stiffed.''

"Did he talk to a man or a woman?'' asked Taylor.

"A man.''

Taylor and Hill were quiet, both adding one and one and getting two. Schumach sees a woman in the house, but the landlord spoke to a man. Was the man he spoke to the killer?

"You think the woman was a dodge to get Schumach out of the office?'' Taylor spoke what they were both thinking.

"I don't know,'' said Hill. "I want to talk to your friend Schumach, ream him out, the fuckhead. Find out what else he didn't tell me.''

"So what do you think, Frank?'' asked Taylor, feeling Hill slipping away, feeling him closing down, lumping Taylor with the enemy. "A nut case? A robbery?''

"I don't know. Could be a religious thing. Gottleib was a Satmarer, and the Lubavitchers and Satmarers are always beating the crap out of each other. Just a few months ago, this Lubavitcher rabbi got beat up, got his clothes torn off and his beard shaved off because he was giving private Bible lessons to a Satmarer kid, teaching him stuff the Satmarers aren't supposed to know, I guess, whatever the fuck that might be.''

"I didn't see anything about that in the papers,'' said Taylor.

"No, the rabbi refused to press charges. I think he was a fag. Probably diddling the kid. Anyway," said Hill, "isn't the Satmarer rabbi's daughter supposed to marry the big Lubavitcher rabbi's kid?"

"That's off."

"I'm not surprised."

"I don't think the Lubavitchers are involved," said Taylor, hoping that was true.

"Fucking Hasids. They're so fucking rich and so fucking weird. You're Jewish, Taylor. Why do they dress like that?"

"One of them once told me it was like a safety belt," Taylor said. "He said, 'How can I get in trouble dressed like this? How can I go places I shouldn't go, see people I shouldn't see? How can I sin?' "

"Makes sense," Hill said.

"Yup," said Taylor.

"What more can I tell you?" Hill asked, sounding bored. "You gonna keep talking to people?"

"I guess. Probably. Maybe I can find Schumach's blond bombshell."

"A bombshell?"

"From the way he described her, yeah."

"Yeah. Like he would know. You know, they're all the time going to whores, the Hasids."

"That true?"

"Absolutely. I guess their wives won't go down on them. I guess that makes my wife Jewish, right?"

Taylor laughed politely, but he hated it when men joked about their wives. Hill's Jew jokes were starting to piss him off, too, although when he was a cop he heard them all the time and they didn't bother him at all.

"My wife's Protestant. The worst. Catholic girls give the best blow jobs," Hill continued. "They think if they give blow jobs instead of fucking, they stay virgins. Well, if you find her, Taylor, the blonde, you come straight to me, right?"

"Right."

"Tell me, is it true they only fuck on Saturdays?"

"The Hasids or Catholic girls?"

"The Hasids."

"No, it's not true," said Taylor.

"A Jewish guy told me that."

"Well, it's bullshit."

"I figured that. Jesus, I see more kids and pregnant girls in Williamsburg than I do in Harlem. How could they make so many babies if they only fuck on Saturday?"

"You got it."

"I mean, all those kids, they must fuck like rabbits. You know, I also heard they fuck through holes in the sheets. They never get naked in bed. Is that true?"

"Some do, some don't."

"You speak the language, Taylor?"

"No."

Hill belched. "Get you another cup of coffee?"

"No, thanks, Frank. I guess I'll be going."

"Okay," said Hill, standing up with Taylor. "Remember what I said. Anything you find out, you come to me."

"And you'll keep in touch with me, right, Frank?"

"Sure," said Hill, who had no intention of doing any such thing.

Hill led Taylor back through the house and out the front door. Taylor was in his car, driving back to the city, before he realized that he had never even given a thought to telling Hill about the Satmarer *rebbe*'s diamond. Well, thought Taylor, fuck Hill. Still, Taylor had not made a conscious decision to keep the diamond from the detective. It was as if the *rebbe* had given Taylor a posthypnotic suggestion to forget about it when he spoke with the police. And perhaps, thought Taylor, he had.

21

West Fifty-ninth Street, Manhattan
Saturday, September 11

Ariel Levin wasn't sure what was making him hotter, Mary Rubel riding his penis—squeezing it with her vagina and then letting it go—or the sight of her heavy breasts bouncing up and down as she leaned over him, her hands pinning his wrists to the bed. Whichever, he knew he was going to come if he didn't do something fast. So he closed his eyes and tried to think about the Mets' infield. Murray at first, Randolph at second, Schofield at short, Magadan at third, and catching . . .

Levin came.

This was the fourth time he had had sex with Rubel—that first night, last night, this morning in his office, and now—and he had never lasted more than a few minutes. This woman, he thought, was like a man. No kissing. No foreplay. Just jump on top and hump away. Levin had never had a woman who was so obviously hot for him, and he wished he could slow things down, show her how much he knew, show her how he could please her. He had been taught certain tricks by the whores in Tel Aviv. He knew he could entrance her, make her yearn for him, but she wasn't giving him the chance.

Rubel rolled off him. "I think we have a little problem, Ariel," she said. "Just stay there. Don't move. I'll get a washcloth."

Levin looked down. Blood. Blood all over his belly, his penis, his balls, his thighs. Shit. The woman was having her period.

Levin felt a twinge of revulsion and then a spasm of anger. Why hadn't she told him? Making love to a woman who was bleeding was something he simply didn't do. It was disgusting.

But how could he complain, how could he stay angry? She was a *shiksa*. What did she know? The *goyim* fucked like that all the time. They were pigs. Besides, not only was she one of the most beautiful women he had ever seen, but maybe she was going to be able to solve his problem: what to do with Gottleib's diamond.

This morning he had taken her to his office and shown her the stone. He had seen her look at him with a new respect, almost awe. And then she had gotten down on her knees, unzipped his fly, and given him a blow job right there in front of the open safe.

It had been the best he had ever had. It had been like sticking his cock in a washing machine built just for him. Afterward she had asked him what he was going to do with the diamond, and he had boasted that he had several buyers lined up, buyers who were bidding against each other. He'd told her that he was going to sell it for a million dollars, and he'd watched her brown, almond-shaped eyes grow wide. Slavic eyes, he had thought. Her ancestors had been raped by Mongols. Now it's my Jewish cock.

And then, to his delight, she had told him that she had an uncle, a very wealthy man, who lived now in Rome and who happened to be visiting New York. He had told her that he had brought a great deal of money with him in order to invest in diamonds. Would Levin like her to call him?

Well, what did she mean by a lot of money? Levin had asked her. Enough, she'd said. Then yes, Levin had said. Why not? The more buyers, he'd said, the better.

Rubel returned from the bathroom with a warm washcloth, sat down on the bed, and began wiping Levin's genitals. "I am sorry, Ariel," she said. "I did not think it had started yet. And I wanted to so badly."

"It's all right," Levin said a little stiffly. "What's a little blood?"

"I am so glad you are not angry," she said. "My husband, he was Jewish, you know, he would never make love to me when I was bleeding. He did not want even to touch me."

"That's old-fashioned," said Levin. "I'm not like that. It's just, well, it makes a mess."

"You are angry. Oh, Ariel, I am so sorry."

"I told you. I'm not angry. Come here," Levin said, opening his arms. "I'll show you."

"No," said Rubel, leaning over to kiss Levin on the forehead and then standing up. "Let me first take care of myself."

Rubel disappeared into the bathroom, and when she returned Levin saw the string of a tampon dangling from between her long, powerful legs. Somehow that made her look all the more naked, and Levin felt himself stirring again. My God, he thought, I can't get enough of this woman.

"Can I get you anything, Ariel?" Rubel asked. "Something to drink?"

"Do we have any champagne left?" asked Levin.

"Yes, I will get some. And then I will call my uncle, yes?"

"Sure. But there's no hurry," Levin said, reaching for her. "Your husband was crazy. There are other things we can do when you have your period. Like we did in the office."

Rubel twisted away from his touch, laughed, and, throwing her head back, ran her hands through her thick hair. The gesture thrust her breasts out, and Levin was hard again.

"You are a bad man, Ariel," Rubel said. "First I will get the champagne. Then I will call my uncle and you will talk with me. After that," she said, pointing to Levin's erect penis, "we will discuss these other things."

Levin stroked Rubel's back as she spoke Polish into the phone. Then she handed it to him.

"Mr. Levin?" said Ladislaw Czartoryski in a lightly accented voice.

"Yes?" said Levin.

"I am Mr. Cartovsky. Mr. Vladimir Cartovsky. My niece tells me that you own an extraordinary diamond, and she tells me that you are willing to part with it."

"Yes, I do, sir," said Levin. "A magnificent stone."

"I am most eager to see it, Mr. Levin. I am very interested in diamonds, and I have come to New York expressly to pursue this interest."

"Well, this is a very special stone, Mr. Cartovsky. Not for

just anyone. It is very old, very beautiful, and, I have to tell you, it is very expensive.''

''I am sure it is, Mr. Levin. If it were not, I would not be interested in it.''

''I must tell you, Mr. Cartovsky, that this diamond has no GIA certificate, and I can't allow it to be appraised. I cannot reveal why.''

Levin had learned long ago that nothing sold a diamond so well as intrigue. A great stone should have a great story to go with it. In fact, mused Levin, Gottleib's stone did have a great, bloody story, but not one that he was about to share with Cartovsky.

''I'm sure you understand,'' Levin continued. ''If people were to learn of it, well, there would be gossip. The government would become involved. The IRS. Therefore, Mr. Cartovsky, we must be discreet.''

''I understand, Mr. Levin. I feel just as you do.''

''This stone, sir, well, it's unique. I can assure you that there's not another like it in the world. I can tell you,'' said Levin, warming to his story, ''that it once belonged to a Persian prince. It has passed through many hands, and, I do not exaggerate, many men have died for it. Over time, Mr. Cartovsky, its very existence has become a secret possessed by a select few. So, I hope your niece did not mislead you. A stone like this, well, I am not anxious to sell.''

''Of course, Mr. Levin. I am, I confess, enormously intrigued. And, by the way, I am quite capable of ascertaining your diamond's worth without the Gemological Institute's pedigree, which in any case I consider of dubious value.''

''Also, Mr. Cartovsky,'' said Levin, summoning up his nerve to take the plunge, ''if you can convince me to sell, I would have to insist upon payment in full, in cash, upon delivery. This is not negotiable.''

''If your diamond is all that you say it is, Mr. Levin, and if it is as beautiful as my niece has told me it is, I can assure you that that would present no problem. I prefer doing business on a cash basis.''

Levin felt a delicious shiver of excitement in his stomach.

Ariel, he told himself, you're going to be rich. You'll tour Israel in a silver Porsche. You'll stay in four-star hotels and buy your old man a dinner that will cost as much as his yearly pension from the Israeli Defense Force. And women. Mary Rubel is just the beginning. You'll have your pick from the world's models and movie stars.

"Excuse me, Mr. Cartovsky. What did you say?"

"I said, when can we meet?"

"Well, why don't you come to my office Monday morning?"

"I would love to do that, Mr. Levin, but I would rather not be seen in the diamond district, as I am engaged in certain delicate negotiations and my presence would surely be remarked upon. I am sure you understand. Could you not bring the stone to, say, my niece's apartment, and we could meet there?"

"I'm sorry, Mr. Cartovsky. I would not be comfortable removing the stone from my office."

"I understand. This is a difficult problem, Mr. Levin," said Czartoryski, "but not insurmountable. Perhaps you would be willing to show me the diamond after business hours. In that way, I would be able to maintain my incognito and you would be able to maintain your security."

"I see no problem with that, sir," Levin said.

"Then Monday evening it is," said Czartoryski. "I will present myself at your building at eight, if that is agreeable."

"Done," said Levin.

"Excellent," Czartoryski said. "I will see you then. It was a pleasure speaking with you, Mr. Levin, and I am quite hopeful that we will be able to do business together. Would you put my niece back on the line?"

Levin handed the phone to Rubel. He could barely keep from shouting for joy. First this beauty falls in my lap, and now her rich uncle. God must love me, he thought, leaning over to kiss the small of her back as she said good-bye to her uncle. Like the Arabs say, Levin thought, *Alah akbah*. God is great. Fucking great.

22

Prince Street, SoHo, Manhattan
Sunday, September 12

Sunday mornings, Dov Taylor went to his "home" AA meeting in the basement of St. Vincent's Church on Prince Street. He knew almost everyone there, and everyone knew him.

It was a discussion meeting that went around the room. Some people spoke about last night, Saturday night, always a rough time for alcoholics. They talked about the parties they went to, or the dinners they went to, and how they didn't drink. Others talked about their problems with their jobs, their problems with their spouses and lovers, and how all those problems were manageable, a day at a time, as long as they didn't drink. A tall, thin, relatively attractive young woman in her late twenties or early thirties, a newcomer to the meeting, introduced herself as Carol and told the group that she was celebrating her first thirty days of sobriety. Everybody clapped. All Taylor said when his turn came was, "My name is Dov, and I'm a grateful recovering alcoholic and drug addict. All I want to say right now is that I'm really glad to be here."

And he was. The coffee, the cookies and doughnuts, the company of his fellow alcoholics, was profoundly comforting. And as he relaxed, Taylor realized that he did have something to say after all.

"It's me again," said Taylor. "Still a grateful recovering alcoholic and drug addict. Yesterday, I was talking to someone and he offered me a drink. He knew I was an alcoholic, and he offered me a drink anyway. I didn't want it—at least I didn't think I wanted it—but I got angry, and I started thinking about what an asshole he was. And I started, you know, taking his inventory. If he wasn't an alcoholic, I thought, he was sure heading that way. I said to myself, See you in the halls, buddy. Anyway, before I knew it, I was screwing up, getting him pissed off, and not getting what I needed to get.

"And I knew I was screwing up, some part of me knew, and I couldn't do anything about it. And now that I think about it, I realize that it wasn't him. It wasn't him offering me the drink. It wasn't him talking about his kids. My wife and I—I mean, my ex-wife and I—we couldn't have kids; it was one of the things that broke us up. Anyway, it wasn't what this guy was doing, it was me, wanting the drink and not even knowing in my conscious mind that I wanted it, and being pissed off that I couldn't have it. I mean, yes, he's an asshole, no question. But that's his problem, not mine. My problem is I'm an alcoholic; I'm the guy he'll meet in the halls. As long as I remember that, and as long as I don't pick up, I'll be okay.

"Like it says in the book, it's a cunning, baffling, and powerful disease. So when I said before that I was glad I was here, I didn't really know how glad. Which is another reason to keep coming. Sitting here, I figure out stuff I didn't even know was bothering me.

"I guess that's all."

After the Lord's Prayer concluded the meeting, Carol, the newcomer, told him how much she enjoyed listening to him. "I mean," she said, "everybody at the meetings seems so together, and I feel so screwed up. I mean, I'm sober, but I'm still screwed up. So it was nice to hear somebody with two years say that he's still screwed up, too."

Taylor laughed. "Well, thank you, I guess."

"You know what I mean," Carol said. "I don't mean you're particularly screwed up. You seem very nice."

"Everybody is screwed up here," said Taylor. "Haven't you noticed? That's why they're here."

"I guess so. Tell me, Dov. That's your name, right? You're Jewish, aren't you?" Taylor nodded. "Me too," she said. "What do you think of the Lord's Prayer ending all the meetings? Does it bother you?"

"No, not really," said Taylor. "It's just a prayer. I don't even think of it as a Christian prayer anymore. It's just the AA prayer, you know, to the Higher Power, whatever that is for you. Does it bother you?"

"A little. I mean, I don't even know the words so well. I just mumble it."

"If you keep coming to meetings," said Taylor, "you'll learn it pretty good. And not all meetings use it, you know. There are Jewish meetings listed in the book, although I've never been to one."

"No. I like this meeting. Anyway," she said, extending her hand, "I just wanted to thank you."

"Anytime," said Taylor, noticing that her handshake was surprisingly firm. Most of the women he had known had weak handshakes, but this one . . .

Uh-uh, thought Taylor. No hanky-panky with newcomers.

He released the woman's hand and stepped back. She was attractive, he thought, and the little white scar above her upper lip was intriguing. But, as he had often discussed with his sponsor, getting involved with someone in early sobriety was a no-no. The newcomer is too vulnerable; the old-timer forgets his humility.

"I guess I'll see you around," said Carol.

"Keep coming," Taylor said, "and you'll see me."

Taylor walked back down Prince to Sullivan Street and his building. He walked through the empty lobby and opened his door. The little red light on his answering machine was flashing. The first message was from Alex, his sponsor, just checking in. The second message was from Naomi, telling him to go to hell. The third message was from his boss at the security agency telling him not to bother showing up for work Monday.

All right, thought Taylor, feeling oddly buoyant, that kills two birds. Now I'm naked. No girl. No job. No booze. And I've just flirted with a pretty woman and I was able to leave it at that. Whatta guy.

The phone rang.

"Mr. Taylor? This is Sarah Kalman."

"Hello, Sarah. How're you doing?"

"My father is angry with you, Mr. Taylor," said Sarah. "You shouldn't have left our home like that, like a thief."

"I'm sorry," Taylor said.

"It's not me you have to be sorry to," said Sarah. "It's the rabbi."

"I'll call him and apologize. I, I had something important to do."

"May I ask if it was about this terrible murder?"

"Yes," said Taylor. "Yes, it was."

"Well, in that case, Mr. Taylor, how can I help?"

"Please, call me Dov."

"Dov. A pretty name."

"My grandmother sometimes called me Doodle."

"I don't think I'll call you that. Do people call you Dovidl?"

"Not since I was six."

"So, Dov? What shall I do?"

"Well, Sarah, I don't really know. Right now, the people I have to speak to seem to speak English."

"My father told me that you are bound to Rabbi Hirsh Leib. He showed me some of your family papers, your grandmother Rebecca's, that said that he was your great-great-grandfather."

"That's what your father says, yes, although I don't know what that has to do with anything. Do you believe that my great-great-grandfather can help me find out who did these murders?"

"I believe that my father is a very wise man."

"Yeah, I think so, too, although he told me Friday night that he didn't want you going to college. That doesn't seem so wise."

"That's his way," said Sarah. "It's *Hasidishe*. College is not important. So, Dov, would you like me to find out about Rabbi Hirsh Leib's history for you?"

"Sure. Yes, Sarah. I would appreciate that."

"Very well, Dov, I will see what I can find out. Then I will call you. All right?"

"Yes."

"And call my father. Explain to him that it was a matter of life and death. Under those circumstances, the *Shabbos* laws must bend."

"Okay."

"Good-bye, Dov. And may the Holy One protect you."

"Thank you, Sarah."

And amen, thought Taylor, hanging up. After all, in this world, it's not just alcohol that's cunning, baffling, and powerful.

23

Eighteenth Street
Bensonhurst, Brooklyn
Sunday, September 12

"Mom!" called Phil Horowitz, crouched in front of the open refrigerator, his white shirt buttoned at the neck, his *tzitzis* dangling over his black pants. The bald spot on the top of his head reflected the overhead light. "We got any fish left? Wait until you taste this fish, Dov. You never had fish like this. This is real Jewish fish. Homemade. The carp is fresh. Then she bakes it. Mom!"

"It's in the icebox," shouted Mrs. Horowitz from the bedroom, "right in front of your face."

"Oh, yeah. I got it."

"You found it?" Mrs. Horowitz yelled.

"Yeah, Mom. I got it."

Horowitz brought a platter of gefilte fish to the kitchen table and set it down in front of Dov Taylor.

"This fish ain't like the crap you're used to," said Horowitz. "It's sweet like sugar. You want a little radish?"

"Sure," said Taylor, and Horowitz got a jar of white horseradish out of the refrigerator.

"The radish is homemade, too," said Horowitz. "It'll

clean your sinuses right out." He got a clear, unlabeled bottle out of the freezer and brought two glasses to the table.

"Not for me," said Taylor.

"This is good stuff, man."

"Homemade?"

"That's right. Vodka. Old Russian guy down in Brighton Beach makes it in his basement. Great stuff."

"No thanks."

"You want something else? I got some Scotch."

"I'm not drinking, Phil."

"Okay," said Horowitz, pouring himself a glass. "Taste the fish. Tell me it's not the best you ever had."

Taylor cut a slice of the cold gefilte fish and put a dollop of horseradish on top of it. First he tasted the sweetness of the fish, then the fire of the horseradish. Tears filled his eyes, and he began to cough. Horowitz laughed, swallowed his vodka, and poured himself another glass.

"I told you it was hot stuff," Horowitz said. "Want a glass of water?"

Taylor couldn't speak. He nodded.

Horowitz filled a glass of water from the tap and put it in front of him. Taylor drank it greedily. "You could kill someone with this stuff," he gasped, dabbing some of the water on his burning lips.

"Not a real Jew," said Horowitz, slathering his own slice with horseradish and popping it into his mouth.

"So I'm not a real Jew."

"No," said Horowitz. "You're some kind of mongrel, some mix. You don't know shit about your own people, your own religion, your own food. You don't belong anywhere, but you're too dumb to know it."

"Thanks, Phil. Thanks for filling me in."

"A cop? I mean, how can a Jew be a cop? How can a real Jew work for the *goyim*? These are the people who oppress your people."

"That's bullshit," said Taylor, "and if I didn't know that you were an asshole, I'd be offended."

"You just don't want to hear the truth," Horowitz shouted, spraying Taylor's shirt with saliva and gefilte fish.

"For chrissakes, Phil. Calm down. Didn't your mother teach you not to talk with your mouth full?"

"Come to *shul* with me. You should see how real Jews pray. I'm telling you, man, becoming a Hasid was the best thing I ever did. My life makes sense now."

Sense? thought Taylor. Behold Phil Horowitz, a balding, pug-ugly fanatic in his late forties, living with his mother, spitting gefilte fish, shouting like a crazy person.

"I need to talk about what happened to that diamond dealer, Phil. Don't tell me you don't know anything about it because I know you do. You're still in diamonds, aren't you?"

"Yeah, I'm still in diamonds."

"So? What do you know about it?"

"I told you before, I don't know nothing. The guy was a Satmarer. You know what that means?"

"Tell me."

"It means he was a maniac. A nut. A superstitious, ignorant, crazy old man. All the Satmarers are crazy, and we don't have nothing to do with them."

"You mean 'we' the Lubavitchers?" said Taylor.

"Yeah."

"You know, I just had dinner with a Lubavitcher rabbi, Rabbi Kalman, and I heard pretty much the same thing. Why do the Satmarers and Lubavitchers hate each other so much?"

"You had dinner with Rabbi Kalman?"

"Yeah. So what?"

"So Kalman is a great man. How do you know him?"

"From the *yeshiva*. From class."

"You've been taking classes from Kalman? You're going to become a Hasid?"

"No. I've stopped."

"Why?"

"Because. Just because."

"Big mistake, man. Big, big mistake. Stupid."

"Maybe. You didn't answer me. What's the problem between the Satmarers and the Lubavitchers?"

"You got a few months to listen?" asked Horowitz. "They're crazy, what can I say? They're anti-Israel. It doesn't matter to them that the Jews finally got a home, they want to tear down the state. When the soldiers go out to fight, they pray for them to lose.''

"I don't believe it," said Taylor.

"It's true.''

"Well, if the Lubavitchers and the Satmarers are such enemies," asked Taylor, "how come the marriage? How come your *rebbe*'s son is marrying their *rebbe*'s daughter?''

Horowitz paused, poured himself another drink, and knocked it back. "Our *rebbe*," he said, clearing his throat, "may his light shine, is a great man. You can't imagine how great he is. Just being near him is incredible. Being near all that holiness. He does miracles, Dov, I've seen them. You know what I was like. A *shtarker*, a thug. One day a guy takes me to 770, and I get on line to see the *rebbe*. I think it's a goof, but when I get up to him he looks me in the eye and it's like he's looking right through me. And before I know it, I ask him what I should do, I'm so unhappy. And he says—I'll never forget it—he says, '*Zay a Yid*.' That's all. Be a Jew. So that's what I did.

"Anyway, the *rebbe* loves all Jews—even Jews like you— and I figure he was trying to help the Satmarers, wake them up. But the Satmarers called it off anyway. You can't help them. Let me tell you, a lot of people were very relieved when it was called off.''

"What people?" asked Taylor.

"Lots of people.''

"So what are people saying about the murder? What are the Lubavitchers saying?''

"I don't hang around the district, Dov. I pick up the stones, and then I'm off. Amsterdam, Antwerp, London, Tel Aviv. I'm a courier, not a dealer.''

"Come on, Phil. You talk to dealers. I know you've heard stuff.''

Horowitz pushed himself away from the table and stood up. "I'm not going to talk about it. I told you that. I don't talk about the business.''

"I'm not asking you about the business; I'm asking you about a murder.''

"I think you'd better go," Horowitz said.

Taylor stood up. "You won't help me, okay. But I'm not going away. I've decided to find out what happened to that dealer, and that's what I'm going to do."

"Take my advice, man," said Horowitz, "forget about it. Walk away. I don't care how much the Satmarers are paying you, it ain't worth your life. This ain't like chasing *shvartzers* up in Harlem. This is serious business, with serious people involved. The Hasidim, all of us, we've become real powerful in Israel, and, well, it's not like before, when we were outsiders."

"I didn't say anything about who was paying me, Phil."

Taylor stared at Horowitz, at his old boyhood idol who had changed so much and, at the same time, had changed so little.

"So?" said Horowitz. "So I hear a few things. Enough to tell me that you're heading for *mucho tsuris* if you don't forget about all this. You don't belong here. This ain't your world. You don't know the players. You don't know what's going on."

"What's going on, Phil?"

Horowitz picked up a knife and cut off a hunk of the gefilte fish. He wrapped it up in plastic and handed it to Taylor. "Here," he said, "my mom would kill me if she knew I didn't give you some to take home."

"You're not going to help me?"

"No, man," said Phil Horowitz. "Because you're a *lantsman*, an old friend from the neighborhood, I'm going to do you the favor of not helping you."

24

Forty-seventh Street, Manhattan
Monday, September 13

The Diamond Dairy opened for business at seven-thirty, and Dov Taylor was there, waiting to take advantage of the $2.25 breakfast special: two eggs, any style, toast, and coffee.

Taylor had his eggs over easy. Next to him at the counter, cops, diamond brokers, cutters, setters, dealers, security guards, and men of unknown avocations—Hasids, blacks, and Hispanics—downed omelets, bagels and lox, and cheese Danishes. When Taylor finished mopping up the last of his egg with his wheat toast it was eight o'clock, and he crossed the cool, still uncrowded morning street to 52 West Forty-seventh.

Frank Hill, Taylor knew, was going to read Morris Schumach the riot act. He was also going to poke around the building, looking for information about Schumach's blonde. Taylor wanted to beat him to the punch, suspecting, correctly, that Detective Hill was not exactly a morning person.

Taylor struck pay dirt immediately. The guard on duty in the lobby, who simply assumed that Taylor was a cop and consequently did not ask to see his shield, remembered a tall blonde visiting the building last week. A babe, he said. A knockout. He checked his book. Wednesday. Mary something with an *R*.

Taylor looked at the scrawl in the book. Yes, the first name looked like Mary. The second was illegible, except for the obviously feminine, elaborately curlicued *R*.

"What's the use of sign-in sheets if you can't read the names?" grumbled Taylor, handing back the book.

"Don't ask me, Officer," said the guard. "I just work here."

The guard told Taylor that Mary R had signed in to see an Ariel Levin, a setter on the ninth floor. Yeah, you wouldn't forget that one, the guard affirmed, carving an ancient and honored shape in the air with his hands.

Discovering that Morris Schumach was already in his office, and that Ariel Levin was not, Taylor decided it would be a good deed to warn Schumach of Frank Hill's coming visit.

Schumach did not seem overjoyed to see Taylor, but he buzzed him in (he had not yet replaced Shirley Stein) and showed him the stains on the carpet. "Terrible, terrible," said Schumach. "But what can I do? Do you know what they want to clean? A fortune. And to replace? Forget it."

Schumach's mood did not improve when Taylor told him to expect another visit from the police, and why.

"So? So I didn't run to them because I see a woman walk into the building? So shoot me. Are they going to take me down to their police station to beat me up?"

"No, Mr. Schumach."

"And did you have to tell them I told you? I thought I was talking to you, not the police. If I wanted to talk to the police, I would have called them. But I didn't call them. I didn't even call you. You called me. And then you run to the police? What the hell kind of business is this?"

Taylor assured Schumach that he was not in any trouble. He told Schumach that Hill would scream and shout, but that if Schumach stayed calm and answered politely, the detective would eventually run out of steam and go away. And then Taylor asked if Schumach knew an Ariel Levin.

"Sure," said Schumach. "A setter on the ninth floor. I think on the ninth. An Israeli. Not a Hasid. Zally threw him some work sometime. Why, I don't know."

"You don't like him?" Taylor asked.

"Did I say that? What, now you are going to tell the police Morris Schumach hates this setter, and maybe you will tell them I killed Zally and poor Miss Stein because, because, I don't know what because?"

"Please, Mr. Schumach. I'm sorry. Perhaps I could have told Detective Hill in another way. But I assure you, you did nothing wrong, and Detective Hill knows that."

"You assure me. Excuse me, Mr. Taylor, if that does not make me want to dance for joy."

"All right, Mr. Schumach. I understand."

"And I don't know anything about this Levin, this Israeli. Understand? He's just a setter, works on the ninth floor. Anybody in this building can tell you that. So, please, do not tell the police, what, I don't know."

"All right, Mr. Schumach."

Taylor left a worried Morris Schumach stomping around his office and took the elevator down to the ninth floor. A sign and an arrow outside the elevator doors directed him to Ariel Levin's small office.

Taylor pressed the buzzer and opened the door to a tiny vestibule. Through a bulletproof window he could see a small, swarthy, muscular man wearing a colorful knitted *yarmulke*, sitting behind a large desk, reading *New York Newsday*'s sports pages. Ariel Levin looked up from his paper.

"Yes?" he asked, his voice sounding thin and metallic as it came through the speaker at the bottom of the window.

"Mr. Levin?" said Taylor, leaning down to what he took to be a speaker grille below the glass.

"Yes?"

"My name is Dov Taylor, and I would like to ask you a few questions."

"Police?"

"No."

"So?"

"Would you let me in? It would be easier not talking through the glass."

"I don't know you," said Levin. "You don't have an appointment. You want a stone set?"

"No, I just want to ask you a few questions. It will just take a minute."

"Questions about what?"

"May I come in, Mr. Levin?"

"What?"

"Will you buzz me in?" said Taylor, raising his voice.

"Tell me what you want to ask questions about."

Taylor sighed. For a moment he sympathized with Frank Hill. These were not easy people.

"Last Wednesday," Taylor began, feeling as if he were shouting, "you were visited by a young woman. I wanted to ask you about her."

"I don't know what you're talking about," said Levin. "Who are you if you're not the police?"

Good question, Taylor thought. "I used to be a policeman," he said. "Now I'm doing a favor for Zalman Gottleib's rabbi, looking into his death."

"So what's that got to do with me?" asked Levin.

"Nothing, Mr. Levin. It's just that perhaps you could help me if you could tell me about your visitor last week."

"What's that got to do with Zally's murder?"

"Mr. Levin, this would be easier if you would just let me in so we could talk without shouting," said Taylor, whose back was beginning to ache from bending over to talk. He shifted his feet, waiting.

"I don't think we got anything to talk about, Mr. . . . what did you say your name was?"

"Taylor."

"Taylor. I don't know nothing about this."

"I'm sure you don't, Mr. Levin. Just tell me, who was the woman who visited you last Wednesday?"

"I see lots of people. Who can remember one?"

"This one was very tall, maybe six feet, blond, and the guard downstairs says she was *zaftig*. I'm sure you would remember her."

"Yeah, I remember now. She wanted a ring reset. I couldn't help her. Too small a job. I sent her to the exchange, maybe she could find someone, help her there."

"Did you get her name?" asked Taylor.

"No name. Look, that's it," said Levin, folding his paper and tossing it under his desk. "I'm busy, okay?"

"The guard in the lobby said she was up here for about a half hour," Taylor lied. "A tall, beautiful blond woman. You sure you didn't get her name?"

"I didn't say I didn't get her name. I said no name. I don't remember her name."

"Are you married, Mr. Levin?"

"No. What business is that to you?"

"According to the sign-in sheet, her first name was Mary. Her last name began with an *R*. Does that ring a bell, Mr. Levin?"

"No."

"Can you tell me what she was wearing?"

"No."

"Can you tell me, did she say where she lived?"

"I don't remember. She didn't say."

"Can you tell me anything about her at all, Mr. Levin?"

"I told you. She came here, she wanted a ring reset, I sent her away, I don't know her name. I don't know who she is. Period. Finished. Okay? Can I go back to work now?"

"Thank you, Mr. Levin." Taylor turned to leave. "Oh, Mr. Levin," he said, turning back. "The police will probably be here today to ask you the same questions I have. If you remember anything then, I would appreciate it if you would give me a call. Let me leave you my number."

Levin shrugged elaborately. Taylor scrawled his name and telephone number on a piece of paper torn from his notebook and left it on the sill below the window.

"Thank you, Mr. Levin," Taylor said, and left.

Walking back down the hall to the elevator, Taylor bounced on the balls of his feet. He loved it when people lied to him, and he was absolutely certain that Levin had been lying, although he had no idea why. But he had a hunch that if he hung around the building today, keeping an eye on Levin, he just might find out.

Ariel Levin waited a moment, then peeked out his door and down the hall to make sure that Taylor had gone. Then, after stuffing the piece of paper with Taylor's number on it into his pocket, he took Zalman Gottleib's locked box out of his safe—partly to reassure himself that the diamond was still there—removed the stone, and put it in his pocket. Now, he thought, he had to sell it quickly, before the police found it and he got himself involved in a murder case.

And what about Mary Rubel? Why were the police looking for her?

Levin thought furiously and unhappily. It was out of the question for Rubel's uncle to come to his office now, even after business hours. They had to meet somewhere else. And they had to meet tonight.

No matter what he offers me, thought Levin, I'll take it. And then Mary and I will go away. Maybe to Mexico. Lie on the sand and drink piña coladas.

He picked up his phone and dialed Rubel's number.

"Mary."

"Ariel?"

"Mary, something has happened. I have to see you."

"What has happened?"

"A man, a detective, he just left my office. He was asking about you, Mary."

"About me? He was asking about me? What did he want to know?" Rubel asked after a moment.

"He just wanted to know who you were. He knew you had come to my office to see me last week. A man in this building was murdered last week, and this man said, he said he was . . . Listen, Mary, can you meet me in twenty minutes at the coffee shop on the corner of Fifty-fifth and Sixth? It's called the Astro."

"Yes, Ariel. But what is this about? A man was killed? What has this to do with me?"

"I don't know," said Levin, but the thought suddenly struck him: What did he really know about Mary Rubel? What did he know about her uncle? Maybe they killed Gottleib and Shirley Stein. And if they did . . . No. This beautiful young woman who was crazy about him? Impossible. How could she be involved in something like that? Still, it wouldn't hurt to be careful.

"Ariel?"

"Just meet me, okay? Twenty minutes."

"Of course, my darling. Ariel? What did you tell the man when he asked about me?"

"Nothing. What's he got to know about us? What business is it of his?"

"Oh, Ariel, you are frightening me."

"I am sorry, my love. Please, don't worry. Just meet me."

"Of course. You will take care of me, I know."

Levin hung up. Yes, he thought, Mexico would be wonderful.

25

The Parker Meridien Hotel
West Fifty-seventh Street, Manhattan
Monday, September 13

Ladislaw Czartoryski threw the telephone against the wall and heard the plastic crack. Stupid, stupid, stupid! he raged. You are an old, stupid man growing soft and foolish.

In the few moments it had taken a hysterical Maria Radziwell to tell him that Ariel Levin had been questioned by a detective, Czartoryski had felt his anger build. Now it boiled over.

Why had he chosen to spare that Jew's life, mounting an elaborate charade to draw him away from the diamond? At the time the Cutter had not said anything, but Czartoryski remembered seeing the question in the old assassin's eyes: Why this comedy? Three throats are as easy to cut as two.

And even as he had told the Cutter that he was merely simplifying—that two deaths constituted murder, easily forgotten, but three deaths were a holocaust—Czartoryski had known he was complicating things. Why?

Vanity, Czartoryski scolded himself. You wanted the Hasid to meet your whore, wanted her to come alive in his dreams, to infect his prayers, to become his Lilith, a succubus. You wanted to enjoy that power.

Czartoryski reveled in watching the effect Radziwell had on men. It tickled him to see lust cloud their eyes as they sniffed the pineapple-sour scent of her vagina. It amused him to imagine them trying to make love to her, mistaking her size for strength, melting in her arms while she herself, Czartoryski knew, yearned to be hurt, humiliated.

So what now, Ladislaw? What about this detective? Whom is he working for?

What about the Israeli, Levin, who is assuredly being watched?

And, most important, what about your diamond?

Too many questions. Suddenly there were too many questions, too much uncertainty. Flee. Save yourself.

Throughout Czartoryski's life, flight had been his most reliable tactic. His ability to disappear—from Poland, during the Allied de-Nazification investigations after the war; from Beirut, after the Mossad and the Nazi hunters had begun to sniff around; and from Poland again, after the Russian cowards went home with their tanks, and his old comrades in the Party faced trials and prison sentences—had earned him his nickname, the Magician. Save yourself, he told himself. Survive. Make a clean break.

Czartoryski walked into his bathroom and splashed water on his cheeks and eyes. "No," he said aloud to his reflection. "Not without my diamond."

It had been during those de-Nazification investigations that Czartoryski had begun to suspect that the Czartoryski diamond was real and not just a family myth, a rainy-day tale told to occupy restless children. Later, through the Odessa, the organization devoted to the survival of the SS command structure, Czartoryski had discovered that the old Satmarer *rebbe* had escaped the camps by purchasing his freedom from that greedy German accountant, Adolf Eichmann—purchasing it with a fabulous diamond.

That had intrigued Czartoryski; it reminded him of those childhood stories. But there had been much to do at that time. From his roost in Beirut, Czartoryski was busily erasing his Nazi past and creating a new one that would earn him a role in the new, Communist Poland. He forgot about the stone until almost fifteen years later, when he learned, this time through the Israelis themselves, that Eichmann had tried to buy off the Nazi hunters who had cornered him in Buenos Aires.

Czartoryski would have loved to be a fly on the wall to witness that farce.

After Eichmann's capture, the description of the bribe that

had made the rounds in the Mossad, and had ultimately reached Czartoryski's ears, left no doubt.

It was the jewel of those rainy-day stories.

Since then Czartoryski had dedicated himself to retrieving what he thought of as his birthright. He pieced together its history from letters, legends, books, and his own intuition, tracing the stone's peregrinations through time and space.

In an old Hebrew text, translated into German, he read how, shortly before Waterloo, the Seer of Lublin had tried to give a "treasure" to Napoleon (why, Czartoryski could not discover). This "treasure," the text went on, had been stolen by Tsar Alexander's agent, Prince Adam Czartoryski, the Magician's great-great-grandfather, who had ruled Lublin for the tsar.

His own family's papers recorded that soon after Prince Adam's death, Joseph Czartoryski, the prince's brother, used a huge diamond to pay off his gambling debts to Nathan Meyer of the Rothschild banking family.

In the Rothschilds' documents, seized by the SS, Czartoryski discovered how, at the turn of the century, the Jewish bankers had loaned a seventy-two-carat stone to Cecil Rhodes, who had used it in his struggle with a Cockney vaudevillian, Barney Barnato, born Barney Isaacs, to gain control of the De Beers Mining Syndicate.

And much later Czartoryski found out about Catherine Maria Radziwell, possibly his Maria's grandmother (although, despite what he had told Maria, he was never sure), who apparently had seduced the dying Rhodes, stolen a large diamond, and, in her syphilitic old age, given it to the current Satmarer *rebbe*'s father-in-law.

Always, in all the papers and books, the diamond was unnamed, and only in the Rothschild papers was it described. But Czartoryski knew. He knew that he alone possessed the knowledge of a treasure that had remained largely a secret for almost two centuries. Then, shortly after he heard about the impending wedding between the Satmarer *rebbe*'s daughter and the Lubavitcher *rebbe*'s son, that American diamond courier, that Hasid whom Czartoryski knew to be a Mossad asset, had contacted him, asking him to recover the stone for the Israelis. So he had dispatched the Cutter to New York, to Williamsburg, and eventually the Cutter had called him with a name, Zalman Gottleib.

It had taken Czartoryski over thirty years, but now the prize was almost his. And what a triumph that would be! The Israelis thought they were so clever. Well, he would show them. With the stone in his hands, he would become the Odessa's *Überführer* and sit at the head of the table. How could he walk away from that?

So far, only Maria had been identified. Send her to London? Tonight? No, he would need her to bring Levin to him. Put her on a plane tomorrow, after.

Tonight he would get the diamond. Perhaps, thought Czartoryski, it will be easier now. The Israeli Levin is probably frightened. All he wants now is to be rid of the stone. That will make him more tractable.

Then, with the Israeli dead, and the diamond in my hands, I can tie up the loose ends and go home to Rome.

And really, thought the Magician, calmer now, there's only one loose end. This detective, whoever he may be.

Well, thought Czartoryski, opening the closet to choose a tie, we will soon find out.

26

West Fifty-fifth Street, Manhattan
Monday, September 13

There she was. Taylor stepped back into the shade of the drugstore's awning on the west side of sunny Sixth Avenue and watched Maria Radziwell, wearing her white linen dress, crossing Fifty-fifth Street. Not hard to spot, thought Taylor. Even in a city as full of beautiful women as New York, this one stood out. She looked like that model, Taylor thought, the one in the Absolut vodka ads, the one with the build, the incredible legs, and the sexy little overbite. No way a woman like this is with our chunky Mr. Levin out of love, he thought.

Radziwell paused in front of the Astro Coffee Shop, looking around. For a moment Taylor felt the blonde's eyes sweep his face, and he retreated deeper into the shadows. Then she turned and walked into the shop where Levin had disappeared a few moments before. Taylor bought a package of Goldenberg's Peanut Chews and kept his eye on the shop's door.

Ten minutes and three Peanut Chews later, Taylor saw Levin leaving the shop. After a moment's indecision, Taylor decided to stay where he was. I can find him later, Taylor thought, watching Levin move uptown.

Away from his office, Taylor noted. He's not going back to work. Is he afraid of the police turning up?

A minute later Radziwell emerged and began walking uptown at a brisk clip, her long gait eating up the sidewalk. Taylor followed her from across the street.

The Cutter was also trailing Radziwell, but not to see where she was going. Staying a block behind her, the Cutter was watching to see if she was being tailed.

Sharp pains were shooting through the Cutter's gut, and he was furious. He had just gotten up off the toilet, where he had spent much of the night and most of the morning, when the Magician had called to tell him to pick up Radziwell at the coffee shop, and why. Holding the phone tightly, he had had to bite back the bitter words that had risen into his mouth. *You old fool*, he had wanted to shout. *You idiot. Look what you've done.* Not for the first time, the Cutter wondered if the Magician's skills were failing him, and he tried to imagine a life without his mentor.

And there he was. The tall man in sunglasses across Sixth Avenue. He was walking fast, pacing Radziwell, and his head was turned, keeping the whore in his line of sight. An amateur, the Cutter thought. So obvious. Well, that will make it easier.

Dov Taylor, still keeping to the opposite side of the street, watched the blonde turn into the apartment building on West Fifty-ninth Street. He waited until she had cleared the lobby, then followed. The doorman was a young Puerto Rican in jeans, sandals, and a fluorescent Hawaiian shirt. Twenty bucks bought Taylor Mary Rubel's name, her apartment number, and the not-so-surprising news that the doorman would sure like to fuck her. Taylor thanked the young man, and for another twenty dollars he had a lifelong friend who would keep an eye out for anything unusual.

Taylor took the elevator to the fourth floor, found Rubel's apartment, and rang the buzzer. A moment later the door, still chained, opened a crack, and Dov Taylor was looking into Maria Radziwell's wide-set, slightly slanted Slavic brown eyes.

"Yes?"

"Miss Rubel?"

"Yes?"

"Mary Rubel?"

"That is correct."

"My name is Dov Taylor, Miss Rubel. I'm a, well, I'm a detective, and I'd like to ask you a few questions."

"You have some identification, please?"

"I'm a private detective, Miss Rubel, a very private detective, you might say, working for the family of Zalman Gottleib, who was murdered two weeks ago in the building where Mr. Ariel Levin works. I could show you my driver's license, and that would tell you that I am who I say I am, but I'm working unofficially. If you don't want to talk to me, well, I understand, but I promise you it would be in your best interests. Unless, of course, you have something to hide."

"I have nothing to hide, Mr. . . . ."

"Taylor. Dov Taylor."

"I have nothing to hide, Mr. Dov Taylor."

"Then let me in and let's talk. It will only take a moment, I promise."

"A man was murdered?"

"And a woman. Zalman Gottleib and Shirley Stein."

"I do not know these people, Mr. Taylor."

"I understand. But I would like to ask you about Ariel Levin and Morris Schumach. Like I say, it will only take a few minutes. May I come in?"

"Just a moment," said Rubel. The door closed.

Well, that's it, thought Taylor. She's gone. Probably calling the cops. I couldn't blame her. But then Taylor heard the chain slide off, and the door opened.

"Come," said Rubel, and Taylor followed her down a hall to a large living room decorated sparsely in white.

Rubel turned and sat on the end of a white couch, crossing her ankles and clasping her hands on her lap like a giant schoolgirl. Taylor felt himself tremble slightly, a melting feeling he had not experienced since he'd first kissed Carol and felt her hard little breasts on the backseat of his Volkswagen bug outside her parents' apartment building in the Bronx. He tore his eyes away from Rubel's breasts only to find himself staring at her long, tanned, muscular legs. He could see the tiny blond hairs flat on her thighs. God, she was delicious.

"I will trust you, Mr. Taylor. What is it you wish to know?"

"Thank you," said Taylor, sitting on an overstuffed white chair set at right angles to the couch. He removed his notebook from his pocket. "First of all," he began, "I'd like to know if you're an athlete."

"Excuse me?"

"I'm sorry, but you look like an athlete."

"When I was a girl, I played basketball in school in Poland. I was not very good."

"I can't believe that. You're being modest. I'll bet you were terrific."

"You are not being like a policeman, Mr. Taylor."

"I'm not? You could be right. I'll start over. Tell me, Miss Rubel, what are you doing in New York?"

"I am in New York because this is where my husband lived."

"Your husband?"

"Yes. He died not so long ago. I am a widow."

"And his name was?"

"Martin Rudenstein."

"Rubel is your maiden name?"

"Rubelski. I made it American."

"And where did you meet your husband?"

"In England. I am Polish. I went to England to escape the Communists. Mr. Taylor. I don't—"

"You called up Morris Schumach two weeks ago to ask him to look at some jewelry of yours. Is that right?"

"Yes. That is correct."

"How did you come to call Mr. Schumach?"

"Mr. Taylor, you must tell me what you want. Perhaps I can help if you will tell me."

"Miss Rubel, Zalman Gottleib and his secretary, Shirley Stein, were murdered the same day you saw Mr. Schumach. Mr. Gottleib was Mr. Schumach's partner. I am just trying to re-create the events of that day. And you have been hard to find, Miss Rubel. You left your house in Queens kind of quickly."

"Yes. It has bad memories of my husband. But I do not know how I can help you, Mr. Taylor. I saw Mr. Schumach, and he buys some jewelry from me. Then I move into this apartment."

"And then you went to see Mr. Ariel Levin."

"Yes, to have a ring fixed."

"Mr. Levin was less than forthcoming about you, Miss Rubel."

"Yes? I am sorry, my English is not so good. What does that mean, forthcoming?"

"It means he lied to me. How did you come to call Mr. Levin?"

"A friend gave his name to me."

"The same friend who recommended Morris Schumach?"

"No, another."

"And his name is?"

"I do not think I should give you his name. I do not want him to become, how do you say, involved."

"Miss Rubel," said Taylor, "after I leave, I'm going to give your name and address to the police. They've been looking for you, too. I don't want to cause any trouble for you, or for your friends, but two people have been killed. I'd advise you to be completely honest with me and with the police. It's in your best interests, believe me."

"I do not know what to say. I have nothing to do with any of this, with murder."

"I'm sure you don't. Just tell me the names of the men who recommended Mr. Schumach and Mr. Levin to you."

"Well, Mr. Schumach's name was in my husband's papers, with a list of the jewelry. You see, the jewelry was my husband's. So I just called the name. Mr. Levin's name was given to me by a man named Jacob Cohen. But he is not in New York. When I want the ring fixed, I call Mr. Cohen, who I know in London, where I live before meeting my husband and coming to New York. He is in the jewelry business, Mr. Cohen."

"Do you have Mr. Cohen's phone number?"

"Yes. Here." Rubel rummaged in her bag and removed a large leather Filofax. She opened it and read off a number to Taylor, who wrote it down in his notebook.

"Thank you, Miss Rubel," said Taylor. "Tell me, how well do you know Mr. Levin?"

"Not so well," Rubel said. "He seems nice."

"Did you know that Mr. Levin worked in the same building as Morris Schumach?"

"No. It is a surprise to me."

"And you didn't know about the murder? You didn't read about it in the papers or see anything about it on television?"

"My English is not so good for the newspapers, I am sorry. And I am not interested in the television."

"May I ask if Mr. Levin is your lover?"

"No, you may not."

"I'm sorry. The police will ask the same questions, Miss Rubel. They'll also ask you if you'll be staying in New York now that your husband has passed away."

"I do not know," said Rubel. "It seems like a very frightening city to me. And now you tell me that the police are going to interrogate me."

"If you tell them what you know, you won't have anything to worry about," said Taylor. "I understand this must be unpleasant for you, but New York is not such a bad place. Did your husband take you around much?"

"No. He was killed soon after we come here."

"How?"

"In an automobile accident."

"Has Mr. Levin? Shown you around?"

"Ariel, he, no, not really."

Christ, thought Taylor, I'm hitting on her.

"Would you like me to show you the town, Miss Rubel?"

"Is that proper, Mr. Taylor?" she said, smiling.

"Why not?" said Taylor, thinking that he must be imagining it, but, no, he could smell her—a fruity scent, mixed with earth.

"I think that would be very nice, Mr. Taylor," she said, smiling, relaxing, and her abrupt shift snapped Taylor out of his erotic fog.

He stood up. "Well, thank you, Miss Rubel. You have been very helpful. I'll call Mr. Cohen and perhaps we can clear this all up."

Rubel stood up with him and stretched, running her hands through her hair. Her breasts rose.

She's putting on a show, thought Taylor.

Rubel walked him to the door, and he was aware of her body close to his. He imagined he could feel heat wafting off her.

"Good-bye, Miss Rubel. Thank you."

"You said you would call the police?"

"Yes, but don't worry. I will call you tomorrow to see how it went. And if you have any trouble with them, don't hesitate to call me. I'm in the Manhattan book. Downtown. Near the Village."

"The Village?"

"Greenwich Village. It's a part of New York. A very interesting part. I'd love to show it to you sometime."

"That would be nice, yes," she said, extending her hand. It seemed to him as if her lips were parted slightly. Is she offering a kiss? Taylor wondered. He started to sway toward her, then stopped himself. Crazy, he thought. This is crazy.

"Well, good-bye again, Miss Rubel."

Rubel let him out, and he walked back to the elevator, both aroused and confused. Something, he knew, was wrong. Not just her answers, which were evasive and vague. And not just the London phone number, which he was sure would turn out to be a dead end. No, there was something about her, the way she switched on the sex. What had Schumach told him? That she reminded him of a hooker? Maybe.

Taylor left the building, crossed the street, and ate another Peanut Chew. Only one left. When he was a cop, on stakeouts, he'd set fire to a whole pack of Merits in a few hours. Now, for the first time since he'd quit, he really wanted one.

He walked the few blocks to the precinct house, and the desk sergeant directed him up the stairs to homicide. Frank Hill was talking on the phone with his feet up on his desk.

"Yeah," Hill was saying, "yeah, I'll pick something up on the way home. . . . I don't know." He paused, listening. "Don't I always? . . . Yeah. . . . Okay. . . . Me too." He hung up. "The wife," he explained to Taylor. "So, you want to see the pictures? Real fucking ugly."

"I've seen ugly before," Taylor said.

"Not like this," said Hill, opening a drawer and pulling out a file. He fished out some eight-by-ten glossies and tossed them, along with the file, across the desk to Taylor. "Want some coffee?" he asked. "Cream? Sugar?"

"Sure," said Taylor. Hill stood up, leaving him alone with the photos.

Bodies like Shirley Stein's, their throats cut, he had seen hundreds of times. Zalman Gottleib, hanging upside down, gutted, was something new. He turned to the medical examiner's report. Gottleib's intestines and lungs had been lifted out of the torso cavity and left dangling.

Taylor turned again to the photographs. Close-ups of the wounds. Something about the pattern of the two cuts—across the throat and from belly to sternum—struck a chord.

Hill returned with Taylor's coffee in a heavy beige mug. "So?" asked Hill. "What do you think?"

"I don't know." Taylor took a sip of the coffee. It was bitter, like cop coffee the world over. "Either somebody's sending a message, or we got a bad nut. Nobody sane cuts somebody up like this."

Hill nodded in agreement.

"I found Schumach's blonde," Taylor said. Hill opened

his pad and took down Rubel's address. "I also talked to the guy she visited in Gottlieb's building, Ariel Levin, an Israeli."

"Well, you've been a fucking beaver, Taylor," said Hill. "What can you tell me?"

"Levin says he doesn't remember her, doesn't know who the hell I'm talking about, but as soon as I leave him he cuts out and leads me straight to her. Then she tells me she doesn't know him too well, but that's clearly bullshit, too. They're obviously fucking, or partners together. She's supposed to be this grieving widow, but I don't buy it. And, Frank?"

"Yeah?"

"Schumach was right. A bombshell."

Hill smiled. "You know, man, I got to apologize for yesterday. I know you're in AA, and I shouldn't have offered you that beer. I was just pulling your chain. I'm a fucking asshole sometimes, can't help it. So"—Hill stuck out his hand—"shake?"

Taylor reached over the desk and shook Hill's hand over the pictures of Zalman Gottlieb's and Shirley Stein's mutilated bodies.

After promising to keep Hill informed, Taylor walked back down to the street. On a whim he ducked into a phone booth and asked Information for a new number belonging to a Mary Rubel on West Fifty-ninth Street. He was informed that it was unlisted at the customer's request. Then he asked for an Ariel Levin in Manhattan and was told there were two residential listings and a business number.

He felt his excitement ebbing. So Levin had lied to him. So he had found Morris Schumach's blonde, and she seemed a little wrong. Why would she need an unlisted number? On the other hand, so what? Maybe they were just having an affair. Who's to say Rubel couldn't find the Israeli attractive? Maybe he had a *shlong* like Wilt Chamberlain's.

For the first time, he felt sad about losing his job at the bank. It hadn't been much, but it had given him a place to go every day. Now he had nothing to do and nowhere to go. Hill would question Rubel and Levin; he would either find out something or he wouldn't. And, Taylor reminded himself, he had been kissed off by Naomi, so he couldn't even get laid. Would he sleep with Mary Rubel? He had the clear sense that that was available if he wanted it. He imagined himself on top of her; he felt himself growing aroused.

"What am I doing?" he asked himself aloud. Playing detective. Tailing mysterious blondes and trying to date them up. Standing in a phone booth talking to myself like a typical New York loony.

He tried to think, but his brain felt thick and slow. A lead balloon of depression began to inflate in his chest. Time to go to a meeting, he thought. Get things in perspective. Then maybe I'll go into Brooklyn, talk to Rabbi Kalman. There was something about Gottleib's corpse that stirred a memory. And maybe I'll visit Sarah Kalman, see her shop.

Feeling heavy but oddly empty, Taylor walked back to Sixth Avenue to catch the train downtown.

The Cutter followed.

27

All Things Beautiful
Kingston Street, Brooklyn
Monday, September 13

Sarah Kalman's dress shop was sandwiched between the Kingston Street Seforim Center, selling religious books, articles, tapes, and records, and Epstein's Travel, advertising trips to the Holy Land. Kingston was the main shopping street in Crown Heights, and dozens of Lubavitcher women, pushing baby carriages and trailed by the usual army of children, strolled up and down in the sunny September weather. They stopped to admire the wigs in the window of the Le Petit *sheitl* store, they turned into the Lubavitcher Congregation butcher shop, with its sawdust-covered floor, to buy freshly plucked *Glatt kosher* chicken for dinner. They crowded into tiny groceries and stood picking over the packages and cans and produce, gossiping in Yiddish while their children darted in and out of the aisles. And some entered All Things Beautiful, to be greeted by Sarah Kalman's sister-in-law, Channah.

Sarah Kalman, sitting and reading by the light of a small lamp at the rolltop desk in the back of her shop, watched the women eye Channah, trying to figure out if she were pregnant yet. Just this morning Channah had been in tears. Here she was, married almost two years, an old married lady of nineteen, and the Holy One, blessed is He, had not yet given her a child. She prayed and prayed, but still no baby. Channah knew that the women in the neighborhood were whispering about her, suggesting that she and her husband were having troubles, and Sarah knew that Moshe was angry and rapidly losing patience. Without children, Moshe's status in the community was at risk, and that meant his income as a rabbi could suffer. Channah was sure that if she didn't get pregnant soon, Moshe would be asking the *sofer*, the scribe, to write up a *get*, a letter of divorce, and although Sarah told her not to be silly, she didn't doubt that Channah was right.

Channah had asked Sarah what she should do, and Sarah had thought briefly of suggesting that Channah see a doctor. A few months before her marriage, Channah's appendix had burst. Perhaps the infection had damaged her tubes. But Sarah knew that she could never explain that to Channah, and that Moshe would never allow her to see a doctor, especially not a fertility specialist. No Hasids became doctors, and they regarded all doctors with suspicion, even the Sabbath-observing physicians who practiced in the community. By claiming to cure people, doctors cast doubt upon God's powers. Most Hasids believed doctors were going to hell. And Sarah did not think much of the neighborhood doctors, anyway—all of whom were well past sixty—believing that they did not keep up with modern medical advances.

Sarah also knew that Channah would never go to a doctor behind Moshe's back, even if Sarah held her hand. Channah was a good girl; she would never act independently or risk giving the slightest offense. Not like me, thought Sarah. So she had told Channah to be patient, *Hashem* would certainly answer her prayers.

Sarah was fond of Channah and felt sorry that she was married to her pompous, thickheaded, intolerant brother, Moshe. Indeed, Sarah sometimes wished she could *be* Channah—a simple, sweet young girl entirely at home in the Lubavitcher world that to Sarah often seemed suffocatingly small.

Sarah sighed and turned back to her book, S. A. Horodezky's *Ha-Hasidut v'ha-Hasidim, Leaders of Hasidism.* By her side was also Simon Dubnov's massive *History of the Jews in Russia and Poland*, and a shoebox containing Dov Taylor's family papers—letters, marriage certificates, and a tattered Bible with a mother-of-pearl cover and his family tree, written in fading blue ink, inside. Reading, studying, was Sarah's drug, the way she escaped from Lubavitch's narrow paths. And now she was deep into the story of Hirsh Leib, Dov Taylor's great-great-grandfather.

A rather mysterious figure, this Rebbe Hirsh Leib. A *zaddik*, to be sure, but a loner, one who never had followers, disciples, or his own congregation. He wrote no books, and very few stories were told about him—and those that did exist concentrated on his physical strength, which was said to be immense, not his erudition or his holiness. He was also said to have had a mystic connection with horses; like Rebbe Schneur Zalman, the author of the Tanya and the first Lubavitcher *rebbe*, he must have known the language of animals. He seemed to have spent most of his life getting into scrapes, wandering from town to town to pray and study with the other *zaddikim* of his time. His wife, thought Sarah, must have loved that.

On the other hand, although a marginal figure in the spiritual and intellectual development of Hasidism, Hirsh Leib certainly had been at the physical center of the third generation of the early Hasidic movement, when the disciples of the disciples of the Baal Shem Tov gained followers all over Eastern Europe. He seemed to have been especially close to Rebbe Jacob Yitzhak, the Seer of Lublin, and to the Seer's closest friends: Rebbes Menachem Mendel of Rymanov, David of Lelov, Naftali of Roptchitz, and Rabbi Bunem, the apothecary. Hirsh Leib knew Rebbe Elimelekh of Lizhensk, the Seer's old teacher, as well as the Seer's troubled disciple, the holy Yehudi. He also knew Rebbe Israel, the Maggid (which meant preacher) of Kosnitz, perhaps the most powerful and worldly *zaddik* of that time, an intimate of Napoleon Bonaparte and Tsar Alexander.

Indeed, as Sarah delved deeper into the stories and histories, this Hirsh Leib seemed to have been everywhere, even at the strange Simkhas Torah celebration of 1814 in Lublin to which the Seer had invited all the Hasidim in the world. It was on that most ecstatic festival day celebrating the completion of the annual cycle of Torah reading that the Seer was said to have fallen to the street from a small window in his study; he died some ten months later, having never arisen from his deathbed, having spoken to no one. Except, perhaps, to Hirsh Leib, the *Zaddik* of Orlik, who, along with Rabbi Bunem, had discovered the Seer that night. Unfortunately, about that same time, Hirsh Leib had also died. He was stabbed to death in the market, it was said, by a Cossack.

That Simkhas Torah night was cloaked in many mysteries. No one knew why the great Seer of Lublin had decided that it should be the largest celebration the world had ever seen. Yet, as thousands of Hasidim danced in the streets with the holy scrolls, the Seer himself went missing. No one, not even his wife, knew where he was. And then came the fall.

Sarah closed her eyes and imagined that night, the narrow, medieval streets of Lublin thronging with men dancing in ecstasy. She could almost hear the singing, the stomping of thousands of feet, the noise rising up to the darkening heavens.

The Seer's fall was another great mystery. The window, it was said, was far too small and too high for a man just to fall out of. And the Seer was found many streets away from the study house, with injuries too severe for him to have walked or crawled.

Sarah Kalman closed the book and pressed her fingers to her eyes. Her thoughts were far from her shop, where Channah chatted endlessly with a stream of customers shopping for new dresses in anticipation of the coming High Holy Days, Rosh Hashanah and Yom Kippur. What Sarah wouldn't give to be able to solve this old mystery, to be able to talk to Hirsh Leib, to ask him what the Seer, who it was said could see backward and forward in time, had told him on his deathbed.

Suddenly Sarah became aware that something had changed. The store was quiet. She opened her eyes. A tall, slender figure was standing in the entrance, silhouetted by the sun. Men didn't often come into her shop, and Sarah rose and squinted to see who it was.

"I'm looking for Sarah Kalman," said the deep voice in English, a language rarely heard in All Things Beautiful. Sarah recognized the detective Dov Taylor and walked up to rescue him from Channah and two customers who were staring at him as if he were a visitor from another planet. Which, in a way, he was.

"Mr. Taylor," Sarah said. "A pleasure to see you."

Taylor was struck afresh by how pretty she was. Usually he was attracted to tall women, the taller the better, like Mary Rubel. But Sarah Kalman, although tiny, had her own charms. There was something intensely self-possessed about her, something that Taylor had intuited at her father's Sabbath table, and he sensed it again right now. She seemed complete, with no loose ends dangling. Somehow she took up space out of proportion to her diminutive stature. Taylor felt a lifting of the agitated depression that had accompanied him on the train down to Crown Heights, the depression that had deepened when Rabbi Kalman had told him that the cuts Taylor had described—across the throat, from belly to sternum, the lungs and intestines removed and left hanging—were the way of *shekhita*, kosher slaughtering.

"Yes," he said formally, "the pleasure is mine."

"You remember Mr. Taylor," Sarah said to Channah in English.

"Yes. Hello, Mr. Taylor," Channah said awkwardly, shrinking away from him even as she spoke.

Sarah then said something in Yiddish to Channah, who

turned and herded the two women shoppers toward the back of the store.

"Very pretty," said Taylor, idly touching the arm of a dress. "You have a lot of nice stuff here."

"Are you surprised?" Sarah asked.

"Well, actually, yes."

"You don't think Hasidic women like to look pretty? You should visit the *sheitl* shop and see the women trying on wigs for hours and hours. Expensive stuff, too. A good wig can cost two, three hundred dollars."

"Would you cut your hair?" Taylor asked.

"Oh, I don't think I'll ever get married," said Sarah. "I'm too old, too set in my ways."

"You're not even thirty."

"Around here, that's old. Come, it's a beautiful day. Let's walk a bit. Let me tell you about Hirsh Leib. That's why you're here, yes?"

"Yes, that, and just to visit," said Taylor, attempting to take Sarah's elbow as they walked out of the shop. She pirouetted away from his touch, talking, covering Taylor's embarrassment with words. She may look like any other woman, he reminded himself, but she's a Hasid; her sense of propriety, of personal space, is different.

As they walked up Kingston Street, Taylor again felt the community's eyes upon him, the stranger, the *goy*. He also felt how Sarah Kalman kept her distance, and he clasped his hands behind his back so that he would not forget and accidentally reach out to touch her.

Sarah told him about Hirsh Leib, about the tumultuous times he lived in, about all the great *zaddikim* he knew, and about the disaster that had befallen the Seer of Lublin. Taylor tried to pay attention. But the events she described—Napoleon's armies sweeping across Europe; *zaddikim* being imprisoned by the tsar or being excommunicated by the traditional Jewish authorities—seemed so distant, so irrelevant, that he found it hard to keep the names straight.

What's all this got to do with diamonds, with murder? he asked himself. What's it got to do with the fact that this murder was apparently committed by a Jew, someone familiar with *kosher* slaughtering? A *shoykhet*, is that what Kalman said? The *shoykhet* hangs the animal upside down so that it will bleed to death because it is forbidden to eat blood. The *shoykhet* examines the lungs and intestines to check for disease. And if the murderer was a Jew, was he a Hasid? Who but a Hasid would know about *kosher* slaughtering?

And what's any of it got to do with me? Tonight, if I wanted, I could sleep with Mary Rubel. Even if I wanted to, I couldn't sleep with this chatty young redhead if I brought her a dozen roses every day for a hundred years.

So what are you doing? he asked himself. Some crazy rabbi tells you that another crazy rabbi who's been dead almost two hundred years is living inside you and *he's* going to solve a murder in the diamond district. And what's really crazy is that you listen, and you're listening right now.

Of course, something told you to ask about the way Zalman Gottleib was cut up. What did you know about *kosher* slaughtering? Nothing, that's what.

Abruptly Taylor stopped and looked behind him.

"What's the matter?" Sarah Kalman asked.

"Nothing," said Taylor. "It's just that I thought I felt someone watching us."

"Here in Crown Heights," said Sarah, "everybody watches everybody. And you're a stranger."

"You mean a *goy*," Taylor said.

"Don't be so touchy, Mr. Taylor," said Sarah. "I mean everybody knows me, and everybody's heard about you, so they watch."

"What do you mean everybody's heard about me?"

"Oh, there are no secrets here. Everybody knows you're the handsome Jewish policeman helping the Satmarers find out who killed the diamond dealer. Everybody knows you went to the *mikvah* and sat at my father's table for *Shabbos*. And now everybody will be talking about how shameless I am, walking down the street with you."

"So why are you walking down the street with me?"

"Because I want to," said Sarah, and Taylor saw her square her shoulders proudly. "I'm used to people talking about me. They've been doing it for years. It makes my father and Moshe, my brother, crazy, but I don't mind. In fact, it's good for business. Women come in to talk to me, it's exciting for them, talking to Sarah Kalman, the *rov's* crazy daughter, and maybe, when they're there, they buy a dress."

"I don't understand. You seem so normal."

"Is that a compliment?"

"I guess. That's the way I meant it."

"What you really meant is that I don't seem as strange as the other Hasidim."

"No. I mean—"

"It's all right. I'll accept your compliment. But it's not true. I'm not normal. Not in my world, and not in your world, either. Probably not in your world most of all.

"But I don't want to talk about me. It's too boring. What's interesting," said Sarah, her green eyes bright, her voice lightly brushed with urgency, "is that no one really knows what happened to the Seer on that Simkhas Torah night except, perhaps, your great-great-grandfather, Rebbe Hirsh Leib."

"Whatever happended to Hirsh Leib, anyway?"

"He died. He was stabbed to death in the street."

"Why?"

"Who knows? Maybe he accidentally kicked dust on a Cossack's boots. I'm sorry, he was your great-great-grandfather, but that sort of thing, you know, it happened all the time."

As they walked down Division Street, Dov Taylor thought about his ancestor Hirsh Leib dying in the street, his blood soaking into the dust as people stepped over him. Another murder. And the Seer of Lublin? Perhaps another. Christ, what a bloody history.

Were they all killed by fellow Jews?

Sarah Kalman was going on about life in Lublin, about the hardships visited upon the Jews, and Taylor tried to pay attention to what she was saying while he tried to shake the feeling that they were being watched.

He could not.

28

The Parker Meridien Hotel
West Fifty-seventh Street, Manhattan
Monday, September 13

Ladislaw Czartoryski could not take his eyes off the huge diamond that Ariel Levin had placed between them on the small pink-marble table by the window overlooking the great, black, nighttime void of Central Park. Ariel Levin could not take his eyes off the dull sheen of the aluminum suitcase packed with money and lying open on the bed.

"It's worth a lot more than that, Mr. Cartovsky," said Levin, giving the suitcase and the money the back of his hand.

"I am sure you are right, Mr. Levin," said Czartoryski, gazing at the diamond, imagining he could see the city's lights twinkling in its depths, imagining how his friends would look at it in awe, "and you can certainly look for another buyer if you wish. Perhaps you will find one who will pay more. However, there, on the bed, is five hundred thousand dollars in American dollars. It is real, tangible. You can feel it, smell it, and count it. And, right now, it is yours."

Maria Radziwell stood behind Levin, her large, tanned hands resting lightly on his shoulders. Her nails were long and unpolished. She looked into Czartoryski's pale blue eyes and saw them shine with triumph. Suddenly she felt as if she were touching a dead man, and she stepped away from Levin.

"Come, Mr. Levin," said Czartoryski. "This is a fair offer."

"I would like at least six hundred thousand," Levin said.

"Yes, and so would anyone," said Czartoryski. "However, I do not have it readily available, and after what my niece has told me about your adventure this morning, I suggest that it is in both our best interests to conclude our business speedily.''

"Yes, yes," Levin said. "You're right. Well, all right." He reached across the table to shake Czartoryski's small hand. "We have a deal."

"Excellent," Czartoryski pronounced. "Excellent." He snatched the stone off the table and produced a blue velvet pouch from the pocket of his gray pinstripe suit. He dropped the diamond into the pouch and the pouch into his pocket.

"Shall we have a toast? I have an excellent brandy here, a Delamain Grand Vesper. You would like one, wouldn't you, my dear?" he asked Radziwell. "My niece," he told Levin, "is very fond of brandy. But why am I telling you? I am sure you have already become familiar with my Mary's tastes.''

Czartoryski fetched three snifters from the suite's bar and poured them each a generous portion. "I would like to propose a toast," he said, swirling the amber brandy in his glass, "to our deal and to this magnificent diamond. May our business bring good fortune and happiness to us all, and may this stone's journeys be over forever."

They drank, and Levin walked over to the bed and closed the aluminum suitcase. "Mr. Cartovsky, it has been a pleasure doing business with you," he said, lifting it up.

"And with you," said the Magician. "Would you and Mary care to join me for dinner? We could dine in my suite. The food here is marvelous. If the French know nothing else—and I'm not sure they do—they know food.''

"No, thank you," Levin said, patting the suitcase. "I'd like to get home.''

"I understand," said Czartoryski. "Mary? Will you stay with me, keep me company?''

"Yes, Mary. Keep your uncle company. I'll call you later this evening at your place," said Levin, who wanted to be alone with the money.

"Very well, Ariel," Radziwell said.

Levin again shook hands with Czartoryski, kissed Radziwell lightly on the lips, and took the elevator down to the Meridien's quietly elegant lobby, leaving the hotel by the

Fifty-sixth Street exit. Outside, he stepped into a waiting cab and gave the driver his address on Seventy-second Street.

After Levin left, Czartoryski poured himself another glass of brandy. "Come here, Maria," he said to Radziwell, who walked over and stood in front of him. He reached up to caress her cheek. Then he tossed off his brandy in one swallow.

"Thirty years I have chased this stone," he said quietly. "I would like to do something for you, Maria. I am very pleased with you, and I would like to reward you. What would you like, my darling? What does your heart yearn for?"

Radziwell looked down into Czartoryski's shining eyes. She saw a few beads of perspiration forming on his forehead and on his upper lip.

"Whatever pleases you, Ladislaw," she said.

"Whatever pleases me," he repeated softly, and again he stroked Radziwell's cheek. He thought suddenly of his mother, standing in her kitchen, kneading and punching dough for bread. A phantom smell of yeast filled his nostrils, and for a second he felt an unfamiliar ache in his chest. "There is something about you," he said almost sadly, "that makes me want to hurt you, you know, Maria?"

Riding uptown in the cab, his hand resting lightly on the suitcase on the seat beside him, Ariel Levin planned his week. Tomorrow he would get in touch with a few friendly, discreet dealers and turn most of the Pole's cash back into diamonds; five- and six-carat stones at five to ten thousand a carat, nothing that would attract too much attention on the street. Oh, sure, people would gossip about the buying spree, but Levin would be paying cash, so no one would be too curious, no one would ask too many questions.

Then Levin would spread the word that he was taking a vacation in Israel, and he would buy the tickets to Mexico City. On Wednesday he'd finish buying stones, and he'd close up his office. By Thursday evening, he figured, he and Mary could be checking into a hotel in Mexico City, in the Zona Rosa, and he'd have maybe $400,000 in gems in his briefcase.

Levin allowed himself a moment's regret. Yes, Gottleib's

diamond was worth ten times what he got for it, but the miracle was that he'd gotten anything at all. This fell into your lap, Ariel, he reminded himself. Be grateful.

Maybe, he thought, in a few months I will go to Israel, buy a house in the hills outside Jerusalem, in a posh neighborhood where the winds are cool. Maybe in a year or two I could set myself up in business in Ramat Gan. But first, enjoy yourself, Ariel. Buy a little cocaine to celebrate with Mary.

Levin got out in front of his six-story apartment building, paid the driver, and pushed through the glass door with the lock that was always broken. He rode the tiny elevator up to his apartment on the fourth floor, let himself in, and closed the door behind him.

Even before he could turn on the hall light, Levin felt a blow between his shoulder blades. He tripped over the suitcase, falling on his face in the dark hallway. A great weight landed on his back, knocking his breath out, and he felt his hair being pulled and his head coming up off the floor. He tried to get his hands underneath him to push himself up, but his arms wouldn't work. He tried to call out, to protest, but he had no voice.

He felt his head being released. Did my head hit the floor? he wondered. You're so clumsy, he told himself. But it wasn't his voice, it was his father's, speaking to him in the clipped, scolding, military fashion Levin hated so much. You've tripped and knocked yourself out, said his father's voice, and now you're dreaming.

The darkness in the hallway assumed a new character, like the inky blue velvet used to line jewel boxes. A crashing sound filled Levin's ears, like waves against a shore.

What's that? he asked. The sea?

It's your heart, his father said.

Really? asked Levin. But it's so loud, it hurts.

There now, thought Ariel Levin. That's better.

It's stopped.

29

Sullivan Street, SoHo, Manhattan
Tuesday, September 14

"You and me got some things to work out," said Frank Hill, sitting in Dov Taylor's efficiency kitchen Tuesday morning. Art Jahnke, Hill's partner, stood leaning against the kitchen counter, his hands jammed into his pockets.

"Look, Frank," said Taylor, sipping his coffee, "I played this straight."

"Yeah? Then how come that security guard on Forty-seventh Street tells me he talked to a cop and that cop turns out to be you?"

"I never told him I was a cop."

"And you never told him you wasn't."

"No, I didn't."

"Well, in my book that's impersonating an officer."

"I can't help what he thought."

"Bullshit. That's bullshit and you know it."

"Okay, Frank, I know it."

"And I didn't appreciate you telling Schumach I was coming. He was hysterical when I walked in the door. I didn't get shit out of him."

"I don't think he knows shit, Frank."

"We don't particularly care what you think, Taylor," said Jahnke.

"Okay," said Taylor, deciding it was better to let Hill blow off steam.

"It also bugs my ass," Hill said, "that you talked to Levin, you talked to this Mary Rubel, or Rudenstein, or whatever her name is, and now they're both gone. Levin never goes back to work, and he's not at his apartment last night, and he doesn't go to work this morning. And the woman doesn't show at her apartment last night, and she's not there this morning. . . .

"I'm waiting for an explanation, Taylor."

"I can't explain it."

"Fuck."

"I don't know where they are, Frank. Get a warrant and wait for them to come home."

"We don't need you to tell us how to do our job," said Jahnke. "We're just trying to figure out what yours is."

"Tell me again about the woman," Hill said.

"She gave me this number," said Taylor, sliding his notebook across the table. "Said this guy Cohen gave her Levin's name. I haven't called, but I think it's a crock."

"Why?"

"Cop's intuition."

"But you're not a cop, Taylor," said Hill, "although you seem to have some trouble remembering that fact."

"We could take you in," said Jahnke. "Obstructing justice. Interfering with an investigation. Interfering with an officer in pursuit of his duties. Impersonating an officer. Christ, you don't even have a private license. You're meat. You got nothing going for you."

"Hey, it's not my fault Levin and the blonde didn't go home last night."

"But how do we know that?" asked Hill. "How the fuck do I know what the hell you've been doing? For all the fuck I know, these are your buddies and you've been going around saying, Cheese it, the cops."

"You're right, Frank. You're right. You don't know. And you're right, I'm not a cop. But I was a cop, a good cop, and you know that, too. And I'm telling you, Levin gave me squat, and Rubel gave me squat, and what I got, you got. Oh, yeah. You might take another look at those pictures. I was going to tell you, before you started yelling and screaming, that my rabbi says that that's the way animals are slaughtered *kosher*."

"What do you mean?"

"You know *kosher*? Well, to make an animal *kosher* so

that religious Jews can eat it, you got to let it bleed to death. You do that by cutting its carotid artery. And after it's dead, you cut open its chest to see if there are spots on its lungs and intestines. If there are spots, you can't eat it.''

"Jesus. Remind me not to eat any more *kosher* franks," Jahnke said.

"Actually," said Taylor, "it's not supposed to hurt the animal. Bleeding to death's not supposed to be painful. That's how the old Romans offed themselves. They sat in a tub and opened a vein.''

"Right. Tell that to the cow," said Jahnke.

"So what are you saying?" Hill asked. "That Gottleib's killer was a Jewish butcher?''

"I'm just saying that it's something to consider.''

"So how many Jewish butchers are there in New York?" asked Hill.

"Not butchers," Taylor said. "Slaughterers. A butcher cuts up meat the *shoykhet* has slaughtered. They're very respected men, the *shoykhets*, because the religious health of the whole community depends on how well they do their job. There can't be too many of them.''

"Fine. We'll check it out," said Hill. "But that still don't make it okay for you to go around sticking your nose into felony murder. You think because you used to be a cop your shit don't stink? You think you can screw around with witnesses, suspects, and not get your ass hauled downtown?''

"Oh, so now I'm getting my ass hauled downtown? Great. Terrific. Well, fuck you very much, Frank. I'm sorry Levin and the girl disappeared, but it's got nothing to do with me. You want to make me a suspect? Fine. Make me a suspect. But that changes the rules, and I want to know if that's what's going on here. Is it, Frank? Am I a suspect?''

"Tell me again about Levin.''

"You didn't answer me.''

"No, you're not a fucking suspect.''

The phone rang in the kitchen. Jahnke looked at Taylor, who got up to answer it. "It's for you," he said to Hill, handing over the receiver.

"Yeah?" said Hill. He listened for a minute. "All right,"

he said, hanging up. "Come on, let's go," he said to Jahnke. He turned to Taylor. "Levin's fucking dead. The body was in a Dumpster behind his building. Throat's been cut."

"Has he been gutted?" Taylor asked.

"None of your fucking business," said Hill. "Listen to me, man. You're not a suspect, not yet, but you're getting close, and now you're sure as hell a material witness."

"Give me a break, Frank," said Taylor.

"No, you give me a break," Hill said. "As far as I know, you were the last person besides maybe the blonde to see Levin alive. Thanks to you, it sure as shit wasn't me. So I don't want you playing detective anymore. No more games or I'll fry your ass. I'll rip your heart out. What they did to Gottleib, I'll do to you. You understand?"

"Yeah," Taylor said.

"I'm not kidding," said Hill. "I don't want you trying to get in touch with the woman; I don't want you talking to anyone who knew Levin; I don't want you talking to anyone. And if anyone calls you, you call me, immediately. No screwing around. You just call me, or I promise you you'll be in a world of trouble. And you don't go anywhere. Period. You got it?"

"I got it." Taylor opened the door to let the two detectives out.

He returned to his kitchen, began brewing another cup of coffee, and conjured up his only image of Ariel Levin—a short, muscular guy with wiry black hair sitting in a sardine-tin office behind a big cluttered desk with a newspaper in front of him, his colorfully knitted Israeli *yarmulke* clashing with the look of suspicion that shadowed his face. No, Levin didn't seem scared, Taylor thought. He acted squirrelly, like a scam artist. Not a good one, either. And, obviously, his scam had backfired.

These are bad guys, thought Taylor. Dangerous people. Evil people.

And at least one of them is a Jew.

He went into his bedroom closet, removed a shoebox from the top shelf, and took out his Police Special wrapped in newspaper. He felt its now unfamiliar heft and, reaching into the box with his left hand, removed a handkerchief tied with a rubber band containing a dozen bullets.

The phone rang. Taylor let it ring until the answering machine cut in. After a pause he heard Phil Horowitz's voice. "Dov? Are you there? This is Philly. Are you there?"

Taylor picked up. "Phil? Yeah. I'm here."

"Look, Dov, I feel bad I didn't help you before. But things have changed a little. I got something I think you should know."

"What? What's changed?"

"I can't tell you over the phone. The phone's not safe, anyway."

"What do you mean, not safe?"

"I mean it could be tapped."

"Who'd tap my phone?"

"Look, I told you before, this is big business. There are people involved, overseas people, and they do that. Among other things, they tap phones. So why don't you just come down here to the Diamond Exchange. I'll meet you in an hour. You know where it is?"

"Yeah."

"Okay. You'll meet me?"

"Yeah."

"Alone, man. Anyone with you, I don't show. I'm serious. I'm taking a big risk, believe me."

"Okay. I'll be there. Alone."

"Good," Horowitz said, breaking the connection. Well, he thought, I tried to warn him off.

Things are starting to pop, thought Taylor, slipping his revolver into his jacket. God knows what I've stirred up, but it must be something.

30

The Diamond Exchange
4 West Forty-seventh Street, Manhattan
Tuesday, September 14

Just before noon, a two-cab fender-bender added its singular note of sour hysteria to Forty-seventh Street's cacophonous daily symphony of trade. The two cabbies standing beside their taxis yelled at each other as a uniformed cop tried to keep them apart, and the drivers in the cars behind them leaned on their horns. Dov Taylor stopped and smiled as he listened to what he had long ago identified as the basic New York exchange.

"You're fuckin' crazy!" driver number one shrieked.

"No, *you're* fuckin' crazy!" screamed driver number two.

Taylor waited two beats and, sure enough, someone watching from the sidewalk yelled out the classic punch line: "You're *both* fuckin' crazy!"

And, thought Taylor, they were. Just as he was, and just as everyone in New York would become, sooner or later. Of course, here on Forty-seventh Street, in the diamond district, it seemed as if the crazy millennium had already arrived. As soon as Taylor had turned off Sixth Avenue onto the street, the decibel level had risen, partly due to the white Lubavitcher trailer parked on the corner. It was pumping out Klezmer music—Yiddish jazz featuring a screechy, frantic clarinet—through a loudspeaker as young, intense Lubavitchers tried to get passersby to accept their pamphlets proclaiming the imminent arrival of the Messiah.

Taylor looked in the direction of the exchange, hoping to spot Phil Horowitz going in. A short Hasid in a sea of Hasidim—fat chance, he thought, and then he glanced at his watch. He still had a few minutes before they were supposed to meet. It was already quite warm, and Taylor wished he could take off his brown silk-and-wool sport coat, but he didn't want to risk having the gun in its pocket fall out. That would be embarrassing, he thought, not to mention dangerous.

Taylor knew he was being stubborn. He thought about calling Frank Hill to tell him what he was doing. Well, he would do that. Later. But if Horowitz really knew something—and he probably did—he'd never say a word with Hill around, Taylor told himself. That's why the *rebbe* had asked him to investigate, precisely so people would tell him things they wouldn't tell the *goyishe* cops.

Just as Taylor was reminding himself to be careful, a voice behind him shouted out something in Yiddish—*a warning?*—and he turned his head to see what was going on. A tall, cadaverous man in a black leather jacket loomed up behind his left shoulder—too close—and instinctively Taylor swung his arm to ward him off.

His elbow caught the Cutter's jaw just as he felt a blow beneath his shoulder blade. He spun away from the dull pain, which immediately began to sharpen and radiate down his back and forward through his chest. Stumbling, he banged his head against a plate-glass window full of jewels, rings, and chains. The Cutter jumped at him, and Taylor raised his arms to shield his face while kicking out, catching the Cutter just below the left knee. His leg knocked out from under him, the Cutter, off balance, fell forward, lunging toward Taylor, and again Taylor felt a burning pain, this time across his left arm.

Taylor, screaming in fear and rage, hit out with his right, striking the Cutter's chest with the heel of his hand. The Cutter lost his footing and fell. A space opened between them, but Taylor's knees had given way and he slid down the window, sitting on the sidewalk. His lungs on fire, Taylor kicked out again, catching the Cutter—who was now on his hands and knees—in the head, knocking him backward. It was only then that Taylor saw the knife in the Cutter's hand.

In the quiet that suddenly seemed to have descended upon the street, Taylor heard the knife's blade drag along the sidewalk, and for the first time he realized that he had been stabbed, that he was, perhaps, dying. He screamed again, the fear gone now, and tried to crawl toward the Cutter. If he was going to die, he would take this man with him. He would pound him to a jelly; he would rip out his throat with his teeth; he would spit his own blood in his eye.

The Cutter scrambled to his feet. Taylor saw several men reach for him. The Cutter swung around in a circle, and the men jumped away from his knife, one falling to his knees, holding his hand and groaning in shock. The Cutter turned, took a step toward Taylor, thought better of it, and then bolted down the street toward Fifth Avenue, knocking people aside as he ran.

Taylor began crawling after the Cutter. He had to get this man. He had to kill him. His stomach churned; he felt like vomiting. Only then did he remember the gun in his pocket. He reached into his pocket.

"Easy," said a voice. Hands on his shoulder stopped him. Hands propped him up against a wall.

The sun was directly in his eyes. He couldn't see the face bending over him. He looked down at his arm. His jacket had been sliced open, and blood pumped sluggishly out of a deep wound that began a few inches below his elbow and snaked down to his wrist, like the rawhide strap that tied his *tefillin*. He reached into his coat with his right hand, and when he pulled out his hand, his fingertips were daubed red with arterial blood. No one will ever know why I died or who killed me, he thought. I made it through 'Nam, but now it's New York; things like this happen all the time.

Taylor leaned his head against the side of the building and closed his eyes against the bright sunlight. It hurt to breathe. He felt the rage seeping out of him, leaving him empty, hollow.

The same voice again said, "Easy." Taylor opened his eyes, and now he saw a man about his own age bending over him, his face shadowed by a large black *shtreiml*, the sun behind his head crisping the edges of his beard. "Make it easy," the Hasid said in a thick Yiddish accent. "Ambulance is already coming."

"I'm hurt," Taylor whispered. It hurt to speak.

"No talk," said the man. "You will be okay."

"I know you. . . ." Taylor felt himself growing groggy, felt himself drifting away. "Who are you?"

The man responded in Yiddish.

"Did he get away?" Taylor asked, gasping.

The man patted Taylor's hand and continued speaking to him in Yiddish even as Taylor heard a siren growing louder and then cutting off as the EMTs arrived. They took his pulse, slapped an oxygen mask over his face, and maneuvered him roughly onto a stretcher, lifting him into the ambulance as the Hasid held his hand.

It was so confusing. He knew he knew this man, even though he had no idea who he was. And even though, rationally, Taylor knew he could not understand a word the Hasid was saying, he had the distinct impression that he was being told that the same thing had happened to the Hasid a long, long time ago.

31

All Things Beautiful
Kingston Street, Brooklyn
Tuesday, September 14

The Cutter, carrying his possessions in a large black leather traveling bag, stood beneath the awning of Rothstein's Bakery and watched Sarah Kalman locking the metal security gate across the entrance to All Things Beautiful. There was very little traffic on Kingston Street now. The neighborhood's women and children were home—the children studying, the women preparing dinner. The men were strolling toward 770 for the evening prayers, taking their time until a few stars would become visible, thereby signaling the proper moment to begin. Finally, after days of heat, the air was cooling off, and the Cutter could smell autumn coming on.

But despite the snap in the air, the Cutter was sweating. He rubbed his palms against his slacks and smoked one cigarette after another. He couldn't believe what he was doing. He should, he knew, be holed up in a room near the airport, waiting for the morning plane to Rome. His work here was finished, even if that detective had survived.

Had he? The Cutter cursed the Hasid who had called out when the Cutter pushed by him to get at Taylor. If not for him, the knife would have punctured Taylor's heart. The detective would have fallen where he stood. By the time anyone in the crowd noticed, the Cutter would have been gone. Instead, Taylor had turned toward the sound, and that had thrown the Cutter off. Still, the blade could have caught one of the major arteries coming from the heart.

No matter. The Magician had the stone; the Cutter would soon be leaving this horrible city behind. And even if the man survived, how would he ever find them, even if he wanted to?

So why was he here, among the accursed Hasidim, wearing a *yarmulke*, watching the rabbi's daughter? Because an unfamiliar need had been growing inside him ever since yesterday, when he'd seen her walking with that detective. He had asked the shopkeepers on Kingston Street about her, and what he had heard convinced him that he needed to know her. All last night, after he had disposed of Ariel Levin's body, he had thought about her as he sat on his bed, smoking cigarettes and staring into the darkness. Alone in his room, he had felt her presence all around him. At times he thought he could almost see her, her small white hands, her fine, sweet features. This was not about sex, he assured himself. This was about the loneliness he sensed in her. He understood her. He felt she was made for him. She could redeem him.

The Cutter made up his mind and crossed the street. He saw Sarah Kalman turn toward him, her hair so vivid it looked like a holy, cleansing fire; her skin like porcelain, her eyes as green as emeralds. So different from that whore Maria, he thought. So small, so delicate, so modestly dressed. She will smell of soap, the Cutter imagined, because this one is clean.

"Excuse me," the Cutter said in Yiddish. Yes, she did smell of soap. "You are Reb Kalman's daughter, Sarah?"

"Yes?" said Sarah Kalman, surprised that a stranger would address her.

"I wish to speak with you. You are perhaps going home? May I walk with you?"

"I live just around the corner," Sarah said.

"Fine," said the Cutter. "What I have to say will take only a moment."

"All right." Sarah tried to place the Cutter's Yiddish. An Israeli, certainly, but not a *sabra*, not native born. Not a Litvak. Not a German. A southerner? A Rumanian? A Hungarian? Maybe a Pole.

They began walking up Kingston Street.

"A lovely night," said the Cutter.

"Yes, but is this what you wanted to discuss with me?" Sarah asked. "The weather?"

"No, of course not. Miss Kalman," the Cutter began, clearing his throat, the sound of his own voice as strange to him as the words he was speaking, "I have watched you from afar. I have admired you. I know you are unmarried. I know you are an accomplished woman, a scholar, and you have your own business. This does not disturb me."

Definitely a Pole, she thought.

"Before you speak, let me say that I know I am much older than you, not a handsome young man. But I am not that old, I have never been married, and I am quite wealthy. I am not a Hasid, but I am a pious, Sabbath-observing Jew. In conclusion, I want to ask your permission to ask your father if he would accept me as a suitor for your hand in marriage."

Sarah stopped. The Cutter turned toward her, and she felt goose bumps that did not come from the suddenly chilly weather. She bit back the casual, sarcastic words that came to her. She felt sure that this tall, hollow-cheeked Polisher was not joking, and something told her it would be dangerous to treat him dismissively.

"I don't even know your name," she said.

"My name is Jacob Rothstein," said the Cutter, combining the name of the bakery with the first name that popped into his head.

"Mr. Rothstein," said Sarah, "I am very flattered, but I'm sure you will understand that I cannot respond to what you are saying."

"All I am asking, Miss Kalman—"

"Excuse me, sir. You are a stranger to me, and, frankly, you have taken me quite by surprise. I am sure you are a respectable man, but what you are doing, what you are saying, is not respectable. I assure you, sir, my father would never accept a man who is not a *Hasidisher Yid* as a marriage possibility. I beg your pardon, Mr. Rothstein, but I must go home now."

The Cutter nodded. "I understand, Miss Kalman. But let me explain. I am being so direct with you because I must go away soon on business, and I wanted you to become aware of me. I understand very well now that my speech must have seemed abrupt, even crude, and I realize now that I have made a mistake. But this mistake comes from an honest heart.

"Listen to me. You are right; I am a stranger to you. But you are not entirely a stranger to me. I know the Lubavitchers, and I know they see you as an outsider. I do not say this to hurt you. Believe me, I understand what it is like to be considered different because one is special, because one is chosen. I know you are a special one, Sarah Kalman, and when I return to this country, I would like to ask you again for your permission, if that is all right."

"I am sorry, Mr. Rothstein. I have said what I can say. Now you must excuse me."

"I will come back, Miss Kalman," said the Cutter. And as he watched her walk away, her heels clicking smartly on the sidewalk, he promised himself, I will come back. You are the chosen one.

32

Roosevelt-St. Luke's Hospital, Manhattan
Wednesday, September 15

Taylor kept going over the attack in his mind. Could he have reacted faster? Could he have gotten to his gun? Could he have been a hero instead of just another victim lying in a hospital bed?

The Demerol he had been given that morning added to his anxiety. He had been nodding when Frank Hill had arrived to ask him for a description of the man who had stabbed him, and even as he told Hill that he had no memory of the man's face, that all he could remember was that he was tall and had worn a black leather jacket, Taylor worried about his sobriety. Did the Demerol count as a slip? What would happen when he left the hospital? Would they give him a prescription for Percodan? Would he need it? Would he fill it? Would he take it?

Hill had been surprisingly decent. He hadn't asked him what he had been doing in the diamond district. That, Taylor knew, would come later, and he would have to tell Hill that he'd been meeting a source, someone who had told him he knew something about the case. But Taylor wanted to speak to Phil Horowitz before Hill did. He wanted to smash his ugly lying face. Then he would give him to Hill.

Taylor did tell Hill he was convinced that the man who had stabbed him was the same man who had killed Ariel Levin, and possibly Zalman Gottlieb and Shirley Stein, too. He saw me talking to Levin, and he thought I was getting close to him, Taylor had told Hill. He overestimated me.

But why did Horowitz set me up? Taylor wondered. Why? Phil is a thug, sure, but a murderer? Could the Satmarer *rebbe* have been right all along? Could all this be some grotesque feud between the Lubavitchers and the Satmarers? After all, isn't the killer a Jew, someone who knows about *kosher* slaughtering? But what had Horowitz said? Overseas people? People who tap phones? Who the hell could that be? Or was that all bullshit?

Well, at least he was alive. Last night the doctor had told him that the knife had nicked his lung and collapsed it—that was why it was hard for him to breathe—but it had missed everything else, most importantly his spleen and his heart. The wound on his forearm and wrist was potentially more troubling. Nerves and ligaments had been severed. There might just be some stiffness, or he might not regain the full use of the hand. But, otherwise, he was going to be fine. And if his lung reinflated, and if he didn't develop a fever, he could leave tomorrow, or the next day, and begin physical therapy at home.

Dumb luck, thought Taylor. Christ, I've been dumb.

How much time had passed since his last shot? He reached over to his bedside table, wincing at the pain in his chest and arm, and looked at his watch. Three hours. That's enough. He rang the bell for the nurse and asked for another shot. The nurse went away, and another nurse arrived carrying a tray of needles.

"Last time, let's see, was the left cheek, right?" she asked. "So let's see if you can shift over on your left side and we'll stick the right cheek."

A few moments after the nurse left, Taylor felt the warmth spreading through his chest, taking the pain away, making him sleepy. It felt wonderful. All the anxiety in his body disappearing, all his muscles relaxing, letting go, all his questions melting away, drifting off into space, gone. He remembered the first time he had ever tasted junk, smoking *touc phins*, heroin and grass, at combat school in Chu Lai. It was the only thing that made the army, the jungle, the war, bearable. Drifting away as the rockets went up, drifting away as the psy-choppers flew overhead, their speakers blaring. Drifting away as he watched the tracers making gorgeous fluorescent arcs across the velvet sky. Drifting away in hell. Drifting away.

Taylor shook his head. What was he doing? The first shot

may not have been a slip, but this one was. Did I need it for the pain, or did I want it for the kick? Once a junkie always a junkie, Taylor thought angrily. Isn't that what they say?

The phone by Taylor's bed rang. He picked it up. It was Rabbi Kalman.

"So, you are all right, yes?"

"I guess so, Rabbi."

"You don't sound so good."

"I've only got one lung working right now."

"That's terrible."

"It's not so bad. They've got me blowing into a gadget, a tube running into a bottle, trying to make a little ball float up in the air. They say it'll get my lung working in no time."

"It still sound terrible. So, Dov, you know who did it?"

"No. I didn't see him."

"You think it was the same one that killed the diamond operator?" Rabbi Kalman asked.

"I don't know, Rabbi. Maybe."

"So what can we do to help?"

"Nothing. The doctor says I can leave tomorrow or maybe the day after. I'll come see you."

"All right. All right. Stop *nudzhing*."

"What?"

"Not you, Dov. Someone here wants to speak with you."

There was a pause, and then Sarah Kalman came on the line. "Mr. Taylor. I'm so sorry."

"It's all right, Sarah. Don't worry."

"May I come visit you?"

"There's no need. You don't want to come to the hospital. It's a creepy place. I'll be out in a day or two and I'll come visit."

"Do you have someone to take care of you when you get home? To cook, to do the shopping?"

"Don't worry about it, Sarah. I'll be okay."

"Because if you don't have someone, I could bring you some food, some soup, and run some errands for you."

"Thank you, that's very kind. But I'll be all right." As soon as I get myself to a meeting, Taylor added to himself.

"Well, if you need anything, please call us," said Sarah. "I will."

"I'll put my father back on."

"Dov. The Satmarer *rebbe* heard about what happened to you," Rabbi Kalman said. "His *gabbai*, Pinchus Mayer, whom you met, called me and asked me to tell you that the *rebbe* is very sorry for your suffering. He prays for you to get better soon. I myself told our master, Rebbe Seligson, may he live long and happily, what happened, and he, too, prays for you. Imagine, Dov, you have two holy men, two *zaddiks*, helping you recover."

"Well, then I should have no problems, right, Rabbi?"

"Mayer also said you should call him because the *rebbe* wants to see you as soon as you get out of the hospital. And he says also you should get the best doctors, a private room, whatever. The Satmarers will pay."

"Good," said Taylor. "Thank him, but that's not a problem. I have insurance. But you can tell Mayer that he should have a check waiting for me. Finding these bastards is going to be expensive."

"I will tell him."

"Also, Rabbi, tell Sarah to be careful. The man who stabbed me, he may have followed me the day I visited her in Brooklyn. For a while she shouldn't walk around alone, she shouldn't be in the shop alone."

"You think she is in danger?" asked Rabbi Kalman, dropping his voice to a whisper.

"No, I don't. But it wouldn't hurt to be a little careful, would it?"

"No, and the same for you, Dov. Get better. Make it easy."

"You know, Rabbi, that reminds me. After I was stabbed, while I was lying there on the street, a Hasid came up to me and told me I was going to be all right. He held my hand and told me to take it easy and I would be all right. The strange thing was, most of the time he was speaking Yiddish, but I swear I understood him, or understood a lot of what he was saying. I think he was telling me that the same thing had happened to him. I guess he meant that he had been stabbed. I don't know. You get hurt, you think you're going to die, crazy stuff goes through your head."

"Not so crazy. He was talking inside you, Dov. Not outside."

"What do you mean?"

"I mean that you are doing good, that you are on the right track. But when you see the Satmarer *reb*, you should tell him about this man. He will understand better than me."

After he hung up, Taylor told his nurse that he didn't want any more pain medication. He told her he was a recovering alcoholic, and he asked her if there was an AA group in the hospital. There was, and Taylor began to feel better.

No, he would not accept a script for Percodan. He'd tough it out. And tomorrow he'd get out of the hospital—away from all the needles and drugs—even if he had to crawl.

I'll talk to Horowitz, he told himself. And something tells me that when I finish with him, I'll find Mary Rubel, too. I'll find her even if I have to chase her to Poland, or wherever it is she lives. Some of my old snitches must be around. A woman like that, someone knows something about her. And when I find her, I'll find the *rebbe*'s diamond, too, I know it.

The *rebbe*'s diamond. His big secret that almost got me killed. Taylor started thinking about how much he would enjoy giving the Satmarer *rebbe* a piece of his mind, and he began rehearsing what he would say to him.

33

The Satmarer Rebbe's House
South Ninth Street, Williamsburg, Brooklyn
Friday, September 17

Taylor awoke with a start as Pinchus Mayer touched his shoulder lightly. "The *rebbe* is ready for you now, Dov Taylor," Mayer said. "You are all right, yes?"

Taylor stood up unsteadily and checked his watch. It was two A.M. He had been discharged from the hospital at noon, Thursday, and the first thing he had done was to call Alex, his sponsor, and tell him about the Demerol.

Alex's voice had grown very grave. "You'll sleep at my place tonight, Dov. What are you doing now?"

Taylor had told him that he intended to go directly to his home meeting in the basement of St. Vincent's, and Alex had approved. "You want me to be there?" Alex asked, and Taylor had said no, assuring him that he'd be all right.

At the meeting he had received a lot of friendly, welcome attention. He told his fellow drunks and drug addicts about that second shot of Demerol and how he felt he could no longer say he had two years of sobriety. Jerry, an auto mechanic in his sixties who had been sober for about thirty years, reminded Taylor that no matter how much time someone had under their belt—two days, two months, two years or thirty— they still had to stay sober one day at a time. Don't fall in love with your slip, Jerry had told him, and don't forget about it, either. Just put it where it belongs—in the past.

After the meeting, Taylor ate a small dinner of linguine and clams with a tossed salad in one of his favorite Italian spots in SoHo, and when he had sat down in the *rebbe*'s crowded parlor at nine P.M., he had been feeling surprisingly good. Now, after falling asleep on the big leather chair, his legs ached, his arm throbbed, and his chest burned.

"I was feeling a whole lot better five hours ago," Taylor said huffily, responding to Mayer's question.

"The *rebbe* wanted to see you last," Mayer explained apologetically. "He did not want to have to think about anything else, yes? Being last is an honor."

"All right, all right. Lead on, Reb Mayer."

Once again Taylor followed Mayer through the still, quiet house and up the broad, polished wooden staircase to the *rebbe*'s office. And when Mayer opened the door and ushered Taylor in, shutting the door quietly behind him, Taylor found the Satmarer *rebbe* much as he had left him just a week before, sitting in his black silk *bekekher* behind a vast desk piled high with books and papers, the only light in the room coming from a small desk lamp. But this time the *rebbe* was alone, and, on the desk in front of him, Taylor noticed a large ashtray, the size of a hubcap, piled high with butts.

Holding a Lucky Strike between his index finger and thumb, taking a deep drag, Rebbe Joel Teitel looked beat. His eyes were red, the dark bags beneath them black. But Taylor thought he detected a small smile of welcome as the *rebbe* nodded for him to sit down.

"You are feeling well, Dov Taylor?" asked the *rebbe*.

"I've felt a whole lot better, Rabbi," Taylor said.

"To me, you look much better than before. You look more like a Jew. Would you like a cigarette?" The *rebbe* held out a crumpled pack. Taylor ignored them.

"I just got out of the hospital today. I was almost killed," he said.

"I knew a pious man," the *rebbe* said pleasantly, "who every day after he got home from his work would lie down in a hole in his garden and let the worms crawl over him. Then he would get up, give thanks, wash his hands, and eat dinner. Every day he did this.

"Tell me, Dov Taylor, when you were stabbed, what did you hear?"

"Excuse me, Rabbi, but how come you're talking to me? Last time you said we couldn't talk. You said you could smell blood on my hands. You talked to Hirsh Leib, remember?"

"Last time you were very far away. Last time you were a

stranger. You frightened me. Now you are known to me. Now you have almost accomplished the *teshuvah*, the turning. The *sefiros*, the ten hidden attributes of the Holy One, Blessed is He, have come close to you. Do you know what they are?''

''I'm not in the mood for a lesson, Rabbi. Maybe five hours ago, but not now.''

''Do you know what they are?''

''No.''

''Yes, you do. Every Jew does. We know them in our souls. You just don't remember them. *Keter*,'' the *rebbe* began, tapping the desk with his tobacco-stained index finger as he recited, ''crown; *khokhma*, wisdom; *bina*, understanding; *khesed*, grace; *g'vurah*, strength; *t'feres*, beauty; *netzakh*, victory; *hod*, glory; *yesod*, foundation; *malkhus*, kingdom. All these things you have come closer to. *Teshuvah*. You are turning. Do you know what means *shema*?''

''It's the beginning of the prayer *Shema Yisroel*. It means 'Hear.' ''

''Very good. You see? You are a Jew. And we say '*shema*' because that is how we learn, through the ears. The Holy One in His Torah, may He be praised, has given us the words, and we learn through hearing them. We are not like the *goyim* with their pictures of the Jesus and their saints. We know we need *khokhma*, wisdom, and *bina*, understanding, to hear what is truly important, what is hidden. And *g'vurah*, strength, to bear it.

''Tell me, Dov Taylor, if a king has a treasure, where does he keep it?''

''What?'' Taylor blinked. It was almost better, he thought, when the *rebbe* was talking to Hirsh Leib. It was less tiring, less confusing.

''When a king has a treasure, where does he keep it?''

''I don't know.''

''You do!'' shouted the Satmarer *rebbe*, making Taylor jump. ''You are not thinking. It is important for what we do here that you think. You are close, very close to the mystery, but you must think. You must use your heart, your ears, your brain. You must use *khokhma*, *bina*, and *g'vurah*.

"I ask you again. When a king has a treasure, where does he keep it?"

"In a safe place?"

"Yes, yes," said Rebbe Teitel. "Of course. He keeps it hidden. Secret. He does not leave it out on the street for strangers to see and maybe to steal it. He guards it. And the more he hides it, the more men he employs to guard it, the bigger the treasure, yes?

"So, when you were stabbed, what did you hear?"

"What?"

"What did you hear? You heard a secret. Something hidden. What was it?"

"I heard a man. A Hasid. He held my hand and told me I was going to be all right."

"And what else did he say?"

"I don't know. He spoke Yiddish."

"But you understood him."

"I told you, he spoke Yiddish."

"But you understood him. Don't tell me what your brain tells you you heard. Tell me what your ears heard."

"I heard him say that the same thing had happened to him. That's what I heard. He said he had been stabbed and that he died, but that I was going to live. It's nuts."

"No, not at all. He told you that he was murdered, yes? He told you something, and you heard it with your ears. But you also heard it with *bina*, with understanding. Your heart is open now, and now you have heard Hirsh Leib himself. That was Hirsh Leib, may his blood be avenged, your great-great-grandfather, his spark, speaking to you. He called out to you; he warned you; he saved your life."

"*Rebbe*," said Taylor, shaking his head, "it's too late for this. I'm too tired, and I don't understand any of it. Please. Listen to me. Another man died because of your diamond. I almost died. I'm going to tell the police what I know about it, about the diamond. And if anyone is going to find the men who did it, if you're ever going to get your diamond back, you're going to have to tell me everything you know about it. Simply. No more riddles, no more stories."

"Shush," said the Satmarer *rebbe*. "Take a breath. Take

a moment. Dov Taylor. You think I am a hard man, I know. Maybe you think I am crazy? A little crazy, yes?'' The *rebbe* leaned forward, and his voice dropped. Taylor felt his eyes burning. It would be so sweet to close them.

"I know that you are in pain, Dov Taylor. How can it not be so? *Eem poga, noga.* If he touches, he is touched. *Eem poga, noga.* You understand? You have touched a mystery. You have touched a treasure. And the treasure is guarded. So you are touched, hurt.

"Has it not always been so? All your life, has it not been so? You have been in pain. Always you think there is something you should do, but you do not know what it is. So you have pain and you finish nothing. You go into the army to become an officer, but you do not become an officer. You get married, but you cut yourself off from your wife. You become a policeman, but then you run away. None of these things you do make you whole. They all leave you empty. So you pity yourself. You drink, or you think about not drinking. What is the difference? The drinking still holds you. It is all the same.

"But now things are changed. Now you could die from this running away. Yes, that is how dangerous this is. You understand? You could die from this."

"Obviously," said Taylor, his voice thick. "You don't have to have mystic powers to see that." Christ, he was tired.

"You refuse to understand," said the *rebbe*. "You think I am talking about men with guns and knives, but I am not. Of course, they will be the servants that will bring you death, but they will be doing your will.

"But," continued the *rebbe*, "you do not have to die. The *teshuvah* is happening. It is happening. I can see it. I can see the sign on your forehead. Those old thoughts of yours—running away, calling for policemen—they will not help you now. You must listen to Hirsh Leib."

"Rebbe Teitel, you have to tell me what you know."

"That is what I wish to do. So I will teach you a *nigun*, a tune, by Rabbi Nachman of Bratzlav. After he died, may his memory be blessed, the Bratzlavers never chose another *zaddik*. This is why we call them the 'dead Hasidim.' This *nigun* of the Bratzlavers was one of Hirsh Leib's favorites. He sang it at weddings, and he sang it whenever he wanted to clear his mind. I will start, and then you say after me. Da, da, dah, da, da-da-dah, da.''

"Please, Rabbi.''

"Listen, Dov Taylor, and say after me.''

Rebbe Teitel began singing the hypnotic, wordless *nigun*, composed over two hundred years ago by Rebbe Nachman of Bratzlav, the Baal Shem Tov's great-grandson. Taylor, exhausted, closed his eyes and gave up trying to follow or even understand Reb Teitel. This is not my world, thought Taylor, even as he began to sing along with the *rebbe*. Well, what of it? he thought. What's so great about your world?

Taylor had no idea how many times he had repeated the simple melody of the *nigun* when he felt himself being shaken, felt the pain shooting down his left arm. He opened his eyes, expecting to see his grandmother. Rebecca. Had he fallen asleep? Had he been dreaming? The Satmarer *rebbe* was shaking his shoulders, his beard and bloodshot eyes not six inches from Taylor's face. The *rebbe* was shouting the *nigun* faster and faster, spit flying from his lips.

"Get up, Dov Taylor, son of Luba, grandson of Rebecca, great-great-grandson of the *Zaddik* of Orlik, the blessed Hirsh Leib!'' said the *rebbe*. "Dance!''

Taylor allowed the *rebbe* to drag him up from the chair. He stood there, shifting his weight from one foot to the other as the *rebbe*, his beard down to his waist, hopped up and down in front of him, singing the wordless *nigun*. Taylor was so tired that his head dropped forward even as he stood. He felt himself falling asleep or passing out, he could not tell which.

The *rebbe* suddenly stopped singing. The room was still. *"Vu zent ir, Reb Leib?"* he asked Dov Taylor in Yiddish. Where are you?

The *nigun* still echoed in Taylor's head, but between the notes he heard Rebecca's voice. *"Zog im, Dovidl,"* she said. "Tell him.'' And words came unbidden to Taylor's lips.

"Kh'bin in Lublin," he said in Yiddish. I am in Lublin.

And at that moment, Dov Taylor began to disappear into

his dream. The fears, the loves, the memories that were Taylor, contracted into a small point of light in a vast, dark universe, where they were greeted by another set of fears, loves, and memories, blazing brightly.

"*Gut!*" said the Satmarer *rebbe*, and it seemed to Taylor that his voice was far off, echoing between the notes of the *nigun* like Rebecca's.

Maybe I'm dying, thought Taylor, frightened. *Don't worry*, a voice in the vastness told him. *You live, and I take nothing from you*. And what was once Dov Taylor relaxed and, perhaps, slept.

"Tell me, master," asked the Satmarer *rebbe*, "why the great Seer of Lublin was slaughtered on *erev* Simkhas Torah? Who was it, old friend, who murdered you? And what are those murderers doing now?"

An hour later, as the rising sun peeked through the drawn curtains, Rebbe Joel Teitel, for the first time in his adult life, skipped his morning prayers. And still, using Dov Taylor as his vessel, Rabbi Hirsh Leib, the *Zaddik* of Orlik, spoke, unfolding the story of the Seer of Lublin, his diamond, and the great conspiracy that he had masterminded unto his death.

BOOK
TWO

34

Lublin, Poland
Tuesday, October 12
1814

IT WAS IMPOSSIBLE TO THINK, IMPOSSIBLE TO FORM THE SIM-
PLEST *thought. The sounds, smells, sights, and sensations
were too strange, too overwhelming. And then there were
those other thoughts, alien yet somehow familiar, jumbling
his own, drowning out his own mind, pushing him deeper
into the dream.*

But whose dream was it?

I am here, thought Hirsh Leib, *in Lublin. The Lord be
praised.*

I am not here, thought Dov Taylor.

It is good, thought Hirsh Leib. *My poor horse is very tired.*

A horse? thought Dov Taylor, *looking down, seeing the
earth rushing past below him, feeling fear.*

I pray the stables are not all filled, thought Hirsh Leib.

Hold on! thought Dov Taylor. *Don't let us fall!*

Ah, the market, thought Hirsh Leib.

Look, thought Dov Taylor. *Lublin!*

We are here!

Hirsh Leib rode down the cobblestones of the King's Road
through Jew's Gate into the city of Lublin. He was a tall,

wiry man with a full black beard and strong, scarred hands unusual in a scholar.

But Hirsh Leib was an unusual man.

His father had been the best tinsmith in Orlik—indeed, he had even roofed the Polish church there—and his son had grown up speaking Polish as well as Yiddish and Hebrew, the holy tongue.

As a child, Hirsh Leib had learned from his father how to work tin, and Rabbi Aaron of Orlik had taught him Talmud, but he had taught himself the language of horses. Anyone who knew anything about those animals could see that just by the way Hirsh Leib sat in the saddle, barely touching the reins. All he ever had to say to his mount was, "Go, my friend, in the name of God," and whatever horse he was riding fairly burst its heart to carry him wherever he willed.

Yom Kippur, the holiest day of the year, had just passed, and all though the *shtot* of Lublin (a *shtot* is a town bigger than a *shtetl*), people were busy building their *sukkahs*, the little thatched huts next to their homes in which they would sleep, eat, and perhaps make love during the eight days of Sukkos that climaxed in the joyous Simkhas Torah celebration. As it is written: "In booths ye shall dwell seven days so that your generations may know that I have made the children of Israel dwell in booths when I brought them forth from the land of Egypt."

In the market square in the center of town, Hirsh Leib could see that the merchants were doing a brisk business selling *esregim* (citrons), *lulav* (palm branch), *mirt* (myrtle branch), and *arava* (willow branch) from the Holy Land, without which no man could properly celebrate the holiday. And today, Hirsh Leib knew, not only would the market be alive with the hum of commerce, it would also be filled with the buzz of rumor and speculation.

Why had Rebbe Yakov Yitzhak, the famous Seer of Lublin, invited all the Hasidim in the world to come celebrate this Simkhas Torah with him?

And Hirsh Leib knew what many people, both simple and wise, ignorant and learned, were thinking: The Messiah is coming.

Certainly times were hard—never had anyone living known them to be harder—and wasn't it written that the Messiah would come when the suffering of His Chosen People had become unbearable? And what better time for the Messiah to come than on Simkhas Torah, when all Jews rejoiced in His law? And wouldn't it be right for Him to arrive just after Yom Kippur, when Israel was clean, freshly atoned for its sins?

Well, perhaps they were right, thought Hirsh Leib, reaching into his saddlebag for the bottle of cherry brandy he had brought from Orlik. Perhaps the Messiah was coming, here, to Lublin.

Of course, as Hirsh Leib also knew, Lublin's innkeepers, cobblers, tailors, and blacksmiths couldn't have been happier even if the Messiah was truly on His way. This massive invasion of pilgrims meant business.

Well, may you all prosper, thought Hirsh Leib, taking a sip of the clear, fiery brandy.

He recorked the bottle, returned it to his saddlebag, and scanned the market. What a windfall for Lublin's money grubbers! he thought. Already Hasidim were arriving from such Polish *shtots* as Pshiskhe and Lodz and from the *shtetls* of Khelm, Kotsk, Apt, and Ger. From the south, those wild, fanatic Hasidim were expected from Belz and Brod, from Lezhensk and Rimanov, and even from as far away as Satmar in Hungary. From the southwest, from Podolia, birthplace of the holy Baal Shem Tov, they were coming from the *shtetls* of Bratslav, Bar, and Mezhbizh. And they were coming from the north, scholars from Bialestok, Karlin, Minsk, and even from far away Vilne, where Hasidim were spat upon in the street and where the famous Gaon of Vilne, the foremost Talmudic scholar of the age, had not long ago declared all Hasidim to be heretics.

These pilgrims would have to sleep somewhere, thought Hirsh Leib. They all could not lay their bedrolls in the Seer's *hoyf*, his courtyard, as he intended to do.

And these pilgrims would have to eat, yes? They all could not squeeze in at the *rebbe*'s table. Many, Hirsh Leib figured, would eat at Berel the drunkard's tavern, where he himself had visited many times on previous trips to Lublin. Berel, it was true, was often too drunk to keep his place stocked with herring and vodka, but his wife, the long and loudly suffering Goldeh, had a good head for business. And in stocking the inn, she would bring business to the bakers, and to the butchers, and they to the *shoykhetim*, the slaughterers.

Of course, the clothes and shoes of the visitors would need mending after their long journeys, yes? They would want to look their best when they danced with the holy scrolls. That was good news for the tailors and cobblers.

And imagine all those horses. They would need to be fed, boarded, and shod, isn't that true? So Yoyne the blacksmith would be busy.

And wouldn't the pilgrims all want to buy souvenirs of their trip, for wasn't Lublin, thanks to the Seer, the center of the *Hasidishe* world? Wouldn't they want to buy *tallisim*, and *tefillim* and books containing the *rebbe*'s wisdom, not to mention little gifts to assuage the wives they had left back home with the children?

So, thought Hirsh Leib, reaching again for the cherry brandy, all you shopkeepers should say a prayer of thanks to Rebbe Yitzhak, the pride of Lublin, the Great Seer. And so should all you fathers and mothers with ugly, unmarried daughters. Surely, among all these visiting scholars, there will be a match for your hunchbacked, cross-eyed darling.

Hirsh Leib knew that even the peasants, the Polish farmers living on the outskirts of town east of castle Czartoryski, were lighting candles in their church (the wooden one with that man on top of it, still shamefully naked and still horribly nailed to that frightening cross) in honor of the Seer and all the good fortune he was bringing to Lublin.

Now, Hirsh Leib, the *Zaddik* of Orlik (although he hated to be called that, and always insisted that as long as his teacher, the Great Seer, lived, there was only one true *zaddik* in the world), tied up his horse and hurried through the market, stopping to ask everyone he met if they knew where the Seer was. Hirsh Leib burned to see his teacher, and he wanted to be the first to tell him that he had seen Reb David of Lelov, and Menachem Mendel of Rymanov, on the road to Lublin.

They were coming, and soon the Seer would bind their *kava-nah*, their holy intents, with his own, and with the *kavanah* of the hordes of Hasidim coming to Lublin, in order to join the upper world to the lower. And when that happened on Simkhas Torah night, the world of men would be shaken and holy fire would rain down from the sky.

In the middle of the market square, Hirsh Leib paused to marvel afresh at the size and energy of Lublin. His home, Orlik, was a tiny *shtetl* of tumbledown shacks. Even on market days, all one could purchase in the square might be some wilted beets, a slice of fish without the head, a pale, skinny chicken. Orlik's shops sold old clothes and old boots, scavenged and mended by the town's tailors and cobblers. But here, in Lublin, one could buy rich silk *kapotes* and gleaming boots that a Polish nobleman might wear. There were *sheitls* and *shtreimels* from Odessa on display that cost more than Hirsh Leib's father, may his memory be blessed, had earned in his entire life. Stands bulged with vegetables and fruit, and an ocean of fish seemed to have washed up on ice in the fishmongers' wagons. Truly, thought Hirsh Leib, his tired eyes taking in the milling crowd, I have come to the center of the world.

Whether that means the center of evil, he thought, we will see.

Just then Hirsh Leib's eyes fell upon a man he knew and loved, Rabbi Bunem the apothecary, who it was said was the Seer's closest friend. Bunem was a short, round, merry-looking man who was famous both for his piety and for his wit. A worldly man, Rabbi Bunem had studied the apothecary's arts in Danzig and in Germany and had studied Talmud with the Holy Yehudi in Pshiskhe, becoming his disciple. When the Yehudi had difficulty in healing a troubled soul, he used to say, "Call the pharmacist; he will help me." And by this he meant, of course, Rabbi Bunem.

"Reb Bunem," called Hirsh Leib, waving over the crowd.

Bunem looked up and saw the tall, fierce figure of the *Zaddik* of Orlik. He is a warrior, thought Rabbi Bunem. But is he fighting a holy war?

Hirsh Leib threaded his way through the crowd to Bunem's

side. "*Sholem aleykhem*, apothecary," said Hirsh Leib. Peace be with you.

"*Aleykhem sholem*, Hirsh Leib," said Rabbi Bunem, taking his ever-present pipe out of his mouth. "What do you think, Hirsh Leib? Lublin is going mad. Have you ever seen so many people? Even the Polish drunkards would be afraid to try to murder us when we gather in such numbers."

"In Orlik, our peasants leave us alone. But we have heard there have been many pogroms in Lublin," said Hirsh Leib.

"Yes. The whole eastern end of the city, where the goldsmiths and the jewelers lived, was set to the torch not two months ago. And when they ran out of their homes, the Cossacks were waiting to cut their throats. Women and children, too. It's that lunatic Count Josep Czartoryski. He wants every Jew dead. Ask the Seer. He'll tell you why."

"But I think you're right," said Hirsh Leib. "With so many of us in Lublin now, we'll be safe."

"Perhaps," Bunem said. "But what do you think these pilgrims would say if they knew the real reason Rebbe Yitzhak had summoned them?"

"I don't think they would care. They're too busy chasing after gold," said Hirsh Leib.

"You are bitter today," said Bunem.

"I'm sorry, Bunem," Hirsh Leib said. "Almost as soon as I entered Lublin, I became angry; I don't know why. Some *dybbuk*, perhaps, some unhappy spirit, entered my body. But maybe it is knowing what the Seer intends, and at the same time seeing all these people buying and selling and yelling that they're being cheated—it makes one wonder how the Seer can ever succeed."

"He cannot," Bunem said simply.

"Surely you have not turned against him," said Hirsh Leib, astounded. "Not you."

"I told him that good cannot come from evil," said Rabbi Bunem, "no matter what, and that we Jews have no business in the affairs of emperors, tsars, and kings. The only king we need to concern ourselves with is the King of Heaven, Blessed be His name."

"And what did he say?" asked Hirsh Leib.

"What do you think, my friend? Our teacher said he understood. What does the Great Seer not understand? He asked only that I not interfere, and, of course, I gave my word."

"And will you try to talk me out of joining him?" asked Hirsh Leib.

"You? Talk you out of something?" Bunem laughed. "You, Hirsh Leib, are like one of your horses. Once you get the bit in your teeth, nothing can turn you, no one is strong enough to pull back your reins. I would not waste my breath. And anyway," said Bunem, "perhaps I am wrong and the Seer is right. I pray it is so."

"I, too, pray for that. Tell me, apothecary, do you know where I can find him? I'm told he is not home, not in the study house, and I wanted to tell him that Lelov and Rymanov will be here soon."

"Well," said Bunem, "I don't know for sure, but if I were looking for the Seer, I would go west down the Old Road, past Berel's tavern, back past the *rebbe*'s *hoyf* and the mill. Walk a little more, and you will see a small hill rising out of the forest. My guess would be that there's where you will find Rebbe Yitzhak, smoking his pipe and looking out over the town. Everyone calls it the Seer's Hill because it is his favorite place."

"Thank you, Reb Bunem," said Hirsh Leib. "Will I see you this afternoon at the *rebbe*'s *shtibl*? Will you be sharing his *sukkah*?"

"If I can squeeze past all the Hasidim trying to get a crumb from his plate, you'll see me there. Tell him I have saved some excellent Turkish tobacco for him. *Gut yontif*, Hirsh Leib." Happy holiday.

Hirsh Leib went off in search of his *rebbe*. He headed out the Old Road, past Berel's tavern (resisting the urge to stop for a quick glass), the inn, and the mill, and soon enough, where the tree line began, he came to a small hill. The sun was now directly overhead, and Hirsh Leib shaded his eyes, peering up the hill. He saw a thin stream of smoke, and then he saw the Seer.

Hirsh Leib waved, unsure of whether the *rebbe* had seen him or not, and began climbing. He had to watch his step, for the path was strewn with rocks and fallen branches. Reaching a clear spot halfway up the hill, he looked up, and for a moment he thought he saw two people standing behind the Seer: a stout woman in a colorful dress with a fur wrapped around her neck and a tall, beardless, strangely dressed but somehow familiar man. Hirsh Leib blinked, and when he looked again, they were gone.

He saw the Seer gesture to him with his clay pipe, and Hirsh Leib resumed climbing. He shook his head. Truly Lublin was a place of mystery, a place, he told himself, where miracles can happen and will happen. In a few minutes he found himself standing in front of his teacher, the *Zaddik*, the Seer of Lublin.

35

The Market Square
Lublin
Tuesday, October 12

Hirsh Leib's thoughts were whirling as he returned from the Seer's hill, and he hungered for the brandy he had left in his saddlebag. He could not get the diamond, or the story the Seer had told him about it, out of his mind. How casually the Seer had taken it from his cloak, as if it were a thing of no account instead of a star that had fallen from heaven.

One night, the *rebbe* had told him, he had left the study house to say the blessing for the new moon under the stars, as it is written. It was very late, and the Seer was alone. When he cast his eyes down from the night sky, they fell upon a strange plant he had never before seen. Something told him to pull it up, and he did. Tangled up in its roots was the diamond.

He had never seen such a gem, he told Hirsh Leib, and as he held it, it seemed as if it contained all the stars in all the seven heavens.

Hirsh Leib knew, of course, that the Seer could see from one end of the world to the other. One of his eyes was larger than the other, and Hirsh Leib knew that with that eye the Seer could see from the beginning of the world to the end and know the history of a man's soul from Adam to the coming of the Messiah.

But try as he would, the Seer said, he could not see to whom this diamond belonged, nor could he tell anything about its past or future. It seemed to him to be the loneliest object in the universe, and that had made him afraid. He ran into the house, he said, and woke up Khaye, his wife. "Look, my dear," he had said to her. "Look what I have found in the earth. Who could have planted such a treasure?"

"Who knows?" Khaye had said. "Perhaps some rich man seeking penance. Maybe it is a secret *pidyan*, an offering to you. You know, secret charity is best."

The Seer told Hirsh Leib how Khaye then praised the Lord and began speaking of all the things they could purchase with the stone: new linens for the table, new Sabbath plates, new dresses. Before he could stop her, she was already talking about fixing the windows in the study and building a new coop for the chickens.

Hirsh Leib had laughed. He'd known what the Seer would say next. "I told her," the Seer said, "that we had no business with such a treasure. I told her I would give the stone to the *kahal*, the town's governors, and they would decide how best to use it to help the community."

So the next day, the Seer said, he went to the *kahal*, which sat in a big brick building next to the market square, and gave them the diamond. Of course, they were overjoyed.

"They weighed it," the Seer said, "and they told me it was seventy-two carats." The Seer paused and looked at Hirsh Leib expectantly.

"Two times thirty-six," said Hirsh Leib, who was always good with Gematria, the study of holy numbers.

"Yes," the Seer said. "Two times the thirty-six unknown holy men for whose sake the Lord preserves the world, the Lamedvovniks. This is when I started thinking that this was a magic stone."

But the Seer said nothing, and the men of the *kahal* kissed his hand and talked about building a new synagogue and a new *yeshiva*. Some of the money, they told the Seer, could be used to bribe the *porets*, the nobleman, Prince Adam Jerzy Czartoryski, to protect the Jews of Lublin against his brother and the endless pogroms.

The treasurer of the *kahal*, the Seer said, put the diamond in his safe and planned the very next day to take a boat up the Vistula to Danzig, where he thought he could get a good price for it.

"But that night," said the Seer, "again at midnight, when I arose to pray in the study house, there was the diamond, lying right next to the holy scrolls."

Again the Seer tried to see the past and future of the stone, and again he failed. Perhaps, he thought, it has been sent by an evil angel to tempt me, and that is why I can't see its history; it is cloaked by the *Tayvil*, the No-Good-One.

When dawn came, the Seer told Hirsh Leib, he took the stone outside the *eyrev*—the wire that defined the area within which men could legally carry objects on the Sabbath—and buried it. Later that morning the men of the *kahal* came to him and told him that a thief had stolen the stone from the treasurer's safe.

" 'No,' I told them," the Seer told Hirsh Leib, " 'the diamond flew back to me, and I have disposed of it. Think of it no more. It was not meant for us.' "

But that night, the Seer said, when he went to pray, there it was again.

"So," the Seer said, "I remembered what my teacher, Rebbe Elimelekh said: The Lord does not play dice. By that he meant that there are no accidents in the world. So I thought to myself: I am not supposed to give this diamond to the *kahal*, and thereby to charity, although the widows and orphans and young scholars could certainly use the help. And I am not supposed to throw it away, although that is what my deepest self tells me to do. So I asked the Lord what to do.

"That night, I did not sleep," the Seer continued. "I prayed, and studied, and stared at this diamond you see in my hand. But as dawn broke, I fell into a light sleep and began to dream. In my dream I saw the diamond, and inside the diamond I saw an army marching into battle under a hot sun. I saw a general on a horse leading this army through steep mountains. I saw the army come through a pass, and beneath them was a shining plain, and beyond that plain was the Holy City of Jerusalem.

"When I awoke, my friend," the Seer said to Hirsh Leib, "I knew that the general was of Gog and Magog, and the plain was Armageddon. And I knew what the diamond was for."

And when the Seer had told Hirsh Leib, and sworn him to silence, Hirsh Leib thought him mad.

Now Hirsh Leib looked up and saw that he was in front of Neshe's soup kitchen on Tailor Street, just outside the market square, where all of Lublin's tailors drank and snacked between jobs. You could get anything at Neshe's, from herring to sour pickles, from cakes to candy, from vodka to brandy— the last two being most important to Hirsh Leib and to the tailors, a rowdy crowd whose *khevreh*, or guild, was full of drunkards.

Hirsh Leib very much wanted a drink, but his way was blocked by a crowd of tailors watching a peasant beat his horse. Most of the tailors were cheering him on, but even though some people in the crowd were yelling for him to stop, the peasant was obviously a powerful man, and nobody even thought of trying to restrain him. Besides, interfering with a Christian, even a drunken peasant, meant, at best, dealing with the police and the civil courts, and that would undoubtedly result in a heavy fine that the *kahal* would have to pay.

Or the peasant's friends might burn Lublin to the ground.

But Hirsh Leib did not care what might happen; all he could hear were the cries of the horse begging him for help. The *zaddik* rushed over to the peasant and plucked the whip out of his hand as if taking a toy from a fractious child. The tailors shut up, stunned at the Hasid's boldness. The peasant, too, was momentarily stunned, but then he ran at Hirsh Leib, swinging his fists and cursing.

Hirsh Leib stepped to the side. As the peasant, made

clumsy by vodka and fury, stumbled by him, Hirsh Leib swung his arm and caught the peasant in the back of the neck, sending him sprawling facedown into the mud and horse droppings. The peasant scrambled to his feet and again rushed Hirsh Leib, who again knocked him down, this time with a blow to the side of his head.

This is a rabbi I like, thought Moyshe ben Areyn, whose family had been butchers for as long as anyone in Lublin could remember, and who, like his grandfather, father, and brothers, was a huge, powerful man. The ben Areyns were not *shoykhetim*, slaughterers; they were both insufficiently learned and pious for that. They were, rather, meat brokers, who bought the animals from Lublin's several slaughterers and then butchered them and sold the meat in their shop. Now, Moyshe burst from the crowd and tackled the peasant as he was trying to get up a third time.

Seeing ben Areyn come to the aid of the stranger, several tailors joined the butcher, piling atop the screaming peasant, kicking and punching and pulling his hair.

"Stop!" cried Hirsh Leib, trying to drag the men off the beaten peasant. "In the name of God, stop. You're killing him."

"Better for you if we do, Rabbi," said Moyshe Areyn, standing up and dusting himself off. "I know this *momzer*, this bastard. His name is Anders Shmielewicz, and if he tells the police what you've done, you won't get to dance with the Torah on Simkhas Torah; you'll be dancing at the end of a Cossack's saber."

"What should we do with the pig eater?" asked one of the tailors kneeling on the now unconscious peasant's chest.

"And what should we do with his horse?" another asked.

"These are weighty questions, Rabbi," said Moyshe Areyn, turning to Hirsh Leib, "and perhaps it would be better for you if you went about your business while we puzzle them out."

"I appreciate your help," Hirsh Leib said, "but I cannot allow any further harm to come to this man."

"That's a pious sentiment, Rabbi," said Moyshe Areyn, "but I assure you, you need not fear for this drunkard. We are not animals. We'll just take him into the forest, and when he wakes up in his own shit and piss, he won't remember a thing. He never does."

"I have your word?" asked Hirsh Leib.

"As a Jew," Moyshe Areyn said. "I like you, Rabbi. You are *eygene mentshen*, one of the people. What's your name?"

Hirsh Leib was about to answer when he heard someone shouting, "Make way for the *rov*," and a short, fat rabbi, gorgeously dressed in a dark suit of Polish cut and a broad-brimmed black hat, burst through the crowd.

"What's going on here?" asked Rabbi Chaim, the official town rabbi who was appointed by Prince Adam Czartoryski for his pliability and not for his scholarship, and who many in Lublin regarded as both a fool and an informer. "What *aveyreh*, what sin, is being committed? What happened to this man?" Rabbi Chaim asked, seeing Shmielewicz lying unconscious in the street. "Another outrage of the Hasidim? You," he said to Hirsh Leib, "who are you?"

"I think, Chaim the Wise," Moyshe Areyn said sarcastically, "that he is a Lamedvovnik."

"I am not speaking to you, Moyshe Areyn," said Rabbi Chaim. "You, I will deal with later. Now I am speaking to this troublemaking Hasid."

Moyshe Areyn gestured behind his back, and while the rabbi was staring at Hirsh Leib, the tailors dragged Anders Shmielewicz into Neshe's kitchen and then out the back, throwing in a few kicks for good measure.

"Well, I am waiting," Rabbi Chaim said to Hirsh Leib.

"I am Hirsh Leib of Orlik."

"So you think you can come to our *shtot* and riot in our streets? No doubt you have come to Lublin to get drunk with Rebbe Yitzhak and his followers."

"I would rather get drunk with the Seer than pray with a *misnagid*," Hirsh Leib said angrily, recognizing Rabbi Chaim as one of those who hated the Hasidim for maintaining that common, uneducated Jews could be as righteous as learned rabbis. Accusing the Hasidim of drunkenness was a frequent slur used by the *misnagdim*.

"Then go to your *rebbe*'s *hoyf* and riot there," said Rabbi

Chaim. "I order you to cease troubling the peace of our streets. I have half a mind to report you to the police."

"Half a mind is right," Moyshe Areyn muttered, and the crowd around him laughed.

"What did you say, butcher?" demanded the rabbi.

"I said, Rabbi," Moyshe Areyn responded, "it is you who are troubling the peace. We have no problem here."

"But what about this man?" asked Rabbi Chaim, turning back to where the peasant was lying a moment ago.

"What man, Rabbi?" asked Moyshe Areyn.

"But, but . . ."

"You see, Rabbi? All is peaceful in Lublin."

"You, Moyshe ben Areyn," said Rabbi Chaim, sputtering, "are a *gonef*, and I assure you that the *kahal* will be looking into the prices you and your brothers charge. It's a scandal."

As Rabbi Chaim stalked off, Hirsh Leib said to Moyshe Areyn, "I'm sorry for the trouble I've caused you."

"No trouble," said Moyshe Areyn. "That man is an ignoramus. He is also unimportant. Threaten me with the *kahal*, will he? Don't I save the best cuts of meat for those *balebatim*, those big shots? And don't their wives all know it? They won't do anything to me; their wives won't allow it.

"But I'd better take care of our drunken friend, and you'd better go off to your *rebbe* in case our *rov* does run to the police. Although I am not a Hasid, I am grateful to Rabbi Yitzhak for the business he brings to Lublin. Tell him that Moyshe ben Areyn thanks him, and begs him to include all the ben Areyns in his prayers."

"I will," said Hirsh Leib, getting back on his horse and riding back to the Seer's *hoyf*. He regretted striking the Pole and causing him pain, but the Torah forbade any man from tormenting any living being.

And how could someone be so cruel as to beat a horse? thought Hirsh Leib, patting his own mount's neck. A horse lived to do his master's bidding, just as a pious man lived to do the Holy One's, blessed is He. And most horses, he reflected, do it better than most men.

Perhaps, thought Hirsh Leib as he stopped in front of the

Seer's courtyard, Lublin is not the *Gan Eyden*, the Garden of Eden, I had imagined.

36
The Seer's Hoyf
Lublin
Tuesday, October 12

The wooden gate of the Seer of Lublin's *hoyf* was open as Hirsh Leib led his horse into the courtyard crowded with Hasids arguing and chatting while chickens ran and squawked among them. Directly in front of Hirsh Leib was the Seer's living quarters—a low wooden building with no windows in front and only one small door. To Hirsh Leib's right, attached at a ninety-degree angle to the living quarters, was the *besmedresh*, the study house, which doubled as the *rebbe*'s *shtibl* and which also contained a kitchen and a dining room for the Sabbath feasts the *zaddik* shared with his Hasidim. To the left were the stables and chicken coops. In front of them was a small vegetable garden in which beets and chard and radishes were now being trampled by hordes of heedless Hasidim ecstatic at being so close to the great Rebbe Yitzhak, the Seer of Lublin.

After tying up his horse, and after pushing and shoving his way through the grumbling crowd of bearded men, Hirsh Leib knocked on the Seer's door. It was opened immediately by a pale young man with a wispy, pubescent blond beard. "We have already told you not to disturb us," the youngster said with more than a little heat. "The *rebbe* sees no one today."

"I am Hirsh Leib of Orlik. The *rebbe* sent for me."

"So that makes you special? The *rebbe* sent for everybody. He sent for the whole world," said the boy.

"No, he sent for me particularly," Hirsh Leib said. "He requests my presence."

"So, tell me what you want to tell him."

"Don't be so proud, young man," Hirsh Leib said angrily. "Your beard is new. If you'd like to see it grow into a man's full beard, go tell the *rebbe* that I am here."

"Wait," the boy said, rudely shutting the door in Hirsh Leib's face.

Hirsh Leib sighed, turned his back, and leaned against the door, looking out over the courtyard. Sometimes, he thought, I prefer the company of men like that big butcher, *heymishe Yidn*, homey Jews, to these overeducated, milk-fed *yeshiva* boys. Grant me patience, Lord, Hirsh Leib prayed silently. My temper will be the death of me.

Smoke rose from the kitchen to Hirsh Leib's right, curling into the blue, almost cloudless sky. His heart, stirred up by the incident in town, began to grow melancholy.

He thought of his wife, Soreh, and his two little girls back in Orlik. He and Soreh had parted angrily. Again, she had said to him, you leave us to fend for ourselves. And what if something should happen to you? What will become of us? You're selfish, my husband.

It's you who are selfish, Hirsh Leib had replied, taking a great swallow of brandy and then riding out of Orlik faster than he had needed to.

My temper, he thought. Soreh is a good wife. If I had taken a moment and allowed her anger to cool, we could have parted with a kiss instead of harsh words.

Always my temper. I could have reasoned with that peasant. Or I could have taken the whip away without striking him. Instead I fought in the street like an animal, or a Pole.

And in Orlik they call you a *zaddik*? What nonsense. You threaten a young man trying to serve the Seer the best he can, trying to protect his peace from all these pilgrims? Shame on you, Hirsh Leib.

The door opening behind him interrupted his painful self-examination. "Come in. Please, sir, come in," said the young man. "A thousand pardons, Rabbi," he said. "I did not know you. When I told the Seer that I had left you waiting, he grew angry with me. 'Don't you know a *zaddik* when you see one?' he said to me. 'Have you been wasting your time in our house?' "

"It's all right," said Hirsh Leib. "What is your name, my friend?"

"Motl, sir. My name is Motl. Please forgive me. Truthfully, sir," the young man continued, "a great sorrow seems to be troubling the *rebbe*'s soul these days. All these Hasidim come to Lublin from all over the world, but he sees no one but a few old friends. He hears no requests from the people of Lublin, he holds no audiences and gives no advice. Marriages go unarranged, and business deals wait for the return of his good humor. He does not even celebrate the Sabbath with his family. He prays alone in his study, or late at night on his hill, and when one speaks to him either he does not hear or he answers angrily.

"So, you see, Rabbi Leib, when you said you wanted to see the *rebbe*, I thought—"

"Enough, Motl. It is I who should apologize to you for letting my anger cloud my understanding, and both of us should apologize to God for disturbing the peace of the *rebbe*'s home with our pride. I will tell the Seer that the fault was mine, not yours."

"Thank you, Reb Leib. But, I insist, the fault was mine. Come, come, follow me. I will take you to the Seer. He is in his study with Rabbi David, Rabbi Naftali, and Rabbi Menachem Mendel."

Motl led Hirsh Leib through the Seer's home with its narrow halls, its wooden floors worn smooth by many feet, and its low, smoke-darkened ceilings. The voices from the courtyard filtered in through the walls, but still the house seemed unnaturally quiet and lifeless, like a forest before a storm.

The house is waiting for something to happen, thought Hirsh Leib. It is waiting nervously.

Motl opened a door at the end of a long hallway, and Hirsh Leib stepped through. Inside, the Seer of Lublin stood at a wrought-iron reading stand, his hand resting lightly upon the pages of a holy scroll. Standing around him were Rabbis

David of Lelov, Menachem Mendel of Rymanov, and Naftali of Roptchitz. The windows that opened to the fields and the distant mountains behind the *rebbe*'s *hoyf* were shuttered. To the left and right of the conspirators were polished tables upon which dozens of scented beeswax candles blazed. And although the men stood still, the guttering candles made their shadows dance crazily on the whitewashed walls.

"Ho, Hirsh Leib," said Naftali, a short, slight young man with sparkling eyes, rosy cheeks, and a beard the color of sunset, "I did not see our Motl with you. Did you give him a good beating for keeping you waiting? I fear he will not survive it. Should we say the mourner's *kaddish* for him right now?

"Our friend Hirsh Leib," Naftali said, turning back to the Seer, "is as strong as one of his beloved horses and, sometimes, as wise."

"You should be as wise as my horses, Naftali," Hirsh Leib bantered back. "They, at least, always know where they're going. But you, I never know where you're headed. And neither do you."

Hirsh Leib and Naftali embraced. Hirsh Leib treasured Naftali for his wit. No one could resist his charm, not even the Seer, who often scolded him for his constant joking.

"I am your balance," Naftali would always say then, "the happy sun to your gloomy moon. You take everything seriously, and so I must take nothing seriously. In this way, we make one whole man."

But Hirsh Leib knew that Naftali took his lightheartedness very seriously indeed, and the effort it took him to find joy and humor in life often plunged him into the deepest melancholy. At such times he would withdraw from the world, and for weeks no one in Roptchitz would see him.

In turn, Hirsh Leib embraced David of Lelov and Mendel of Rymanov. Both of them had been students of Rabbi Elimelekh, and both had followed the Seer when he left their teacher to set up his own court in Lublin. But although while David considered himself one of the Seer's disciples, Menachem Mendel still called Elimelekh, may his memory be blessed, his teacher.

Both David and Menachem Mendel were older than the Seer, even though only Mendel looked it with his white beard, crooked back, emaciated neck, sunken cheeks, and rheumy eyes. David of Lelov's eyes, on the other hand, gleamed with a fiery light that Hirsh Leib sometimes thought was a mark of holiness and sometimes saw as the sign of possession by a dark, violent spirit. Of the four of them, it was David who fasted most, lived in the direst poverty, and practiced the most rigid asceticism. Particularly, he denied himself sleep.

"How can I serve the Lord when I am sleeping?" David would ask. "I will be dead soon enough, and then I can sleep all I want." And when the Seer would tell him that by sleeping one took care of the body that God had given him, David would reply that he was only renting his poor body for a little time, and what renter spent time improving his landlord's property? David's soul, however, had been entrusted to him by God, may His name be praised, as his responsibility for eternity, and David could not let a moment pass without bathing and oiling it in His holy word.

Finally Hirsh Leib turned to face Rebbe Yitzhak. As always, even as he did this morning when he met Rebbe Yitzhak on the hill, Hirsh Leib felt a shudder of love mingled with fear course through him.

The Seer was tall, well over six feet, and he always stood absolutely straight. His face was immensely long and his forehead hugely high. Most extraordinary were his eyes. Both were a wintry gray, but one was significantly larger than the other, and it was with this eye that the Seer could look into a man's soul and read everything therein, no matter how well hidden. It was with this eye that the Seer could see from one end of the world to the other, from ages gone by to epochs to come. And it was with this eye that years before the Seer had spotted a little Corsican lieutenant rising to prominence in the west and had known him to be the one foretold.

"I have received word that Prince Czartoryski has agreed to meet me," began the Seer. "He will carry our message to Napoleon."

"Do we not trust our own strength that we need the help of a Christian?" asked David of Lelov.

"Remember, David?" the Seer said. "Remember—what was it—fifteen years ago when we first heard of him? It was Purim, and he had called upon the Jews to come to his side to throw the Turk out of the Holy Land. Remember how I summoned you and Mendel, and I reminded you how Don Isaac Abarbarrel had said that the occupation of the land of Israel by strange peoples was caused by God in the nature of bait to catch the nations of Gog and Magog?

"And didn't we then join our holy intents even as his armies were fighting in the valley of Jezebel against the armies of the Sultan? And were not our efforts then in vain?"

"Perhaps," said Mendel of Rymanov, "the Frenchman is not the one. Perhaps we are mistaken."

"We are not mistaken," said the Seer.

"The *Maggid* believed we were wrong," Naftali said. "He asked, 'What have we to do with Frenchmen and Russians?' The *Maggid* said it was not for us to make what is wicked stronger. He said it was our duty only to oppose God's enemies. And Bunem agrees."

"The *Maggid* was a friend to the tsar," said Hirsh Leib.

"A friend of Alexander's?" said Naftali, laughing. "Our holy little *Maggid* and the tsar? Friends? I didn't know that. Tell me, Hirsh Leib, did they go riding together? Did they go hunting? Did they feast and get drunk and make sport with the tsarina?"

"You know what I mean, Naftali. The *Maggid* knew and feared the tsar," said Hirsh Leib. "He feared that if the tsar learned of what we were doing, he would unloose a pogrom that would be the death of us all."

"And so now we include this friend of the tsar's, this Czartoryski," said David of Lelov. "This indeed will be the death of us."

"We must bring the Frenchman to us," said the Seer, "and only Czartoryski can accomplish that."

"Napoleon is wicked," said Mendel.

"And what would you have the general of Gog be?" the Seer asked. "The world is poised between darkness and light. Is it not written, 'Strange is His work'? And is it not also written, 'Truly, Thou art a God who hides Himself'? So, where does He hide? In the light, where all can see? What sort of hiding is that? No, as it is written, 'He makes the darkness His hiding place.'

"Mendel, it is dreadful to seek Him there, but seek Him we must."

"It is written," said David of Lelov, " 'Lo, the storm wind of the Lord.' "

"The storm is supposed to come from the north," said Naftali. "A little thing, perhaps, but I thought I'd mention it."

"It is written, 'The storm wind blows according to His command,' " David said angrily.

"Shall we argue amongst ourselves?" asked the Seer. "Listen. God himself uses evil. Hatred, suffering, even murder—they prepare the way for the birth of the Messiah."

The men were silent. Hirsh Leib could hear his own heart beating. He noticed how the four of them had drawn closer, shoulder to shoulder, around the holy scrolls. Even Rabbi David, who hated to be touched.

"I see him," the Seer said slowly, his deep voice a hoarse whisper, his great eye wide and far-seeing.

"He has come from an island, and he has swum ashore.

"He was beaten back to an island, but he will return.

"First he was small and gaunt, but he puts on more and more flesh.

"He has fallen, but he will rise, rise again in his might.

"His legs are short, but his head is huge.

"He loves no one and desires to be loved by all.

"He calls himself the lion. But he is no lion. The sign of the scorpion is upon his head.

"He will sting the whole world to death, and then he will sting himself.

"His name is Ruin."

"Have our sages not warned us?" asked Naftali, his voice hoarse, his usually merry face filled with fear. "Do they not say, 'Seek not to press for the end'?"

"We will push him to Vienna!" said David of Lelov, his eyes blazing. "We will dance with God's Torah, and one hundred and twenty thousand prayers will push him on to

Moscow! And the people of Israel will march in his wake to
the Holy Land.''

Could it be? thought Hirsh Leib. Could it truly be? Can
the French emperor bring the Jews to the land of Zion? Well,
who says it cannot be done? In Lublin, miracles happen.

The Seer bowed his head and extended his hands left and
right. David of Lelov, wrapping his own hands in his *tallis*
to avoid the impure touch of flesh on flesh, took the Seer's
left hand, and Menachem Mendel took his right. Hirsh Leib
took Mendel's right hand, and Naftali took Hirsh Leib's left.
Joined in a circle, they prayed silently.

The night prayer came into Hirsh Leib's mind: ''Lord of
the World, I forgive everyone who has angered or hurt me or
committed a trespass against me. Let no man be punished on
my account.'' And then he asked the Lord to protect him
from the evil impulse, which even in this holy circle among
these holy men, Hirsh Leib felt to be close. Too close.

The *zaddikim* agreed to meet again for evening prayers,
and each took their leave. ''Reb Leib,'' said Naftali, casting
off his trepidations as one shrugged off a shawl when the sun
grew too warm, ''will you come with me to seek out Bunem
the apothecary? I miss him, and perhaps I can still convince
him to join us. If nothing else, he can tell us what goes on in
the great world. We can smoke his excellent tobacco and let
him buy us a glass of good brandy. I am sure Bunem knows
the best places to drink.''

''Yes, Hirsh Leib, go with Naftali,'' said the Seer. ''But
first, Naftali, we need a moment alone with our friend. Then
he will join you.''

Naftali left the room, and Hirsh Leib was alone with his
teacher.

''You will come with me tonight, my friend, to meet with
Prince Czartoryski,'' said the Seer. ''Tonight we will give
him the diamond to give to Napoleon.''

The Seer reached into the folds of his flowing silk robe and
removed the jewel.

Again Hirsh Leib stared at it in wonder. It was the size of
a goose's egg, and it seemed as if the light from all the candles

in the room were flickering inside it, multiplied a hundred times. And each tiny point of light was surrounded by a minute rainbow. Hirsh Leib could not tear his eyes away from it.

"We must bring Napoleon to us," said the Seer. "He must come here, to Lublin, on *erev* Simkhas Torah. He must stand before the Torah and let the strength of the Lord enter his limbs. He must enter into a covenant with Israel, leading us out of Poland like a new Moses, opening to us the Holy Land. This diamond is the bait that will hook him. And if he is truly the one, then I will give him the stone, and it, along with our prayers and the Holy One's right arm, will purchase for him the victory that will be our redemption.

"This I share with you, Hirsh Leib, and with you alone. You are the strongest. Tonight, when I go to meet Czartory-ski, your strength will be by our side."

Hirsh Leib looked up into the Seer's face, and despite the Seer's words, he saw uncertainty, sorrow, and even fear there, a fear he felt reflected and magnified in his own soul even as the diamond reflected and magnified the light of the candles.

"If?" asked Hirsh Leib. "If he is the one? You have not seen it?"

"I have seen both victory and defeat. I have seen the desert bloom, and I have seen the desert blasted. Always, I have seen death. I have seen such terrible things, Hirsh Leib, that I cannot speak of them."

"How can we do this, then?" asked Hirsh Leib. "How can we take such a terrible step if we are not sure?"

"We leap into the darkness," answered the Seer, "because the fire rages at our back."

37

Berel's Tavern
Lublin
Wednesday, October 13

Later, as he sat in Berel's tavern listening to Naftali and Bunem argue about whether what was happening at the Congress of Vienna was good or bad for the Jews, Hirsh Leib kept thinking about Prince Czartoryski's gloves.

They had been, Hirsh Leib was sure, pigskin. And when he had handed the Seer's diamond to the prince, and his hand had touched the nobleman's glove, it seemed to him as if it were covered with butter, it was so smooth and soft. For a moment, before Czartoryski returned it to him, the stone had rested in the aristocrat's palm, catching the moonlight, and Hirsh Leib had shuddered thinking of this jewel, upon which rode so many of their holy plans, sitting on the skin of a pig covering the hand of a Christian prince.

Why hadn't the stone fled from the touch of pig? Hirsh Leib thought now. Wasn't it a Jewish stone? Soft pigskin covering the hands of a Polish pig. And my hands, too, are unclean. I am unclean.

I'm drunk, Hirsh Leib realized. I'm drunk again.

Rabbi Bunem, ripping off a hunk of brown bread from the loaf on their table, was saying that the Austrian Metternich was good for the Jews because he would keep Poland tied to Russia, and the tsar was better than the Polish *poretsim*, who were all bloodthirsty drunkards.

Rabbi Naftali, stuffing a slice of herring into his mouth, said that Metternich, and Talleyrand, too, were part of the old order, and that the men meeting in Vienna to divide up Europe were trying to turn back the clock and undo the French Revolution. And that this was terrible for the Jews.

"Don't be so naive, Naftali," said Bunem. "Unlike you, I have seen the world. I have walked the streets of Paris. You think the French care about the Jews? You think their revolution was about the Jews? Napoleon used the Jews, and"—Bunem lowered his voice—"he is still using them, as you know very well."

What are they saying? thought Hirsh Leib, staring into the amber brandy in his glass and then closing his burning eyes. If they had only seen what I have seen tonight, he thought, they would realize that the noise of their silly argument is about to be drowned out by the trumpets of the Lord.

Hirsh Leib and Rebbe Yitzhak had stood silently shivering under the cold stars on the Seer's hill, watching Prince Adam Jerzy Czartoryski, his long blond hair flowing down his back, lead his horse through the brush. When the prince reached the *rebbe* and his disciple, Hirsh Leib took the reins of Czartoryski's horse from his hands.

The Seer had prepared Hirsh Leib for this meeting. He had told him that Prince Adam was a friend to the Jews. Or, at least, as good a friend as the Jews could expect. He also told Hirsh Leib about the prince's brother, Count Josep, who hated the Jews and was always stirring up the peasants against them.

Several years ago, the Seer told Hirsh Leib, at the prince's son's baptism, Adam had told his brother the story of how the *Maggid* of Koznitz had helped him. Adam had been married to the Princess Grushinka for six years, and they had had no children. Adam had gone to the priests, gone to the physicians, and finally, in desperation, he had asked the Seer of Lublin what to do. The Seer told him to visit Rabbi Israel, the *Maggid*, who, the Seer said, was a wonder worker.

So Czartoryski rode all day and all night and arrived in Koznitz to meet the *Maggid*, a tiny, feeble-looking man who, from birth, was so sickly and weak that he spent most of his life in bed, wrapped in warm rabbitskins, rising only to pray.

The prince told the *Maggid* of his wife's barrenness, and in a small, almost inaudible whisper, the *Maggid* agreed to pray for him, assuring him that when he returned to Lublin, his wife would conceive. And here, Czartoryski had said to his brother, holding up his infant son, still dripping from the holy water of the baptismal font, is the fruit.

Josep, whose own strapping four-year-old son—already something of a bully like his father—was standing by his side, proposed a bet. "Let's go see this Jew, this so-called holy man," he had said, "and I'll show you he doesn't know apples from fish. If I'm right, you will give me your best hunting falcon."

"And what if you're wrong? What will you give me?" Adam had asked.

"I'll name my next son Adam."

So, said the Seer, they rode to Koznitz together, and Josep said to the *Maggid*, "Oh, holy Jew, I beg you. My son is sick; I fear he is dying. Please pray for him."

The *Maggid* said nothing, only closed his eyes. "Please," said Josep, winking at his brother, "please pray for my son."

The *Maggid* opened his eyes. "Go," he whispered sadly. "There's nothing I can do. Go quickly. Perhaps you will be in time to see your son while he still breathes."

The two brothers left, and all the way back Josep teased Adam and mocked the *Maggid*. But when they returned to the castle in the morning, Josep's son was dead. He had fallen off his horse and broken his neck.

From that time on, the Seer said, Josep had hated the Jews with a black, never-flagging passion.

Now Prince Adam Czartoryski addressed the Seer of Lublin. "Only for you would I come out so late on such a night, Rabbi," said Czartoryski. "You are well, I trust?"

"Yes, thank the Lord. And you also?"

"Very well."

"And your wife and son?"

"Yes, well, thank God."

"The Lord be praised."

"Yes. Well, Rabbi," said Czartoryski, "Lublin is certainly stuffed with your followers. I think tonight there are more Jews sleeping in Lublin than in any city in Poland. You must be pleased."

"It is the will of the Lord."

"Of course. Well, Rabbi," Czartoryski said jocularly,

"what are these affairs of state you wish to discuss, and why must we discuss them here, now, like conspirators?"

"You once told me, my lord, of your respect for the French emperor, Napoleon Bonaparte," said the Seer. "Do you respect him still?"

"No," Czartoryski said gravely. "He went mad. Anyway, Bonaparte is finished. He will die on that rock the English have sent him to."

Said the Seer, "Napoleon is in Warsaw."

"Nonsense."

"It is true."

"Some Jewish magic tells you this?" asked Czartoryski.

"The rabbi of Warsaw tells me this," said the Seer. "Napoleon is with his mistress, Countess Marie Waleska. He travels freely now. In disguise, of course."

Prince Adam Jerzy Czartoryski folded his arms across his chest. He thought the Jews a strange, somewhat repellent people, but he did not hate them. As far as he was concerned, the best of them were better company than most of the vain, foolish noblemen he spent much of his time avoiding; their rabbis were more trustworthy and probably more pious than most of the priests he knew, and the poorest, humblest Jew in Lublin was far more sophisticated than any of his peasants. The Jews, at least, could read. And they bathed from time to time.

Tsar Alexander, Czartoryski knew from their many conversations, felt the same way. The Jews, he often said, paid their taxes; they facilitated trade by providing loans to Christian merchants at reasonable rates of interest. Didn't Alexander himself keep a Jewish physician? Of course he did.

But Czartoryski knew that the tsar's relatively benign attitude toward the Jews was changing because of Napoleon. The last time Czartoryski had visited the tsar, meeting him in his summer palace on the Black Sea, Alexander had been fretting about Napoleon, exiled to Elba only a few months before. At one time Alexander had been enthralled by the French emperor. But with Napoleon's renegade minister, the clubfooted Talleyrand, whispering in one ear and the Russian Orthodox priests whispering in the other, Alexander had come to believe that, if not the anti-Christ himself, Napoleon was certainly an enemy of Christianity. And, of course, Alexander could never forgive Napoleon for burning Moscow, forgetting that it was he himself who had given the order to put the holy city to the torch.

Now the tsar was saying that the Jews, especially the Rothschilds, were secretly financing a new Bonaparte adventure, preparing to return him to his throne in Paris. Didn't Napoleon in 1799 call upon the Jews to help him in his wars against the Turk? In 1806 didn't Napoleon give the Jews of France a year's grace in the payment of all their debts to their landlords? And hadn't the Jews in return declared France a homeland, promising to defend it unto the death?

For God's sake, the tsar had raged, that fat, arrogant, dwarfish Corsican who dared call himself an emperor gave the Prussian Jews all the rights of citizenship just six years ago.

Prince Czartoryski himself had mixed feelings about Napoleon. Years ago, when Czartoryski met the first consul, he had been bowled over by Bonaparte's energy and vision. This man, Czartoryski had thought, must be followed. And in the ensuing years Bonaparte had teased Czartoryski over and over again with the promise of his support for Polish independence. But then he would conclude another pact with Alexander, and the subject of Poland would be forgotten.

Now Czartoryski thought of Napoleon as a glorious ruin—a missed opportunity—and, unlike the tsar, he did not think the emperor would ever return from Elba.

Until this moment. What was this Jew saying? Bonaparte in Warsaw? Less than 150 kilometers away?

Czartoryski knew, of course, how infatuated Napoleon had been with Marie Waleska when Czartoryski had introduced her to him in Warsaw seven years ago, after Bonaparte had taken most of Poland from the tsar. Indeed, Czartoryski had coached the eighteen-year-old Countess on how to flatter her French conqueror. Czartoryski had told her that she could be the Polish Esther. As Esther had saved the Jews from Haman by seducing King Ahaseurus, Marie could take Bonaparte into her bed and convince him to grant Poland its freedom.

I underestimated him, Czartoryski recalled now. Yes, Marie had bewitched him. How could she not? Even today she is known as the most beautiful woman in Poland. And seven years ago she seemed a goddess come to earth, her hair the color of the sun, her skin the color of the dawn. Yes, she took Napoleon to her bed and bore him a son. But the French emperor had not allowed his pleasures to interfere with his politics.

And that must still be the case, thought Czartoryski. If Bonaparte is in Warsaw, it is not just to lie in Marie Waleska's lovely white arms.

"Even if what you say is true, Rabbi," said Czartoryski, "why are you telling me?"

"Because I know that you are a patriot, my lord," said the Seer, "and today Poland's future is in the hands of the Austrians and the tsar. And you know that they will never grant Poland its freedom."

"So? What is this to you, Rabbi?" asked Czartoryski.

"I am telling you, my lord," the Seer said, "that Napoleon has returned. He is gathering strength. A man who would help him now will reap a rich reward for his country."

"You are speaking treason, Rabbi. You should not involve yourself in such matters, in politics. You forget yourself. Go back to your temple, go back to your prayers, and I will forget this conversation. This world is not your world. If you play in this world without armies, without power, you and all your people will be crushed."

"I have the power of the Lord, blessed be His name," said the Seer. "What armies are as great as His? What power greater? And the Lord gave me this"—the Seer brought out the diamond from beneath his cloak—"to bring Napoleon here to Lublin. Reb Leib," said the Seer, "give the stone to the prince."

Hirsh Leib took the diamond from Rebbe Yitzhak and handed it to Prince Czartoryski, his hand brushing the prince's yellow pigskin glove.

"I beg you," said the Seer, "go to Warsaw. Go to Napoleon. Tell him of this treasure. Tell him it is his if he will come to Lublin to receive it from my hand. In six days, when we remove the Torahs from the synagogue and take them into the streets, if he will meet me by the steps of the great *shul*, the diamond will be his. Tell him that the Jews bless his endeavors, and that the God of the Jews blesses him also. Poland, Prince Czartoryski, I leave to you."

Prince Adam Czartoryski stared at the diamond in his hand. Could such a stone be real? He had never seen its match, not even among all the treasures of Moscow and Paris. Even in the darkness it seemed to shine, gathering the light of the moon and stars. And this jewel belonged to a Jew in his own town of Lublin?

"Where did you come by this stone, Rabbi?" Czartoryski asked sternly.

"It was a gift of the Lord's, blessed be He," said the Seer. "As your son was a gift. And as your country's freedom will be a gift."

Czartoryski thought of Alexander, flush with his victory over Napoleon, and how when Czartoryski had tried to bring up the restoration of the grand duchy of Warsaw, Alexander had brushed the subject aside. Later, the tsar had said to Czartoryski, we'll discuss it later. And then, last June, in Vienna, Alexander's representatives had agreed to divide up Poland with Austria and Prussia. What the rabbi had said was true: Poland would never receive justice from the hands of the men in Vienna.

"Will you do this, Prince Adam Czartoryski?" demanded the Seer.

"Hirsh Leib, Hirsh Leib," said Bunem, shaking him. "Do you find our conversation so boring that you have fallen asleep, or have you had too much brandy?"

Hirsh Leib opened his eyes. The stars above the Seer's Hill were replaced by the smoking candles of Berel's tavern.

"You are a fool, apothecary," Hirsh Leib said angrily. "And you, too, Naftali, a fool. You babble about Metternich and Talleyrand and Vienna and Moscow. We are the center of the world right now. Lublin is the center of the world. And this is where God's plan is being formed. Right here in holy Lublin. Not in Vienna or Moscow or Warsaw, where the

Christians roast pigs and have orgies and sleep with their mistresses.''

"Our friend is drunk," said Rabbi Bunem. "We'll take him to my home, Naftali. We're going home, Reb Leib."

"I'll have another brandy," Hirsh Leib said.

"I don't think that's a good idea, my friend," said Naftali.

"You don't think, you don't think," Hirsh Leib said scornfully. "You want to go home? Go home. You too, Bunem. Both of you, go home. Sleep. Sleep while the world spins. Sleep while the pigs fornicate. I'll have a brandy with our brother Berel, an honest Jew, a learned Jew. Berel," Hirsh Leib shouted to the tavernkeeper, who was sitting slumped over by the door. "Wake up, Berel. In the name of the Holy One, wake up. Have a last brandy with Hirsh Leib of Orlik."

Hirsh Leib threw off the hands of his friends and staggered over to Berel, shaking him violently. As Berel blinked awake, sputtering, Goldeh, his wife, came down the stairs from their rooms above the tavern.

"Shame, shame on you," shouted Goldeh, a stout, red-faced woman. "What are you doing? Go home, you crazy men. Go home to your wives and children and leave us in peace."

"Hirsh Leib," said Naftali, pulling him from behind. "Please, let's go away from here."

Hirsh Leib spun around and struck Naftali across the face with the back of his hand. Naftali fell in a heap to the tavern's floor.

"You murderer!" Goldeh screamed. "You crazy drunkard! Look what you've done. You murderer."

Hirsh Leib looked down at his friend in horror. He closed his eyes and saw, quite vividly, a small boy, a black-skinned boy, lying on the ground, bleeding. A man was standing over him, rocking and weeping. Hirsh Leib felt the man's sobs in his own chest, as if it were he himself who was crying. Hirsh Leib opened his eyes.

Naftali rolled over onto his knees, his head hanging. Then he vomited bread, brandy, and herring. Bunem kneeled down next to Naftali and stroked his head.

"He's all right," said Bunem, looking up at Hirsh Leib.

"Go home. Go home, Hirsh Leib, and for the sake of heaven ask God to give you rest from the Evil Impulse."

"I beg your forgiveness, Reb Naftali," said Hirsh Leib. "I, I am not myself."

"Naftali forgives you," said Bunem. "Isn't that true, Naftali?"

Naftali, gasping, nodded.

"Now go home, Hirsh Leib. We know it was not you who struck our friend. It was the Evil Impulse. Not you."

Hirsh Leib covered his face with his hands and staggered out of Berel's tavern into the cold. The street was quiet, the square empty. The sky above was black and filled with stars.

What is wrong with me? thought Hirsh Leib. What is happening to me? Was the boy I saw Naftali as a child? Why was his skin black? Is it because my deed is black? And who was the man?

Hirsh Leib forced himself to think of the Torah. He saw the page of Exodus before his eyes: "He who raises his hand against another is called *rasha*, wicked." And in a hoarse, trembling voice, Hirsh Leib recited aloud to the empty square, " 'And he said to the *rasha*: Wherefore wilt thou strike thy neighbor?' "

This was not like hitting that drunken peasant who was beating his horse, thought Hirsh Leib, shame and remorse rising up in his throat, choking him. It is forbidden to cause needless pain to a dumb animal, and I struck the Pole only to protect myself. That is permitted. But now I have committed a grave sin, and God will punish me. Of course, he has already punished me, as there is no before or after, earlier or later, in the Torah. As God said, "Before Abraham was, I am." Is that black child a sign of my punishment? Is the weeping man my father or my son? I must ask the Seer.

But I am unfit to stand in the Seer's presence. I am unfit. I am unfit, and I am unclean.

Where is the *mikvah*? thought Hirsh Leib. I must get clean.

It's too late for the *mikvah*, Hirsh Leib told himself. You will wake the *rebbe*'s household, and everyone will see your shame. Go to the river. Yes.

Hirsh Leib began walking unsteadily down Tailor Street,

toward the small stream that skirted the eastern boundary of Lublin. Looking down the street, beyond the slaughterhouse, above the trees, Hirsh Leib could see the cross of the Polish church, and behind it the heavens turning gray with the coming dawn.

The cross reminded Hirsh Leib of Prince Czartoryski. Is he on his way to Warsaw right now, as he promised the Seer, with our message to Napoleon? Hirsh Leib wondered.

Or is he lying on his silken sheets in his castle, plotting to nail us all to that horrible cross?

38

The Seer's Bedchamber
Lublin
Wednesday, October 13

The sun fell across the Seer of Lublin's face. He opened his eyes and sat up, and his soul went out of his body. It flew across the forests and entered the great city of Warsaw. Later, he would tell Hirsh Leib what he saw there and what he understood:

The morning sun was leaking through the shutters as Countess Marie Waleska poured water over her hands from a blue filigreed glass pitcher by her bed. Then she dabbed her eyes with her fingers, wiping away the sleep. In a corner of the countess's bedroom, Napoleon Bonaparte, the exiled emperor of France, squatted over a porcelain chamber pot and groaned.

He's grown so fat, thought Waleska, regarding Napoleon with a critical eye. He used to be so beautiful. She wrinkled her nose at the odor filling the room from Napoleon's tortured bowels and reached for a flacon of perfume to drive away the smell.

Seven years ago, when Prince Adam Jerzy Czartoryski—

with whose robust, blond good looks, so like her own, Marie Waleska was entirely smitten—suggested that she take Bonaparte to her bed, the eighteen-year-old countess was terrified. She wasn't concerned about her sickly sixty-seven-year-old husband, Count Waleska, who rarely stirred from his house in the country and who hadn't visited his bride in Warsaw for almost a year. But she had heard such stories, she told Czartoryski. Wasn't it true that the French had insatiable appetites—surely the prince knew what she meant—and wasn't it true that their equipment compared favorably with that of their horses? And wasn't it true that their emperor was chosen to lead them because his equipment was the largest of all? And weren't these French violent, savage beasts who, it had been said, devoured babies, ripping them from their mothers' arms?

Czartoryski took her into his arms, kissed her, and assured her that these were just stories told to frighten women and children and make them behave. But although she was prepared to believe whatever her adored Czartoryski said, even if he had told her that the French were angels come to earth in Christ's name, her fears did not entirely depart until she finally saw Napoleon at the duke of Warsaw's palace.

The thirty-seven-year-old conqueror of most of Europe had a high, noble brow and a thin Roman nose. He was, it was true, rather short—far shorter, certainly, than Marie herself—but beneath his simple uniform his body looked powerful, his shoulders broad, his thighs and calves muscular. Wherever he moved in the duke's grand ballroom, walking with a heavy tread and almost comically long strides, as if to compensate for the shortness of his legs, people would give way, allowing him space, as if to touch his person to be dangerous. To Waleska he looked like a rough Mars, god of war. And when Prince Czartoryski brought her over to him, he bowed deeply and kissed her hand. Looking up into her eyes, he murmured softly, only for her to hear, "Now I know why I took Warsaw."

She slept with him that night.

He was a strong, gallant lover, impetuous and somewhat crude, more like the boys she had slept with in the duke's stables and forests than her husband. In time, however, she was able to teach Napoleon how to kiss her between her legs, how to lie back and do nothing while she straddled him, how to accept the loving slaps and bites that allowed Europe's conqueror to be himself conquered. In Marie Waleska's bed Napoleon could escape from the responsibilities of empire and become, once again, a child suckling at his mother's breast.

And time and time again he would return to her bed, riding night and day to reach her from some far-flung battlefield. Marie Waleska was sure that he was falling in love with her. And when she told him that she was carrying his child, she was sure he would offer her a seat next to him on France's, and therefore Europe's, throne.

Instead, of course, he divorced Josephine and married—on April Fool's Day 1810—Marie Louise, the blandly pretty, blond, bovine nineteen-year-old daughter of the Hapsburg emperor, Francis of Austria.

"Politics," he told Marie Waleska, as if that excused his treachery.

If she had not known it before, she knew it now: her dominion over Napoleon, absolute though it may have been, extended no farther than her bedroom door.

Now, watching her lover of seven years straining over the chamber pot, Marie Waleska savored her revenge. Marie Louise had brought Bonaparte nothing, not even the loyalty of her father, who had turned against him last January and, as Paris fell, brought his army onto the field on Tsar Alexander's side. Marie Louise had not even accompanied her husband into exile, fleeing to Italy with a lover and taking with her Napoleon's tiny son, the magnificently if idiotically titled king of Rome.

Of course, Napoleon's marriage to Marie Louise never prevented him from turning up regularly at Marie Waleska's door and begging from her the sweet punishments upon which he had grown to depend.

"Marie, get me a cloth," said Napoleon, squatting.

Waleska swung her long legs across the sheets, picked up a linen from the table next to Napoleon's side of the bed with her toes, and tossed it to him. It fluttered to the floor well out of his reach.

"Please, Marie. I don't want to soil myself."

Waleska rolled off the bed. After picking up the linen handkerchief, monogrammed with his royal *N*, she walked over to Napoleon and dropped it into his lap.

"But, Marie," said Napoleon, looking up at his mistress towering nakedly over him, his loins, even in his bowels' distress, stirring at the sight, "this is my handkerchief."

"Why should you dirty one of my linens?" said Waleska, noting the sweat running in rivulets down the folds of fat in Napoleon's red, swollen face and noting, too, his growing erection. "They are expensive to clean. You may not be poor," she said, referring to the annual two million francs granted Napoleon by the victorious rulers of Prussia, Austria, Russia, and England upon his abdication last April, "but I am."

"I deny you nothing," said Napoleon, accepting the handkerchief and cleaning himself.

Waleska turned away and sat on the edge of the bed. Napoleon gathered his dressing gown around him, stood up, and walked over to Waleska.

"Get rid of the pot," Waleska said. "It stinks."

Napoleon swung open the window, picked up the chamber pot, and poured its contents onto the gardens below.

"Russia," muttered Napoleon, returning to the bed and sitting beside Waleska.

"What does that mean?"

"My bowels have never recovered from the Russian campaign," said Napoleon.

"Before Russia," Waleska said, "you blamed Spain. Your digestion has always been bad, and that's because you stuff yourself like a pig."

"Marie, why are you so angry with me?" asked Napoleon, placing his hand lightly on her thigh. "What have I done?"

"I would not know where to begin, *mon empereur*," said Waleska, brushing his hand away.

"Marie, I have told you before, I was wrong. Marrying Marie Louise was a mistake. It was Talleyrand's idea, that fop, that sneak, that shit inside the ass of a worm. But it was my mistake. I have paid for it. What more can I say?''

Waleska shrugged.

''You are the only person in the world to whom I have ever apologized for anything. You are the one person who has stood beside me in this terrible time. The rest are all traitors. They will drown in their own blood and shit. But you, Marie. When I take back the throne, when the French people throw themselves at my feet and beg me to restore their honor, their glory, you will sit at my left hand, I promise you.''

Waleska stood up, and Napoleon wrapped his arms around her ass, burying his head in her belly. She rested her right hand on the top of his head and idly brushed his hair. He's getting bald, too, my emperor, she thought, lifting up a thin brown strand and studying his pink scalp. His hair used to be a warrior's helmet. Fat already, and soon bald.

She didn't doubt that he would reclaim France. What could Napoleon Bonaparte not accomplish? But put a poor Polish countess on France's throne? He'll marry another Marie Louise, she thought. A younger and stupider version with a royal father who has a big army or a big purse.

Waleska sighed, and Napoleon, mistaking its meaning, lowered his head to her groin. She pushed him away and broke his embrace. ''Not now,'' she said. ''I am not in the vein. Besides, I must be about breakfast.''

''Just coffee and milk,'' said Napoleon.

''And bread and butter and jam and cheese and eggs and ham and raspberries and pears,'' said Waleska, throwing on her gown. ''When have you eaten less? If you stay longer, I'll have to sell my jewels to feed you.''

''Coffee and milk,'' said Napoleon. ''Perhaps some bread. You joke. Can't you see my agony?''

''Yes, *mon empereur*. You suffer so terribly, and so terribly well.''

Waleska swept out of the bedroom to see to her servant and ready breakfast. A sharp, burning pain, like a saber thrust, cut through Bonaparte's guts. From his dressing gown pocket he removed a small ivory-and-gold box and opened it. He removed a tiny black ball of opium—his rabbit turds, he called them—and swallowed it. Then he swallowed another. The spasm subsided. In a little while he would be himself.

There was a knock on the door. Napoleon stood up and smoothed his robe. "Enter," he said.

Marcel Betrand, a sergeant in the palace guard who had accompanied him to Elba and now guarded his person during his secret trips off the island, peeked into the room.

"Yes, Marcel?"

"You have a visitor, *mon empereur*," Marcel whispered.

"Impossible," said Napoleon.

"Prince Adam Jerzy Czartoryski is here, *mon empereur*. He says he has ridden all night and all morning and has not slept. He says he has a message for you."

And hearing that, the Seer knew that there would be no turning back. The cosmic conspiracy had begun.

39
The Seer's Hoyf
Lublin
Wednesday, October 13

In the market square Hirsh Leib, his head throbbing and his body aching, bought a citron and the sheaf of bound palm, myrtle, and willow branches with which one celebrates the holiday of Sukkos. They were expensive—the merchant swore that they came all the way from the Holy Land—but they were perfect: the citron without blemish; the leaves fresh and green. Hirsh Leib brought the willow up to his face, its sweet, earthy odor helping him to clear his head. He sniffed the citron, then placed them all in his saddlebag and rode out of the noisy market toward the Seer's *hoyf*.

Last night Hirsh Leib had fallen asleep by the banks of the river. After awakening, he had gone to the public bathhouse on Tanner Street, where he'd washed, put on his *tefillin*, and prayed. From there, he'd gone to Neshe's for a glass of tea, some black bread with salt, a slice of onion, and a small glass of sweet brandy. By the time he had left the market, his hands had stopped shaking and the storm in his soul had begun to pass.

Riding down the Old Road, Hirsh Leib told himself that brooding on his sins would only make him their captive. You stir filth, he thought, and what do you get? Stirred filth. Is it not written, "Depart from evil and do good?" You have done wrong, Hirsh Leib? Well, then, balance it by doing right. Is this not the message of Yom Kippur, the Day of Atonement? The gates of repentance are always open.

At that moment Hirsh Leib saw an elderly Jew with a beard the color of tin sitting in the dust by the side of the road. He was dressed as a peasant in rough clothes, a leather cap, and old, cracked boots. Hirsh Leib reined his horse and called to him.

"Are you all right, Rabbi?"

"If I were all right, would I be sitting here in the dust? I am old, and I am exhausted from my travels," said the old man.

"Are you going to see the Seer?"

"Are you a *melamed*?"

"No. Why do you ask?"

"Because like a *melamed*, like a teacher of idiot children, you ask stupid questions instead of helping."

"Come, Rabbi, you can ride with me."

"You call that help? If I could lift myself up to walk, why would I need you?"

Hirsh Leib dismounted, stroked his horse's neck, told him to stay, and walked over to where the old man sat. He lifted him up by his elbows, feeling the man's bones beneath the thin material of his black coat and the even thinner material of his flesh.

"You're hurting me," the old man whined. "What's the matter with you? You don't know your own strength?"

Hirsh Leib apologized, thinking, This is a sour one; look at his eyes. They were so red, it was if he had a fever. The old man took a deep breath, and with the *Zaddik* of Orlik's right arm around his waist, he shuffled toward Hirsh Leib's horse.

"What's your name, Rabbi?" asked Hirsh Leib.

"Yekl."

"And where are you from, Reb Yekl?" asked Hirsh Leib.

"From everywhere," the old man said, "and from nowhere. I have been all over the world looking for an honest Jew. Most recently, I have been in Pshiskhe."

"Did you see Reb Yitzhak there?" asked Hirsh Leib, referring to the *Zaddik* of Pshiskhe, the Holy Yehudi. "Certainly," he said, smiling, "he is an honest Jew."

"Yes, indeed he was," Yekl replied. "But last night the Jew died, and my search continues."

Hirsh Leib was stunned. Rebbe Yakov Yitzhak, who shared the Seer of Lublin's name, was the Seer's disciple. He was called the Yehudi, the Jew, because once, with a fellow student, he had put on peasant clothes to search for the prophet Elijah, who often wandered the world in that disguise. Walking through the Pshiskhe market, the Yehudi had suddenly grabbed his friend's arm and, pointing to a peasant leading a horse by a rope, said, "There he is!" The peasant had turned to Reb Yitzhak, crying angrily, "Jew! If you know, why do you boast?" And then the peasant had vanished, for it had been, indeed, Elijah. After that people simply called Rabbi Yitzhak the Yehudi, or, later, the Holy Yehudi.

Hirsh Leib felt tears gathering behind his eyes and in his throat. While the Yehudi lay dying, he thought, I was brawling in a tavern with Reb Bunem. While the Yehudi was saying the *Shema* for the last time, I was calling for brandy. It is not the common, *prosteh* Jews who delay the Messiah and prevent the unification of the upper and lower worlds; it is righteous hypocrites like myself.

"Well," said the old man, "are you going to help me onto your horse or are we going to stand here all day?"

"How did Rebbe Yitzhak die?" asked Hirsh Leib.

"Like all men, when it's their time. He stopped breathing," Yekl said.

"How can you be so unfeeling, old man?" said Hirsh Leib.

"Surely, having met the Yehudi, you know that he was the holiest man in the world."

"Is that saying such a great deal? I think not. Anyway, did not *Hashem* say, as it is written, 'You are not permitted to be more compassionate than I am'?

"*Hashem* decided that it was time for the Yehudi to leave this world. Is it for you or I to say, No, it was not time, we know better? Are you always so arrogant, young man? And were you lying when you said you would give me a ride? My tired feet and my aching back tell me you were."

Hirsh Leib felt confused and angry. This man was sent as a torment, he thought, but I will treat him with the kindness he does not deserve.

So Hirsh Leib lifted the old man—who weighed no more than a child—onto his horse, then swung himself into the saddle. Yekl put his arms around Hirsh Leib's waist, and they set off down the Old Road.

"So," said Yekl, "you are a *shiker*, a drunkard, yes?"

Hirsh Leib turned his head to look at his passenger. The old man was smiling merrily now, showing broken, tobacco-stained teeth. His red eyes seemed to glitter like rubies. His breath reeked of garlic.

"Don't look at me like a thundercloud," Yekl said. "I don't care if you're angry. People don't like to hear the truth, but I'm an old man, and I'll be dead soon, so I don't have time for lies. And the truth is, you're a *shiker*.

"You don't have to be, you know," added the old man. "You don't have to be a drunkard, sucking on a bottle as if it were your mother's tit."

"You're feeling better now that you're off your feet, yes?" said Hirsh Leib. "Good enough to insult me?"

"What insult? Since when is the truth an insult?"

"What do you know about it, old man?"

"I know that I can smell the brandy. It comes through your flesh even though you've bathed. And I know what I saw in your eyes. And I know that your hands were shaking even though you're young and strong. And I know also that if you keep drinking, my friend, soon you won't be able to keep your wife happy in bed."

Hirsh Leib decided not to respond. Better to let him rave on, he thought, than to encourage him. This Yekl is one who loves to make trouble and stir things up.

And, sure enough, Yekl fell silent, not saying another word until they were within sight of the Seer's gates. Then he spoke again: "If you want to cure yourself of this sickness, you must comfort a policeman. There will be a time when a policeman will be consumed by fear. The Angel of Death will have his thumbs at his throat. You must tell him that he will be safe. He will not believe you. He will not even understand you, but you must make him understand. Then, he will redeem you."

A lunatic, thought Hirsh Leib. Perhaps he was also raving when he said that the Yehudi had died.

They rode through the Seer's gates and into the courtyard, now filled with even more Hasidim than before. They packed the courtyard like crows, spitting and smoking and calling out to one another. Hirsh Leib dismounted and helped the old man down.

Hirsh Leib slipped the bridle off his horse, and when he turned around, Yekl was gone. Without a word of thanks, Hirsh Leib thought. He shrugged and, shooing away a black cat that had appeared at his feet, led his horse to the stable. After making sure that he would be watered and fed, Hirsh Leib retrieved his citron and palm fronds from his saddlebag and pushed and shoved his way through the crowd toward the *rebbe*'s *shtibl* for the afternoon Sukkos service.

The Seer's *shtibl* was a humble affair. It was nothing like the great Lublin *shul* with its ceiling of carved lions and fantastic birds, its high balconies and gleaming curved staircases, its walls decorated with biblical passages painted in gilt letters. The Seer's *shtibl* was a simple room with an earthen floor, a low, smoke-stained ceiling, and freshly washed windows along the northern and southern walls. Along the eastern wall, with the *Aren Kodesh* and the *sefer* Torahs, were bookshelves and benches made by Meyer the carpenter, who had given them to the *rebbe*. The wooden *bimah*, from where the Torah was read, was in the middle of the room, facing a row of benches. To the right of the *bimah* was a small wood stove, and to the right of that was the charity box and the enameled washbasin.

Hirsh Leib entered and washed his hands. The *shtibl* was packed with Hasids, so Hirsh Leib leaned back against the western wall, standing on his toes to see if he could see the Seer. He could not, and then he remembered what that student Motl had told him: the *rebbe* had taken to praying alone. Probably, thought Hirsh Leib, he's praying in his *sukkah* right now.

Hirsh Leib had arrived before the service had begun, and the noise in the *shtibl* was deafening. Men were greeting friends, laughing, gossiping, arguing. A man whom Hirsh Leib took to be the *shammes*, the one who managed the *shtibl* for the *rebbe*, was standing at the *bimah*, trying to outshout the crowd. Hirsh Leib heard him say something about the *eyrev*—the wire strung around the town that defined it as private property—being torn somewhere, and therefore no one would be allowed to carry anything to somewhere else—Hirsh Leib could not make out where—this coming *Shabbos* for fear of breaking the injunction against removing objects—by carrying, throwing, or handing them—from a private to a public place, and vice versa. Then Hirsh Leib heard a name he recognized.

"On orders of the *rov* and the *kahal*," the *shammes* was saying, "I hereby announce that meat sold by the ben Areyn family is *treyf* and *posl*, unfit and forbidden, and anyone who has bought meat from them should appear before the *rov* to see if your knives are still *kosher*."

The shouting in the *shtibl* grew louder, for the ben Areyns cut meat for most of Lublin's Hasidim. So despite his brave words, my temper has, after all, brought misfortune to the butcher, thought Hirsh Leib.

Suddenly the rich baritone of the *hazzan*, the cantor, cut through the tumult: "*Borekhu es Adonoi hamvorokh*." Praise the Lord, to whom our praise is due. It was the call to prayer, and Hirsh Leib and all the men responded loudly and clearly:

"*Barukh Adonoi hamvorokh leolam voed*." Praised be the Lord, to whom our praise is due, now and forever!

Later, after he had joined the congregation in shaking the

palm fronds east, south, west, and north, after he had marched
around the *bimah* and kissed the Torah with the fringes of his
tallis, after he had chanted the mourner's *kaddish* for the Holy
Yehudi, Hirsh Leib felt whole again. He remembered that the
Baal Shem Tov had called prayer the daily miracle, and
leaving the *shtibl*, Hirsh Leib felt that miracle afresh. The
sky was bright with the Lord's light as Hirsh Leib repeated
the words of the psalm: "Light is sown for the righteous."

The Hebrew word for "righteous" was *zaddikeh*, and
Hirsh Leib thought, If they will call me a *zaddik*, however
wrongly, I can at least act like one.

Now he felt that the harmonious unification of all the worlds
above and below was, indeed, possible. And wouldn't that
joining release the holy light that the Zohar, the Book of
Brightness, said filled the universe before God made the sun
and stars?

Hirsh Leib yearned to be bathed in that light.

He worked his way across the courtyard and walked behind
the Seer's residence. There, standing alone in the field that
seemed to stretch all the way to the distant, purple Carpathian
Mountains, was the Seer's *sukkah*, built by his own hands for
the holiday, as was commanded.

For a moment Hirsh Leib stood there quietly, smelling the
fresh autumn air, relieved to be out of the crush of Hasidim,
relieved to be alone and at peace. He could hear the wind
rustling the leaves of the trees; he could hear the crows complain. Then he heard a honking, and looking up, he saw a
chevron of long-necked geese flying south. "Blessed art
Thou, our Lord our God, King of the Universe," whispered
Hirsh Leib, "who hath such as this in His world."

Content, he felt reluctant to move, and he let his mind paint
a picture of the inside of the *rebbe*'s *sukkah*. It would have
rich rugs piled in profusion on the floor, he thought, with the
sunlight coming through the *sukkah*'s roof of bound branches
dappling them. There would be a long rustic table at which
the Seer would break bread with his Hasidim. There would
be bowls of fruit and olives on the table, and loaves of braided
bread, and citrons would hang from the walls, filling the
sukkah with their sweet scent.

Suddenly Hirsh Leib felt a change in the air. The bucolic scene in front of him darkened, as if a cloud had passed across the sun. He realized that he was hearing shouts from behind the Seer's house. Then he heard something that sounded like a rifle shot, then another, and a third, and the cries doubled in volume.

The Seer of Lublin, dressed in a white silk robe, appeared in the doorway of the *sukkah*.

"Something's happened," said Hirsh Leib.

"Go, I'll follow," said the Seer.

Hirsh Leib began running back toward the courtyard. When he turned the corner of the Seer's residence, he saw Hasidim rushing toward the gates. Hirsh Leib grabbed a man from behind and spun him around.

"What's happened?" Hirsh Leib demanded. "What's going on here?"

"Save yourself," said the man, knocking Hirsh Leib's hand away and plunging back toward the gates.

Hirsh Leib followed, throwing himself into the crowd like a swimmer diving into a dark, rough sea. He saw Hasidim running down the Old Road, back toward Lublin, and then he was outside the gate, where a group of men were standing in a stolid circle. Hirsh Leib pushed them aside and saw a man and a woman lying on the ground in a widening pool of blood. He knelt down and saw that they were dead.

"Pogrom," said a Hasid in the circle.

"Who did this?" asked Hirsh Leib. "Did anyone see?"

"I saw," another man said. "It was Shmielewicz with some others. The others, I don't know. But Shmielewicz, I know."

"It's a pogrom," said the first Hasid.

The circle parted, and Hirsh Leib saw the Seer standing above him, looking like a ghost in his white silk robe.

"The Yehudi is dead," said Hirsh Leib.

"I know," said the Seer.

"Pogrom," repeated the first Hasid.

"Yes," said the Seer. "It has begun."

40

Neshe's Tavern
Tailor Street, Lublin
Thursday, October 14

I am not drunk, Hirsh Leib told himself, and I will not become drunk. This brandy is just to help me think.

Suddenly five men burst into the inn and began shouting for wine. They were covered with mud and dust, their clothes were torn, and Hirsh Leib could see that they were angry.

"What's the matter, my friends?" he called to them. One of them, a rough-looking man, walked over to where Hirsh Leib sat. "I have a story, young rabbi," he said, "that will make your beard go white."

"Tell me," said Hirsh Leib.

"You know Hannah, the butcher's wife?" the man asked.

"The butcher Moyshe ben Areyn?"

"Yes, that one."

"I do not know her," said Hirsh Leib, "but I have met her husband."

The man covered his face with his hands, and Hirsh Leib could see that he was overcome. Then the man composed himself.

"This is what Moyshe ben Areyn's wife has just told me," he began. "She was sitting in her kitchen with her poor son, Shmuel, who is five years old."

"Why do you call the boy 'poor'?" asked Hirsh Leib. "Is he sick, a cripple?"

"Wait," said the man, "let me finish, and you will understand."

And this is what the man told Hirsh Leib:

* * *

Hannah, Moyshe ben Areyn's stocky wife, was telling Shmuel to stop playing with a skinny, piebald cat that had strayed into her kitchen. "You play with a cat," she told the boy, "you lose your memory."

Shmuel looked up at his mother and coughed.

"Still that cough." Hannah sighed and fetched some raspberry syrup—good for coughs, diarrhea, rheumatism, impotence, and just about whatever ailed you—from a shelf in her cupboard.

"I don't want any," said Shmuel. "I want to go out."

"I told you," Hannah said, "today we go nowhere. You understand, Shmueli? Today we stay inside."

There was a knock at the door, and Hannah froze. Such terrible things had been happening. Those dirty *balebatim*, those big shots at the *kahal*, had declared her Moyshe's meat *posl*. Then, yesterday, two Hasids, a man and a woman, had been shot and killed in front of the Seer's gates. Last night, before going to bed, Moyshe had told her that he feared a pogrom, and he wanted her to stay inside the house with Shmuel tomorrow. He didn't even want them to take their meals in the small *sukkah* he had built attached to the house.

So, she had asked, more frightened than she had let on, who's going to bring us food? Are you going to market? How will you know what to buy? How will you know what to pay? How will I prepare for *Shabbos*?

The hell with *Shabbos*, Moyshe had said, and then Hannah knew that Moyshe was also frightened, if not for himself, then for his family. Her husband was not a religious man, but he loved the *Shabbos*. On that one day, he always said, the poorest Jew was a king. On that one day, you could spit out *olam hazeh*, this world, and taste *olam habo*, the world to come. So on that one day Moyshe would sleep late, eat at his leisure, and even read those passages in the *Shulhan Arukh* concerning the Sabbath laws, slowly sounding out the Hebrew a letter at a time.

Hannah had wanted Moyshe to hold her, to comfort her, but it was her time of the month, so she went to sleep with Shmuel on his small pallet in the kitchen and drew whatever comfort she could from her son.

Hannah went to the door.

"Open up, Hannah," said a woman's voice. "It's Altah. I've come for Hakhnosses Kaleh."

Because the ben Areyns were relatively well off, their home was visited constantly by representatives of Lublin's dozens of *tsdokeh khevros*, charitable organizations. There was Malbish Arumim, clothes for the needy; Bes Yessoymim, the house of orphans; Talmud Toyreh, the school for poor children; Bikkur Khoylim, which helped the sick; Hakhnosses Orkim, which provided board for travelers and indigents; Khevreh Kadisha, the burial society that handled funerals for rich and poor alike. And on and on. Hakhnosses Kaleh provided dowries and proper weddings for brides whose parents were too poor to afford them.

Giving to charity was more than a duty; it was a *mitzvah*. It assured your place in the world to come.

Hannah, of course, was always glad to give—there were at least ten small tin boxes in her kitchen, each marked for a different charity, into which she put a few pennies every day—but she was usually reluctant to invite Altah in. The woman stayed too long and talked too much. But today Hannah was glad of her company.

Hannah made tea, and the two women sat in the kitchen. They quickly agreed that the Seer, although a wise and holy man, had made a mistake inviting all these Hasidim to Lublin. Lublin's own Hasidim were well behaved, but these others from crazy places like Belz and Brod and Satmar were troublemakers. Could you blame the *goyim* for being upset by all these fanatics filling up the town? asked Altah. They should all go back where they came from, Hannah agreed. Look at the problems they've already created for Moyshe. I heard, said Altah, shaking her head sadly.

After discussing the blight of Hasidim, Hannah and Altah moved on to the ever-fascinating topic of their neighbors: who kept a clean house, meaning they were putting on airs, and who didn't, meaning they were lazy slobs. Who was pregnant and who was not, and was that because that one was too busy flirting with the Polish boys in the market to pay attention to her husband, the poor fish? Who was making a match with whom, and wasn't it ridiculous for such a pretty young girl to marry such an old man, even if he was richer than he let on. Altah, who made the rounds collecting for brides every day, was a fount of such information, and Hannah was able to forget about *kahals* and pogroms until Moyshe came home for lunch.

Moyshe ben Areyn gave Altah a menacing look, and Altah jumped up, said a hurried good-bye to Hannah, and fled next door—where she would ask Feygel, the shoemaker's wife, how Hannah could bear to live with such a brute as that Moyshe ben Areyn.

"That Altah," said Moyshe, "a terrible gossip. Why do you talk to her?"

"I should better sit here alone and worry?" asked Hannah, who actually agreed with her husband but would have her tongue fall out before admitting it. "So?" Hannah asked. "Did you see the *rov*?"

"*Tateh!*" yelled Shmuel, running into the kitchen and throwing himself into his father's lap.

"No," said Moyshe, stroking Shmuel's head and wondering at the softness of his hair. Like an angel, Moyshe thought. "And I'm not going to. That ignoramus. I'm going to appeal his decision to the Bes Din. The other rabbis on the court know what I do, and they know what the *rov* is. Don't they, Shmueli?"

"Yes, *Tateh*."

"But the Bes Din won't meet until after the holidays. Until then, how will we live?"

"Have we ever gone hungry?" Moyshe asked angrily. "Do you think I would let you and the boy go hungry? What kind of man do you think you've married?"

Hannah was about to answer sarcastically when the door exploded off its hinges. Three men burst in.

Moyshe ben Areyn jumped up. Shmuel ran to his mother. "Are you crazy?" Moyshe asked Anders Shmielewicz.

"The butcher wants to know if you're crazy," said a young blond boy, no more than a teenager, to Shmielewicz. The boy's face was filthy, his hair matted. In his left hand he carried a half-empty bottle of vodka, in his right a rifle. They all carried rifles.

Anders Shmielewicz, smiling, his broad face red, held out his hand, and the boy passed him the bottle. He took a huge swallow and handed the bottle to the third boy, who could have been the first one's brother.

"You don't scare me, Anders," said Moyshe. "And these boys you've brought with you, the ugly twins, they don't scare me, either. If you want to fight, let's fight. I've whipped you before and I'll whip you again. I'll fight all three of you. But let's go out into the street. My wife just cleaned, and I don't want to dirty her kitchen with your blood."

The first boy swung his rifle into Hannah's cupboard, smashing the Sabbath dishes that had been her dowry.

"Run!" barked Moyshe.

But Hannah, her heart beating raggedly in her throat, froze as Shmielewicz drove the butt of his rifle into Moyshe's face, splitting open his cheek and knocking him to his knees. At the sight of blood, Hannah shrieked and threw herself at Shmielewicz. The boy holding the bottle swung it into Hannah's face, catching her across the bridge of her nose. She fell to the floor, stunned and sobbing.

Shmielewicz stepped over Hannah and grabbed the hair on the back of Moyshe's head, bringing his knee up into his mouth. Moyshe fell backward, spitting teeth and blood. Shmielewicz, straddling him, unbuttoned his fly and urinated on him.

"What should I do with the boy?" asked the dirty-faced blond.

"What should we do with your son, Reb ben Areyn?" asked Shmielewicz with elaborate courtesy, putting his penis back into his trousers. "What should we do with this young Jewish calf? He'd make good veal, Jew cutlets, don't you think, butcher?"

"Don't," said Moyshe.

"I can't hear you, butcher." Shmielewicz bent over to bring his face close to Moyshe's. "Speak up."

Moyshe saw Shmielewicz's huge face looming over him, and he spat. Shmielewicz wiped the spittle off his lips and then hooked his right index finger under Moyshe's eye and popped it out of its socket.

Moyshe ben Areyn screamed as the pain exploded in his head. He flipped over onto his belly and tried to push his eye back into place. He wanted to stop screaming, but he couldn't. He wanted to faint, but the gift of unconsciousness would not come. Then he vomited. Shmielewicz laughed, and the twins joined him.

"What's the matter, butcher?" Shmielewicz asked. "Did you eat some of the meat you sell to Christians?"

Moyshe crawled toward Shmielewicz, his right hand cupping his eye, holding it up to his face. "Anders," he moaned, spitting blood. "Don't do this. All your life you've known me. For God's sake, don't."

"Maybe you're right, butcher," Shmielewicz said, winking at the boys. "Yes, God knows, I've known you all my life. All my life you've been an arrogant piece of filth. But I'll tell you what. If you kiss my foot, maybe I'll let you live. I'll think about it. If you kiss my foot. Will you kiss my foot?"

Moyshe reached for his boot.

"No, Jew. Not my boot. My foot."

Shmielewicz sat down, pulled off his left boot, and stuck his foot into Moyshe's face. "Now kiss it, Jew. Kiss my foot."

Through a red haze, Moyshe saw Shmielewicz's chalky-white foot. It was covered with red-and-black sores and cuts; the nails of his toes were brown, ragged, and chewed. The smell, like spoiled milk, hit Moyshe's nose and he gagged.

"Come on, Jew, before I change my mind. Are you too proud, you bastard, you piece of filth? Kiss it now."

Moyshe bent down toward Shmielewicz's foot, took it in his hand, and then shoved it into his mouth, biting down as hard as he could, shaking the foot back and forth like a dog with a bone. Blood, hot and salty, filled his mouth as he heard Shmielewicz roar.

"Get him off me!" yelled Shmielewicz, sliding off the chair to the floor.

The two boys began beating Moyshe with their rifles, but still he held on, biting, chewing, feeling the bones in Shmielewicz's foot crack between his teeth.

"Shoot him, shoot him, for Christ's sake!" Shmielewicz shrieked.

The boy with the dirty face pressed the barrel of his rifle into Moyshe's ear and pulled the trigger. The sound of the explosion made the boy jump, as blood and brain and bits of bone spattered the kitchen floor.

"He won't let go," Shmielewicz moaned.

"He's dead," cried the boy. "He's dead."

"He won't let go, I tell you!" Shmielewicz shouted.

"He's dead, he's dead," repeated the frightened boy, while the other kneeled down to try to pry Moyshe ben Areyn's dead jaws open.

"Smash his jaw with your rifle, smash his head in," said Shmielewicz.

The two boys began pounding Moyshe's shattered skull. His other eye fell and dangled from its broken socket. Finally they crushed the jaw, freeing Shmielewicz's mangled foot, which gushed blood.

"Help me, get me out of here," Shmielewicz cried, and the boys lifted him off the floor and dragged him into the street.

A small crowd, drawn by the screams and shots, stood silently in the mud in the narrow street in front of Moyshe ben Areyn's home. Other people leaned out their windows and watched.

"Get out of here or I'll shoot," yelled one of the boys, waving his rifle.

The crowd fell back a few paces. The boy fired a shot into the air, and the crowd fell back a few steps more. The boys, Shmielewicz hanging heavily from their shoulders, edged sideways down the street, their backs to the houses, their eyes wide with fear.

"Take me home, and then tell Count Josep," said Shmielewicz, his voice strangled with pain. "Tell him I need him."

* * *

"Then we went into Moyshe ben Areyn's house," the rough-looking man told Hirsh Leib. "And when we saw what we saw, what I have just told you, you could hear our screams all along Butcher Street. Women and men. If you had seen it, Rabbi, you would have screamed, too."

41

The Jewish Cemetery
Lublin
Thursday, October 14

The men of the Khevreh Kadisha, the Burial Society, carried Moyshe ben Areyn's shattered body out of his house. Because he had been murdered, they did not perform the rite of *taharah*, purification of corpses. They did not pour water over his body, wash his head with wine and egg beaten together, clean and trim his hair and nails, and wrap him in his *tallis* and a white shroud. As a sign of wrath, Moyshe ben Areyn would be buried as he was found, in his blood-soaked clothing.

When the Khevreh Kadisha notified the gravediggers at the *bes-oylem*, the cemetery, they began to dig. If they hurried, Moyshe ben Areyn could be buried before candlelighting. As it is written, "His body shall not remain at night, but thou shalt surely bury him the same day." Let the Christians leave their mothers and fathers, their sons and daughters, to lie rotting in their homes and churches for days and days. Jews would not insult their dead so.

The sun was low in the sky, and the air had an autumnal chill as the ben Areyns began carrying their brother's body, lying face up on a wide board, down the narrow streets of Lublin to the *bes-oylem*. Only the grotesque ruin of his shattered head was covered by a cloth. As they carried their burden east toward the river and Death Bridge, people began to fall in with the procession, some tearing their clothes, others weeping. As it was written, "The Holy One, Blessed be He, counts the tears shed for the death of a virtuous person, and He stores them up in His treasure house."

It was said that one who saw a funeral and failed to join it was like one who mocked the poor. And it was also said that by joining a procession one prevented the death of little children, God forbid.

The beggars had also heard of Moyshe ben Areyn's murder, and dozens lined Death Road, chanting, "*Tsdokeh* saves from death." And no one passed them without reaching into their pockets for a little something.

By the time the procession had crossed the old, creaking Death Bridge, and the body had reached the *bes-oylem*, at least a hundred people were walking slowly behind it, including Hirsh Leib and Rebbe Yakov Yitzhak, the Seer of Lublin.

The bodies of the couple murdered at the Seer's *hoyf* had been taken away earlier by the suddenly busy Burial Society. But as no one knew their identities, the Seer had declared that their funeral could be put off until tomorrow morning while an attempt was made to find their relatives, if any. Of course, it could not be delayed longer than that, as soon it would be the Sabbath when graves could not be dug.

Hirsh Leib and the Seer stopped at the *bes-oylem* gates. It was not permitted for *kohanim*, firstborn sons of Israel's ancient hereditary priest class, to defile themselves by coming too close to death. So they stood apart—like two old crows, thought Hirsh Leib—and watched the burial, as Moyshe ben Areyn's body was laid in its grave with two boards on either side of the corpse and one on top of it. (The ben Areyn family had always scorned coffins as an indulgence of the rich.) A bit of earth from the Holy Land was placed in the body's mouth.

The butcher's rabbi, Reb Shelomo, recited the *kaddish* and then chanted a psalm. Then Moyshe ben Areyn's brothers took turns shoveling dirt until the grave was filled and the earth smoothed over.

"So much death," said Hirsh Leib, who had torn the lapel

of his coat twice to signify his mourning for both the Holy Yehudi and Moyshe ben Areyn.

The Seer remained silent. Some people, leaving the *besoylem*, began to approach him, to ask him for his blessing, but when they saw that he had cloaked himself in distance, his eyes fixed upon the setting sun, they turned away with mumbled apologies.

"All this evil," Hirsh Leib said when the cemetery was again empty of all but the dead.

"It is only with our poor, human understanding that we look at events and call them evil," said the Seer. "Once, Rabbi Zusya of Hanipol was asked to explain the existence of evil. 'What is evil?' he replied.

"You must try to cultivate that inspired innocence, Hirsh Leib. In time, you may even come to understand what Elijah told you about your sickness."

Hirsh Leib felt shame color his cheeks.

"Do you think I do not know about your drinking, my friend?" asked the Seer. "And do you think I do not know that you met Elijah on the road yesterday and gave him a ride to our home? What did he tell you?"

"I don't remember," said Hirsh Leib. "It made no sense."

"But if you know it made no sense, then certainly you remember what it was," said the Seer. "Come, tell me."

"That nasty old man was truly Elijah?"

"Of course."

Hirsh Leib walked a few steps in silence, asking himself how he could have failed to recognize the prophet. The Yehudi had known him. The Seer had known him. Of course, what did the Seer not see with that one, huge, gray-blue eye that alternately warmed and chilled Hirsh Leib's soul? Finally he responded.

"He said I should comfort a policeman. He said that would redeem me. But the police rob and kill us."

"Remember, my friend, there is no before or after in the Torah."

"You mean this policeman may have already lived?"

"Or has not yet been born," said the Seer.

"But how can I comfort someone who has not yet been

born? The dead, at least, I could summon in prayer, in memory. But the unborn? It is impossible."

"As Rabbi Zusya might have said, what does impossible mean? Anyway, you have already seen this man. When you arrived in Lublin, and came to see me on the hill, he was standing behind me with a woman. I did not see them, because they are not bound to me. But when you saw them, I felt their presence."

"I don't understand," said Hirsh Leib.

"I pray you will. Come," said the Seer. "It's time to return to the *sukkah* for our evening prayers. The stars will soon be out."

The Seer and Hirsh Leib turned their backs on the cemetery and the setting sun and began walking in the gathering gloom, their shadows running down the road before them.

"You see, Hirsh Leib," the Seer said suddenly, "as the Yehudi, may his memory protect us, said, 'The important thing is not to mix the good with the bad. A hair of goodness is enough if only it has not the slightest trace of bad.'

"And what is the test of goodness? How can we know it? The Yehudi said it is the love of Israel. And by that he meant the love of our fellow man, for all men are Israel, Jew or Christian. This is why we have summoned all the Hasidim to Lublin. We gather here for the love of Israel, may it grow in our hearts.

"The brandy you drink, Hirsh Leib, separates you from Israel. It poisons your heart, and you turn away from those who love you. You look around and you see evil, and you forget that the Holy One, Blessed is He, has created this world for His pleasure and yours.

"These terrible times," the Seer said, stopping and placing his right hand on Hirsh Leib's shoulder, looking into his eyes, "only tell me that the hour is approaching. Prepare yourself, Hirsh Leib. Simkhas Torah is only a few days off, and the Corsican is on his way. I have seen him, disguised, accompanied by a prince and a beggar."

"Tell me, Rabbi Yitzhak," said Hirsh Leib, "why did the Yehudi die? Why now?"

The Seer walked a few paces. "He could not be a part of this thing we do," he answered, sighing.

"Did he, perhaps, see a trace, a hair of bad in this good, Rabbi Yitzhak?" asked Hirsh Leib.

"Perhaps," said the Seer.

"And if we fail?"

"As Rabbi Yitzhak, I see suffering beyond measure. But if I were Rabbi Zusya, I would say, What is failure?"

They had just reached the river upon whose banks Hirsh Leib had slept the night before when a dark-haired, richly dressed man on horseback rode up the decrepit bridge from the Lublin side and halted in the middle.

"So, Jew," said Count Josep Czartoryski, his horse's hooves clattering on the bridge's rotting boards, "you must be that great fraud, the so-called Seer of Lublin."

"I am Rabbi Yakov Yitzhak, my lord," said the Seer.

Czartoryski spurred his horse over the bridge and pulled up right in front of the Seer and Hirsh Leib. Hirsh Leib could smell the horse's breath and see the foamy sweat on his flanks.

"You are the devil himself," said Czartoryski, "and I would be doing God's will by cutting off your beard and head. But why should I soil my hands with your blood? The people of Lublin will do it for me."

"As you will, my lord," said the Seer.

"Don't play the humble Jew with me, you devil," said Czartoryski. "I can smell your pride. You," he said, addressing Hirsh Leib. "I do not recognize you."

Hirsh Leib stared at the count.

"Answer me, you insolent pig. Who are you?"

"I am Hirsh Leib, of Orlik."

"The people of Lublin are tired of all you filthy Jews," said Czartoryski. "I know. They come to me and they tell me that they're tired of being robbed in their homes and in the market by scheming, lying Jews. They tell me that they're tired of seeing their land cursed by your blasphemies. They're tired of seeing their children murdered so that their innocent blood can be used to bake your ceremonial bread."

"That's a lie," said Hirsh Leib. "A blood libel."

"Is it?" asked Czartoryski, smiling. "Well, perhaps you should petition the tsar. Tell the tsar your troubles. Or maybe you should go to Elba and tell Bonaparte. Bonaparte loves the Jews, doesn't he? Or is Elba too far away? He is in Elba, isn't he? Isn't the anti-Christ still dwelling in Elba? . . .

"What's the matter?" asked Czartoryski. "You're so quiet. Jews usually have so much to say.

"By the way, who was it you buried today? A butcher, wasn't it? Your butchers are the ones who slaughter our children, aren't they? I was just going to ride over to your cemetery to let my horse relieve himself on the butcher's grave."

Czartoryski jerked the reins and his horse reared, pawing the air. The Seer and Hirsh Leib fell back, and Czartoryski laughed.

"You Jews think you're so clever. But the people are rising and soon there won't be a Jew left in Poland. At least not a living one."

"Amen," whispered the Seer as Czartoryski spurred his horse toward the cemetery.

"Do you have any doubts now, Hirsh Leib?" asked the Seer. "This *porets* speaks the truth. We can stay in Poland no longer. Only death awaits us here."

"He knows," said Hirsh Leib, terrified. "He knows everything. Napoleon. The diamond. His brother told him."

"If he did, it doesn't matter," the Seer said. "We will all be murdered unless we can get to the Holy Land. Our fate lies in the hands of the Lord, and in the hands of his instrument, Napoleon."

42

The Seer's Study House
Lublin
Friday, October 15

Had Prince Adam told his brother about the diamond, about Napoleon? Once again the Seer let his soul go forth, flying over the forests, over the roofs of Warsaw. Once again it flew through the windows of Marie Waleska's home and hovered there. And this, as the Seer would tell Hirsh Leib, was what he saw and what he understood:

He's completely mad, thought Prince Adam Jerzy Czartoryski as he sat on the edge of Marie Waleska's bed and watched Napoleon adjust his false beard in Waleska's bedroom mirror. For the past day and a half Czartoryski had listened to Bonaparte complain about Talleyrand's treachery, Tsar Alexander's stupidity, his wife's, Marie Louise's, promiscuity, the physical decline of his first wife, Josephine (particularly the sad state of her once magnificent ass), the shrewishness and cruelty of his mistress, Marie Waleska, the horrible conditions under which he was forced to live at Elba, and the pitiable state of his bowels. It was an endless river of words, a ceaseless torrent of abuse and self-pity that was interrupted only when he turned his attention to consuming the astonishing amounts of food Waleska brought to his table four and five times a day.

There were baskets of eggs—boiled, baked, and fried. There were meats served in sauces, and meats baked in dough, and meats ground into sausage. He devoured fish and fowl of every description, fruits and vegetables without number, and, it seemed to Czartoryski, every pastry devised by every chef in Warsaw. And he washed it all down with buckets of coffee and jeroboams of champagne, claret, port, and brandy. There was nothing, it seemed, that Napoleon would not lower into his guts with an appetite that did not seem in the least diminished by the violent cramps that doubled him over every morning and every evening.

And now, to Czartoryski's exhausted despair, the exiled emperor was determined to journey to Lublin disguised as a Jew.

Napoleon's adjutant, Sergeant Betrand, had managed to scrounge up a battered black coat and an equally disreputable black hat for his emperor, and now he presented Napoleon with the pièce de résistance, the beard that he had purchased from the Grand Theater of Warsaw.

"They were performing *The Merchant of Venice*, *mon empereur*," Betrand said. "That, they told me, is the beard of the Jew Shylock."

"And what will Shylock wear?" Napoleon asked.

"I do not know, *mon empereur*," said Betrand.

"It doesn't matter," said Napoleon. "I know the plays of that Englishman. Shakespeare, yes? *Hamlet*. *The Moor of Venice*. Poor stuff. Very poor. Lacking in nobility, in grace, in grandeur. Completely lacking. I am surprised the Grand Theater wastes its time with such nonsense. Now, Racine— there was an artist. But such is the decline of the world. What is excellent is ignored, what is common is exalted. That's rather well put, don't you think, Czartoryski?"

"Yes, my lord. Very well put."

"So, Prince," said Napoleon, turning around triumphantly, "how do I look?"

Like a perfect idiot, though Czartoryski. "You look like a Jew," he said.

"But a noble Jew, yes?"

"Of course."

"A king of the Jews. Perhaps, when your rabbi, the one they call the Seer, sees me, he will proclaim me king of the Jews. What do you think the pope will think of that? What do you think your Alexander will think of that?"

At that moment Marie Waleska entered her bedroom, saw Napoleon, and burst out laughing. Sergeant Betrand slipped out of the room.

That part of Napoleon's face that was not covered by black whiskers turned purple.

"My lord," said Czartoryski, "I believe that you may attract more attention in that disguise than you would otherwise. People will wonder why I would be traveling with a Jew."

"Then you should disguise yourself as I do," said Napoleon, "and we would be two Jews."

"But then," said Czartoryski, horrified at the thought, "we could not be assured of safe conduct. What if we were stopped?"

"Enough!" said Napoleon. "I have decided to wear this disguise. You, Prince Czartoryski, you can do as you will. And you, Marie, I'm hungry. Fetch me some fruit and wine."

"The way you stuff yourself, I'm surprised you don't burst," said Waleska. "You're the fattest-looking Jew I've ever seen."

Napoleon took two stiff, angry steps toward Waleska, his hand raised as if to strike her. She threw back her shoulders and lifted her head high as if to emphasize the difference in their heights. The little tyrant and his Amazon, thought Czartoryski. This is farce, he thought, looking down at his boots, sheer farce. This is not Racine; it's Molière.

"Don't be embarrassed, Adam," said Marie Waleska, pronouncing his name with a tenderness that surprised him and made him realize that she was still available to him. Did Napoleon also hear that note? A frightening thought.

"The emperor and I are beyond embarrassment," she continued. "Aren't we, *mon empereur*?"

Czartoryski, still looking down, heard Waleska leave. He looked up. Napoleon was standing over him.

"You see, Adam?" he began with that all-too-familiar whining note of complaint, and instantly Czartoryski knew that Napoleon was deaf to any subtleties in his mistress's voice, even the subtleties of love. "You see how she treats me? With scorn. With contempt. This is how it is when great men fall. This is a theme for an epic poem, for an artist like Racine. But I will write a new last act, yes? I will crush them all, beginning with that sack of shit Talleyrand. And

Alexander. I will force Alexander to kneel at your feet, Prince Czartoryski, and sit a Pole on a Polish throne. And then, you and I," said Napoleon, reaching out and clasping Czartoryski's hand, "we will humble the English. We will close the continent to them, and their shopkeepers will starve. We will take India from them. Like Alexander the Great, we will march east to India. Do you see?"

"Yes, my lord."

"Without markets, without ports, the English are helpless. There is no need to waste an army crossing the Channel. A Channel crossing is always hazardous. But it is not necessary. Instead, we starve them. That was always my intent, but Alexander was weak. Alexander let the priests and those drunken barons lead him around by the nose. If only he had listened to me.

"But all that is past, yes? We are beginning a new adventure. And the Jews will finance it. The baron de Rothschild is behind me. And now this magician and his diamond. Do you believe in his magic, Adam, or do you just believe in his diamond?"

"I have seen both, my lord."

"So you have said. So how can I insult him by not dressing as a Jew? You see? By wearing these clothes, I tell him that I am with him."

"Yes. As you will. But we should be off, my lord."

Marie Waleska returned carrying a silver platter piled high with pears and grapes. Behind her, her servant carried a bottle of claret.

"Of course," said Napoleon. "But first we fortify ourselves. An army travels on its stomach, Czartoryski. Isn't that so?"

"Yes, my lord," said Czartoryski, watching the juice of a large pear splash onto Napoleon's false beard. "That's very well put."

The Seer closed his eyes and felt his soul return to the study house. He let his head fall to his chest, and then he lifted it, opened his eyes, and saw an old man sitting on the bench in front of him, his coat covered with dust. The Seer leaned

*forward and tapped the stranger on the shoulder. The man
turned around, and the Seer saw his tin-colored beard. The
man smiled, showing broken teeth, and then put a finger to
his lips, telling the Seer to remain silent. The man turned
back around, and the Seer felt his soul again lifted from his
body, this time as if someone were taking it on a journey.
And this is what he saw and what he understood:*

Czartoryski and Napoleon were entering the woods that lay
between Warsaw and Lublin. With the sun setting, and night
coming on, they would not be seeing many fellow travelers
until they arrived at the inn where Czartoryski had decided
they would spend the night. It was, Czartoryski knew, owned
by a Jew. He must remind Napoleon to keep his mouth shut
around the innkeeper, or he surely would be unmasked.

Napoleon had decided to leave Betrand behind with
Waleska, and Czartoryski had seen that Marie was pleased to
have the grizzled sergeant for company. She always did have
a healthy appetite, thought Czartoryski, recalling their few
times in bed together in the days before he had procured
her for the French Caesar. Most vividly he remembered her
flesh—how smooth it had been, like butter, but how alive. It
responded to his every touch. He could run his finger across
her sweetly rounded, down-covered belly as lightly as he
could, yet there would be a red trail marking its passage—a
trail that would vanish an instant later. Indeed, although she
had told Czartoryski all about her many adventures with her
husband's stable boys—discussing their techniques in bed
and comparing them, always unfavorably, with his own—
she seemed to him forever virginal, a true Diana. A perfect
mistress, thought Czartoryski. Never a wife.

As if he were afraid Napoleon could read his thoughts,
Czartoryski turned in his saddle to check on the emperor,
who was sitting easily and contentedly on his mount, that
ridiculous black hat pressed firmly upon his balding head.

Napoleon nodded to Czartoryski. When Czartoryski turned
back around, he spotted an old Jew with a tin-colored beard
sitting in the dust by the side of the road. He wasn't there a
moment ago, thought Czartoryski. Where did he come from?

Czartoryski reined in his horse, and Napoleon came up to his side. The Jew sat where he was, smiling at them with brown, broken teeth.

"Ask him, Adam," said Napoleon, "why he is sitting in the dust."

"Why shouldn't I sit in the dust?" the Jew responded in perfect French.

"How extraordinary," exclaimed Napoleon. "You're a French Jew?"

"As French as you," said the Jew.

"Remarkable. Well," Napoleon said, "I suppose there is no reason why you shouldn't sit in the dust, but, on the other hand, why should you?"

"That is a deep question indeed, Rabbi," said the Jew. "But I am too old and too tired to discuss Talmud with you."

"He takes me for a rabbi," Napoleon whispered to Czartoryski, enormously pleased.

"Where are you going, old man?" Czartoryski asked.

"Nowhere, obviously," said the Jew.

"We can see that, my good man," said Napoleon. "But before you sat down, you were, probably, going somewhere. Where was that?"

"Such wisdom!" exclaimed the old man. "Such a mind! You are perhaps a *zaddik*, Rabbi?"

"No, not at all," said Napoleon, who had no idea what the old man was talking about.

"Such modesty!" said the Jew. "Such brilliance wrapped in such humbleness is truly pleasing to the Lord. Before I sat down in the dust, Rabbi, I was going, as I'm sure you are, to Lublin, to celebrate Simkhas Torah with the great Seer. But now I fear I am too weak to get there in time."

"Nonsense," said Napoleon. "You can travel with us. Adam, he will ride with you."

"I do not think this is wise," said Czartoryski.

"It is fate, Adam. Help the man onto your horse."

As Czartoryski dismounted, Napoleon smiled and nodded at the old Jew. "What is your name, sir?" he asked.

"Yekl," answered the old man, his red eyes glittering. "You can call me Yekl."

* * *

And when the Seer's soul returned once more to his body, he was alone.

43

The Seer's Sukkah
Lublin
Friday, October 15

In the *sukkah*, the Seer was crooning the "Song of Songs," welcoming the Sabbath. Hirsh Leib had never heard it sung so sweetly.

O that he would kiss me with his lips. Indeed, your caresses are better than wine.

With Hirsh Leib at the Seer's table were Rabbis David, Naftali, and Menachem Mendel. It was the first time the conspirators had assembled since last Tuesday.

He brings me to the house of wine, and looks at me with love. Sustain me with raisins, refresh me with apples, for I am lovesick.

The Seer's head was thrown back, his eyes closed, as he sang in a soft baritone, his voice rising and falling. Hirsh Leib could imagine the angels in heaven listening, enthralled. He closed his eyes, leaned back in his chair, and inhaled the rich smells of the *sukkah*: the sweet scent of the beeswax candles, the sharp acid of the citrons hanging from the walls, and the piny tang of the fir branches that made the *sukkah*'s roof.

On my bed at night I sought him who my soul loves; I sought him, but I did not find him.

Hirsh Leib's mind leapt to his home, back to Orlik. Would Soreh, his abandoned wife, be thinking of him as she lit the Sabbath candles? Would his two little ones be by her side? Were they safe?

Your lips, my bride, drip honey; honey and milk are under your tongue; the fragrance of your garments is like the fragrance of Lebanon. A garden enclosed is my sister, my bride, a spring enclosed, a fountain sealed.

Hirsh Leib saw his Soreh bending over the candles, her eyes closed as she recited the prayer in a low, musical voice, one of her mother's pearly linens draped over her head, covering her long, beautiful red hair, hair down to her waist. He saw her tiny white hands, white like milk, white like the finest porcelain, hovering over the candles, cupping the Sabbath flames, bringing the orange tips of the candles close to her breasts as his girls stared up at their mother, their eyes the very models of his Soreh's eyes, green eyes, as green as the sea. Then he saw her lying in his bed, her hair fanned over the pillow, her breasts, full, white as cream, white as pearl—always a surprise, every night, such large, womanly breasts on such a little girl. . . .

I opened to my beloved; but my beloved had turned away, had gone; my soul failed when he spoke.

"No," whispered Hirsh Leib as the Seer sang. He would never turn away from his beloved. What had he not learned from his Soreh? How to be a husband. How to be a man. Even Torah. Even *kabbalah.* His Soreh, he thought pridefully, was a scholar, as learned as any rabbi. How she loved her books. He had taught her. They would study during the Sabbath, and her eyes would get wide and her face would shine in the candlelight as she read the holy words. Afterward she would thank him. She would kiss the palms of his hands, the tips of his fingers, and tell him how he had opened her soul for her. "All the women talk about is their children, and shopping and cleaning, and the way other women raise their children, shop, and clean," she would say. "Without you, I would have been just like them. My world would have been that small, that narrow.

"Come in to my soul, my love," she would say. "You have opened it. You have made me more than a woman. Now take that woman part of me."

How could he have left her for a moment, even to save the world?

Their last night together. Hirsh Leib had looked into her sea green eyes and said, "You know I'd die for you, my love. For you and the girls. I'd die for you."

"That's easy," said Soreh. "Dying is easy. Live for us, my love. That's what I want, all I want. Live for me."

How beautiful are your steps in sandals, O Princess; the curves of your thighs are like ornaments made by an artist. Your chest is like a round goblet filled with wine; your body is like a heap of wheat set about with lilies.

Hirsh Leib imagined himself falling into Soreh's arms once again, her arms encircling him, crushing him to her heavy breasts, fitting herself to him, her nipples pressed against his, her legs wrapped around his waist, her breath warm in his ear, sweet in his mouth.

He opened his eyes and looked at David of Lelov and Menachem Mendel. An hour before, in the Seer's *mikvah*, he had seen their pale blue skin, their withered loins, as they'd walked haltingly down the stone steps to immerse themselves in the dark, chilly water. Have they ever known love? Hirsh Leib wondered. Their wives cannot be like my Soreh, so what does the "Song of Songs" mean to them? Do they think only of an abstract Sabbath bride and the love Israel has for the Holy One, Blessed is He? How can they know the love of heaven if they don't know love on earth?

Let us go early to the vineyards, to see whether the grape-vine has budded, whether the vine blossoms have opened, if the pomegranates are in flower. There I will give my love to you. The love-plants yield their fragrance, and at our doors are all kinds of precious fruits, both new and old, which I have kept for you, my beloved.

Yes, Soreh had yielded everything to him. She had welcomed him into her secret garden, and he had picked her fruit. Why, then, was he still hungry? Why did he leave, time and again, to sit at the Yehudi's feet, the Seer's, always searching?

How can I find my true soul? thought Hirsh Leib. In Orlik, with Soreh, and here, in Lublin, in the Seer's *sukkah*, surrounded by *zaddikim* welcoming the *Shabbos*, still my soul fails me.

Make haste, my beloved, be like a gazelle, or like a young deer, on the mountains of spice.

I will, Soreh, thought Hirsh Leib. I will.

The song was over; the Seer's voice drifted away. As if by a signal, Khaye, the Seer's wife, entered the *sukkah*. The Seer stood up and sang to her: "A good wife, who can find? She is worth far more than rubies." After he finished, she smiled and poured wine from a silver pitcher into the *kiddush* cup. The Seer made the blessing and passed the goblet to Hirsh Leib.

Hirsh Leib looked into the cup, his mind, heart, and soul still in Orlik, still with Soreh. Suddenly the wine looked like blood, a deep ruby pool encircled by a lip of silver. Could it be? He looked up at the Seer, but the Seer had turned away. He looked around the table, but Naftali, David, and Menachem Mendel were all staring at their plates. Was this a trick? Hirsh Leib thought. Why have they given me a cup of blood? Or is this a sign that I will never see my Soreh again?

Grief filled his chest. No, that is impossible, he thought. Not to see Soreh again. That is too cruel.

My mind betrays me, Hirsh Leib thought, lifting the cup to his lips.

"Wine is injurious to him."

"What did you say?" Hirsh Leib asked the Seer, putting down the cup.

"What?" said the Seer.

"I thought I heard you say something," said Hirsh Leib, adding, "although you sounded very far away."

"Nobody said anything, Hirsh Leib," Rabbi David said, annoyed that the ceremony was being interrupted.

"Are you all right?" Naftali asked. "Perhaps," he said gently, "you shouldn't drink the wine right now."

Hirsh Leib flushed with embarrassment, remembering how he had struck Naftali. The concern in Naftali's voice enraged him. He picked up the *kiddush* cup, drained it in one swallow, and then, thrusting it toward the *rebbetzin*, said, "Here, it's empty."

Here, he thought, I'm empty.

At that moment Motl, the Seer's young student and servant, entered the *sukkah*, his eyes wide.

"Excuse me, Rabbi," he said to the Seer. "Count Czartoryski is here. I tried to stop him. I told him you couldn't be interrupted, but he—"

Pushing Motl aside, Josep Czartoryski burst into the *sukkah*. The Seer and Hirsh Leib jumped to their feet.

"What could be so important, my lord," demanded the Seer, "that you should come into our holy place and disturb our prayers?"

"Your lives?"

"What do you mean?" asked Hirsh Leib.

"Right now," said Czartoryski, "there's a mob gathering in the market square. It will soon be here. The people of Lublin are tired of your lawlessness, Rabbi. They're tired of your people's lies and blasphemies. They've gathered in the name of Christ to cleanse their city of your minions."

David of Lelov began to pray, rocking back and forth on his chair. Menachem Mendel stood and backed up against the wall of the *sukkah*.

"Why are you telling us this?" asked Naftali.

He means to kill us all, though Hirsh Leib. He means to keep me from my Soreh's side. Never to see her again. Never to see the children. Never to celebrate the Sabbath with my flesh-and-blood Sabbath bride, my beautiful, red-haired Sabbath bride.

"Go away," Hirsh Leib said in a hoarse, croaking voice that sounded far off to his own ears. "You have no business here. Go away."

"You're a rude, impertinent fellow," said Czartoryski. "I should let the mob have you."

"It is your duty to the tsar and to God," said the Seer, "to protect the Jews of Lublin."

"Don't lecture me on my duties, wizard," said Czartoryski. "How dare you call upon the tsar's protection even as you betray him. The Lord's name," he continued, crossing himself, "is foul in your mouth.

"But I'm a Christian, and as much as I despise your false

religion, I don't wish to see you all slaughtered. I'm prepared
to quiet the mob and save your skins if you will turn over to
me that diamond you intend to use to bribe the exiled French
emperor, Napoleon. In return, not only will I save your lives
now, I will also keep your treachery from Tsar Alexander."

We're lost, thought Hirsh Leib. That pig Prince Czartoryski
has betrayed us to his brother and now he will kill us all and
I shall never see Soreh again.

Grief lifted Hirsh Leib to his feet. Tears filled his eyes.
Rage set his heart aflame, and fire coursed through his veins,
making him tremble. He felt a hand grab his sleeve; he shook
it off. He stared at Czartoryski.

Murderer, he thought.

"Murderer," he cried aloud, leaping up on the table and
then throwing himself at Czartoryski, his weight carrying
them both back through the *sukkah*'s entrance, out into the
night, onto the dirt.

They landed, Hirsh Leib on top of Czartoryski and the
Zaddik of Orlik's hands closed around Czartoryski's throat.
He felt Czartoryski buck beneath him, like a fractious horse,
but he was determined not to be thrown. His thumbs searched
for the Pole's Adam's apple and found it.

It's like a nut, thought Hirsh Leib.

Let me crack it.

He felt hands on him, weak hands, pulling at him, picking
at him. No, he thought. Give me a little time. I must crack
this nut.

"Stop."

Who was that?

"Stop."

It was the Seer.

"Stop."

Hirsh Leib felt his rage suddenly vanish, as if the Seer's
voice had overturned a bucket of rainwater on his flaming
heart. His hands relaxed. The nut slipped away and hid from
his thumbs. All right, he thought, stunned in the aftermath of
the storm that had swept him up and then, just as quickly,
had dropped him.

But it is a pity, Hirsh Leib thought, releasing Czartoryski

and standing up. He turned to the Seer and met that great, chilly, gray-blue eye.

I might have saved us, thought Hirsh Leib. In another minute I might have saved us all.

"Some things are not worth the price, Hirsh Leib," said the Seer. "The price you were about to pay was too steep. Let someone else pay it."

Josep Czartoryski lay on the ground, coughing and spitting, trying to get air down his tortured throat into his burning lungs. His mind could not accept what had just happened. Struck by a Jew? Beaten by a Jew? This Jew was stronger than you. He could have killed you, throttled you like a child.

Czartoryski scrambled to his feet. "You're all dead," he said, spitting phlegm and blood, his voice a raspy whisper. "I'll kill you all. You"—he pointed at Hirsh Leib—"I'll cut your heart out."

Czartoryski ran away from the *sukkah*. The *zaddikim* watched him go. Motl stood transfixed.

"What have you done, you madman, you drunkard?" shouted David of Lelov, his eyes blazing at Hirsh Leib.

"What was he talking about?" Naftali asked the Seer. "What's this about a diamond? What diamond?"

"A bribe," said Menachem Mendel. "A bribe for Napoleon. A foolish bribe that the Lord despises."

"He's murdered us all," continued David of Lelov, his face red, spit flying from his lips. "This *meshuggeneh*, this crazy man, has signed our death warrants."

"Don't trouble yourself, Reb David," said Naftali. "Have we made another Christian enemy? So? What's one more? Isn't that so, Hirsh Leib?"

But Hirsh Leib did not answer him. Indeed, he hardly heard him. He was staring at Menachem Mendel, who had known what he should not.

Hirsh Leib turned to the Seer to denounce the traitorous *zaddik*, but something in the Seer's face stopped him.

He knows, thought Hirsh Leib. He has always known that Mendel would betray us. And he doesn't care. He is using this evil, just as he is using the diamond, the pogroms, perhaps even my drunkenness and rage.

What kind of man is this? Hirsh Leib wondered, and he felt fear.

44

The Seer's Study
Lublin
Sunday, October 17

Hirsh Leib stood in a corner of the Rabbi Yakov Yitzhak's private study, staring at his teacher's back. The Seer of Lublin gazed out the small window that overlooked his courtyard. As it had been for days, it was crowded to bursting with chattering Hasidim.

"Like crows," the Seer muttered. "Tell me, Hirsh Leib, is our drab dress, our black hats and black coats, a rejection of vanity, or is it a kind of self-righteousness, a kind of pride?"

Hirsh Leib did not answer. He had been trying to discuss Menachem Mendel, the traitorous *zaddik*, but the Seer had refused.

"Ah, they are just men," the Seer said, his hand taking in the Hasidim. "The Lord judges, not us. They are men like all men. Some mostly good, others mostly bad, all of them both good and bad.

"Can men such as we are ever please the Lord most High?" the Seer wondered aloud. "Is it folly to expect men such as we to unite the upper and lower worlds? Is it vanity to think that we can hasten the coming of the Messiah? Is it madness to put our trust, our lives, in the hands of that monster, Napoleon?"

The Seer shuddered. "What we are doing *is* mad," he said, "but what choice do we have? To remain here, in Lublin, until some drunken Pole fires a bullet through my window? To remain here, in Lublin, until Count Czartoryski or some other nobleman decides to throw all the Jews out of Poland? To remain here, in Europe, until some king or emperor or tsar decides to put all our homes to the torch?''

"You could go to Zion," Hirsh Leib said. "You yourself could lead us to the Holy Land."

"But what of those I leave behind?" asked the Seer. "And what will the Lord think, Blessed be His name? He showed me the Corsican, waging war on the plains outside the Holy City of Jerusalem. He gave me the stone. How can I deny what He has revealed to me?"

Beyond the courtyard, the Seer could see the wooden and tin roofs of Lublin. The market square, he knew, would be deserted. The people were afraid.

The Seer lifted his eyes, and there, on top of the hill, almost touching the clouds, he could see that crucified man on the roof of the church.

"They believe we killed him, Hirsh Leib," the Seer said. "A rabbi. They believe we held the hammer and drove the nails."

"They say their Jesus was betrayed by a man named Judas," Hirsh Leib said. "We have been betrayed also."

"If Menachem Mendel told Czartoryski of our plan, it was because he feared for the Jews. It was because he thought he was following a righteous path. And from righteousness, no evil can come."

The Seer sighed. He knew Hirsh Leib did not understand.

Their mass will soon be over, Hirsh Leib thought. Will the Poles come spilling out to continue their pogrom? Or will they be calmed by praying to the soul of that tortured rabbi?

So much hate has gathered around us, so much anger. Help me, Lord, Hirsh Leib prayed.

Help me, Lord, the Seer of Lublin prayed. Help me to see what is to come.

The door to the Seer's study opened, and Khaye, the *rebbetzin*, poked her head in. "Can I get you anything, Yakov?" she asked. "Oh, excuse me, Reb Leib. Can I bring you something, too?"

"Thank you, dear," the Seer said. "A glass of tea would be nice."

"Nothing for me, thank you," said Hirsh Leib.

The door closed, and the Seer turned back to the window. He saw the clouds thicken, billowing up. "Look, Hirsh Leib," he said. "Look there. Can you see two horses upon whose backs ride three men?"

"You know I cannot," said Hirsh Leib.

"He comes," said the Seer. "He will be here tomorrow. By tomorrow evening we will know if we have succeeded or failed. We will know if we live or die."

The Seer took the diamond from his coat and placed it on the windowsill.

"What do you see in the stone?" asked Hirsh Leib.

"It carries my eye in a spiral," the Seer said. "It is this and not this, that and not that. It cloaks and reveals. It is clear, and yet it is obscure. It is a picture of the world. It is like the *sefiros*, the ten hidden attributes of the Lord. This will be a good exercise," said the Seer. "This will quiet my mind and help me see. Do you mind if I think aloud?"

"Of course not," said Hirsh Leib.

"First," said the Seer, holding up one finger, "the stone reveals its surface—oil floating on water, rainbows swimming through the oil. That's its *t'feres*, its beauty."

The Seer reached out and tapped the diamond. "Its surface is hard," he said. "That's its strength, it's *g'vurah*. Beauty and strength, that's its glory, *hod*."

The Seer ran his finger over the top of the stone. "That's its crown," he said, "*keter*. From the crown, it flares out. That's the foundation, *yesod*. The combination of the crown and the foundation define *malkhus*, kingdom.

"Now my eye is drawn inside. It is so deep. It has no bottom. Just facets reflecting facets infinitely. One can get lost in its recesses as one can get lost in Talmud. But to see what is hidden in its flashing lights requires *khokhma*, wisdom; *bina*, understanding; and *khesed*, grace."

The Seer glanced at the stone. "Something's missing," he said.

"*Netzakh*," said Hirsh Leib. "Victory."

The *rebbetzin* entered with the Seer's tea. "Are you all right, Yakov?" she asked.

"Yes, Khaye. I'm fine."

"May I speak?"

"Yes, of course," said the Seer.

Khaye glanced at Hirsh Leib. "I'll go," he said.

"Nonsense," said the Seer. "Is it so private we must be alone, Khaye?"

"I'm frightened, Yakov," she said. "Is that private? I don't think so. Hirsh Leib is frightened, too. I can see that. You think women don't see. We see more than you think."

"Tomorrow is Simkhas Torah, Khaye. We will dance with the holy words, and no harm will come to us."

"I wish you would bury that," she said, pointing to the diamond on the windowsill. "Bury it in the woods, far away. It frightens me."

"I will do that, Khaye. Tomorrow."

"With you, it's always tomorrow. And you, Hirsh Leib," she said. "You look like a sick man. You're so pale. I think you should leave Lublin."

"Khaye," said the Seer, angrily.

"I don't care," Khaye said. "It's the truth, and since when does it make you angry to hear the truth? The way you attacked the count," she said to Hirsh Leib, "like a crazy man. You know the count won't forget. He'll tell his brother, the prince, and that will make trouble for you, for all of us."

"Shush, Khaye. Hirsh Leib is suffering. What kind of friend would I be if I sent him away? Besides, he's strong, and we need his strength."

"You're wrong, Yakov. You know it, don't you, Hirsh Leib. There's something terrible happening inside you. You've changed. I don't know you anymore. Wednesday, when you came to the *hoyf*, the day those poor people were shot, there was an old beggar riding with you?"

"That's right," said Hirsh Leib.

"I think," Khaye said, her voice dropping to a whisper, "it was 'That One.'"

"Khaye," the Seer said, laughing, "you couldn't be more wrong. That old beggar was Elijah. I saw him in the study house just the other day."

"It was the Angel of Death, Yakov, I'm sure of it. His

beard was the color of tin. And then I took a needle from my dress. I looked at him through its eye, and I saw him holding a wooden sword over his head. I closed my eyes, and when I looked again, he was gone. But, right where he was standing, there was a black cat that Hirsh Leib kicked. You know what that means. Wasn't there a black cat, Hirsh Leib?''

"Stop, Khaye,'' said the Seer. "I don't know what you saw, but you know as well as I do that if it was 'That One,' and you saw him, you'd be dead now, and Hirsh Leib, too.''

"Maybe. Maybe not, Yakov. Maybe he's waiting to get us all at once.''

"Enough of this,'' the Seer said, kissing his wife on her forehead. "It was Elijah. I know. Now go. Leave us alone to discuss these things.''

"Yes, *Rebbenyu*,'' said Khaye, closing the heavy wooden door softly behind her.

The Seer turned back to the diamond. "Why else would you be given to me,'' he asked, "if not to save us?''

"Could you have mistaken the Angel of Death for Elijah?'' asked Hirsh Leib.

The Seer closed his eyes and recited the prayer "Blessed be He who in His holiness gave the Torah to the people of Israel.'' Then he began rocking silently.

"What do you see now, my teacher?'' asked Hirsh Leib.

"I see what I have seen dozens of times before,'' the Seer said in a voice as soft as the sound of the wind ruffling the feathers of birds in the trees.

"I see the Hasidim dancing in the streets of Lublin.

"I see the silver crowns of the Torahs bouncing up and down above the throng.

"I hear the singing and rejoicing.

"I see hands reaching up to touch the Torah.

"I hear children screaming happily.

"I see myself, my *tallis* over my head, my face covered, moving through the crowd.

"I hear my Hasidim whispering as I pass: 'Where is our *rebbe*? Where is our Seer? Why is he not with us?'

"I see myself coming face to face with a short, fat man with a curly black beard and a battered black hat.

"It is the emperor Napoleon.

"I hear Napoleon say, 'I have come.'

"I see myself reaching into my coat.

"I feel the hardness of the diamond.

"I see myself extending my hand toward Napoleon, the diamond shining in my palm.

"I hear myself saying, 'In the name of the Lord, Blessed be He, take this from the Jews of Lublin. Take this as a sign of victory.'

"I see Napoleon reach out."

The Seer fell silent. He stopped rocking.

"And then?" asked Hirsh Leib.

"Nothing. I lose the vision."

"Does it ever change?"

"Never. Sometimes the faces are a little different. Sometimes Napoleon does not have a beard. Sometimes Prince Czartoryski is there, sometimes not. Sometimes, different faces."

"How can you not go mad?" asked Hirsh Leib. "I feel I am going mad."

"I am afraid you have had very little peace since you've come to Lublin, my friend."

"My sickness grows, Rabbi," Hirsh Leib said in a low, hollow voice. "Khaye is right. I feel him stalking me, Death. Only the brandy seems to make him go away."

"We need you, Hirsh Leib," said the Seer. "Tomorrow evening, when the scrolls are removed from the ark, when the tribes of Israel participate in the seven *hakkafot*, dancing seven times around the great *shul* with the Torah, Prince Czartoryski will bring Napoleon into our midst. We will go to him to hand him the jewel. You must be by our side. Together, we will recite the *kohanim*s' first *hakkafah*: 'O Lord, save us; O Lord, prosper us; O Lord, answer us when we call. God of all souls, save us; Examiner of hearts, prosper us; Mighty Redeemer, answer us when we call.'

"You must guard us from harm, Hirsh Leib. Your eyes must be clear, your ears open."

"Choose someone else, Rabbi Yitzhak," said Hirsh Leib. "*Hashem* has turned his face from me."

"No, Hirsh Leib. *Hashem* has not turned from you. You have turned from Him. Now you must turn your face back to the Lord. That turning, that *teshuvah*, will create a prayer so sweet that all the angels in all the heavens will join you in praising the Lord.

"What is the greatest *mitzvah*, Hirsh Leib? What is the holiest deed a man can perform?"

"The ransoming of captives," Hirsh Leib answered.

"Exactly," said the Seer. "Today, Hirsh Leib, you are a captive. Tomorrow, with the help of the Lord, Blessed be His name, you, and all of Israel, will be ransomed. Tomorrow, we will all be freed.

"So prepare yourself, Hirsh Leib," said the Seer. "There is very little time."

45

The Church
Lublin
Sunday, October 17

When the Seer was again alone, his soul went forth, and this, as he would later tell Hirsh Leib, was what he saw and what he understood:

Thin clouds raced overhead as Count Josep Czartoryski stood chatting with Father Karol Wojtyla, congratulating him on his sermon. Its theme, suggested to Father Wojtyla by Czartoryski earlier in the week, had been the sins of the Jews.

"The sin that towers over all the others," the young priest, expanding on his sermon, was explaining to Czartoryski, "is the sin of pride. Of course, the peasants do not understand that, nor do they need to. They simply know the Jew as our Savior's executioner, and that is sufficient. But as sophisticated men, Count, we shun the Jew not because he crucified our Lord—all men share in that sin—but because in the face of Revelation, in the face of the Resurrection, the Jew in his pride refuses to accept Christ as his savior. That is why the Jew is damned.''

"Of course," said Czartoryski, whose voice was still hoarse and whose throat, hidden by a white silk scarf, bore the purpling bruises left by Hirsh Leib's fingers.

The mood of the men leaving the church was sullen. Tomorrow was Anders Shmielewicz's funeral. After that, there was talk of heading into Lublin and killing Jews.

Joseph Czartoryski had heard their mutterings and could sense their mood, but he had no desire to speak with them. Let them stew, he thought, mounting his horse and riding back to the castle. If they kill a few Jews today, good. Tomorrow we'll kill a lot more.

The Seer's soul flew over the trees.

When Czartoryski returned to the castle, a groom took his horse and told him that his brother had arrived. Czartoryski made for the library, where he knew the prince would be warming himself by the fire after his journey. He entered the room and saw his brother and a short, stout Jew standing in front of the hearth.

"Now you bring them into our home!" shouted Czartoryski. "You've lost your mind, Adam. The peasants will first kill the *kapotes*, and then they'll turn on us."

"Be quiet, Josep," said Adam Czartoryski. "Try using your brain before you open your mouth."

"Get him out of here," said Josep. "I'm serious. I won't stand for it."

"You won't stand for it? You? Since when are you the master here?"

"I must say," said Napoleon, "and I mean no offense, Adam, that yours is an impossible language. It sounds like you are being sick after having bitten into a bad oyster. I simply cannot understand a word you're saying. I presume this is your brother. He does speak French, doesn't he?"

Josep Czartoryski stood staring.

"Ah, yes," said Napoleon. "My disguise. I have grown so used to it." He removed the false beard. "Now, Count Czartoryski, do you recognize me?"

"I apologize, *mon empereur*," said Josep, bowing.

"Allow me to present my brother, Count Josep Czartoryski," said Adam.

"Charmed," said Napoleon, extending his hand. Josep bowed again and kissed it.

"The emperor will be staying with us tonight and tomorrow," said Adam Czartoryski. "I have instructed that his room be prepared. You understand, of course, that no one is to know. No one. And that includes Nikola. As far as she and the servants are concerned, the emperor is a holy man who has come to Lublin to celebrate the Jews' holiday, and we are honoring him."

"I have met your wife, Nikola, Count," said Napoleon. "You and your brother must be married to the two most beautiful women in Poland."

"Thank you, my lord," said Josep. "But, Adam, I must tell you that since you left, a Jew killed a peasant—he bit off his foot—and the people have killed a few Jews. Tomorrow the peasant is being buried. If it gets out that we're keeping a Jew in our home, they'll be angry. I don't know what could happen."

"I want no pogrom," said Adam. "Any peasant who interferes with the Jews' celebration tomorrow will be lashed fifty times. I'll do it myself, Josep. You let them know that. It's very important to the emperor that there be no trouble tomorrow. Do you understand?"

"Yes. But why should we care about the Jews' holiday? My lord," Josep said to Napoleon, "I don't understand your interest in these matters."

"Don't be rude," said Adam. "When and if the emperor wishes to inform you of his plans, he will do so. Until then, he relies upon your discretion. You won't disappoint him, will you?"

"Of course not," said Josep.

"Good," said Napoleon. "Excellent. We all understand each other. And that reminds me, Count Josep. Your French is rather poor. Really quite, quite execrable. Your brother's is much better. So, for that matter, is your wife's. You should practice. I would suggest speaking with them in French at all times. In that way, in time, you may improve.

"And now, Adam," Napoleon said, rubbing his hands together, "I'm positively faint with hunger. Would you believe it, Count Josep? Since we left Warsaw on Friday, I've literally had nothing but bread and water. So, Adam, shall we eat?"

46
The Great Shul
Lublin
Monday, October 18
Simkhas Torah

Hirsh Leib was to meet the Seer on his hill at sunset, but now, really for the first time, the *Zaddik* of Orlik was enjoying Lublin.

All through the day, from the morning prayers on, the mood in Lublin's great wooden *shul* on Synagogue Street had become progressively more playful. Children ran up and down the temple's aisles as their mothers, leaving the balcony reserved for women, chased them. Men who normally would have become enraged by such riotous behavior, who normally would have scolded the children and berated the women, smiled indulgently. Some even produced dried and candied fruits from their pockets as treats for the children.

Not even on the High Holy Days, on Rosh Hashanah and Yom Kippur, was the *shul* so crowded. On those days many Jews went to their own *shtibls*, leaving the great *shul* for the big shots. But on Simkhas Torah everyone went to the great *shul*, not only because it had more Torahs than any five *shtibls* combined—thereby increasing one's chances of getting to carry a Torah around the *bimah* and out into the streets—but because it was an opportunity to revel in their numbers, to be surrounded, engulfed, and succored.

On Simkhas Torah it felt good to be a Jew.

As the sun sank lower in the sky, the *hazzan*'s singing had also become more playful, more outlandish, more theatrical. By the afternoon service he was singing the closing *Aleinu* to the tune of a popular Polish folk song while the congregation clapped and laughed and sang along.

In the market square, Berel the drunkard's tavern was so crowded that Goldeh, Berel's long-suffering wife, had set up a table out on the street with bottles of sweet wine and brandy. The day was warm, and men lined up three deep, as they did at Neshe's soup kitchen, and in the dining rooms of Reb Leyzer and Reb Moyshe's inns.

For the first time in days, the Hasidim from Pshiskhe and Lodz, from Khelm, Kosk, Apt, and Ger, stopped arguing, stopped bragging about the relative merits of their respective *rebbes*, and joined in spontaneous song and dance. Soothed and excited by drink, by their teeming numbers, and by the surprising warmth of this sunny day—surely a sign of God's pleasure—Lublin's Jews began to forget the terrors of the previous nights. As they looked around them at the crowded, festive streets, as they stood on the steps of the great *shul* listening to the singing, the very idea of a pogrom seemed ludicrous, like a bad dream from which they had finally awakened.

Hirsh Leib, as he had on his first day in Lublin, approached the Seer's hill and saw Rabbi Yakov Yitzhak sitting on a tree stump, smoking his pipe, his eyes closed. Beneath Hirsh Leib's feet the pine needles made a soft cushion. He could hear birdsong, and from far off he could hear the voices of the Jews of Lublin.

He knew that to the Seer the diamond, in itself, was of little importance. It was nothing more than a snare to bring Napoleon to Lublin. As the Seer had explained to him, what was important was to see the emperor, to look at his forehead and read there the history of his soul, backward and forward. Then and only then would the Seer really know if he was the one who would bring about the final battle between good and evil on the plains of Armageddon.

As a boy Yakov Yitzhak had been remote, withdrawn, and melancholy. His teachers had recognized his swiftness of mind, but they worried about his heart. He seemed to take no joy from the games of the other boys, and his prayers seemed to hover low to the ground, not fly up as they should have. So they sent him to Rabbi Zusya, who quickly divined that when Yakov's soul had been created, it had been endowed with the power of seeing from one end of the world to the other. But that power, for which so many men would have schemed and even murdered, tortured the young boy.

Wherever he looked, young Yakov saw pain. Wherever he looked, he saw evil. Only by keeping his eye fixed on the holy words could he escape his dark visions. He told Zusya that seeing every man's sins lessened his love for Israel. So he had begged him to do something to take away that power. But Zusya reminded him that the Lord did not take back his gifts.

So Zusya taught Yakov how to rein in his visions, how to limit them so he was not continuously assaulted by all the world's horrors. He taught Yakov how to use music and song to defeat, or at least hold at bay, his melancholy. He encouraged Yakov to go into the woods, to listen to the birds and mice and deer, because their lives were untouched by evil, because they were perfect, just as *Hashem* had made them.

Zusya had even given Yakov his pipe and told him to smoke it whenever he grew too sad. And by the time Yakov Yitzhak had founded his own school in Lublin, his heart had been healed. After Zusya, he gave his wife, Khaye, some of the credit for healing him, and for the rest he thanked *Hashem*.

But now, as Hirsh Leib climbed up the hill toward him, the Seer summoned his vision. Now he opened his gray-blue eye, the large one, and his heart sank. He saw the shame that burned inside Hirsh Leib, and he saw him reaching out for wine to extinguish the flames. Tears filled the Seer's eyes.

The Seer blinked and looked from the sky to the town lying beneath him and back again, bringing the heavens and the earth together, binding them so that the clouds became the floor upon which Lublin stood. Now it seemed to the Seer as if all the buildings had turned to crystal, and he could see into every room. The people, too, had turned to glass, and he could see into every heart.

Now, above the city, he could see Castle Czartoryski, and in its many rooms he could see the blond prince, his dark brother, and the man he had glimpsed so many years before, leading a great army outside Jerusalem. Now the man looked like a Jew, a Hasid, and even though the Seer knew it to be a disguise born of a twisted vanity, he prayed that it was a sign.

Rabbi Yitzhak, the Seer of Lublin, saw the prince and the emperor leave the castle together, and he stood up. He looked around him, banishing his vision by concentrating on what was in front of him. The last rays of the sun were painting the leaves red. Night was coming on. It was time to go. With the lighting of the stars, the evening prayers would begin.

He knocked the ashes out of his pipe. He touched the diamond in his pocket and began walking down the path toward Hirsh Leib, down the path to Lublin.

47

The Great Shul
Lublin
Monday, October 18

The eighteen blessings for Simkhas Torah were beginning. Inside the *shul* every seat was filled, and sweating men, standing beneath the smoking candles, lined the walls three deep. Behind the *bima*, along the eastern wall, in their white holiday robes, sat Rov Chaim, Lublin's official rabbi, the puffed-up members of the *kahal*, and the cosmic conspirators, Rebbes David and Naftali, who, with their eyes tightly shut, sent their words up to heaven and prayed for the coming of the Messiah. No one had seen Rebbe Menachem Mendel.

The *hazzan* sang the first blessing—*You have learned to know that the Lord is God; there is none else besides Him*—and the congregation repeated it at the top of its lungs. The joists of the wooden *shul*—built, like the legendary temple in Jerusalem, without a single nail—vibrated and hummed with the sound of a thousand voices. The roar spilled out into the street, where men holding prayer books stood shoulder to shoulder in the gathering dusk and rocked and prayed.

Hirsh Leib repeated the second blessing under his breath—*To Him who alone does great wonders; His mercy endures forever*—and darted through the crowd that pressed around the steps of the *shul* and spilled out and down all the streets of the town. Pushing, shoving, craning his neck, and standing on his toes, he searched the dark throng for the Seer, from whom he had become separated.

Hirsh Leib felt sick. The heat, the press of people, and the wine he had drunk to calm himself had combined to make him dizzy. He cursed himself for his weakness.

The third blessing rose from a thousand throats around him: *There is no God like Thee, O Lord; there are no deeds like Thine.*

The prayers went on, washing over Hirsh Leib while he strained to find his teacher, his master.

The Lord is King; the Lord was King; the Lord will be King forever and ever.

Hirsh Leib felt time collapsing.

I have searched through such a crowd before. I have rushed through such a press of men. Not once, but twice. But when did this happen? Whom was I looking for? How can this be?

Thy kingdom is an everlasting kingdom, and Thy dominion endures throughout all generations.

Suddenly, standing in front of him, was the man he knew as Yekl.

"I know who you are," said Hirsh Leib.

" 'Thy dominion endures throughout all generations,' " Yekl said, repeating the words of the prayer, translating the

Hebrew into Yiddish. "Did you hear that, Hirsh Leib? Do you understand what that means?"

"Where is the Seer?"

"Don't worry about the Seer. Think about what I told you before. You are not lost; there is still time."

"I don't know what you're talking about," said Hirsh Leib. "I must find the Seer."

"But here he is," said Yekl, stepping aside, his face breaking into a broken-toothed smile.

Hirsh Leib looked past Yekl, and there, his head covered by an enormous blue-and-white *tallis* woven through with silver threads, was Rabbi Yitzhak.

Merciful Father, may it be Thy will to favor Zion with Thy goodness; mayest Thou rebuild the walls of Jerusalem. Truly, in Thee alone we trust, high and exalted King and God, eternal Lord.

"Amen" roared through the streets, and there was a sudden rush toward the temple. The *shemonai esrei* were concluded. Next would come the *hakkafot*, as all the tribes of Israel— first the priests, the *kohanim*, then the Levites, their cup bearers, and finally the Israelites, the common folk—would carry the Torahs out of the ark, carry them seven times around the temple and then out into the streets. It was an honor to carry the Torah. It was a blessing to kiss one, and nobody wanted to miss his chance.

"Elijah is here," Hirsh Leib said to the Seer.

"Where?" the Seer asked urgently. "Let me see him. I have seen him but once, and that only briefly. And I have never seen him in my visions."

Hirsh Leib looked around. "He's gone."

Men rushing up the temple steps collided with Hirsh Leib and the Seer; they struggled to keep from being swept off their feet. Hirsh Leib held the Seer's arm to anchor him to the ground.

"How will we find Napoleon in this madness?" asked Hirsh Leib.

"He is almost here. Czartoryski will bring him to the steps of the *shul*. I have seen it," said the Seer.

A shout came from the throng, and Hirsh Leib turned to

see the silver crown of one of the Torahs emerge from the *shul*'s doorway, glittering and shining in the light cast by a dozen torches. Then it was swept up as if by a huge wave, first washed down the *shul* steps, then spun in widening gyres as the crowd danced, singing the first *hakkafah*: *O Lord, save us; O Lord, prosper us; O Lord, answer us when we call! God of all souls, save us; Examiner of hearts, prosper us; mighty Redeemer, answer us when we call!*

"Blessed be He; He has answered us," said the Seer.

In front of them, holding a torch, stepping forward like a ray of sunlight breaking through a storm-tossed sky, was Prince Adam Jerzy Czartoryski, tall, blond, erect. Beside him stood a short, stout Hasid.

Prince Czartoryski leaned toward the Seer. "The emperor greets you, Rabbi Yitzhak," he said.

The Seer took his *tallis* off his head and, draping it over his shoulders, stood silently gazing at Napoleon's broad forehead in the torchlight. On it he saw ambition, an appetite that would never be satisfied. He saw the mark of Cain, the bloody sign of fratricide. How many deaths has this monster been responsible for? the Seer wondered. Millions? Yes, millions.

"Is this what you wanted?" Czartoryski shouted.

Is it? wondered the Seer. May the Lord preserve us.

Hirsh Leib, still holding his master's arm, felt the Seer tremble. The Torah was slowly making its way to where they stood. It seemed to Hirsh Leib as if a glass jar had been dropped over the four of them. He could still hear the singing and shouting; he could still feel the press of the thousands; but it all seemed far off, unreal. Then he saw three or perhaps four rough-looking peasants moving among the Hasidim.

Napoleon was speaking. "What does he say?" Hirsh Leib asked Czartoryski.

"He says he can look at him for as long as he likes. He says he's not afraid. He means he's not afraid of Rabbi Yitzhak. But, please, Rabbi," Czartoryski said to the Seer, "it's not good to tarry here. We're conspicuous. At least, I am."

The Seer continued to stare at Napoleon.

He saw him on the battlefield, roaring amidst carnage, delighting in slaughter.

He saw him riding in his carriage, wrapped in blankets, speeding through the frigid Russian night while his army starved and froze in the icy fields.

He saw the huge head. The fat beneath the flesh.

A creature of chaos. A thing from the abyss.

Well, what did you expect? the Seer asked himself.

He tried to force his vision beyond this meeting. He tried to see himself leaving, returning to his study, the diamond still in his pocket. He could not.

So? Let it be done.

The Torah was coming closer. Hirsh Leib could see the silver bells on its crown bouncing up and down, but he could not hear them ring. He felt himself being pushed from behind as first one man, then another, tried to approach the Torah, reaching out to touch it with their prayer books, leaning over Hirsh Leib, shouldering him aside. Suddenly Hirsh Leib's hand was no longer on the Seer's arm.

Pushing back, trying to regain his position by the Seer's side, Hirsh Leib saw the Seer reach into his pocket and then extend his right hand toward Napoleon. At that moment he saw the peasants, shouting, knocking people aside with clubs, throw themselves on the Seer. He heard Prince Adam Czartoryski shout also, flinging himself on the peasants, and then, standing behind them, he saw the cruel face of Josep Czartoryski.

A voice screamed in Hirsh Leib's ear. "Look out!" A body crashed into him and knocked him off his feet, knocked him to his knees.

There, lying on the ground in front of him, was a beardless yet familiar-looking man his own age wearing a brown coat of strange cut. The man's white shirt was stained black with blood. His head was resting in Yekl's lap.

"This policeman has redeemed you," Yekl said calmly. "Now you must comfort him."

"What?" shouted Hirsh Leib, trying to get his feet beneath him as bodies tumbled over and around him. He felt as if he were being held under water by a strong current. He felt as if he were drowning.

"This man has won your battle with wine," said Yekl. "It was hard. You owe him your soul."

"The Seer," said Hirsh Leib, panicking. "Czartoryski. The diamond. I must get up."

"You must leave all that to this man," said Yekl.

"But what can he do?" Hirsh Leib asked.

"He is already doing it," said Yekl.

Can this be? wondered Hirsh Leib. Yes, he answered himself. Yes, it can. What does Hashem care for time?

"Blessed be God," Hirsh Leib said to the bleeding man. "Easy," he said to him. "You'll be all right."

Instantly Hirsh Leib felt as if a cloud had been lifted from his mind. The fire of shame that had, it seemed to him, forever burned in his chest, flickered out, leaving not an emptiness, but a fullness.

"You're not Elijah, are you?" asked Hirsh Leib, looking up from the bleeding man to Yekl.

"No," said Yekl.

"Who are you?" asked Hirsh Leib.

"Soon," said Yekl. "Soon you'll know."

"This man?" asked Hirsh Leib.

"Will live," said Yekl.

"Good," said Hirsh Leib. He patted the man's hand and then stood up, easily. His mind was full of questions, but somehow, oddly, they didn't seem urgent.

A dream, he thought. This is all a dream.

Hirsh Leib looked around. The Seer, Napoleon, Prince Czartoryski, his brother, Josep—all gone.

Hirsh Leib looked down. Yekl, the bleeding man—gone, too.

A dream, he thought again. I will wake up in Orlik, next to Soreh.

The Torah was in front of Hirsh Leib. He touched its velvet coverlet, then he kissed his fingers.

They were wet.

He looked at his hand.

It was covered with blood.

Shocked, Hirsh Leib pushed through the throng, staggering. He could see three, four Torahs dancing in the street, their bells and crowns bobbing in the torchlight, their shadows rushing up and down the walls of the shops. He stumbled into a man, who pushed him away. "Drunkard!" the man shouted. "Shame!"

Hirsh Leib reeled into another man, who also pushed him off, and he fell into another's arms. Looking up, he saw it was Reb Bunem, the apothecary who had held back from the conspiracy.

"Are you drunk, Hirsh Leib?" asked Bunem.

"No. Not anymore," said the *Zaddik* of Orlik.

"You're covered with blood," said Bunem. "My God. Come, come to my shop. Let me help you."

"I'm not hurt," said Hirsh Leib. "It's not my blood. But the Seer. Help me find the Seer."

"What has happened? Is it the Seer's blood?"

"I don't think so." Hirsh Leib pulled away. "But come. We must find him."

Hirsh Leib and Reb Bunem elbowed and shoved, fighting their way away from the *shul*. Men grabbed for them, asking where was the great Seer, why was he not in the synagogue, why was he not leading the celebration?

Finally they broke free of the crowd, moving into dark streets that had been transformed into rivers of mud by the feet of thousands of Hasidim.

"My God!" said Bunem, pointing to a man lying face-down. They ran to him and turned him over. It was Rebbe Menachem Mendel, his throat cut.

"The Lord Himself will weep," said Bunem, horrified.

"Perhaps," said Hirsh Leib.

"How can you be so hard?" Bunem asked.

"I will tell you later," said Hirsh Leib. "Now we must find the Seer."

"But we must take care of our brother here."

"He is in the Lord's hands. The Lord will deal with him as He sees fit."

"What have you done, Hirsh Leib? What have all of you done? What has happened? Does the Seer live?"

"I don't know," said Hirsh Leib.

They crossed Lublin's almost empty market square, the sounds of the celebration at the temple fading behind them. They moved down another street and then another, eventually finding themselves walking down the Old Road toward the Seer's hill.

For the first time that evening, Hirsh Leib looked up at the sky. Never, it seemed to him, had he seen the stars brighter. Who needed a moon, he thought, when the angels lighted their own candles in the heavens?

There is joy in my heart, Hirsh Leib realized with a shock. In the midst of defeat, I feel only joy.

"Look," said Bunem.

There, lying against a building, was a man wrapped in a blue-and-white *tallis* that glistened in the starlight.

Bunem pulled the *tallis* off the Seer's face and gasped. His high forehead was covered with black mud. Both his eyes were black, swollen, and bruised, as were his lips. Blood trickled from his nose, and hanks of his beard had been torn out by their roots, leaving the flesh beneath raw and bleeding. The Seer's chest heaved, and he coughed up blood and phlegm as Bunem lifted him to a sitting position.

Bunem ran his hands gently over the Seer's chest, arms, and legs, discovering broken bones wherever he touched. He tore a strip of cloth from his *kapote* and wiped the Seer's mouth inside and out.

"I must get help," said Bunem, handing the cloth to Hirsh Leib. "You stay with the Seer. Keep his head back so he can breathe. If his mouth fills up with blood, clean it out. I'll go find some men to help us carry him to my shop. I'll be back as soon as I can. May the Lord protect and keep you both."

"Amen," said Hirsh Leib as Bunem rose and began trotting back toward the square and the great *shul*.

Hirsh Leib took the cloth Bunem had given him and wiped the mud off the Seer's forehead.

"It's quiet here," said Hirsh Leib. "Rest."

The Seer opened his eyes.

"Blessed be the Lord, you'll be all right," said Hirsh Leib.

"No," said the Seer.

"The diamond?" asked Hirsh Leib.

"I could not," the Seer whispered, reaching into his coat. There, in his palm, was the stone.

"Take it," said the Seer.

"I cannot," said Hirsh Leib. "I will not."

The Seer coughed, and a bubble of blood formed in the corner of his mouth, broke, and ran down his beard. "You must," said the Seer.

"This stone," said Hirsh Leib, not wanting to touch it but unable to take his eyes off it, "this stone has destroyed you. It is from the Evil One."

"No," said the Seer. "The diamond is an angel's heart. See how it shines with the Lord's light. But the world, and the men in it, are broken vessels. They are jealous of such completeness, of such purity, of such beauty. They are jealous of the Holy One Himself, and so it has been since the first man. I thought, perhaps, enough men had changed to mend the world. I saw too much, and I was fooled. Now I know. The stone cannot purchase paradise; it cannot bring the worlds together until the broken vessel, man, is mended.

"So take the angel's heart, Hirsh Leib, and return it to the earth. Bury it deep, my friend. When it is once again found, perhaps then . . ." The Seer coughed. "Take it, Hirsh Leib."

Hirsh Leib reached out and took the stone from the Seer's hand. As his hand closed over it, he felt fear.

Relieved of the stone, the Seer felt his heart slow. He tried to summon his vision once more, but the world refused to change. The sky and the earth remained in their places; the buildings remained solid. He closed his eyes, sighing. He was free.

"I'm thirsty," said the Seer.

"I'll get you something," Hirsh Leib said, standing.

"Hirsh Leib," said the Seer, "I can feel that you are yourself again."

"Yes," said Hirsh Leib. "Now rest. I will find us some water. It is a beautiful night."

The Seer nodded, and his heart praised the Lord.

Hirsh Leib began walking back the way he had come, back toward the market square. He turned a corner onto another dark, deserted street and saw a man on horseback galloping toward him. Hirsh Leib raised his hand, signaling for help, and the horseman stopped in front of him.

Suddenly, out of the darkness, something came flashing down. He blinked, raising his arm to protect himself. He felt his face and neck burn as his arm was knocked aside. He felt his knees buckle, and he sank to the muddy street.

No! Hirsh Leib's mind roared.

"No!" Hirsh Leib shouted.

"No!" Dov Taylor screamed.

"Still alive?" said Josep Czartoryski, leaping from his horse. "We'll fix that."

Czartoryski stood over Hirsh Leib for a moment, then kicked him in the ribs. Hirsh Leib felt them break, and Dov Taylor felt the air rush out of his lungs.

"Remember me?" Czartoryski asked, crouching beside Hirsh Leib and taking him by the throat. "You remember me, don't you, Jew? I told you I would cut your heart out, didn't I? A gentleman always keeps his word, Jew.

"But did your cursed wizard give it to you?"

Czartoryski plunged his hand into Hirsh Leib's pocket. "Yes!" Czartoryski shouted. "Thank God." He held the stone in front of Hirsh Leib's eyes.

"Can you see it, Jew? Can you see it? Can you see your death in it?"

Hirsh Leib looked at the stone, glittering in the starlight. In its recesses he thought he saw his Soreh's face, and each star the diamond reflected was a *Shabbos* candle she had lit.

I love you, thought Hirsh Leib, and Dov Taylor felt love well up in his heart.

I won't go away anymore, Hirsh Leib told Soreh.

"You see? You've failed, Jew," said Czartoryski. "I don't know from whom you stole this diamond, but it's mine now. Your wizard is dead. Napoleon will slink back to his rotten island, and the tsar will learn of your people's treachery. You've failed. I want you to die knowing that you've failed."

"What is failure?" Hirsh Leib asked.

Czartoryski's sword caught the starlight above Hirsh Leib's head.

"*Shema, Yisroel*," said the *Zaddik* of Orlik. "Hear, O Israel. The Lord is our God. The Lord is One."

"Amen," said Rebbe Joel Teitel, opening the curtains in his study on South Ninth Street in Williamsburg and then turning again to face Dov Taylor, who had buried his face in his hands and had begun to sob convulsively, his face red and his whole body trembling like an infant who had awakened starving from a troubled sleep.

BOOK
THREE

BOOK
THREE

48

Crown Heights, Brooklyn
Sunday, October 20
The Present

DOV TAYLOR STOOD IN A GENTLE EVENING RAIN ON THE
FRINGES of the crowd that filled the broad street outside Lubavitcher World Headquarters at 770 Eastern Parkway in Crown
Heights. It was Simkhas Torah. Taylor's gun was in the
pocket of his overcoat.

Somewhere in the crowd, perhaps inside the synagogue,
Rabbi Kalman was praying. Somewhere in the crowd, perhaps in the balcony with the other women, was Rabbi Kalman's daughter, Sarah. Taylor had promised he would meet
them. He had promised Reb Kalman that he would go up to
the *bimah* with him to receive a Torah to carry around the *shul*
and then out onto Eastern Parkway, where a huge projection
television screen had been set up on a flatbed truck so that
the thousands of Hasidim outside could see the service.

But Taylor did not want to see the Kalmans. Tonight,
leaning against the brick wall of an apartment building across
the street from the synagogue, watching the scowling,
bearded, ten-foot-high face of the ninety-year-old grand Lubavitcher *rebbe*, Menachem Seligson, on the television
screen, Taylor held his solitude close, taking refuge in it.

How could he explain to Reb Kalman and Sarah what had
been happening to him? How could he make them understand

that he had been dreading this night for weeks? How could he admit to them, and especially to Sarah, that it had taken every last ounce of his dwindling reserves of courage to leave his apartment tonight to come to the *shul*? And that the only way he had been able to make it this far was to have brought his revolver?

He had awakened from his dream, or vision, or memory—he still wasn't sure what to call it or even how to think about it—to find himself as unprotected, as easily rattled, as a newborn infant. It felt as if his skin had been peeled off.

A car backfiring in the street brought his heart into his mouth. Every time a door slammed in his apartment building, he had to fight the urge to reach for the gun, which he now kept loaded—the safety off—on the table by his bed. He kept turning down the volume of the bell on his phone, but every time it went off, he still jumped. Eventually he'd placed a pillow over it, and when that hadn't done the job, he'd put another one on top of that.

He wondered, often, whether he was having a nervous breakdown.

He had called Phil Horowitz a dozen times, only to be told by his mother again and again that Phil was gone, away, overseas, and she didn't know when he'd be back.

He had had lunch with Frank Hill once, meeting him at a midtown coffee shop, and although Hill had been friendly, Taylor could not bring himself to tell him about the diamond. He'd given Hill a description of Horowitz, told him how Horowitz had set him up, and Hill had taken down the information. After that they had seemed to have little to say to each other. Hill had talked about new cases, new homicides, in a distant, offhand way, and Taylor could see that the distance between cop and civilian had reestablished itself between them.

He had gone back to Rebbe Teitel once, three weeks ago, hoping that somehow the rabbi could take his dread away. But the Satmarer *rebbe* had been busy with preparations for his daughter's wedding—which, on the strength of Hirsh Leib's story, he had decided to permit—and he had been impatient with Taylor.

"What do you expect?" the *rebbe* had asked. "You think you can be a Jew so easy? Why shouldn't you be afraid? I'm afraid. Everyone is afraid. All Jews are afraid. That is because we touch a great mystery. We call it Torah. You think you are so different?

"He who touches, is touched. So, you have been touched. And it hurts. So what? That is what it means to be a Jew. Now you know.

"You know more than me now. You know everything," the *rebbe* had told him. "If I spoke Yiddish to you now, you would understand."

"I wouldn't," Taylor had said.

So the *rebbe* had begun speaking Yiddish, and Taylor had understood nothing.

"You are just stubborn," the *rebbe* had said. "Like Hirsh Leib, a stubborn man, may his memory be blessed."

"All right, I'm stubborn. But what am I supposed to do now?" Taylor had asked.

"Find the diamond," the *rebbe* had said as if that were the simplest thing in the world. "The wedding will be November fifth, the full moon, and that, and the Seer's stone, will be the blessing. Also, that will be a Tuesday, and it was on the third day that the Lord said 'It is good' twice."

"I can't," Taylor had protested. "It's impossible. There are no leads. How can I find these people? They could be anywhere."

"The *Zaddik* of Orlik has given you a map," the *rebbe* had said, exasperated. "And you know the thief, that murderer Josep Czartoryski, may his blood boil in his veins."

The fact that Czartoryski had been dead for over one hundred and fifty years did not trouble the *rebbe*. "You, of all people," he said, "should know that time exists for man, not the Lord, Blessed be He."

And then the *rebbe* had begun twisting his beard and speaking Yiddish again.

Taylor gave up.

He had told Rabbi Kalman and Sarah about the Seer's conspiracy to bribe Napoleon into returning the Jews to the Holy Land, and about Hirsh Leib's murder, and they had been impressed. Sarah had told him that he had made a great contribution to Jewish scholarship. Reb Kalman had declared it all a miracle. He told him that if Taylor returned to his studies, perhaps he would now become a *zaddik* himself.

But to Taylor's own ears, his story sounded like nothing more than a dream. With every passing day, Lublin grew less vivid to him. The faces—of the rabbis, of Moshe ben Areyn, of Yekl and the Czartoryskis, and even the great Seer with his one huge, gray-blue eye—seemed to fade. And with each successive telling Taylor felt that he had left out, or forgotten, something else, something important.

Only the fear remained, the fear that paralyzed him.

When had fear ever been such a constant companion? He had to think back to Vietnam, back to the night when the 707's doors opened at Tan Son Nhut Air Base in Saigon and the war instantly enveloped them all: the incredible, unbelievable heat; the stench of the rotting garbage; the stomach-churning explosions; the crazy beauty of the tracers ripping the velvet sky. Here, he had known instantly, was a place for dying.

And now, on Simkhas Torah night, he knew he had come to a similar place in time.

Pinchus Mayer, the Satmarer *rebbe*'s *gabbai*, had given Taylor a checkbook. "The *rebbe*, may his light shine, has told me to make sure that you have everything you need," Mayer had told him. "Just keep good records," Mayer had added, frugally.

But Taylor had yet to write a single check. He could not make anyone understand that when Josep Czartoryski's sword had pierced Hirsh Leib's heart, it was his own heart that had bled.

I should be dead, Taylor thought. Why aren't I dead?

His AA meetings were, of course, a comfort. And now he felt as if he were going not only for himself, but for Hirsh Leib, too. No matter how crazy it sounded, he knew that if he stopped, Hirsh Leib would not die sober. And he would not, therefore, be able to say good-bye to Soreh with a clear mind and a whole heart. To Taylor, nothing seemed more important than that.

But he couldn't see himself standing up in his home meeting, surrounded by people he had known for years, saying, "My name is Dov and I'm a grateful recovering alcoholic and drug addict. I just saw my great-great-grandfather murdered, and it's really been fucking with my head. In fact, the one-hundred-and-seventy-ninth anniversary of the day he was killed is coming up, and I'm scared shitless someone is going to sneak up behind me with a saber.

"And, by the way, Napoleon was a pig."

Once, desperate to talk about it, he looked into the *New York Area Meeting Book* and found a meeting called "Sober Sam's" on the Bowery. It was, naturally, filled with men and women who were, in AA parlance, "damp in the attic." Many of them were active drunks who showed up only for the watery coffee and stale cookies.

So Taylor told his story there, standing up after a woman had mumbled on for fifteen minutes about having fallen into the East River. It seemed that she had been rescued by the mayor himself, who was, she had said, pretty nice for a black guy. Now, she had said, they were lovers.

At "Sober Sam's," Taylor's story fit seamlessly into a web of self-deception and madness. It fit too well.

He never went back.

He continued to go to his meetings. He listened to other drunks tell their stories, and when he got home he triple-locked his door. And when he went out, he carried his gun.

Sarah Kalman was his only visitor. At first he had tried to discourage her, but she had ignored him. Uninvited, she'd showed up at his door with Tupperware containers of chicken soup, roasted chicken, carrot *tsimmes*, sweet noodle pudding, boiled potatoes, and dense chocolate layer cake for dessert. The sheer quantity of food made him laugh. She heated it all up in the microwave and watched him while he ate. She, of course, would eat nothing. Nothing in his kitchen—his plates, his silverware, even the microwave—was *kosher*.

He loved to watch her putter around his apartment, picking things up, putting them down. It wasn't boredom or nervousness, he knew, that kept her on the move. It was curiosity. His life was as much a mystery to her as hers was to him.

But neither of them had the vocabulary to penetrate the other's secrets.

So Sarah touched the things he had touched, trying to read their message. And Taylor watched.

Her size fascinated him. It seemed to be constantly changing. When she sat at the table with him, her hands touching her hair or resting in her lap, she seemed big, like the type of women he usually found sexually attractive. But when she would pick up a glass of water, or a book, the size of the object in her hand would remind him of how tiny she truly was.

Looking at her across his living room as she straightened the magazines on the coffee table or opened the blinds on the window, she seemed statuesque: muscular calves atop clunky high-heeled shoes, the tresses of a queen. But as she walked toward him she grew smaller, defying the laws of perspective.

He had decided, finally, that she was a little woman who took up a lot of space in his mind.

"Why do you look at me like that?" she had asked him.

"Look at you like what?"

"I don't know. Like you're studying me."

"You remind me of someone, I don't know who."

"I know who," she had said. "You told me. When you described Hirsh Leib's wife, it was like you were describing me."

"But I never saw her. His wife."

"Of course you did."

Taylor grunted.

"You're not comfortable with what has happened to you," Sarah had told him. "It doesn't fit into the way you know the world. It's not like you want the world to be. That's all right. It takes getting used to."

"I'm not getting used to it," Taylor had said.

"Yes, you are. Your eyes are getting clearer. Not so far away. You're getting stronger. I can see it."

"It's all the food you're bringing me."

"You eat like a bird," Sarah had said, laughing.

Just like Rebecca, Taylor had thought. That's what my

grandmother always said when I ate in her kitchen. Dov, like a bird you eat.

On the screen in Eastern Parkway, Rebbe Seligson droned on in Yiddish, his voice guttural and monotonous. The picture occasionally cut to the crowd in the temple, showing bearded men in dark fedoras rocking back and forth as if praying. For them, Taylor understood, everything their *zaddik* said was a prayer. Pale little boys in *payes* sat next to their fathers, their eyes wide, their mouths hanging open, trying to pay attention to the *zaddik*'s stream of Torah. Other boys had given up and, restless, poked and teased each other. Taylor, who despite what the Satmarer *rebbe* believed could understand nothing of what Reb Seligson was saying, decided to go home.

Just as well, he told himself. I've been spending too much time with Sarah as is.

She had been coming to his apartment more often, bringing her books and papers along with her home-cooked meals. As he ate she studied, lifting her head from time to time to tell him about something new she had discovered about Hirsh Leib, or the Seer, or about the Czartoryskis, Prince Adam and Count Josep.

It seemed that the Seer had died slowly, lingering on for six months after Hirsh Leib's murder, not speaking to anyone. Prince Adam had passed away shortly after the Seer. It was rumored that either Tsar Alexander or his own brother had poisoned him. Certainly Count Josep had become lord of Castle Czartoryski, as Adam's son had been too young to assume the responsibility. In fact, the young princeling died of consumption a few years later, and Grushinka, Adam's wife, left the castle to enter a convent. After that Josep began gambling heavily, and he began raising taxes in Lublin to cover his enormous debts.

Taylor didn't really want to hear any of it—he wanted to put Lublin behind him—but he loved listening to Sarah's low, serious, musical voice. Sometimes, in order to distract her from the history he found so disturbing, he would ask her to teach him a little Yiddish. He found her a wonderfully patient teacher.

Stop it, he told himself, turning up his collar against the rain. You're getting moony over a woman who makes sure to keep a good three feet between you at all times. Once, as she was leaving, he had tried to help her put on her coat, and she had just stood there waiting for him to hand it to her. He had felt ridiculous.

She's not interested in you, he told himself. She just feels sorry for you.

But not as sorry as you feel for yourself.

"Poor me, poor me, pour me a drink," he whispered to himself. You'd understand, Great-Great-Grandpa, he thought. You were a drunk like me.

Taylor turned onto Kingston Street. Four men were standing at the top steps of the subway entrance. Three very dark young blacks with dreadlocks spilling out from beneath huge red-and-green knitted hats (probably Jamaicans, possibly posse members, dreads, they called themselves—Taylor's cop-mind ticked off the relevant data) were shouting at a short, stocky Hasid.

Taylor slowed his steps, feeling for the revolver in his pocket. He smelled violence in the air, and he didn't want to walk between the men. The dreads were probably armed. At least knives. Taylor glanced behind him. The street was empty. There's never a cop around when you need one, he thought.

He saw the Hasid reach into his coat and pull out what must have been a gun. Shit, he thought. Fucking Simkhas Torah night. Right.

"I shove dat ting up your ass, mon," one of the blacks yelled in a thick West Indian accent.

"Fuckin' Jew bahstad," said another.

"Get away from me," the Hasid shouted, waving the pistol at them.

Taylor, his heart racing, found himself walking toward them, his hand on the gun in his pocket. He forced himself to be calm, to breathe. An AA saying came to him: "Right action, right attitude."

You've done this before, he told himself. You know how to do this. Cool them down.

"Hey, what's going on here?" Taylor asked, taking his hand out of his pocket and trying to keep his voice calm and steady, keeping the four men in front of him.

"Who the fuck are you, mon?" asked one of the blacks, taking a sliding step to Taylor's left.

"Take it easy, man," said Taylor, taking a step backward. Don't let anyone get behind you, he reminded himself. Just wait. The more time passes, the better the chance that nothing will happen.

He turned to the Hasid, who was now pointing his gun at him. It was an automatic, maybe a Walther. Taylor felt his stomach knot as if expecting a bullet. Sure, he thought. Simkhas Torah. Time to die.

Again.

Taylor summoned up some of the Yiddish he had picked up from Sarah. *"Vos tutstu, Yid?"* What are you doing? He pointed to the Hasid's gun. *"Dos iz gornit helfn."* That's not helping.

The Hasid began screaming at Taylor, who couldn't understand anything except the word *shvartzers*, blacks, which the Hasid kept repeating over and over.

"You tink I don't know what you sayin', mon?" shouted one of the blacks. "You call me dat again, motherfucker, I fuck you up bad."

"Put the gun away," Taylor told the Hasid, pitching his voice so that it remained soft yet could still be heard. "Come on, it's not worth it. Put it away."

The Hasid scrunched up his face as if smelling something bad. Suddenly he spat at Taylor. Taking advantage of the distraction, one of the blacks grabbed the Hasid's gun hand and pulled it up. There was an explosion. Two quick shots, the noise blurring the space between them. Then another.

Out of the corner of his eye, Taylor saw one of the dreads rush toward him. Taylor stepped into him, catching the man's right wrist with his left hand even before he actually saw the gravity knife that he knew would be there. Using the man's momentum, he spun him around, pulling the man's right arm across his chest, driving his left shoulder into the back of the man's elbow. He heard it crack. The man screamed. The knife fell to the pavement. Taylor let go, and the man dropped to his knees, his right arm bent grotesquely, his hat falling off his head, his dreadlocks spilling out over his face and shoulders.

The second black took a step toward the knife lying on the street. Taylor pulled out his revolver. "Don't," he said, at the same time kicking the knife down the street. He whirled on the man and the Hasid still wrestling over the gun. "Drop it!" he shouted.

The Hasid and the black looked at Taylor, saw the gun, and froze. "Drop it," Taylor shouted again. The Hasid let go of his gun. It clattered to the sidewalk.

"Step back," Taylor ordered, and the black man let go of the Hasid. The Hasid bent to retrieve his pistol. "Touch it and you're dead," Taylor said.

"Let me get my gun, Officer. You can arrest these men."

"We not doin' nothin'. Him the mon with the gun," protested the man who had been struggling with the Hasid.

"Help your friend," Taylor told the man. "Take him to a hospital. I think his elbow's broken."

"You let them walk away, these murderers? Sure, why not? This is the New York police. All you care about is the *shvartzers*. Some Jew you are."

Taylor kept his gun pointed at the Hasid as the men helped their friend up off the sidewalk.

"You gonna bust him, mon? I see everyt'ing now."

"Get going," said Taylor. "Beat it."

The dreadlocks walked away down Kingston Street, supporting their injured friend between them.

"I'll call your captain," said the Hasid. "I'll tell him what you're doing. You, give me your name."

"Fuck you," said Taylor, picking up the Hasid's gun and slipping it into his pocket. It was a Walther.

"You're taking my gun?" the Hasid asked.

"Evidence." Two-gun Taylor, he thought. He felt elated. "It's Simkhas Torah," he said. "Why aren't you in *shul*? It's time for the *hakkafot*." It's ten o'clock, thought Taylor, do you know where your Hasidim are? He laughed. "By the way," he said, "what was this all about, anyway?"

The Hasid just glared at Taylor.

"Okay. Be that way. Now get lost."

The Hasid stuck his hands in his pockets and spat on the pavement. He looked at Taylor defiantly.

"All right, you little shit," said Taylor. "Stand there. Catch pneumonia. I'm going."

As the train crossed the Brooklyn Bridge, Taylor leaned against the door and stared at the lights of Manhattan below. He could see the FDR Drive, backed up as usual, and that made him feel good. He was exhausted, but for the first time since he had awakened a month ago in the Satmarer *rebbe*'s study, he felt as if he had come home.

In a couple of hours, he thought, Simkhas Torah will be over, and I'll still be alive.

I'm not going to die.

Now, thought Taylor, I can start to live again. Tomorrow I can go to work, looking for the diamond and Hirsh Leib's killer.

Look out, Czartoryski, Dov Taylor told a man he knew to be nothing more than rotting bones in a Polish tomb, I'm coming after your ass.

49

The Savoy Hotel
The Strand, London
Monday, October 21

When he first landed in London, Ladislaw Czartoryski sent Maria Radziwell ahead to check in at the Savoy. Then he took a taxi to the train, and the train to an Odessa safe house in Ashwell, Hertfordshire, about ten miles north of London. There he waited for Phil Horowitz, who was expecting Czartoryski to hand over the stone in exchange for a quarter of a million dollars American that Moskowitz was carrying in his rented Chevrolet.

When Moskowitz arrived, Czartoryski shot the chunky, balding Hasid once in the neck, once in the eye, and once in the roof of the mouth, dragged the body down into the basement for the Odessa janitors to dispose of, quickly found the money in the boot of the car, and thereby concluded his arrangement with the Israelis to his satisfaction, if not to theirs.

Now he sat in his hotel room, watching Maria. She stood facing the window overlooking the Thames, her broad back to the room. Rain puckered the surface of the river, and fat drops of water hurried down the window. She was putting on her raincoat, pulling her thick blond hair out from underneath the collar.

"So, where are you going today?" asked Czartoryski, sitting in a silk maroon dressing gown on an overstuffed lime-green chair. He sipped his morning coffee from the Savoy's gold-rimmed china, the *Times* spread out on his bed.

"Brompton Road," said Maria.

"You went shopping there yesterday."

"Yes, and I am going back today. Unless, of course," she said, turning to face him, "you would like to take me someplace."

"No," said Czartoryski. "Unfortunately, I cannot. I have a business appointment."

"How unusual," Maria said dryly, putting her hand on her hip.

Like a fishwife, thought Czartoryski, disgust filling his chest. Or rather, like a Polish whore.

"Do you need some more money, my dear?" asked Czartoryski, turning his contempt into sarcasm. "There may be some items you have not yet bought."

"No," said Radziwell, turning back to the window to study the bleak London sky and the gray, sluggish river. "Not at the moment."

"Feel free to ask," Czartoryski said. "I wouldn't want you to feel deprived, my dear."

"I will be back sometime this afternoon, Ladislaw," she said, drawing on her fawn-colored gloves.

"As you will," said Czartoryski, watching Radziwell sweep out the door.

He was losing her, he knew. Well, there was nothing he could do about it. She had grown used to the money—he couldn't dazzle her with it; even the Savoy, with its beautiful view of the river, had become . . . what did the English say? Old hat. Not being able to make love to her was gradually but surely dissolving their connection. They were becoming strangers. Polite strangers, usually, but nothing more than that.

Which would make it easier, he thought, to draw the curtain on what had become a tiresome charade.

In a way, his impotence, finally settling into a permanence, had come as a relief. He no longer had to worry about whether or not it would be there. It just was. And, to his surprise, it did not make him feel any less a man. Indeed, in certain ways, he felt more forceful than ever. Perhaps the cooling of the blood had liberated his mind. He felt he was thinking more clearly than ever.

He picked out a gray suit with the faintest red pinstripe; matched it with a dark blue Hilditch & Key white-collared shirt with white French cuffs, and a rich, red Charvet tie. He looked at himself in the huge bathroom mirror and adjusted his pocket square to his satisfaction. Then, on impulse, he walked through the bedroom into the small sitting room of his suite and opened a mahogany cabinet in which sat a small television set and a smaller safe. After spinning the tumbler and opening the safe, he removed a blue velvet bag, much like the one General Gehlen had tossed over to him forty-five years ago. But now, instead of containing a dozen diamonds, the bag held only one.

As Czartoryski held the Seer's stone up to the light, marveling once again at its size and beauty, at the fires burning inside it and the rainbows it threw off so prodigally, his resolve hardened. He had never intended to hand it over to the Israelis. As far as he was concerned, it had never belonged to them. But now, he realized, he could not allow it to be cut. There was a power contained in this stone that was worth more to him than the money that could be realized by dismembering it and selling it off piecemeal.

So that meant putting off the Odessa. And that meant betraying his old comrades.

He detected a yellowish glint in the stone, and he thought, Daffodils, his lips forming the word silently. And that brought it all back to him. It was his age, he knew, but there was no resisting these memories when they came flooding through him, bathing his mind in the radiance of the past.

It had been May 1945. May 18, to be precise. He remembered standing amid the daffodils on the lawn at Misery Meadow, his back turned to the sprawling chalet nestled in a lea of the Bavarian Alps above the resort town of Fischhausen. Below him he could see several white sails tacking across sparkling Lake Schilersee. The mountain breezes were sweet, and Czartoryski remembered wondering if he had, perhaps, died somewhere on the road and this was, indeed, heaven.

At the time, that seemed as likely as anything else. Less than three weeks before, he had been staggering away from the burning ruins of the Belzec work camp as Allied planes strafed and bombed. With a blood sausage stuffed into his shirt and some hard, crumbling black bread crammed into his trouser pockets, he had made for the woods, the map that Hermann Baun had showed him and told him to memorize fixed in his head.

Baun had arrived unannounced at Belzec a few nights before the bombing had begun and, one by one, had interviewed the guards. His dusty black uniform carried no sign of rank, but the glittering silver death's head on his cap had told Czartoryski all he needed to know. This dark, slender, pock-marked man was SS, one of the elite. He was a man to be respected, a man to be feared. And, Czartoryski remembered thinking, he could be his savior.

For months everyone at Belzec had known that the war was lost, that the German army was disintegrating as it fell back across the Rhine. Even the Jews knew. They had become defiant as their already meager rations were cut to nothing. For Czartoryski, they had ceased to be amusing. He wanted their voices out of his ears, their stink out of his nostrils. At any moment he expected the order to come to shoot them all and bury them in lye-filled pits. (It would have been better to burn them, but the camp was out of petrol.) They could not afford to have them roaming around when the Russians arrived, and the Russians were expected momentarily.

But the commandant was continually drunk, and discipline had given way to anarchy. There was no doubt in anyone's mind that the Russians would kill them all. Shoot them on the spot and mutilate their bodies. That's the way it was with the Russians. So most of the guards talked about heading west, toward the British and American lines, or slipping back into the cities, into Lublin and Warsaw, into Rudem and Lodz, and trying to blend in there.

Czartoryski did not expect them to make it. They would be caught by the Russians or informed upon and turned in to the Red Army by their neighbors. Either way they would be dead meat.

So he waited—for the order to exterminate the last of the camp's Jews and for a plan to come to him. You have to have a plan, he had told himself. In the midst of chaos, the man with a plan can survive.

(You are a planful man, he told himself. As you were then, so are you today.)

Then Hermann Baun arrived.

Czartoryski entered the commandant's office, stood at attention, and saluted. Baun, sitting behind the commandant's desk, did not return the salute. His hat rested on a stack of files on the desk, and his hair was plastered down on his skull. To Czartoryski, he looked a little like a death's head himself.

"Your commander is dead," Czartoryski remembered Baun announcing. "The shithead tried to shoot himself. He made a botch of it. I did him the favor. He's out back. Do you want to say good-bye?"

"That's not necessary, sir."

"Then tell me. Now that the war is over, what do you want to do?"

"I want to fight, sir," Czartoryski responded.

Baun smiled, and then he began to laugh. He laughed until he began coughing. He pulled a dirty handkerchief from his pocket and blew his nose.

"Thank you, Sergeant," he said. "You're the first Pole I've met in this shithole with any balls."

"I'm an officer, sir. A lieutenant."

"I don't like lieutenants," Baun said. "I like sergeants. And corporals. The Führer himself was a corporal. So I'm promoting you, even higher than the Führer. You are now a sergeant."

Baun then asked him about his background, and Czartoryski told him that he was descended from an old aristocratic family whose lands and fortune had been stolen by Jewish bankers. Baun asked him about the Communists, and Czartoryski responded that they were the real enemy—not the English, not the Americans—and that someday the Allies would realize to their regret that Germany, and National Socialism, had been their best defense against Jewish bolshevism.

"So, you want to fight?" Baun said. "Good. Because, Sergeant, although the battle has been lost, the war will go on." And then Baun showed him the map and told him to make his way to Fischhausen, where he would be given further orders. Baun congratulated him. He had just been recruited, Baun said, into the Organization of Veterans of the SS, the Odessa.

"You must be in Fischhausen by the nineteenth of May," Baun had said. "After that, it will be hard."

As if it had been easy to get there at all, Czartoryski recalled. For weeks he kept to the woods, avoiding towns, drinking filthy water from puddles and streams. He stole crumbs from the corpses of German and Russian soldiers. At night, the sky above the trees glowed red with the light of cities burning.

That color, too, was in the diamond, Czartoryski thought. Red fire. Red blood. It had been a journey through hell, but it had ended in paradise or, at least, a picture postcard of paradise: a house sitting in a field of daffodils.

The chalet itself, Czartoryski recalled, a small smile creasing his face, was grand—a rustic pleasure palace of huge oaken beams and yellow gingerbread shutters. White wicker swings graced a deep, shady porch. The air was alive with birdsong, and Czartoryski had realized with a shock that at one time spring had meant more to him than mud and death. He hoped that he would be given a chance to bathe before he met whomever it was he was supposed to meet. Maybe they would even have fresh clothes for him.

Hermann Baun, wearing white flannel slacks and a crisp blue shirt with the sleeves rolled up, had emerged from the chalet and fairly skipped down the porch steps to the lawn. He looked ten years younger than he had at Belzec, and Czartoryski knew that Baun's journey to Misery Meadow had been quite different from his own.

Czartoryski remembered drawing himself rigidly to attention and saluting.

"No more saluting," Baun said. "That's over. Congratulations, Sergeant. You're just in time for dinner. Tomorrow we surrender to the Americans."

Turning away from the safe, Czartoryski laughed. He had been so angry. God, he had been so young. Had he come so far, he remembered demanding of Baun, only to turn himself over to the Allies? Was this his reward? The pleasure of being hanged by the Americans rather than being shot by the Russians?

"Not you," Baun said. "Us. For you, we have other plans. Come."

Baun led Czartoryski inside the chalet and then up a broad stairway to the second floor. They walked down a long hall lined with lithographs of hunting scenes and mountain vistas until they stopped and Baun opened one of the doors. "Inside," he said, "you'll find clothes, a basin, soap, and washcloths. Unfortunately we have no running water, and no razors. You have fifteen minutes before dinner."

Czartoryski thanked him, shook his hand, and closed the door behind him. He stripped off his clothes and began wiping the encrusted mud and dirt off his body.

A mirror leaning behind the washbasin told him that he had lost a great deal of weight. His cheeks were hollow; dark bags hung beneath his eyes. His forehead felt hot. Perhaps a touch of typhus, he thought, from drinking contaminated water.

Naked, he opened the clothes closet and understood for the first time that, for him, the war was over. It was filled with dozens of trousers, shirts, and sport coats. He wandered over to the bureau and opened a drawer bursting with undershirts, boxer shorts, and socks. The drawer below it was filled with silk ties. It was like being in one of Warsaw's finest haberdashers before the war, and Czartoryski recalled that tears had actually come to his eyes. He had always loved dressing up; he had especially loved ties. And these were so beautiful.

He dressed quickly, choosing tan gabardine slacks, a silky blue shirt, a brown-and-heather-tweed shooting jacket, and a yellow tie with blue medallions.

He left the room and walked down the hallway the way he had come. He went down the stairway and saw other men—all unshaven, all looking slightly ravaged even in their holiday tweeds and flannels—funneling through a narrow doorway. Czartoryski fell in with them.

How could he ever forget that room? It was enormous, with dark brown wainscoting halfway up the walls. A huge, wooden, candlelit chandelier hung from the ceiling above a long dining table covered in white linen, surrounded by heavy wooden chairs with ball-and-claw legs. Opposite the door, at the very end of the room, was an outsize flagstone fireplace.

He remembered counting the men to cover his nervousness. There had been twenty-five, all between the ages of twenty and forty-five. At least half of them clustered around a slight, unremarkable man who looked to be in his early forties. His clothes seemed to hang off him like a scarecrow's. Czartoryski began edging toward that group when he spotted Baun, standing apart. Relieved, Czartoryski walked over to him.

"Ah, Sergeant," Baun said. "You look better."

"Thank you, sir. I feel better."

"Too bad about the razors. Shortages, you know."

"Yes, sir."

"And the pump for the well is broken. Unfortunate."

"Yes, sir."

"Still, it's not a bad place, wouldn't you say? Bormann

built it. Fancied himself lord of the manor, the silly shit. Used it for skiing and hunting. And entertaining.'' Baun leered. ''The Führer stayed here many times,'' he added more soberly.

''Yes, sir. Tell me, sir. Who is that man over there, the one everybody is listening to?''

''That, Sergeant, is Brigadier General Reinhard Gehlen, commander of the Reich's Foreign Armies East.''

''He was on the eastern front?''

''General Gehlen was in charge of organizing sympathetic forces in the occupied territories.''

Czartoryski, who had never before heard of a General Gehlen, was not so uninformed that he didn't know what that meant. He knew about the Ukrainian B Faction, the Vanagis of Latvia, the Turkish Grey Wolves, and many others. These were the world's best Jew hunters, better and bloodier, some said, than the SS itself.

Wine and brandy were brought into the room on silver trays by women in white blouses, black skirts, and lacy aprons. Someone tapped a fork against a wineglass, and the room grew still.

''I would like to propose a toast,'' said General Gehlen in the thin, reedy voice that would forevermore cause Czartoryski to snap to attention. ''A toast to all those who have traveled so far, and under such difficult circumstances, to be with us tonight.''

This is a toast to me, Czartoryski recalled thinking, lowering his head and lifting his glass.

''Tomorrow,'' Gehlen continued, ''we end one phase of the struggle and begin another. Many of our comrades perished in order to bring us to this place. Let us pledge ourselves to their memory and to their cause so that they will not have died in vain.

''To the *Schutzstaffel*, our beloved SS, and to its newborn child, the Odessa, may it flourish for a thousand years. Heil Hitler!''

After the toast, dinner was served—game birds in a brandy-and-fruit sauce, boiled potatoes, and red cabbage. Czartoryski made sure he sat next to Baun.

"So, Sergeant," Baun said, "this is better than the woods, yes?"

"Yes, sir. Sir . . . ?"

"You have questions, Sergeant? I know you have questions."

"Yes, sir. You said we were surrendering tomorrow?"

"Tomorrow we shall turn ourselves over to the Americans in Miesbach."

"Why?"

"Because the Americans will take good care of us."

"And why is that, sir?"

"Because we have something they want."

"And that is, sir?"

"You said it yourself, Sergeant. Soon the Americans and the Reds will be at war. You know it, I know it, they know it. Even the Reds know it. And in a war, you must have intelligence. You must have assets behind your enemy's lines. And that's what we have. Assets. Networks. Armies. In the Ukraine. In Yugoslavia. In the Caucasus, and in the Baltics. In Russia itself. We have names, lists, radio operators. We have them and the Americans don't. That's why they will turn to us. They need us."

"You said you had plans for me, sir."

"After dinner."

Coffee was served and then brandy. Men began drifting away from the table, their faces red, their eyes tired and shadowed in the candlelight. Czartoryski noticed that Gehlen had left the room, and then Baun had tapped him on the shoulder.

"Come with me, Sergeant."

Baun led him across the chalet's broad parlor and through a small door into a library. The room was broiling hot, and Czartoryski immediately began to sweat. Reinhard Gehlen stood bent over by a small fireplace, arranging the glowing logs with a poker.

"Allow me to introduce Ladislaw Czartoryski, Reinhard," said Baun.

Gehlen straightened up. His sandy hair was receding, and

his small, cold, gray-blue eyes provided the only spot of color in a dead white face. He looked, Czartoryski thought at the time, like one of the "goners" at Belzec. He could not have weighed more than one hundred and twenty pounds. Czartoryski found his very sickliness somehow frightening.

"A Pole?" Gehlen asked, turning back to the fire, warming his hands in the overheated room.

"Yes, Reinhard," Baun said, taking out a handkerchief to mop his brow. "But his German is good, and he speaks English. He's an aristocrat."

"Where did you find him?"

"At one of the work camps. What was its name?" Baun turned to Czartoryski.

"Belzec, sir."

"And you found your way to us. You must be a magician."

"I don't know, sir."

"He's very polite, isn't he, Hermann?" said Gehlen.

"Very polite, Reinhard," said Baun, smiling.

"Good. I like that. So many people are coarse these days. You are now a member of the Odessa, Mr. Czartoryski." Gehlen turned from the fire to address him directly. "That means I am now your commanding officer. Do you understand?"

"Yes, sir."

Gehlen walked over to a large teak desk, opened a drawer, and pulled out a small blue velvet bag. He tossed it to Czartoryski.

"Open it," Gehlen said.

Czartoryski loosened the bag's drawstring and looked inside.

It was full of diamonds.

"We will need British sterling or American dollars," Gehlen said. "Until we can become fully funded by the Allied intelligence organizations, we will need currency. There are many travel arrangements to be made. There are many comrades who will need to be relocated. To the Middle East. To South Africa. To South America.

"There is nothing better than diamonds, Mr. Czartoryski,"

Gehlen said professorially. "They are easy to carry, easy to hide. They maintain their value because the Jews in Johannesburg control the supply.

"You must turn that little bag into pounds sterling or dollars. Swiss francs will also be acceptable, but we prefer pounds or dollars. No Polish kroners, please, and certainly no rubles.

"We have friends who will help you out of Germany. Hermann will brief you. After that, we will rely on your initiative. I suggest Amsterdam as a good place for the transaction, but I have always allowed my agents to make their own decisions in the field."

"How will I turn over the money, sir?"

"When you have completed your mission, you will arrange for an advertisement in the London Sunday *Times*. It will read 'Spiders for Sale,' and you will provide a place and a time where you may be contacted.

"Tell me, Mr. Czartoryski," said Gehlen, "do you know anything about the diamond business?"

"Not really, sir."

"Then you must begin to learn."

And I did, thought Czartoryski, returning the stone, his stone, to its bag, and the bag to the safe.

I did indeed.

50

The Satmarer Rebbe's House
South Ninth Street, Williamsburg, Brooklyn
Monday, October 21

Pinchus Mayer, the Satmarer *rebbe*'s *gabbai*, his personal secretary, lit another cigarette and tried not to think of Lily's phone number. It was impossible.

His hand went to the phone on his desk in the small office

off the *rebbe*'s study. He looked through the doorway. The study was still empty. He punched the number: 555-1601. The phone rang twice. A high, breathy voice answered, "Hello?"

Mayer hung up.

This was madness. This was an abomination. This he could not do. Not this time. Not ever again. Did it not say in the *Shulhan Arukh*, the Code of Law, that one out of a thousand men die from other diseases, but nine hundred and ninety-nine die from sexual indulgence?

It's the pressure, he told himself, calling up his daily calendar on his IBM personal computer. There. You see? He had left a note to himself to call that *gonef*, that Lubavitcher thief who rented flatbed trucks, and explain to him again that for ordering three, there should be a discount. The stage for the *khupa*, the wedding canopy, which had to be set up outside the synagogue on the flatbeds so that the bride and groom could be married under the open sky (as it was written: "Thus, like the stars, shall your children be"), needed to be large enough to accommodate the bride's party, which, Mayer knew, would be enormous, and the groom's party, whatever that would be, since he could never get Reb Kalman to set a figure.

He had also made a note to himself to call that Italian police captain who was supposed to be looking for off-duty patrolmen to hire to guard the gifts at the reception and to make sure that no one—blacks, Nazis, who knew?—tried to disturb the wedding.

And he had to go down to the police station to pick up the permits for closing down Rodney Street. Then, he thought, I should go to the health department to get the permits for serving hot food at the Pratt Institute gymnasium, where the reception would be held.

It was all too much. And when Mayer protested to the *rebbe* that it was impossible to plan a wedding for twenty thousand guests—to set up the travel arrangements, to find lodgings for people coming from Europe, Israel, and South Africa, to set up the kitchens, plan for the food and wine, prepare the *khupa*, the sound system, the video system, not to mention coordinating security—all by November 5, the *rebbe* would just shrug and insist that that was an auspicious day.

"I have always dreamed that my daughter would be married at the end of the third day," he had said. "You know, when the Lord, Blessed is He, created the world, at the end of the third day He said twice, 'It is well.' Therefore, that day above all others is blessed for making a wedding. Pinchus, I trust you," the *rebbe* had said, "and I trust the Lord, Blessed be He."

Now November 5 was just two weeks away, and so much remained to be done. Not only would Reb Kalman not specify how many were to be in the groom's party, he was also dragging out the negotiations on the *ketubah*, the wedding contract. Not that Mayer himself was so anxious to negotiate the *ketubah*. In the first place, one should never seem to be in a hurry to conclude a deal, even when one is negotiating for a bride. And in the second place, the *rebbe* had insisted that Esther Teitel's dowry include a diamond that Mayer had never even heard of. All the *rebbe* would say was, "A diamond the size of an angel's heart."

Well, thought Pinchus Mayer, the *rebbe* of course knows how many carats that is, but I don't, and I suspect that Reb Kalman doesn't, either, so what will I say when he asks? And he will ask.

It was all so expensive. The money had already begun to flow out, and this was just the beginning. Again, Mayer wondered why the *rebbe* was insisting that that detective should have his own checkbook to draw against the Satmarer account. Of course, Mayer would never ask, but it frustrated him. It was so unbusinesslike.

Again, Mayer looked at the telephone. Two years ago, that Lubavitcher convert, that diamond courier he had met at a gathering in honor of poor Zalman Gottleib, may his blood be avenged, had handed Mayer a little piece of paper with a phone number on it.

"Sometimes," the Lubavitcher—Horowitz was his name—had said, "even a pious man needs a little pleasure."

Mayer was astounded and offended—of course, what could

you expect from a Lubavitcher; and not even a real Hasid, a convert—but instead of throwing away the paper, as he should have, the Evil Impulse had led him to put it in his wallet. And sure enough, not two days later he had yielded to the Evil Impulse and called.

She lived in a basement apartment in a brownstone near the Williamsburg Bridge. When Pinchus Mayer had rung the bell, and the door had opened, he'd been too shocked to run away. She was an Oriental, but not Chinese. Her skin was brown, not yellow. Her face was broad, and her thick black hair was cropped short. She wore a black dress that barely covered her crotch and barely contained her breasts.

"My name is Lily," the woman had said in a little girl's sibilant whisper. "I'm from Singapore. What's your name?"

Mayer had lied and told her the first name that popped into his head: Joel. For that alone, for using the name of the *rebbe*, he would burn in hell.

Mayer picked up the phone. He looked through the door into the *rebbe*'s study to make sure that it was still empty. He punched the number. Lily answered.

"This is Joel. Can I come over? . . . In thirty minutes? . . . Good."

Mayer hung up. This is the last time, he promised himself, the absolute last time.

Mayer pulled his black raincoat off the hook behind the door in his office and went out through the *rebbe*'s study and down the broad staircase of the house. At the foot of the stairs, he saw the *rebbe*'s curly-haired *zaftig* daughter, Esther, bouncing toward the kitchen.

This is the sort of woman I should be thinking about, Mayer scolded himself. A good Jewish girl with rosy cheeks and juicy, like this one.

"*Gutn tog*, Esther," said Mayer. Good day.

"*Gut yor*, Reb Mayer," said Esther, wishing Mayer a good year, as was the custom.

Esther watched him go out, thinking briefly that he always seemed to be worried, always in a hurry, no matter what he was doing. Then she dismissed little Pinchus Mayer from her mind. She had more important things to think about than her father's *gabbai*. Soon she would be a *kaleh*, a bride.

Esther had been beside herself with joy when her mother had told her that her father had changed his mind and had decided to permit her to wed the Lubavitcher *rebbe*'s son, Adam. Not that she loved Adam or even desired him. In fact, she had met him only once, and he looked like any other young Yeshiva *bukher*—a thin, pale-faced scholar. But this one was to be her *khossen*, her bridegroom, and not only was he a learned scholar, with the *yikhus*, the prestige, of his father, he would be the one who would give her what she wanted more than anything else in the world: a baby. And once she had a child, she would finally be the equal of any woman in the community.

Esther was tired of being treated like a little girl. She was, after all, seventeen, and she really should have been married already. And she would have been if that poor Mr. Gottleib, the one who had been murdered, had not lost her dowry. But now the diamond must have been returned. Why else would her father have approved the wedding?

Esther went into one of her home's four kitchens—the one used for dairy—and found her mother peeling potatoes.

"Ah, Estherel, you've come to help me," she said.

"No, Mama. I'm going out."

"Where are you going?"

"To see Rivka."

"At that restaurant?"

"Yes."

"You spend too much time with that girl. She's a no-gooder. You should stay here and help your mother."

"Oh, Mama," Esther wailed. "I'm just going out for a little while. I'll be back soon, and I'll help you then."

Esther flounced out of the kitchen, grabbed her coat from the coat rack in the hall, and went out, saying hello and good-bye to the two silent men who always stood outside her father's door.

Soon, thought Esther, I won't have to tell my mother where I'm going and who I'm meeting. Soon I'll have a baby, and then they'll all have to listen to me.

* * *

As Esther Teitel hurried down South Ninth Street to meet her friend, the talkative Rivka, and as Pinchus Mayer sat in his car trying to talk himself out of ringing Lily's doorbell, Ladislaw Czartoryski was grabbing his umbrella and folding his raincoat over his arm. He took the elevator from his fifth-floor suite down to the Savoy's lovely Victorian and Art Deco lobby.

The doorman hailed a cab, and Czartoryski handed him a pound note. Settling onto the roomy backseat of the big black taxi for the ten-minute ride into the City, and the offices of Gemstones International, Ltd., on Central Street, Czartoryski gave himself up to the contemplation of London, his favorite city.

He remembered how it had appeared to him in the fall of 1945, its ancient and regal beauty framed and highlighted by the rubble to which the V2s and the Luftwaffe had reduced it.

Czartoryski had taken a circuitous route to London. On the evening of the day Reinhard Gehlen, Hermann Baun, and the others had surrendered to the Americans in Miesbach, Czartoryski had found himself lying under a pile of blankets in the back of a Red Cross truck, the pouch full of diamonds in his pocket. Late that night, the truck had stopped at a small country church, and Czartoryski had changed into a monk's habit.

For the next two weeks the truck traveled almost exclusively by night, keeping to back roads. Czartoryski was alone with the driver, an Italian who spoke hardly any German. During the day they hid in various churches, subsisting on thin soup, stale bread, a little salt, occasionally some dry cheese. Eventually the truck stopped in the courtyard of a monastery. Czartoryski stepped out into the warm, moist night air, and below him the lights of a vast city twinkled beneath the stars. His heart swelled. It was Rome.

Later Czartoryski would learn how hundreds of other Odessa agents had followed similar routes to freedom, all mapped out and arranged by Reinhard Gehlen months before the war had ended. The Allies called these escape routes the "rat lines.'' In the Odessa, the network was known as *Der Shpinner*, the Spider.

In the courtyard, a priest had come out of the darkness to hand Czartoryski a pouch containing a Swiss passport, five hundred pounds in Swiss francs, and papers identifying him as Father Franz Mayduch, a priest attached to the Vatican relief agency. The priest led Czartoryski into the monastery's kitchen, showed him a sideboard on which rested a half round of Neufchâtel cheese, most of a loaf of fresh, crusty bread, a glass, and a sharp, fruity red wine in a clay carafe. The priest then excused himself.

After eating, Czartoryski went in search of the priest and his driver. Both were gone. Indeed, the monastery seemed to be deserted. Czartoryski understood that he was now on his own.

After spending a few days in Rome—and a sizable portion of the Swiss francs on food and women—Czartoryski made his way to Amsterdam. He found a small room east of Dam Square, on the fringes of the red-light district, and after drinking a vast amount of beer and Genever, the Dutch gin, in various hotel bars, he found his first buyer—as luck would have it, an American Office of Strategic Services captain—at Papeneiland, the oldest tavern in the city. With the money from this first sale, Czartoryski was able to purchase new papers and bid farewell to Franz Mayduch and his priestly attire.

The American OSS captain led the newly minted Helmut Ellenbogen, a Swiss businessman, to other buyers—mainly American and British intelligence officers who seemed to have more cash than they knew what to do with. In three weeks Czartoryski had sold off all but one of the diamonds Reinhard Gehlen had given him in the chalet on Misery Meadow.

Czartoryski had thought briefly of arranging for the Sunday *Times* ad from Amsterdam, but with almost ten thousand pounds in his suitcase, he decided to indulge a long-deferred dream, and, after buying a ticket on the boat train, he traveled to London.

* * *

The taxi pulled up in front of a tall, modern office build-ing—a gaudy gift of the Thatcher years—in the heart of London's financial district. Czartoryski paid the driver and took the silent elevator up to Gemstones International's mod-est twelfth-floor office.

Gemstones International, Ltd.'s provenance extended back to 1944, when it was one of the hundreds of businesses established outside the Third Reich by Minister for the Econ-omy Dr. Hjalmar Horace Greeley Schacht. (His father had been an admirer of the famous American newspaper editor who had said, "Go west, young man.") As early as the spring of 1944, Schacht understood—as did Deputy Führer Martin Bormann and Brigadier General Reinhard Gehlen—that the war was lost, and Schacht began thinking about how to pre-serve the Reich's capital. Working through agents abroad, and in close communication with Bormann and Gehlen, Schacht began moving the Reich's monies—its gold reserves, some of it ripped out of the mouths and off the fingers of Jews in the death camps, and its foreign currency holdings—into straw companies in the United States, England, South Africa, and South America. Eventually, after the war, these businesses became fronts for the Odessa.

"Hello, Stanley," Czartoryski said as he was ushered into Stanley Featherstone Ukridge's office.

"Hello, Ladislaw. Please, sit down," said Ukridge, gestur-ing toward a small sofa against the wall to the right of his desk.

Ukridge was a tall, sandy-haired, pink-faced pukka sahib, a former British Office of Naval Intelligence officer with startlingly blue eyes that made him appear much younger than his sixty-odd years. He had been recruited by the Odessa in the early fifties after the English had been "ejected," as he put it, from Palestine by "those Zionist thugs." Czartoryski had never been able to learn why he had chosen to throw in his lot with the Odessa. All he knew was that Ukridge had been a Middle East hand and had been one of those "ejec-tees." Perhaps, Czartoryski sometimes conjectured, Ukridge had had friends staying in the King David Hotel, the one the Cutter had helped blow up.

Anyway, Czartoryski knew all he needed to know about Ukridge: operating as president of Gemstones, he had turned Odessa diamonds into cash and back into diamonds, always at a profit, again and again.

"Would you care for some coffee or tea, Ladislaw?" Ukridge asked, sitting next to him on the sofa. "I can have either sent in. And very good stuff, too."

"No thank you, Stanley. I've just had breakfast. I must say, you're looking tremendously fit."

"We try," said Ukridge. "We avoid fried and fatty foods, and we eschew all forms of exercise. You look well yourself."

"Kind of you to say so. Tell me, Stanley," said Czartoryski, who enjoyed listening to Ukridge expound, "what's new in London?"

"In what area?"

"The high points, Stanley. The zeitgeist."

"We're reeling, old man. Times are very hard. The old empire is sinking beneath the waves for the third time. In a very few years, England, as we know and love it, shall, I'm afraid, be swallowed up in some sort of awful European stew, like some sort of amoeba engulfing its lunch."

"Won't there always be an England, Stanley?"

"I always thought so, but now . . . ? Well, I'm just a bitter old man, a relic. What did Hamlet say? ' 'Tis an unweeded garden that goes to seed. Things rank and' . . . something-or-other . . . 'possess it merely.' Emphasis on the 'merely,' old man. You should see the wogs swanking about London as if they owned the old place. Well, I imagine they do, now. So if they wish to swank, what's to stop them?"

"Nothing, I suppose."

"Of course, sometimes things do happen. Turned up a dead one, a bearded brute, positively apelike, in our place in Ashwell. Circumcised. Something you'd like to tell me, Laddy?"

"Not really. A minor affair. He ran errands for the Israelis and had become a nuisance. Nothing to concern yourself about.''

"Fine. Good enough for me. Anyway, Laddy, we hear that things have been looking up in your corner of the world. Quite exciting, yes? I presume that that, and not my scintillating company, is what has brought you to our humble offices.''

''You are correct, Stanley, although your company is always a pleasure.''

''As is yours, Laddy, as is yours. Well, you can be sure that we've been all a-bustle since receiving the news.'' Ukridge leaned forward, his enthusiasm palpable. ''In fact, we've already arranged for the time of an excellent man in Antwerp. Quite an artist, I'm told. Top drawer. He'll be able to chop up your stone smartly. Wouldn't trust it to anyone else. But, of course, I assume you'll want to discuss it with him directly, huddle over the loupe with him, an old diamond hand like yourself. . . .

''What's the matter, Ladislaw? Have we been too forward? You don't seem very pleased.''

''I've had second thoughts, Stanley.''

''Really?'' Ukridge leaned back, sighed, and then stood up. He wandered over to his desk and sat down behind it. ''Are you sure you won't have some coffee, Ladislaw?''

''Whom do we have at De Beers, Stanley?'' asked Czartoryski.

''What do you mean?''

''We do have someone in Johannesburg or London, someone at De Beers, don't we? Am I wrong?''

''No, you're not wrong. We usually have someone there. Never anyone too-too high up, of course. The Jews run the show, you know. Anyway, right now we've got a youngish chap in the Diamond Trading Company. Half the year he's here, half the year he's in Jo'burg. We also have an older fellow working for the De Beers appraiser in London. He collects the rough crystals, puts a price on them. But what's this all about? I mean, you can't seriously be thinking of trying to sell the stone to De Beers.''

"Of course not. But these men, what are their prospects?"

"I'm not following you, Ladislaw."

"Do you think either one will ever sit on the board of directors? Do you think either one will ever have a major role setting the price of the boxes in the sights? Will either one ever determine who gets the lion's share of the rough, and at what price?"

"I'm still not there, Ladislaw. I don't have the foggiest notion of what you're getting at."

"Say we were to implicate a syndicate director in the theft of one of the world's great diamonds," said Czartoryski. "And say that that director's dastardly scheme were to be uncovered by our friend in the Diamond Trading Company. Or our friend the appraiser. Wouldn't that be a feather in his cap? Don't you think it might improve his prospects within the Syndicate? And don't you think it would be quite wonderful to have a man there with influence, our man, who would be able to provide us with an unlimited flow of stones at our price? And, conversely, someone able to deny them to anyone we wished to cut off?

"Imagine, Stanley, controlling even a portion of the Syndicate. Wouldn't that be far more valuable to us than the few million we'd get from selling my stone?"

"I like the way you so airily say a few million," said Ukridge. "I had no idea you were so well off."

Czartoryski laughed.

"You're suggesting that we give the diamond to this man?" Ukridge asked.

"Give is not what I had in mind, Stanley. Loan, perhaps. Make available to, as a prop in a show. The actor does not own the prop; he borrows it to create an effect in the play we will write."

Ukridge leaned back in his leather chair. "Do you have anyone in particular in mind, Ladislaw? A De Beers director who could be compromised?"

Czartoryski had the name ready, the name supplied to him by the Mossad. "Alfred Berg."

Ukridge sniffed. "Ridiculous."

"Did you know that Berg is a gambler, a very serious

gambler? He owes quite a lot of money to a great many people.''

''No, I did not know that.''

''Mr. Berg is in an extremely vulnerable position.''

''Listen, Laddy,'' Ukridge said after a moment. ''Even if what you say is true, even if we could, shall we say, frame Berg and advance our own man, this is not a decision you can make on your own. There are others involved, as you well know. There are others who have been counting on an immediate return on your stone.''

''You, Stanley?''

''What about me?''

''Were you counting on a commission?''

''I won't dignify that with a response, Ladislaw.''

''All right, Stanley. As you will. I am more than willing to discuss this, to consult with whomever, but I am absolutely convinced that this is the right way to proceed. I am quite determined.''

Three hours later, after a rather pedestrian lunch in the second-floor dining room of Rouxl Britannia, beloved of the City's younger expense account lions, Czartoryski returned to the Savoy. There was a message waiting for him at the front desk from a Mr. Anderson of the Suisse Credit Bank of London, where both Czartoryski and Maria Radziwell kept accounts. Czartoryski had previously asked Anderson to keep him informed of Miss Radziwell's comings and goings, explaining that his ward was somewhat eccentric.

After returning to his suite, Czartoryski called Anderson, who informed him that not more than an hour ago Miss Radziwell had closed her account, a withdrawal of some five thousand pounds.

Czartoryski thanked him and hung up. He opened Maria's closet. Yes, her clothes were still there. He walked over to the suite's picture window and opened the curtains the maid had closed. Rain and wind still ruffled the surface of the Thames.

Taking the money, he knew, could mean only one thing: Maria was getting ready to run. For an instant he conjured a vision of her, lying on a small bed in that whorehouse in

Warsaw so many years ago. All that white skin, almost luminescent in the dim light. Her broad, powerful shoulders. Her breasts, youthfully defying gravity. Her long, muscular legs. The fine blond down on the inside of her thighs. The lushness of her. If it were true that she was Catherine Radziwell's great-granddaughter, and if Catherine had resembled Maria at all, it was easy to see how she could have seduced that great English faggot Cecil Rhodes.

Czartoryski bowed his head. Her odor filled his nostrils. Pineapple and musk. A gust of wind blew a spattering of rain against the window.

After this is all over, a vacation in Capri would be nice, he thought, turning to place a call to Tel Aviv and the Cutter.

How *triste* that I will be going there alone.

51

Mario's Butcher Shop
Red Hook, Brooklyn
Tuesday, October 22

"So it's my old pal, the Hebe detective," said Joey della Francesca, practicing his putting on the carpet in his office.

It occurred to Dov Taylor that he had never in his life seen anything so incongruous as Joey with a golf club in his hands. "Practicing for the Greater Mafia Open, Joey?" Taylor asked.

"I've never been able to decide, Taylor," said della Francesca, tapping a ball across the orange carpet into a frosted Tom Collins glass, "whether you were born an asshole or whether you practice. What do you want?"

From Sarah Kalman to this punk, thought Taylor. Just a few hours before, he had been sitting on a couch in Rabbi Kalman's study with Sarah as she read from the Lublin "Memory Book."

Sarah had thought that the book might help him. "After the war," she had told him, "The Lubavitchers started the 'Memory Project.' We didn't want that life to be forgotten. We didn't want to give the Nazis that victory. So we asked survivors to tell us what they remembered of life in their *shtetls*, and we put their memories into these books."

Taylor realized that he had never been so close to her. Their knees were almost touching. She had looked up from the book and had caught him staring at her.

"What are you looking at?" she asked.

"At you," he said.

"And what do you see?" she asked, smiling.

"I see a *sheyne meydele*," he said, using the Yiddish she had taught him.

"I'm not so beautiful," she said, pulling her hair off her forehead and looking away. She looked radiant, a human candle burning with light and intelligence. Looking at that face, he thought, you had to believe in God. Biology alone could not have created that.

"Have you found any of the people I dreamed?"

"Oh, yes," said Sarah. "Here is a man, Nathan Birnbaum, a shoemaker, who recalls a family of butchers, the ben Areyns, and how it was said that one of them was horribly murdered in a pogrom. And, of course, all the people mention the Seer. He made Lublin famous. They're all proud of living in his city, even those who weren't Hasids. It gave them a sense of being important."

Sarah turned some more pages. This close, I can smell her, he thought. Soap, bread, and a sweetness.

"What about the Czartoryskis?" he asked.

"All I can find is the castle," she said. "Many people mention an old castle on the road outside town called castle Czartoryski."

"Can the book tell me where they are today?"

"I don't think so. Here," Sarah said, "in the memory of a Rabbi Dov Baer. He says his father told him there was once a great *farbrengen*, a gathering, of all the world's Hasidim, and a pogrom broke out during which the Seer fell out of his window and died.

"These people," said Sarah, her eyes meeting Taylor's, "they lived all their lives with death and violence and stories about killing. But what's amazing is that mostly they remember the good things—weddings, songs. They remember the streets filled with children. I think that's what we do, the Hasidim. We try to fill the streets with children so we can forget the horrors around us. You and your wife never had children?"

"No," said Taylor, feeling again the frustration and disappointment that had become the defining character of his marriage. "We tried, but . . ." How could he explain? How could he tell Sarah Kalman about making love because the thermometer said that it was time? Or watching while some doctor injected his sperm into Carol's vagina as she lay in the stirrups on an examining table? Or going on a bender every time she got her period? Why go through all that again?

"What about you?" he asked. "Don't you want children?"

"Of course I do. But first I need a husband, and that's not so easy."

"I can't believe that."

"You don't understand the Hasidim."

No, he did not understand the Hasidim. He did not understand how a woman as beautiful as Sarah Kalman could be an outcast among them.

But, he told himself, I do know Joey della Francesca. I know that he's a thief, a pimp, and probably a murderer. And that's why I should forget about Sarah Kalman. Because I feel comfortable with Joey.

Taylor had known della Francesca, it seemed, for most of his life. Actually, they had met in a bar at LaGuardia Airport in 1968. Taylor was on his way to Infantry Officers School at Fort Benning, Georgia. He was miserable and needed a drink.

When Taylor had enlisted—against the almost hysterical objections of his family and the bitter ridicule of his friends—he'd figured that he'd be made an officer. That sounded better to him than what he had been doing—driving a cab, cutting classes, and hanging out at City College.

Taylor didn't like the hippies who lolled around the south

campus cafeteria at CCNY; they were pompous, phony, and the girls didn't shave their legs or pits. But he did like the effect it had on them when he told them that he was thinking of enlisting. The girls especially. First they'd call him a fascist bastard; then they'd go to bed with him. Eventually Taylor had told so many people that he was enlisting that it became real. He got drunk one day and did it.

The army told him he could choose between four officers candidate's prep schools. Armor-tanks sounded too hot; who wanted to sit in a tank in the jungle? Aviation was too exotic; he couldn't see himself as a flyboy. Infantry was too deadly; the average life expectancy of an infantry lieutenant was, what? five seconds? So he'd picked artillery.

Of course, after basic training, and after eight weeks of advanced artillery training at Fort Sill—being taught to operate the RDFs, range direction finders, and the FADACs, the field artillery direction auto computers, learning his way around the penny-nickel-nickels (the 155-mm Howitzers) and the dime-nickels (the 105-mm Howitzers)—he was assigned to Infantry Officers School anyway.

It was the army way.

In the bar, Taylor spotted Joey immediately: he was wearing his green uniform with absolutely no tags or insignias. He was the anonymous soldier incarnate.

They got drunk together and discovered they were both on their way to Fort Benning in order to train to become corpses.

"No way I'm staying in infantry," Joey said. "I plan to come out of this alive."

"What are you going to do?" Taylor asked.

"I'm just going to tell them I ain't officer material."

"And you think they'll listen?"

"Hey? What are they going to do to me? Send me to Vietnam?"

They showed up at Fort Benning a day late, hung over and stinking.

Neither of them became officers.

Both of them were sent to Vietnam.

After that, they seemed fated to be stapled at the elbows. They flew the same World Airlines transport from Fort Dix to Anchorage (where they managed to cadge some beers) to Tokyo (where they were kept in the hangar for forty-eight hours) to their final destination: Tan Son Nhut Air Base in Saigon.

From Tan Son Nhut they were flown to Jungle World, which was what they called combat school, in Chu Lai, hard by the South China Sea, and from there they were piled into half-ton trucks for the ride to Arty Hill, HHB, the headquarters of Head Q Battery of the 3/18th Artillery I-Corp, the proud Americal Division, where Private First Class Joey della Francesca quickly set up a good business selling *touc phins*, opiated reefer, in ten-joint party packs, and Private First Class Dov Taylor set about seeing how many of them he could smoke and still stay sharp enough to make the right decisions necessary to staying alive.

For two years Taylor sat in a hole at Alpha battery, twenty yards from the big guns, twenty-five miles from Arty Hill, Route One, and the South China Sea, and directed fire into a patch of jungle they called the Rocket Pocket. Every day Viet Cong B-40 rockets would fly out of the Rocket Pocket, killing soldiers, and ruining the days and nights of I-Corps' top brass. Every day Alpha, Bravo, and Charley batteries would pour 160- and 200-pound shells into the Rocket Pocket.

Like everything else, it was an exercise in futility. First the Rocket Pocket would go quiet, and then, after a while, the VC would crawl out of their holes and the rockets would fly again.

PFC della Francesca gave PFC Taylor some good advice during those years. He convinced him to stay away from the body shops—"If you don't get some fucking horrible Asian clap, you'll get your throat cut by the hooer's brother"—and he convinced him not to transfer from Alpha battery to Bravo, even though Bravo was a much cooler place—"They're a bunch of fucking junkies, and they got bad vibes; I feel it." Sure enough, one day on the Quang Tra Bong Road to Tam Ky, Bravo company was ambushed and wiped out.

But Joey was never able to talk Taylor out of smoking his *touc phins*. "That shit fucks you up too much," Joey would say. "You can nod out all you want in the world, but here, if you crap out, you *really* crap out."

But Taylor needed the warm, safe feeling the opiated dope gave him; he knew he'd go crazy and do something stupid without it.

One day Taylor asked della Francesca what he planned to do when he got back to the world.

"Go into my uncle's business," he said.

"And what's that?" Taylor asked.

"Meat," Joey said. "What are you going to do? Go back to school like the dumb motherfucker you are?"

At that time, Taylor was unsure, but as the days of his hitch dwindled, the idea of becoming a cop began to tickle his brain. Then, one day, after seeing Joey attack a soldier over something or other and beat him bloody, Taylor felt as if he had been given a gift, an understanding of why guys like Joey could be frightening—for by this time Joe had dropped enough hints for Taylor to figure out that Joey's uncle's business was more than just sausages and steaks. Their strength, Taylor decided, came from the way they could switch on their rage, instantly, and act on it without fear. While everyone else was thinking, they were moving. Suddenly. Violently. It was also the great truth about war. You had to give it your all without losing yourself to it.

I can do that, Taylor thought. I can match that anger. And I can do it without turning off my brain.

The idea of becoming a cop began to feel right. It would be fun to challenge guys like Joey, and, as a bonus, it would be a very un-Jewish thing to do.

Taylor returned stateside a few months before Joey and stopped thinking about him until a year later, when he saw a story in *Time* magazine about a Joseph della Francesca who had been busted just as he was about to spill a mountain of betting slips recorded on dissolvable paper into a vat of boiling water. In the story, Joey took credit for the technological breakthrough. Taylor, who was just about to take the police exam, cut out the article and carried it around in his wallet for weeks.

Over the years, Taylor was careful never to use della Francesca as a source, never to ask him a direct question. But from time to time Joey would call him with a piece of information—about who may have shot whom; about who may have ripped off a certain party. The information led to several busts and helped Taylor make detective. He knew that Joey was using him to drop dimes on his enemies, but if Taylor could help himself by helping Joey, why the hell not?

But this was different. Taylor couldn't wait. The wedding was set for November 5.

"I need some help, Joey," Taylor said. "Last month somebody cut up a Hasid in the diamond district. I'm wondering if you heard anything about it."

"I don't know nothing about it," said Joey, sinking another putt. "My business is meat."

"I know, Joey. But you know the Hasidim."

In New York, *kosher* meat was big business. Each Hasidic sect considered the other's meat *treyf*, unfit for consumption. That meant that each sect had to purchase its own animals, establish its own slaughterhouses, truck its own meat. Five years ago della Francesca had leased a slaughterhouse to the Kozlovers and convinced them to use his trucks. They had paid top dollar, and that had given della Francesca ideas. One day the Satmarer slaughterhouse had mysteriously caught fire, and della Francesca had suggested to the Kozlovers that he would be glad to help the Satmarers out of their difficulty. Soon della Francesca had the Satmarer franchise. Over the next few years he brought the Belzers and the Gerers into the fold. Just two years ago he'd scored his biggest coup —the Lubavitchers.

That was why he was so upset when he heard about the planned marriage between the Satmarer *rebbe*'s daughter and the Lubavitcher *rebbe*'s son. If the two sects started eating the same meat, it would cost della Francesca almost half of his business. And that was why today he was so pissed off at that fucking Polack, Czartoryski, who had told him that it had all been taken care of.

"You play golf, Taylor?" asked della Francesca.

"No, Joey. I'm not retired."

"Fucking great game. Play it until you're ninety. Get out in the fresh air. Walk around. Good for your heart. Good for your soul, you know what I mean?"

"Can you help me, Joey?"

"You're not a cop anymore?"

"No."

"Good. About time you gave up that racket. You need work?"

"No. I'm okay."

"So you got work. This? Is this it?"

"The guy who was killed was a Satmarer. The Satmarers asked me to look into it."

"They paying you good? They should. They got money up the wazoo, I ain't kidding."

"They're paying me so good, I'm thinking of taking up golf."

"Go ahead, break my balls. I'm trying to help you."

"And I like you, too, Joey."

"Was a guy in town," said della Francesca after a moment, "last month. A Polack. Old guy. Must be seventy, maybe more. Heard he was hanging around the diamond district with this other guy, a scary old fuck, about sixty, supposed to be good with a knife."

"This Polack have a name?"

"Czartoryski. Don't know his first name. Don't know the other guy's name."

For a moment Taylor thought he heard hoofbeats. He closed his eyes. A glint of steel flashed. It was all true. His vision was true.

"You know where he is?" Taylor asked, his voice low.

"No idea."

"Know anybody who might?"

"Maybe. This guy Czartoryski is international. Wired in, you know. Nobody knows much about him. Not even me. But if I was looking for somebody like that, I'd go to Miami, look up this old Jew broad. Teddy. If she's sober, and if she ain't lost all her marbles yet, she knows everybody. Bring her a bottle of Scotch, she'll go down on you."

"How would I contact this person?"

"Here . . ." Della Francesca wrote down a name and a number on a slip of paper. "You can even use my name."

"Thanks, Joey," Taylor said, looking at the paper and slipping it into his wallet. "Teddy Lansky? Any relation to Meyer?"

"His wife. His widow."

"You're kidding me."

"Nope. Her old man told her everything he knew. All his old wop buddies support her now, keep her lushed up and happy, she don't go writing her memoirs, *The Boss's Wife*.

"You learn to play golf," said della Francesca, "you give me a call. We'll play."

"Sure. Tell me, Joey. How did this Czartoryski fuck you?"

"I don't know what you're talking about. I don't even know the guy."

But I do, thought Dov Taylor. I do.

52

Heathrow Airport
London
Thursday, October 24

Late in the afternoon, the Cutter checked into the Post House alongside the M4 just outside the airport. Then he took a cab into Soho. The Magician was meeting him at Bahn Thai, and the Cutter already knew that everything there would be too hot for him to eat.

It was dark when the Cutter arrived. Czartoryski was sitting at a red leather banquette, a bottle of Thai beer on the table in front of him. Oriental parasols with red, blue, and gold dragons hung open and inverted from the ceiling. The Cutter slipped onto his seat across from Czartoryski, who slid a menu over to him.

"The food here is excellent," Czartoryski said. "Thai

food, in my opinion, is one of the world's great cuisines, yet it's largely unappreciated. As are most Asian cuisines apart from the Chinese. That is part of Chinese cultural hegemony. Do you know the Chinese are called the Jews of the East? That is because of their shrewdness in business."

The menu was huge, and the Cutter's eye fell upon the warning on the top of the page: "All these sauces tend to be hot and pungent and often not to the taste of non-Thais." He closed the menu.

"Would you like a beer, my friend?" Czartoryski asked. "It goes very well with the food. In fact, apart from beer, only champagne can be drunk with Thai food, and the wine list here is very poor. They do, however, have an '86 Clicquot. Would you like that? . . . No? Then a beer it is. Thai beer is very spicy, fuller than Chinese beer, lighter than Japanese beer."

The Cutter nodded, and Czartoryski signaled for a waiter. "I'll order for you. The menu is rather daunting. You like fish, don't you? They have a wonderful whole fish here—a sea bass—marinated in honey and ginger and charred over an open fire. I'll tell them to serve the chile sauce in a bowl and you can employ as much or as little as you wish."

"I'm not hungry," said the Cutter.

"You will be when you see this dish," said Czartoryski, giving the order in French to a slender young Asian. "It's magnificent."

"So," said Czartoryski, "your flight was tiring, no doubt. I can see that. But beneath all that, you look fit and rested. Was Tel Aviv as you left it?"

Tel Aviv was precisely as the Cutter had left it, but he had changed. He had thought that when he returned home his guts would heal and he would be able to sleep. But the pains continued—the awful cramps, the explosive diarrhea—and he had spent almost every night smoking cigarettes, sweating, and staring out the window. In the street below, he imagined he could see Sarah Kalman walking away from him, her long red hair fanned out behind her like a biblical queen's.

A waiter poured the beer; the Cutter took a sip.

"There," said Czartoryski. "That's what you need."

The Cutter felt the cool beer sliding down his throat into the black hole of his stomach, and he winced. He imagined it splashing on the tumor he felt sure was there, lying in wait, preparing to blossom and kill him. He was sure he had cancer, but he would not go to a doctor. He knew about doctors. He knew them from the camps. He would rather die in agony than allow one to touch him, even a Jewish one.

But Sarah Kalman's touch, that would be another matter. Perhaps her soft hands could convince the tumor, the black excrescence of his sins, to shrink, to vanish.

Czartoryski regarded the Cutter. He was thinner than ever. He looked, Czartoryski thought, like a fright mask: his skin waxen, his cheeks sunken, dark purple circles under his red-rimmed eyes. Delicately, Czartoryski sniffed. Yes, the Cutter smelled of the camps. After all these years, Czartoryski thought, I can still smell death.

But you can't die just yet, my friend, he thought. No, not quite yet.

"Maria is preparing to run away," Czartoryski said.

The Cutter looked up from his beer and smiled thinly.

"Ah, that's better," said Czartoryski. "For a moment I thought you were not happy to see me. I see now that you have just been bored. Did you think I brought you here just to share a meal with me? Not that I don't relish your company. You, Maria, and I, we have been an excellent team, don't you think?"

The Cutter grunted.

"You have never cared for her, have you?" said Czartoryski. "You object to her, to my relationship with her."

"Your whore," said the Cutter.

"Yes, that. You are quite bourgeois, my friend."

"When?" asked the Cutter, imagining his knife opening Radziwell's white belly, making a red grin appear above the goatee of her pubis. He smiled again.

"I want her away from here," said Czartoryski. "We shall let her run. You will keep watch on my hotel. Most probably she will go to Rome. She will feel safe there. You will follow her. I don't want her found. She is too closely associated with me, especially here in London."

The Cutter's fish arrived. He looked at it with loathing.

"You must eat, my friend," said Czartoryski.

The Cutter took a pack of Marlboros from his pocket and tapped one out.

"If you're not going to eat," said Czartoryski, "please allow me to do so without tasting your smoke. I have become very American in that way."

The Cutter put the cigarette back in its pack and stood up.

"You will enjoy this," said Czartoryski, reaching across the table for the Cutter's fish. "She likes being hurt."

"I know," said the Cutter.

Czartoryski finished his meal alone and returned to the Savoy. After asking at the front desk, he was informed that Miss Radziwell was out. Up in his room, Czartoryski again checked her closet. Her clothes were still there.

When she had not returned by eleven, Czartoryski went to bed. He awoke in the night and looked over at Maria's bed. It was empty.

A sudden, terrible thought struck him. He sat up and pulled on his robe and slippers, then walked into the sitting room and spun the tumblers on the safe. He opened its door.

It, too, was empty.

53
Wolfie's
Collins Avenue, Miami Beach
Thursday, October 24

Dov Taylor fell asleep as soon as he sat down in the plane leaving Kennedy for Miami International Airport. He awoke just in time to see the ribbon of golden beach below him, the shadows cast by small, puffy white clouds scooting across the stacked-up hotels, and the tiny power boats offshore churning up slender, creamy, crisscrossing trails in the turquoise sea.

Getting off the plane and walking down Concourse D, the airport—all neon lights and black tile, filled with men in *guyaberas* and women in tight, rhinestone-studded jeans— was profoundly disorienting. Taylor thought of an old joke. A Hasid in a long black coat and beard steps off a bus some- where in the Deep South, and little children begin following him, jeering and throwing sticks and stones. After trying to ignore them, the Hasid finally turns and demands: "What's the matter? You never seen a Yankee before?"

Over the phone, Teddy Lansky, her voice smoke-cured, had told him that she didn't know "nothing about nothing," but she agreed to meet him for lunch if he was buying. Taylor gave the cabdriver the name she had given him, and thirty minutes later he was stepping out of the air-conditioned cab into the tropical heat in front of Wolfie's on the corner of Collins and Twenty-first Street. A line of elderly Jews waiting patiently for tables snaked halfway down the block.

Taylor entered the freezing restaurant. To his left, hard, wrinkled salamis hung by the score over a long, gleaming steel-and-glass case containing smoked sturgeon and white- fish, sliced Nova and belly lox, tubs of coleslaw, bowls of hot and sweet red and green cherry peppers, sour tomatoes, and *kosher* dills. To his right, sitting on a stool behind the cash register, a bald man broiled crimson by the Florida sun studied the *Daily Racing Form* and chewed an enormous unlit cigar.

"You want a seat, you gotta wait," the man said without looking up and without taking the stogie out of his mouth. "An hour for a table, half hour for the counter." A tiny bubble of brown saliva formed in the corner of his mouth.

"I'm meeting Mrs. Lansky," Taylor said. "If she's here, she's expecting me."

"What's your name?"

"Mr. Taylor."

"Wait a minute." The man took the cigar out of his mouth, and the brown bubble burst. He wiped his chin and called to a young Latino and whispered in his ear. The boy left, and the man put the soggy, ragged end of the cigar back in his mouth, staring at Taylor with a lack of enthusiasm that bordered on distaste.

"Good cigar?" asked Taylor.

"The best. Cuban," the man said.

"You ever light up?"

"Nah. Too good to smoke. Lasts longer this way."

Even through the air-conditioning, Taylor could smell the boiled cabbage. It reminded him of his grandmother's kitchen, and because of that he felt at ease and eager to meet Meyer Lansky's widow.

As a boy, Taylor had heard the names of Jewish gangsters pronounced with the same reverence accorded Jewish baseball and basketball stars. Before the Israelis stomped the Arabs in the '67 war, it was men like Arnold Rothstein, Dutch Schultz, Jake Guzik, Lepke Buchalter, Bugsy Siegel, and, of course, Meyer Lansky who gave the lie to the belief that Jews were weak. These were men who defied the *goyishe* world and made their own way with balls, brains, and muscle.

The Latino boy returned and whispered in the cashier's ear. He nodded, looked at Taylor, and said, "Follow him." Then he returned to the *Racing Form*.

Taylor followed the boy through the crowded restaurant to a red Leatherette booth in the back. Teddy Lansky, a small, chubby woman, her blond hair cut in a pageboy, sat smoking a long brown cigarette, a Manhattan and a small bowl of maraschino cherries in front of her.

"So sit down already," she rasped.

"Thank you," said Taylor, sliding into the booth.

"You want a drink?"

"No thanks," said Taylor.

"Tony!" Lansky yelled, and another young Latino appeared at the table. "I'll have another Manhattan," she said, tapping her drink with a long red fingernail. "What do you want, mister?"

"You got a cream soda?" Taylor asked Tony.

"Of course they got cream soda. Dr. Brown's. Just like in New York. Tony, bring him a can and a glass with lots of ice."

Tony went away, and Taylor studied Teddy Lansky. Her small face and hands were leathery, deeply tanned. This was someone who put in a lot of pool time. She wore red lipstick on her bee-stung lips, red rouge, and her eyes were a bright blue. Her dress was tight, and she showed a little cleavage. Forty, even thirty years ago, she must have been a knockout, thought Taylor. Lansky had divorced his first wife to marry her. She had been a trophy, and even now, at seventy-something, she still looked like an old Jew's idea of a prize.

"What are you looking at?" Lansky demanded.

"I was just thinking that you're a very attractive woman," said Taylor.

"Don't give me that crap," said Lansky. "I'm too old for that crap. You tell me I'm gorgeous and I'm supposed to tell you my life story? Forget it. That may work with the chippies you know, but it doesn't work with me. You're a good-looking guy, but you're wasting your time buttering me up. Better-looking guys than you have tried. You want to know something, ask."

"Okay, Mrs. Lansky."

"Nobody calls me Mrs. Lansky. You ain't talking to Eleanor Roosevelt here. Call me Teddy."

"All right, Teddy. Well, a friend of mine in New York—"

"Now you're going to tell me about that *putz* Joey. For chrissakes, you think I got Alzheimer's? You're just like all those lawyers. Whenever something happens, they send some kid to talk to me, and the first thing he says is how good I look and the next thing he wants to know is who's running the organization. Like I got a private line to Meyer in heaven, God rest his soul."

"I'm sorry, Mrs. Lansky."

"Teddy, for chrissakes. Oh, you're a peach."

Tony returned with Lansky's drink and Taylor's cream soda, and Taylor felt grateful for the break. Teddy Lansky certainly seemed to have all her marbles, and, at the moment, she seemed relatively sober, but she was hardly the nice old Jewish lady he had been hoping for.

"You should have the pastrami," said Lansky. "It's good. Not too fatty. I'll have the usual, Tony. So, you're going to have the pastrami?" Taylor nodded. "He'll have the pastrami, Tony. And tell them to cut it nice and lean. Fat will kill you. It's the worst thing in the world."

Lansky popped a cherry into her mouth, lit a fresh cigarette, and blew a cloud of smoke across the table into Taylor's face. "Maraschinos," she said. "My only vice. So, *nu*? What do you want to know, mister?"

"Taylor. Dov Taylor."

"Taylor, Shmaylor. I'm not going to remember. Dov, is that an Israeli name?"

"Actually, it was a compromise. My mother wanted to name me David, my father wanted Dionysus."

"Dionysus?" Teddy Lansky started a laugh that quickly turned into a cough. She bolted down what was left of her first Manhattan and ate another cherry. "That's a good one. Your father Greek?"

"No, he was an English teacher. He loved mythology."

"So did my Meyer. You know, he went to that library across the street every day. Every day. He read everything. He had a library card. The man never had a driver's license, he never had a credit card, he never had a goddamn Social Security number, but he had a library card. That tells you something.

"He should have been a teacher. Then I'd have a pension now." Lansky's eyes narrowed. "Everybody thinks Meyer left me millions. You know what he left me? *Bupkis*. *Gornit*. He died broke. If it wasn't for some of his friends, I'd be in the poorhouse."

"I'm sorry to hear that."

"Sorry I've heard all my life. Sorry is crap. You don't believe me, anyway."

"Of course I do."

"Don't shit a shitter. You think I'm full of it. You read the stories. What did they call him? The chairman of the board? What a load of crap. You know what happened to Meyer? Castro, that bastard. He took the Riviera, and we didn't get a nickel out of it. Do you know how much money Meyer sunk into that hotel? His own money? If I told you, you wouldn't believe me.

"But Meyer loved Havana, he loved hotels. He understood hotels. That's what that movie, *The Godfather*, they didn't get. All they showed was a gangster. Meyer said he liked that actor, Lee Strasberg, who played him. What was his name in the movie? Hyman Roth? I didn't like it. It was so violent. It was terrible seeing him get shot like that. But Meyer and his friends watched it over and over again and bust a gut. Anyway, what was I saying?"

"About hotels."

"The Riviera. He poured his own blood into that place. I said, Meyer, don't work so hard. But let me tell you, mister, you could get the best meal you ever ate in your life there. Everything was the best. Meyer was always in the kitchen, checking everything. He cared more about the kitchen than the casino. He always said, If you want people to spend money, you got to give them the best steaks, make them feel like kings and queens."

"That makes sense," Taylor offered.

"A wonderful place. We should've killed that bastard Castro," Lansky continued. "Kennedy, he should've killed him. But he was too busy with his whores, his *nofkes*, that Marilyn, God rest her soul. He was so ugly, with that beard. It made me nauseous."

"Castro?"

"Of course Castro. We had dinner with him, Meyer and me, two, three times, and there was always pieces of food in that beard. It was disgusting. Finally, I couldn't take it anymore. I told him, I said, 'Mr. Castro, you should cut off the beard. Without the beard, you'd look like a human being. Maybe then you wouldn't have so much trouble with our government and businesspeople would want to invest in Cuba.' Meyer was so angry with me, but I can't help it. I tell the truth. People don't like it, but what can I do?"

Teddy Lansky leaned back in the booth as Tony brought the food. Taylor's sandwich was huge, the pastrami piled six inches high. Lansky's usual seemed to be a tuna-fish salad with sliced eggs and Russian dressing.

"Is that enough pastrami?" Lansky asked.

"Plenty."

"So," said Lansky, "old stories from an old broad. I'm putting you to sleep."

"No," said Dov Taylor. "Not at all. It's fascinating."

"Sure. You flew down to Miami to hear my life story. You still haven't told me what you want to know."

"There's a man," Taylor began, chewing his pastrami, "I want to find. His name is Czartoryski, a Pole."

"What's his racket?" asked Lansky.

"Diamonds, I think. The pastrami is excellent."

"As good as New York?"

"Absolutely."

"They fly it down. The bagels, too. I used to have some beauties. Diamonds, not bagels. I had to pawn them. The newspapers never write about that. It's always Teddy Lansky, the widow of the millionaire gangster. What a laugh. If I had so much money stashed away, why am I living in a crummy apartment in Miami Beach, tell me that? Not even a good neighborhood. Thank God it's paid for. Thank God I don't have to ask my children for anything. His children wouldn't give me the time of day."

"If you could help me, Teddy, I think I could pay for more than lunch."

"You know, you should get in the sun more. You're so white, like a fish. You'd be a pretty good-looking man if you got some sun."

"There's not a lot of sun in New York."

"What's the matter? You never heard of a sun lamp?"

"Czartoryski, Teddy. You know him?"

"Nah. But if he's in diamonds, I know a man who knows everybody in diamonds. He's right here in Miami, retired, like everybody else. What do they call Miami? God's waiting room? Hey, this guy you're looking for, he's not an Israeli, is he?"

"I don't think so. Why?"

" 'Cause they're bastards, that's why. Me and Meyer spent a year in Israel when Meyer was trying to get his citizenship. The bastards wouldn't give it to him. It broke his heart. It killed him. I blame them for his death. All his life, he supported Israel. He raised a fortune for them; he even made his Italian friends give money, buy bonds. And then, when he needed them, they turned him over to the *goyim*. Imagine, Jews doing that to another Jew. After that, we never gave a nickel."

"You were saying, Teddy, this man you know who knows everybody in diamonds? This man in Miami?"

"All of a sudden you're in a hurry. We're having a nice *shmooze*, and now you can't wait to get rid of me."

"I'm sorry. I didn't mean to rush you. And, like I said, I can pay for more than lunch."

"A grand."

"What?"

"You heard me."

"All right."

"Just like that?"

"Just like that."

"Cash?"

"If I can cash a check."

"My bank can cash it."

"Then cash."

"Good," Lansky said, smiling. "I like your style, mister. All right. His name is Jan Pleesis. South African. He used to be a diamond cop. He used to do favors for Meyer. I'll give you his number. What's the name of the man you're looking for again?"

"Czartoryski."

"Write it down so I remember."

Taylor finished his sandwich, paid the bill, and got up to go with Teddy Lansky to her bank to cash the Satmarers' check. As he walked through Wolfie's, steadying Lansky by her elbow, Taylor felt observed. Old men, tanned black by the sun, squinted through their cigar smoke at him with hard eyes. Retired gangsters, thought Taylor. Tough *Yids* who knew the great Meyer Lansky and now watched out for his widow. The thought made Taylor smile.

"You have a lot of fans," said Taylor, his arm taking in the men in the booths.

"Bunch of old farts," Lansky said. "*Alte kockers*. When they're not trying to *shnor* money off me, they sit around talking about what big shots they used to be. *Shtarkers*. Tough guys. Killers. Hah! My Meyer would have squashed them like cockroaches."

54

An Apartment in Knightsbridge
London
Friday, October 25

Standing by the window, wrapped in a blanket, Maria Radziwell shivered and waited for the sun to rise. Sleep was out of the question. Lying in bed, the young Englishman she had picked up at the bar slept curled up on his side like a pink shrimp, his lipstick smeared.

In the gray predawn light, Radziwell looked at his pale, delicate face, his long lashes fluttering in a dream, his dark blond hair plastered to his skull. How do the English ever make babies? she wondered. It seemed to her that every Englishman she had ever met was queer. Last night, as soon as they had gotten to his flat, this one had disappeared into his bathroom and emerged in fishnet stockings, garters, and black lace panties. Teetering on high heels, he'd carried a strap-on dildo that he'd wanted her to wear. Why didn't he go find a man if that's what he wanted? she had thought. But she had needed a place to stay, so she'd put it on and fucked him with it until he'd come and then instantly fallen asleep.

She would have much preferred it the other way around.

She was, she knew, close to hysterical with fear, and being made love to violently, even by this effete young Englishman—if he could have managed it—would have been a relief. Perhaps then she could have slept. But perhaps not. Awake or asleep, the nightmare was the same.

Yesterday, still not sure of what she was going to do with the money she had taken from the bank, still not sure of when, or where, or even how she was going to flee from this man who was beginning to look at her like a disappointing whore he had ordered up from room service, she had followed Czartoryski.

And seen the Cutter getting out of a cab.

First, she'd run. She'd run down Frith Street to Old Compton Road, and then up Compton to Charing Cross Road. She'd run until her heel broke, and then she'd taken off her shoes and run some more. She'd run until her lungs burned.

She wrapped the blanket around herself more tightly, but—damn these English—the cold was already inside her bones, shaking her like a rag doll. Her stomach heaved at the thought of what the Cutter might do to her, what he would enjoy doing to her.

When she had stopped running, she had hailed a taxi and returned to the hotel, planning to pack some clothes. Then, in the empty room, she had decided against it. Leaving her clothing would give her a little more time before Czartoryski realized that she had gone. And then, terrified and angry, wanting to strike back at him, she had taken the stone, having memorized the combination from watching him on those evenings when he'd taken it out to gaze at and play with.

Now what? she thought. I could hide the diamond. He won't kill me if he doesn't know where it is.

No, she thought, he won't kill you; he'll just torture you until you tell him. Then he'll kill you.

Where could she go? Where could she go where Czartoryski and all his Nazi friends (oh, yes, she knew about that) could not find her? Rome? Would she be safe in Rome? And who could help her there?

"What time is it?" the Englishman asked, lifting his head from the pillow.

"Go back to sleep," said Radziwell. "It is not yet dawn."

"You must be cold," the young man said sleepily. "It's freezing. Come to bed."

"In a moment," said Radziwell.

"You were wonderful," the man said. "Last night. Today, I'd like to show you London. Not the tourist's London; my London. I'll take off from work. Take you around, you know. We'll have fun."

"Maybe. Now go to sleep."

"Say yes."

"Yes. Go to sleep."

The boy mumbled something and turned over, pulling the blankets up over his head.

So he'd like to take me around London, Radziwell thought ruefully. Show me the city. Perhaps he'd like to wear my clothes, too. They'd fit him, and he'd look good in them. Better than I would right now.

Why do men always want to show you the city they live in? As if you would think they owned it, that it belonged to them and they were giving it to you. As if a million other people didn't live there.

That detective in New York, Radziwell thought. He also wanted to show me his city.

Her wide-set brown eyes narrowed as she recalled Dov Taylor standing in her doorway in Manhattan, smiling. What had he said? He wanted to show me a village? In New York?

But he liked me, she thought. He wanted to make love to me.

The Cutter tried to kill him and failed, she thought. Had that ever happened before?

The room began to lighten. Soon, she thought, this English boy will get up and start pestering me. Soon Czartoryski will know I have gone, and know that his beloved diamond is gone. And soon the Cutter will be on the street, his knife in his pocket.

Radziwell walked over to the bed and shook the young Englishman.

"Hello," he said.

"You must take me to the airport," she said.

"What?"

"I have to go. If you want to be nice to me, hurry up, put your clothes on, and take me to the airport."

"Wait a bloody minute," said the Englishman. "The airport? You didn't say anything about going anywhere. Where the hell are you going?"

"New York," said Maria Radziwell. "I must go to New York."

55

All Things Beautiful
Kingston Street, Brooklyn
Friday, October 25

Her mother was sick with the flu, and Sarah Kalman had promised to help her get ready for *Shabbos*. There was the cleaning, the shopping, and the cooking to be done before the candlelighting. Tonight, as usual, there would be guests, and their rooms had to be prepared—their beds made, towels laid out for them, extra places set at the table. Mrs. Kalman also wanted to go to the *mikvah* in the afternoon, and Sarah had said she would go with her. But first, she'd told her mother, she had work to do at the store.

"Why can't Channah take care of it?" her mother had asked, and Sarah had simply said that although Channah was a great help, her sister-in-law did not like to be left in the store alone. In truth, Channah had become completely useless in recent days, which was too bad because the store had been very busy with women buying new dresses for Adam Seligson's wedding. Everybody in Crown Heights discussed little else.

The bride—she wasn't so pretty, they said, very dark, like all the Satmarers. The groom—such a brilliant young man, someday, God forbid not soon, he would be a wonderful *rebbe*. The reception—with all the Satmarers' money, it should be the most lavish the world had ever seen.

But Channah did not join in the talk. She spent all her time staring out the window or crying, positive that Sarah's brother, Moshe, was preparing to divorce her because she had failed to become pregnant.

And, indeed, Sarah knew that to be true. She had gone to Moshe and pleaded with him to take Channah to a doctor, an infertility specialist. She had suggested that Moshe have himself checked out, too. Moshe, as Sarah knew he would, scoffed at both suggestions. He had asked her, his voice dripping with sarcasm, to tell him when and how doctors, a notoriously impious class of people, had discovered the Lord's secrets. He quoted the Law to her in that pompous way she detested, saying that fulfilling the precept of propagation was one of every Jew's most important duties—perhaps the most important of all—and therefore it was a man's duty to divorce a wife who was sterile. Finally he'd told her to mind her own business. What did she, an *alte moyd*, an old maid, know about men and women and what transpired between them?

Sarah had looked at Moshe and cursed him silently. A man like this, she thought, a cruel, narrow-minded, pusillanimous man, did not deserve children. Go ahead, she thought, divorce your sweet Channah. You don't deserve her. And may your next wife be barren as well.

Sarah stared at the book in front of her, the real reason she had told her mother that she had to go to the store this morning, even though both mother and daughter knew that no one in Crown Heights would be shopping for dresses on the eve of *Shabbos*. The book she was reading was a history of the Satmarer Hasidim. Sarah was trying to discover how the Seer's stone had ended up in the possession of the Satmarers, hoping that that could help Dov Taylor's investigation. But Sarah had quickly realized that the book, which was little more than a recitation of miracles performed by the various Satmarer *rebbes*, would be of little use. What she needed was the Satmarer *rebbe*'s own personal history, and that, she knew, as a Lubavitcher—not to mention a woman—she would never be allowed to see.

Sarah closed the book, and her thoughts returned to Dov Taylor. This was a man, she believed, of vast potential. The vision the Lord had given him was, she thought, a call. The Lord Himself was asking Taylor to help Him right something in His world, something that had gone terribly wrong. And she knew Taylor was afraid of answering that call, afraid of what would be expected of him, afraid of making a commitment. Sometimes it seemed to her that Taylor was the loneliest man she had ever met.

Sarah had tried to discuss Taylor's vision with her father, but Rabbi Kalman had shrugged and been uncharacteristically reticent, speaking vaguely of how difficult it was to know what went on inside the hearts of men such as Dov Taylor. It dawned on her that her father had divined her true feelings for the detective, and he disapproved.

And Sarah knew he was right. Despite the fact that she considered herself to be an educated, modern woman, despite the fact she felt set apart from the rest of Lubavitcher world, she knew that she would be lost outside it. She would not want to live without the sweetness of *Shabbos*. She could not imagine herself eating pork, or shellfish, or meat with milk. Even drinking a harmless glass of water in Taylor's apartment filled her with anxiety.

Furthermore, a man like Taylor would expect things from her that she knew she could not give. And how much could he change? How far could she expect him to come over to her side, to the side of religion and piety, a man whose life had been spent with violence and criminals, a man who had had sex with women who danced in bars and wore short skirts and sheer stockings and did who knew what in bed? Even though Sarah knew that Taylor was attracted to her, did he realize that she was a virgin? Did he understand what that meant? How could he? And how could she ever satisfy him? It would be a disaster for them both.

Moshe was right, Sarah thought ruefully. I am an *alte moyd*. What do I know about men and women?

The phone in the shop rang. It was Taylor, calling from Miami, telling her that he was about to meet with a man who might know Czartoryski, asking her if she had discovered anything new. She told him she had not. He told her about meeting Teddy Lansky, the widow of a famous gangster. Sarah had never heard of him.

"Didn't you see *The Godfather*?" Taylor asked.

"No," she said. She found it hard to pay attention to his words. All she heard was the warmth in his voice, and all she could listen to was her own inner sense saying, Sarah Kalman, you're a fool.

"I have to go now, Dov," she said. "My mother isn't feeling well, and I have to help her get ready."

"I'm sorry," she heard Taylor say. "Give her my best. *Gut Shabbos*, Sarah. I miss you already."

"It's not *Shabbos* yet," said Sarah.

There was a silence, and Sarah wondered if he was waiting for her to say that she missed him, too. But that's precisely what will get you in trouble, she told herself sternly. But she did miss him. And she was just about to say so when Taylor said, "All right. I'll call you when I get back."

"All right," said Sarah, hanging up, furious with herself for sounding cold when she didn't mean to be and furious with Taylor for making her feel that way. And then it occurred to her that there might be a way to get her hands on the Satmarer *rebbe*'s personal history. He could not deny it to his son-in-law-to-be, the Lubavitcher *rebbe*'s adopted son, Adam Seligson.

There is something you can do right, she told herself. There is a way you can help Dov Taylor.

Feeling somewhat buoyed, she closed up the shop and began walking her well-worn path home, enjoying the feel of her community getting ready to close down and turn in on itself in celebration. But as she was figuring out how best to ask her father for help in approaching Adam Seligson, again she heard that voice in her head, her own voice:

Sarah Kalman, it said, you *are* a fool.

56

International Hotel
Miami
Saturday, October 26

Dov Taylor sat in the sauna connected to the health club on the twelfth floor of the International Hotel overlooking Biscayne Bay, breathing in the fumes of Jan Pleesis's Scotch and water. Taylor had not been to an AA meeting since he'd arrived in Miami, and he was beginning to feel antsy. Once, at a meeting, he had heard someone describe his alcoholism as doing push-ups in the next room, and now Taylor could feel his own disease breathing heavily. He resolved to find a meeting as soon as he finished with Pleesis.

Teddy Lansky had been as good as her word. Soon after Taylor had left her and returned to his hotel, the phone had rung and a man with a thick accent that Taylor could not place had been introducing himself. They'd arranged to meet at the hotel this morning, and Pleesis had arrived exactly on time.

A huge, bald, red-faced Afrikaaner with hands the size of baseball mitts, Pleesis was obviously a drinker, and obviously suffering, his eyelids at half-staff behind his horn-rimmed glasses, his hands shaking. "This joint got a sauna, mate?" Pleesis had asked as soon as they had shaken hands. "A sweat and some firewater will put me back on my feet, and then we can have a nice chitchat about my favorite subject."

"Diamonds?" Taylor had asked.

"No, mate. Lunch."

Pleesis poured himself two tall Scotch and waters from the courtesy bar in Taylor's room and toasted Taylor's health in Afrikaans: "*Gesunheid.*" Pleesis swallowed one drink at a gulp and took the other with him into the sauna.

Now, the dry, superheated air was working on the drink, filling the redwood paneled sauna with the peaty smell of Scotch.

"Not a drinking man, eh?" Pleesis asked.

"No," said Taylor.

"But you were, right?"

"I was."

"Never met a cop who wasn't," said Pleesis. "Couldn't handle it, eh?"

"That's right. I couldn't handle it." Taylor was becoming increasingly annoyed by the man's bluff heartiness, which he suspected was an act. Oh, well, thought Taylor, picturing Pleesis's liver as a gray, fatty, alcohol-ravaged blob, he'll be dead soon.

"Me neither," said Pleesis. "But I'm sixty-five, retired, and don't give a bloody fuck. Cheers." Pleesis finished off his drink. "So," he said, "my dear old darling Teddy tells me you're looking for someone in IDB, a master criminal type."

"IDB?"

"Illegal diamond business."

"I think he stole a diamond, so if that puts him in the illegal diamond business . . ."

"No, mate. That just makes him a thief. IDB is mainly smuggling."

"Was that your beat?"

"You mean when I was with IDSO?"

"What's IDSO?"

"You don't know anything, do you, mate? Babe in the woods, eh? Everybody knows IDSO. That's the Syndicate's International Diamond Security Organization, the best bloody cops in the world. Say, you think they'd bring a man a drink in the sauna?"

"You could try."

"Think I will. I'm starting to feel human again, and I like it. Back in a jiff."

Taylor watched Pleesis's mottled back disappear through the sauna door. He wiped the sweat out of his eyes with a towel. Christ, it was hot. Personally he preferred steam baths.

Steam baths made him think of old Jews in Coney Island, sitting around and complaining; saunas conjured up blond, big-breasted Swedish girls rushing out of the heat pink and naked to pelt each other with snowballs and whip each other's bottoms with birch branches.

He shook his head to get rid of the Nordic bimbos. I'm wasting my time with this old lush, he thought.

He imagined Sarah Kalman sitting in the back of her shop, a book on her lap. He could always summon up a vivid image of her. What does that tell you? he asked himself. It tells you that you've got a hard-on for the rabbi's daughter, he answered, and you're an idiot. Haven't you figured out that even if Sarah were interested in you, a relationship would be impossible? And if you haven't figured it out, she has. She wasn't too thrilled about you calling her, was she?

Taylor shifted on his towel. He felt drained.

Pleesis returned with another drink and sat down. "They got a bar right in the club, God bless 'em," he said, taking a big swallow. "So, the thief you're looking for, he got a name?"

"Czartoryski. I don't have a first name."

"Doesn't ring a bell. Tell me about the diamond."

Taylor felt a wave of nausea sweep over him. He took a swallow of hot air. "There's not a lot I can tell you," he began, and then stopped. Black-and-purple blobs began chasing each other around the sauna. Lie down, he told himself. It's cooler on the floor.

He closed his eyes and saw the diamond, shining like the sun. Purple clouds drifted across it. And then he saw Josep Czartoryski's sneering face, and then Czartoryski turned into Pleesis.

"You all right, mate?"

Taylor realized he was lying on the floor. Pleesis put a meaty palm on his chest. "Don't rush it, son. Take it easy. It's cooler on the floor."

"I'm okay," said Taylor. "I feel fine now."

Pleesis put his arm around Taylor and helped him sit up. "Jesus," said Taylor. "I fainted?"

"You fainted. You have breakfast?"

"No," said Taylor. "Just a cup of coffee."

"Well, there you go. Let's get some food into you."

Taylor, still woozy, dressed next to Pleesis in the club's blue-carpeted locker room. Then they rode the elevator down to the coffee shop off the lobby.

When the waitress came over, Pleesis told her that they wanted some toast and butter, "chop-chop, on the double." She brought it quickly, and Pleesis buttered a slice for Taylor. "Eat up, mate," he said. "Get something in your gut. He'll be wanting the fat man's breakfast, darling," Pleesis told the waitress. "Pancakes, eggs, a rasher of bacon, pot of coffee. I'll have the same. That all right?" he asked Taylor.

Taylor nodded yes and chewed his bread. It was pleasant, he realized, being taken care of.

"You were going to describe the stone," said Pleesis.

"Yes. Well, I don't know much about diamonds, but it was about the size of an egg."

"Oh, really? A pigeon egg or a chicken egg?"

"It was about so big," said Taylor, cupping his hand.

"That's a bloody big rock. You should be able to trace it through the Syndicate. Where did you see it?"

"I can't exactly say."

"Well, why don't you say approximately."

"I just can't tell you."

"All right," said Pleesis. "I'll just finish my breakfast and then you can go about your business and I'll go about mine."

"Look, Jan," said Taylor. "I can't tell you because you'd think I'm crazy, so why don't you just trust me on this. I'm looking for a man named Czartoryski, and I want to know whether you can help me get a line on him or not. I'm sure Teddy told you I can pay."

The waitress spread the food out in front of them as Pleesis stared at Taylor. When she left Pleesis leaned across the table. "Listen, mate," he began. "I spent thirty years chasing some real world-class bastards, killers every last one of them, and I didn't stay alive by trusting people. I don't know you, laddie, and even if I did, I still wouldn't trust you. Trust is what ladies give you before they take off their knickers. Bugger trust, if you follow me."

Taylor looked at Pleesis, at his peeling scalp, at the rum blossoms blazing on his nose, at the tracery of red lines in his eyes, and at his sagging, unshaven, hound-dog jowls. A drunk. And, therefore, a brother. Not only to Taylor, but to Hirsh Leib, too.

So Taylor told him his story, beginning with Zalman Gottleib's murder, continuing through his own stabbing and his vision in the Satmarer *rebbe*'s office. As Taylor spoke, Pleesis's face assumed the sympathetic, encouraging expression that Taylor knew was pure cop and meant nothing at all.

"You think I'm crazy?" Taylor asked.

"Crazy? I'm South African, mate. Crazy don't mean a lot to me. Some people say the whole country is crazy, and I wouldn't argue with them. I once saw a *kaffir*—that's what we call our blacks—tell a perfectly healthy pal of his that he'd be dead in two hours. Two hours later, on the button, the man keels over deader than the queen's pussy. And when it comes to diamonds, shit, mate, nothing's crazy. The things I've seen. So let's just say that you seem sane enough to me."

"Can you help me?" Taylor asked.

"Well, if there's some fucker running around playing with big rocks, we'll have him on file."

"What if he's never been caught?"

"Don't matter. Most of the boys on file have never been pinched. IDB is the biggest racket in the world, my son. Everyone does it, from *kaffirs* sticking diamonds up their arses to little old ladies slipping them through customs to some of the biggest *bwanas* in the world driving from Antwerp to Brussels with a few hundred thousand in submarined stones in the boots of their BMWs. It's all IDB. The Syndicate knows all."

"I'm impressed."

"If you're in diamonds, mate, you kiss the Syndicate's ass every day and twice on Sunday. Let me tell you a story. In the seventies the Syndicate opens a new building at Seventeen Charterhouse for the London sights. It lets the sight holders know that gifts will be appreciated. To furnish the new building. It tells the sight holders that more than ten thousand would be in bad taste. Well, you can bet every bloody one of them kicks in, and ninety-nine point nine percent of the checks are for ten thousand, not a penny more or a penny less. Now when they go to Seventeen to get their stones, they can see their money hanging on the walls. Makes 'em sick.''

"A shakedown.''

"But nobody had the testicles to complain. You complain, you're finished. You get coal in your stocking. You screw up, same thing. Back in the sixties the Israelis screwed up, and the Syndicate practically croaked their whole bloody government.''

"I'm listening.''

"It dropped the price on industrial-grade diamonds about fifty percent. Bang. Pow. Just like that. That meant that Israeli reserves were worth about half of what they were the day before, and Israel had just about cornered the market. More than a billion pounds sterling, gone just like that." Pleesis snapped his fingers and smiled. "They screamed like stuck pigs.''

"How did they screw up?''

"At that time, about half the sight holders in the world were Israeli. And the Israelis were cheating. You know the rules for sight holders?''

"Not really.''

"Say you're one of the three hundred or so sight holders. You say to your De Beers broker, I want a million dollars' worth of rough this month. You show up at the sight in London—there are ten a year, one every fifth Monday—with a check in your hand, and they hand you a cardboard box, like a shoebox. Nice touch, that. Makes you feel like a bleeding beggar. Anyway, inside the box are your stones, whatever De Beers decides is a million's worth. If you don't like it, tough shit. No negotiating allowed. You say, Thank you very much, sir.

"Now the deal is, you've promised De Beers you'll move the stones, individually, on the open market, for jewelry. That way, if anyone's hoarding, the Syndicate knows. But the Israelis were selling the unopened boxes to speculators for a twenty-five-percent markup. Sneaky bastards. So the

Syndicate was losing track of its diamonds, which it didn't like at all.''

"All right," said Taylor. "The Syndicate knows all, sees all. So it should be able to ID my man."

"Maybe. But, you know, at the highest levels, mate, there's no bloody difference between the *bwanas* and the crooks. If your guy is connected, well, he's just another businessman. For all you know, he could be doing the Syndicate's business."

"He's a murderer."

"So?"

"So I want him in jail," said Taylor, "and I want the diamond back."

"Noble sentiment, mate," said Pleesis, "but as far as prison is concerned, I wouldn't bet on it. The *bwanas* never go down that way. Maybe they lose their yacht. Maybe they retire early. And chances are your rock's already been cut up and sold in London, Rio, or Bombay, slipped into a package with a bunch of other stones."

"It hasn't been cut."

"You know that, eh? You've seen it in a dream?"

"I know what I know."

"Well, we'll just leave that alone, okay? Your man, Whatski, what is he? A Pole?" asked Pleesis.

"I think so."

"An old guy? Old enough to have been in the war?"

"Yes."

"Did you know that Hermann Göring's dad, Robert, was once governor of German Southwest Africa? Hermann Göring? Hitler's Luftwaffe *bwana*?"

"What's that got to do with anything?" asked Taylor.

"Well, old Bob Göring was also on the board of directors of Consolidated Mines Selection. That's the Premier Mine, near Pretoria. That's the mine old Cecil Rhodes used to start the De Beers Syndicate."

"So?"

"So I'm saying that the Nazis were heavily into diamonds before and after the war. Could be your guy was a Nazi.

Could be your diamond belonged to them, and they're just getting it back.''

"Nothing belonged to the Nazis. They stole everything," said Taylor.

Pleesis shrugged. "All right. Could be Mafia. I'm just thinking aloud, but if the guineas get their hooks into a dealer, they can do some serious IDB. They buy on the dealer's credit, sell the stock, and then bust him out. Declare bankruptcy. Could be someone is using your stone as bait to work the scam or something like it. Anyway, it don't make no difference.''

"What do you mean?"

"I mean, whatever he is, your fish could be very hard to catch. I'm just telling you.''

"But you'll help.''

"I'll make the calls, ring up the old pals.''

Later, back in Taylor's room, Pleesis poured himself another Scotch and water and started working the phone. He called Tel Aviv, Antwerp, London, and South Africa. While they waited for callbacks, they talked about police work. Pleesis drank but never seemed affected by it. A midstage lush, thought Taylor. Eventually he'll get drunk reading the label. Then he'll get the DTs. Then his liver will fail, or his heart will stop, or he'll forget whether a red light means stop or go. That, thought Taylor, will be too bad, but there's nothing I can do, nothing anyone can do.

Two hours later the phone rang. Taylor handed it to Pleesis and watched while he nodded and made notes. Then he hung up.

"IDSO's got a Czartoryski on file," Pleesis said. "First name, Ladislaw. Lots of AKAs. Age unknown. No photos in the file, although it says there should be. Sloppy bastards. Former Polish cultural attaché. That means spy. Former Party member, of course. File's pretty old, mate. No entries since '85, and that's just a spotting in Rome. Marked down for some suspicious diamond business in London. Involved with a company called Gemstones International. Never been pinched. Also, suspected drug and LCN connections.''

That's how della Francesca knew him, Taylor thought.

"Another thing," said Pleesis.

"Yeah?"

"File says he could be Mossad."

"Israeli secret service?"

"Unconfirmed, of course, but there's signs that point that way. That's what the file says, anyway."

Taylor closed his eyes and again saw Josep Czartoryski's cruel face. "That's impossible," Taylor said. "That can't be." But then, what about Phil Horowitz? Hadn't Horowitz set him up? Wasn't Horowitz working with Czartoryski?

"The Arabs have a saying," Taylor heard Jan Pleesis say. " 'The enemy of my enemy is my friend.' The Israelis do business with everybody." Seeing the look on Taylor's face, Pleesis added, "Lot of shit goes on in this world, son. Nothing's impossible."

57

The American Bar
Savoy Hotel, London
Sunday, October 27

Ladislaw Czartoryski stared balefully at the elderly waiter. "This," he said, indicating his martini, "is utterly vile. If I had wanted a warm vermouth and water, I would have ordered one."

"Would you like me to bring you another, sir, or perhaps something else?"

"I daren't risk another. Bring me a Delamain Grand Vesper."

"Very good, sir."

Czartoryski's meeting with Piet Vermeer had not gone well. The man had been obstinate. How could he go to the Syndicate, he had asked, with a story about a stone he had never seen? And such an incredible story, too? That he had been asked to appraise a flawless seventy-two carat diamond that the unnamed owner swore he had purchased from Alfred Berg, who sat on the board of the Diamond Trading Company, the wholly owned De Beers subsidiary that ran the London sights? Didn't Czartoryski know that Berg was a personal friend of Henry Oppenheimer, the chairman of De Beers?

Czartoryski had told Vermeer about Berg's IOUs, held by Czartoryski's Italian friends. He told Vermeer about Berg's German mistress and about the man Berg had hired to keep her in heroin. It would be easy, Czartoryski had said, improvising, letting his imagination run riot, to arrange for an overdose, what the Americans called a "hot shot." Wouldn't a corpse in Berg's apartment, and the revelation of his gambling debts, lend credence to the charge that Berg was dirty?

Vermeer had only shaken his head. The board would never, ever turn against Berg. Didn't Czartoryski see that bringing such an outrageous story to the board could only discredit Vermeer, thereby destroying his usefulness to the Odessa?

Czartoryski had wanted to slap this pompous little Dutchman. The Magician didn't care about Berg. The whole Berg business was just a way to stall the Odessa while he figured out how to get away with his stone. But how dared Vermeer lecture him? When Vermeer was in knee pants, Czartoryski was cutting throats in Bonn and Belgrade, training assassins in Paraguay and El Salvador. While Vermeer was peering through a loupe, Czartoryski was running agents in Cairo and Paris. He had risked his life for the Odessa a hundred times while Vermeer grew fat and rich appraising gems.

It was Ukridge, Czartoryski thought. Vermeer would never have dared refuse me without Ukridge's support. Ukridge wanted the stone, Czartoryski's stone, cut up and sold. He wanted his commission, and perhaps a piece of the diamond for a souvenir.

Well, thought Czartoryski, he can't have it. The stone is mine. It belonged to my great-great-grandfather, and now it belongs to me.

But you don't have it, Ladislaw, he reminded himself as the waiter brought his cognac. Your tart has taken it. And how will you tell Ukridge that? He will not believe you, and you will become a marked man. One did not steal from the Odessa.

Czartoryski swirled the cognac in its snifter and then knocked it back. He felt it burn the back of his throat, and tears formed in his eyes. He slammed down the glass, and people turned to look at him. He stood up and hurried out of the bar.

He stopped at the front desk. No, there were no messages. Where had the bitch gone?

Czartoryski took the lift up to his room. He went into the sitting room and switched on the television. Next to the television he saw the safe, and he threw the television's remote control at it.

Damn her, he thought. I won't let the Cutter kill her; I'll do it myself. And damn Ukridge. What is he doing now? Having a drink with Vermeer? Laughing at me? Or is he on the phone with our friends in Cairo, telling them that my diamond—the diamond I don't have—will soon be cut up and sold, telling them that their money is on the way?

I'll have it out with him, thought Czartoryski. I'll have it out with him right now.

He took the lift back down to the lobby, hailed a cab, and gave the driver an address in Kensington, not far from Ukridge's flat.

Czartoryski leaned back in the cab and watched the streetlights twinkle in the evening fog. It was, as usual, raining lightly. One must never trust the English, Czartoryski reminded himself. People think that it's the Germans who consider themselves the master race, but it's the English who truly think themselves better than everyone else on earth.

Czartoryski knew that General Gehlen, when he was head of the Bundesnachrichtendienst, the West German Federal Intelligence Service, had tried to warn the CIA about Kim Philby, the Russian mole working for MI6. As far back as 1951, Gehlen had been tipped off by the Mossad that Philby might well be a double agent run by the Kremlin. Hadn't he married a Jewish Communist? At the very least, Gehlen had said, that should disqualify him from being allowed access to CIA files.

Of course, MI6 had assured Jim Angleton, the CIA's neurotic, foolish director, that Philby could not possibly be a traitor. He was, after all, an old Etonian, an Oxford man, "one of us." So Gehlen and the Israelis had watched in horror as Philby became MI6's liaison to the CIA, and not even the pleasure of being proven right made up for the havoc Philby had wreaked right up to that day in 1962 when he disappeared from Beirut and surfaced nine months later in Moscow, wearing the uniform of a general in the Komitét Gosudárstvennoĭ Bezopásnosti, the Committee for State Security, the KGB.

Czartoryski knew the story because it was he who had supplied the Mossad with the information about Philby.

Czartoryski remembered coming home to his apartment in Warsaw in 1950 to find two men in his room. They told him that they worked for Israel, and they knew who he was. They warned him that unless he agreed to supply them with intelligence—about Soviet activity in Poland, about what the Party leaders were doing and saying—they would turn his file over to the government, and he would certainly be executed as a war criminal.

He had turned to General Gehlen for advice, and the general, to Czartoryski's surprise, had told him to cooperate. "You can trust these Jews," he had said. "We understand each other now."

And the first piece of intelligence Czartoryski had given his new friends in the Mossad was the story of Philby's secret wedding in Vienna.

Naturally, it was ignored. An Oxford man. Just like Ukridge, thought Czartoryski. Another traitor.

Czartoryski got out of the taxi and walked one block in the opposite direction from Ukridge's apartment. Then, circling the block, he walked back.

He paused a few houses down from Ukridge's flat. The street was empty. He walked up to Ukridge's door and rang the bell. After a moment Ukridge opened the door, a drink in his hand.

"Ladislaw, what on earth are you doing here?"

"I had to speak with you, Stanley. It's very urgent. May I come in?"

"Of course, of course. Can I get you a drink?"

"No, thank you," said Czartoryski, sweeping past Ukridge into his book-lined sitting room. A fire was burning in the hearth, and a piano concerto was playing on Ukridge's stereo.

"Can I take your coat, Ladislaw?" Ukridge asked.

"You told Vermeer not to agree," said Czartoryski, turning to confront Ukridge. "You told him it would be all right."

Ukridge stuck his hands into the pockets of his baggy gray flannel pants and rocked back on his heels. "I told him to use his own judgment," he said.

"Bullshit!" Czartoryski shouted. "You told him to refuse me."

"Very well, Ladislaw, if you insist on being unpleasant. Yes. You're quite right. I told him to say no. I told him not to compromise himself. I told him that he would be protected."

"You bastard."

"Listen, Ladislaw. I can see that you're upset. You've grown attached to the stone. I understand that, too. But your plan was no good. It was too convoluted. Surely you can appreciate that. The fact is, we have the diamond. We will convert it to cash. It will be simple, and we will all profit, you most of all. You will come out of this a rich man, Ladislaw. A richer man, I should say. In any case, I have spoken to the others and they agree."

"But I do not agree. I do not agree at all."

"I'm sorry, Ladislaw. This is all settled. I should like you to produce the stone as soon as possible—tomorrow, in fact—so that we may proceed."

"But I don't have it," said Czartoryski.

"What?"

"It's been stolen."

"Come, come, Ladislaw. This won't do."

Czartoryski looked at Ukridge, slouching with his hands in his pockets. Look how relaxed he is, Czartoryski thought. He is so confident, so self-assured. He feels no need to protect himself from me, and why should he? I am an old man, older than he, and he is in his own home. A lovely fire is burning. A glass of warm Scotch and lemon rests by his chair. A book is open on the table. He was reading before I arrived. He was listening to his music.

Czartoryski moved closer to Ukridge and smiled. Ukridge smiled back, thinly. Czartoryski bent his knees slightly and then drove the heel of his hand into Ukridge's nose, forcing the cartilage up into Ukridge's brain. Ukridge took a step backward and then collapsed in sections. First his legs buckled, and he fell to his knees. He tottered there for a moment, and then pitched forward at the waist, his forehead striking the floor, his hands still in his pockets. He looked, thought Czartoryski, like an Arab praying toward Mecca.

Czartoryski hooked a foot under Ukridge and flipped him over on his back. His eyes were open and filling with blood. His lips were still parted in a smile.

Good, thought Czartoryski. Excellent. And it came to him suddenly that there was something he used to like to do. The stirring in his groin reminded him. He unzipped his pants, and, straddling Ukridge, he urinated on his face, the last few drops squeezed through a growing erection. Then he dragged Ukridge to the fire, opened the grate, and heaved his head into the glowing logs.

As the air filled with the smell of Ukridge's flesh going up the chimney, Czartoryski surveyed the room. Satisfied that he had not touched anything, he let himself out and strolled several blocks before hailing a cab to take him back to the hotel.

The night air was wet and fresh, and Czartoryski felt tremendously revived, as if Ukridge's dying breath had somehow entered his own lungs to give him new life. This is how I used to feel all the time, he reminded himself. This is why I loved Belzec.

When he returned to the hotel, there was a message for him at the desk. Back in his room, he dialed the number. It was the Cutter. "New York," he said. "She went to New York."

"How do you know?" asked Czartoryski.

"What can a whore do? A whore uses men. I found the man she used," the Cutter answered.

"Then New York it is," said Czartoryski, thinking that his luck was changing. Act, he told himself, and you control events. Be passive, and they control you.

Tonight, he thought, for old times' sake, he might engage the services of a prostitute, a tall one, a blond one.

"I love New York," he told the Cutter.

58

The Satmarer Rebbe's House
South Ninth Street, Williamsburg
Monday, October 28

Standing in front of the Satmarer *rebbe*'s door, staring at his feet, the Kalman woman by his side, Adam Seligson shivered in the chill morning air and thought that he had never been more uncomfortable in his life. Bad enough that he was going to see his future father-in-law, a man he both despised and feared, but to have to see him in the company of this strange old woman—it was almost too much to bear.

Seligson looked at the two guards flanking the *rebbe*'s door. Typical Satmarer brutes, he thought. Fanatics. Mindless *golems* who lived only to do their *rebbe*'s bidding. Do they ever study? Seligson wondered. He sniffed the air. Do they ever bathe?

Walking from the subway to the *rebbe*'s house had been a trial. In all of his twenty years, Adam Seligson, the Lubavitcher *rebbe*'s adopted son, had been to Williamsburg only once before, and that was just a few months ago when his future father-in-law had tested his Torah knowledge for three hours, grilling him so fiercely that Seligson, who was prouder of his erudition than of anything else, had left the *rebbe*'s home feeling like a boy just beginning his *aleph-bes*.

Now, the thought of being surrounded by so many Satmarers made him uneasy. Would they recognize him as the Lubavitcher's son? And if they did, would they attack him? Would they rip his beard out by the roots as they did a few years ago to that poor Lubavitcher teacher who had tried to lift the veil of ignorance from a Satmarer boy's eyes? And would they think that this brazen Kalman woman was somehow associated with him, the man who was to marry their *rebbe*'s daughter?

He sneaked a peak at Sarah Kalman and shuddered again at the sight of her red hair spilling over her shoulders and down her back. It was obscene. Even though she was unmarried, an old maid, she should cut it off so as not to be such a temptation. When his father had told him to accompany her to the Satmarer *rebbe*'s home, and to do whatever she asked, he thought immediately of her red hair, the red hair he had seen so many times on the street, and the fact that, as it was written, Lilith, the temptress, also had red hair.

Seligson felt himself becoming aroused. Damn the woman, he thought.

Sarah Kalman could feel Adam Seligson's angry eyes upon her, and she resisted the urge to glare back at him. He reminded her of her brother, Moshe. Though still a boy, Adam had the same arrogant stare, the same potbelly. Most annoying, he had that same air about him that said that any time he spent with Sarah was *bitel* Torah, a waste of Torah, a waste of time.

The door opened and a man who introduced himself as Pinchus Mayer led them into the home, up a broad staircase, and into the *rebbe*'s study. "The *rebbe* cannot see you now," Mayer told Seligson, who could not prevent himself from sighing in relief. "He instructed me to give you this book," Mayer continued, pointing to a large, leatherbound notebook on the *rebbe*'s desk. "He said that you may read it in here, but it may not leave the room. You have three hours. Spend it wisely." Then Mayer went into an office off the study and closed the door behind him. He had never once looked at or acknowledged Sarah Kalman.

Adam Seligson walked over to the bookcases and began

perusing the *rebbe*'s collection, humming tunelessly. Sarah Kalman sat down behind the *rebbe*'s desk and began to read.

The book, the collected personal diaries of all the Satmarer *rebbes*, was handwritten in Yiddish with a multitude of incomprehensible words that Sarah Kalman took to be transliterated Hungarian. It was difficult going at first—full of Torah commentary, references to sages and *zaddiks* she had never heard of, banal entries of marriages and births followed by philosophical discourses about the number and nature of the hidden worlds. Sarah skipped ahead to the entries written by the current Satmarer *rebbe*'s grandfather, and there she found a reference to a *briliant*, a diamond. She soon found herself swept up in the story, all the while imagining how she would recount it to Dov Taylor.

An old woman, it was written, appeared one day at the Satmarer *rebbe*'s door in Budapest. According to the diary, it was the tenth day of Ab, 5675, or July 1914. The Great War was about to begin.

The woman said her name was Princess Catherine Maria Radziwell, the daughter of an exiled Polish count living in Russia. She had married a Prussian prince, Wilhelm Radziwell, in 1873, and had been banished from Berlin in 1886, accused—falsely, she said—of intriguing with the tsar.

But despite her innocence of that particular charge, her life, she had confessed to the *rebbe*, had been spent in wickedness. Now, dying, she wanted to make amends. The diamond she had brought would, she hoped, purchase the *rebbe*'s blessing.

It was not unusual, the *rebbe* wrote, for *goyishe* women to come to him for cures and blessings after reaping the fruits of their sinful lives. And the *rebbe* could tell that this was indeed a woman upon whom the Lord's justice had fallen. Her eyes were feverish, her skin a deathly white. But the *rebbe* told her that he could never accept a tainted *pidyan*—a gift to buy redemption—even one as beautiful as this diamond.

But the diamond belongs to your people, the woman said. I am returning it to you.

And the *rebbe* knew then that this diamond was the fabled

Seer's stone mentioned by his grandfather's friend, Menachem Mendel of Rymanov.

The woman recounted how she had gone to South Africa as a correspondent for the *Times* of London to meet Cecil Rhodes, and how she was surprised to discover that the great English imperialist, the king of the diamond mines, was not a real man. ("An abomination," the *rebbe* had written.) Still, Radziwell, by flattery and persistence, had gained entry to Rhodes's home and confidence. Then, one night, Rhodes had shown her a magnificent diamond that, he told her, he had used as collateral for the loan he received from the American millionaire J. P. Morgan. He had used the money, he boasted, to defeat his enemy, Barney Barnato, and gain control of the Kimberly Mine.

The deal between Rhodes and Morgan had been brokered by the Rothschilds, who had given Rhodes the stone in return for an undisclosed position in the new company he was forming: the De Beers Mining Syndicate.

The woman told the *rebbe* that she had indeed stolen the diamond from Rhodes, taking it after he had gone to sleep, but that it had brought her nothing but misery. She had hoped to sell it back to Rhodes, but he died just days after she left South Africa. Then she brought it to Barnato, Rhodes's rival, but by that time Barnato had gone mad. Soon he would drown himself by jumping off a ship bound from Johannesburg to London.

She told the *rebbe* that upon finding out that she had a loathsome disease and would soon die herself, she slipped back into Poland, and there discovered that the diamond had been stolen from the Jews by Josep Czartoryski, a Polish count who had lost it to the Rothschilds through gambling. Now, she said, all she wanted was to die in peace. And to do that she must return the stone to its rightful owners, the Jews.

So the *rebbe* accepted the diamond from her hand, gave her his blessing, and never saw her again.

Skipping ahead in the diaries, Sarah Kalman read how the current Satmarer *rebbe*'s father had used the diamond to purchase his freedom, and the freedom of his Hasidim, from the Nazi murderer Adolf Eichmann. And how when Eich-

mann was captured by the Israelis in 5721 (1960), he'd tried
to bribe them with the *rebbe*'s stone. One Israeli agent, unnamed in the diary, described only as the one pious Jew
among the godless Israelis, returned the stone to the *rebbe*,
whose son was named Joel Teitel.

The diaries went on to recount how no lesser personage
than Isser Harel, the chief of all Israeli intelligence, had come
to Williamsburg to demand that the *rebbe* return the diamond
to Israel. And how the *rebbe* had refused, telling Harel that
it belonged to Jews of faith, Jews who kept the Messiah alive
in their hearts, not to Jews who had replaced the Messiah
with a Golden Calf they called the state of Israel.

The door off the *rebbe*'s study opened and Pinchus Mayer
entered the room. He cast a disapproving eye at Sarah Kalman
and then addressed Adam Seligson, who was sitting on the
windowsill, reading by the light that filtered through the dirt-
encrusted window. "You must go now, Reb Seligson,"
Mayer said.

"What?" said Seligson, looking up from his book, blink-
ing through his wire-rimmed glasses.

"It's time to go," said Mayer.

Sarah Kalman got up from her chair and replaced the book
on the *rebbe*'s desk.

"Thank you, Reb Mayer," Sarah said softly. "And thank
the *rebbe*."

Mayer grunted and opened the study door, shooing Seligson and Kalman in front of him.

As soon as they were back on the street, Adam Seligson
muttered something about an appointment and began rushing
down South Ninth Street toward the subway. Sarah Kalman
was glad to be rid of him, glad to be alone with her thoughts.

Could the Israelis have stolen the diamond and murdered
that poor diamond dealer? she asked herself. After all, treachery and deceit seemed to be the provenance of this diamond.
Well, unlike the Satmarers, the Lubavitchers had many
friends in Israel, and perhaps they could find out for Dov
Taylor. But if it was indeed the Israelis who had taken it, she

thought, it would never be returned, and all that Dov had done, and all he had gone through, would be futile.

Her heart ached for the detective.

59

Prince Street
SoHo, Manhattan
Monday, October 28

"Hi, I'm Dov Taylor, and I'm a grateful recovering alcoholic and drug addict."

"Hi, Dov," responded the forty or so people in Taylor's home meeting in the basement of St. Vincent's Church on Prince Street.

"My life's been pretty hectic," Taylor began, not sure where he was going, "and I haven't been getting to as many meetings as I'd like. I've been down in Miami. I was with a heavy drinker, an active alcoholic. It didn't make me want to pick up, but I felt bad that I couldn't do anything for him. He's pretty far gone, but, you know, what can you do?

"Let's see. I'm also, well, I think I'm getting involved in an impossible situation. A woman. I'm not really involved with her, but I have feelings for her, and it just can't work. I don't know what to do about it. Well, actually, that's not true. I know what to do. I shouldn't see her. I should find somebody else.

"I guess there's not much else. The business I'm doing, it doesn't make much sense. I'm looking for a man, and I just found out that he might be working for people I thought would be the last people in the world he'd be working for. I can't really explain that. I'm sorry if this doesn't hang together, but there's not a lot making sense for me these days. But I'm okay. Thanks for listening. I guess that's all."

After Taylor sat down, a tall, slender, pretty young woman stood up. Taylor remembered having seen her before. Her name was Carol. She was a beginner, claiming a little more than two months of sobriety.

"I thought everything would get better once I stopped drinking," she said, "and, in a way, that's true. And in a way, it's not. I mean, yeah, I'm sober, and that's great, but my life is still all screwed up. Yesterday I was in my car, going up the West Side Highway, and I thought I'd just like to drive into the river. I thought thoughts like that were supposed to go away once you stopped drinking."

Carol went on to list her troubles; the usual, Taylor thought ungenerously. She had quit her job because she had had an affair with her boss, tried to break it off, and he didn't want to. Her boyfriend was, as she said, "a heavy drinker, probably an alcoholic," and he was pissed off that she had stopped. And she wondered how long she could stay sober if she continued to see him. She also talked about taking a sip of nonalcoholic beer at a party and wondering if that was okay or not.

Taylor, and everybody else in the meeting, knew that if she kept drinking the phony beer, she'd pick up a real one sooner or later. But AA was supposed to be supportive, and it was difficult to tell someone that what they were doing was wrong or dumb. After Carol had finished, a man Taylor knew only as Joe, an old-timer, stood up.

"I'm Joe," he began, "and I'm an alcoholic, and I'd just like to say that, for me, nonalcoholic beer is, like, crazy. I mean, maybe some people can do it, but for me, it's Russian roulette. It's like going to bars and drinking Cokes. You can do it, sure, but why risk it? Why risk your sobriety? I just want to say to Carol that I would think about that."

A few more people chimed in, talking about the dangers of nonalcoholic beer and about sober drunks hanging out with active drunks, mostly without addressing Carol directly. Soon it was time to join hands for the Lord's Prayer. As Taylor was getting ready to leave, Carol walked up to him and asked if they could go someplace, have a cup of coffee. She reminded him that they had met over a month ago, and that she had thanked him for talking about how screwed up he still was after two years of sobriety.

Taylor remembered—although that month seemed so long ago it was like another life; it *was* another life—and he remembered finding her attractive then. Now, up close, she seemed older to Taylor, in her thirties, not her twenties, but no less attractive. She had brown eyes and light brown hair, pulled away from her face by a red hairband. Her most distinctive feature was a small white scar on her upper lip. She was wearing new jeans and an oversize black sweater with embroidered red flowers. She seemed very demure, very shy. Taylor thought that it must have cost her something to approach him, and he said yes.

Over espresso in a little Italian place down the street from the church, Carol recited her drunkalog. She had started drinking as a teenager. She didn't like pot, it made her paranoid, and when her friends smoked, she drank. She drank through college, drank before, during, and after dates. Eventually she was drinking alone in her apartment every night, vodka and orange juice mainly, but she never thought she had a problem until she woke up one morning next to her boss and couldn't even remember making a date with him.

"It was weird, you know," she said. "I didn't even like the guy. I asked him, you know, where we had dinner, stuff like that, and he thought it was funny. I thought I was going crazy."

Taylor thought about how so many people's stories were the same and regretted his previous impatience with Carol's. Perhaps his story was more dramatic, but that was just an accident of his having been a cop. It was as if the booze wrote the script, and the drunk acted it out. And the booze was a simpleminded playwright, using the same plot over and over again. The bottle was always center stage, and there were only two endings: you stopped, or you died.

Because they shared the same disease, because they were fellow performers in the same play, Taylor immediately felt close to this woman who just a few hours before had been a stranger. So when she told him that she didn't want to be alone tonight, it was easy for him to invite her up to his apartment.

There was a taste of desperation in the way Carol made love. She had strong, sinewy arms, and she held on to him tightly as if to convince herself that he was real. Taylor felt her shyness dissolving beneath his kisses, felt her mouth relax, and that excited him. He knew he was breaking one of the unwritten rules by having sex with a beginner. In AA, it was called Thirteenth Stepping. But with her legs wrapped around his waist, her mouth open in a silent scream, and tears rolling down her face, he made excuses for himself. He wasn't taking advantage of her; he was helping her. They were helping each other. And anyway, when he had put his finger inside her, he had felt a diaphragm. She had been looking for someone to spend the night with; it might as well have been him.

Afterward she curled up next to him. "You must think I'm a slut," she said.

"Don't be silly," he said.

"I feel a little embarrassed," she said. "Believe me, I don't do things like this."

"Things like what?"

"You know," she said, punching his chest playfully.

"I don't know."

"Promise me you don't think I'm a slut."

"But I like sluts." She punched him again. "All right, all right," he said. "I don't think you're a slut."

Taylor felt himself drifting away, growing sleepy.

"Dov?"

"What?"

"I'm really not a slut."

"I know."

Taylor woke up in the dark and looked at the glowing clock by his bed. It was three A.M., and he was alone. He sat up, listening. He heard a sound in the living room. He slid out of bed, and careful not to make a sound, he opened the bedroom door. Carol was sitting at his small desk, the light from the old-fashioned green-shaded banker's lamp illuminating her face. She was wearing his shirt. She was looking through his papers, through his address book.

"What the fuck are you doing?" he said, and his voice sounded shockingly loud in the three A.M. quiet.

Carol's head snapped around. The light from the lamp framed her now, giving her a halo. She stood up. The shirt fell open, revealing her breasts, her belly, the dark triangle of her crotch.

"I was restless," she whispered. "I couldn't sleep."

"What were you looking for?"

"Nothing," she said, walking toward him. "I'm sorry. I guess I just wanted to know more about you."

There was something alarming about this woman, Taylor thought suddenly. She was too comfortable in her nakedness. It didn't jibe with the sense of her he had received in bed.

Taylor turned, went back into the bedroom, and flipped on the light switch. He saw Carol's brown leather shoulder bag on the floor at the foot of the bed. He picked it up and opened it. Carol ran through the bedroom door. "What are you doing?" she said angrily, grabbing for the bag. Taylor ripped it out of her hands, and when she tried to grab it again he pushed her away. She fell backward onto the bed.

"Fair is fair," he said, taking out her wallet and flipping it open. Her charge cards and her driver's license agreed that her name was Carol Rosenberg. The license listed an address in the East Seventies.

"Pretty far from home, aren't you, Carol? No meetings uptown?"

"Are you going to give me back my bag?" she asked, her voice sharp and annoyed.

"Awfully heavy, isn't it?" Taylor turned the bag over and spilled its contents onto the sheets. He looked briefly at the makeup kit, a leatherbound date book, a pack of Merit Ultra Lights, a hairbrush, keys, a vial of pills. He picked up the bottle and looked at the prescription label. Tylenol and codeine. For pain. Filled two weeks ago. "Hurt yourself, Carol? Alcoholics shouldn't take codeine," Taylor said. "Even with only a few months, you ought to know that. But you're not really an alcoholic, are you, Carol?"

"You're crazy," she said.

The bag still felt heavy. There was a zipper on the inside.

Taylor opened it and retrieved a small, flat, automatic pistol. A Mauser. He turned to face Carol, who was lying on her back, propped up on her elbows. Her face was calm, composed. Taylor thought that she seemed utterly transformed. The affinity he had felt for her before was gone, and now she lay on his bed, naked but for his shirt, a complete stranger.

"This is a very fancy weapon," said Taylor. He popped the clip into his palm. "Loaded, too."

Carol shrugged. Taylor sat on the edge of the bed and lightly poked her foot with the gun. "So, lover," he said, "I'll bet you have something interesting to tell me."

Carol Rosenberg sat up and pulled Taylor's shirt around her, covering her breasts. She brushed a comma of hair off her forehead. "We'll make a trade," she said finally. "You tell me where you think Ladislaw Czartoryski is, and I'll tell you why we want you to forget about him."

"Who's we?" Taylor asked.

"The Israeli government," said Rosenberg. "May I have my cigarettes back?"

60

Dov Taylor's Apartment
Sullivan Street, SoHo
Tuesday, October 29

When Sarah Kalman called to tell him that she had found out what had happened to the Seer's stone after it had been stolen by Josep Czartoryski, Dov Taylor told her that he was no longer interested, that he was off the case. Carol Rosenberg had done her job.

Sitting on his bed, smoking her cigarettes, Rosenberg had told Taylor that Czartoryski had been an Israeli asset for many years. After the war for independence in 1948, the fledgling Israeli secret service, the Mossad, needed covers for its agents. It needed passports, birth certificates, work histories. It needed everything, in short, that would allow its people working to get the surviving Jews out of Europe and into the new state of Israel to operate. And, as many of its agents had been born speaking German and Polish, it was only natural that the Mossad would look to those countries for help.

But they were Nazis and anti-Semites, Taylor had protested. War criminals. They were the enemy. Precisely, Rosenberg had answered. How do you think we got them to do what we wanted? Whether we had proof of their Nazi pasts or not, we said we did.

"You blackmailed them," Taylor said.

Of course, Rosenberg said. The man you're looking for, she said, provided our people with Polish documents. And in return we kept his past a secret from his superiors, from the Communists.

"But I thought Israel hunted war criminals. I thought you brought Nazis to trial," Taylor said.

"Of course," said Rosenberg. "But we also needed allies. The American government didn't need our help back then, so we couldn't count on them. The same was true for the British and French. But the Germans and Poles, we had something to hold over them. The Austrians, too. In '48, they were all we had.

"Besides, German scientists and military men were all running to the Middle East, to Cairo and Beirut and Amman. They were especially busy in Egypt, helping build their army. Once we identified them, they could provide us with wonderful intelligence about the enemy, intelligence no one else could supply.

"So, once upon a time they tried to kill us. Now they could keep us alive. What was more important? Vengeance or survival? We chose to survive."

"And Czartoryski is one of them."

"Yes."

"He was a Nazi, a war criminal."

"Yes."

"And he worked for you, for Israel."

"He has been useful in the past."

"And that's why you don't want me to find him."

"Yes."

"No deal," said Taylor.

"You don't understand, Dov. This man, he's no longer of any use to us. For many reasons. He was supposed to do something for us and he hasn't. We're not asking you to leave him alone so we can protect him. Do you understand? We're not going to protect him."

"You're going to bring him to trial?"

"No. That would be impossible."

"You mean embarrassing. It wouldn't look good, would it, if people found out that Israel's been working with ex-Nazis."

Carol Rosenberg stood up and began to get dressed. "Believe it or not, Dov, we don't want to see you get hurt. We don't want you interfering, getting yourself killed. We know about the diamond, too. Trust me, it does not belong to the people who hired you."

"Who does it belong to, then?"

"To us."

"Tell me about it."

"I've told you what I can. I hope that's enough for you to make the right decision. It has to be enough."

"How did you find me?" Taylor asked.

"We've had you under surveillance for a long time. Ever since you visited the Satmarer *rebbe*. When anyone visits the *rebbe*, we notice. The Satmarers are very anti-Israel, you know. We're interested in all the Hasidim. They're becoming very powerful."

Where had Taylor heard that before? Then, suddenly, it all fell into place.

"Phil is one of yours, isn't he? Phil Horowitz. He's Mossad."

"May I have my bag back?" Rosenberg asked.

"A diamond courier would make a terrific agent, wouldn't he? He travels all over on a legitimate passport. And he could give you information on what the Hasids were up to. Did you recruit him before or after he became a Hasid? Or is he a Hasid? Is he a phony like you?"

"I don't know anyone except the man I work for."

"You bastards set me up, didn't you? You used Horowitz to set me up because you were protecting Czartoryski. 'We don't want to see you get hurt,' " Taylor said, mimicking Rosenberg. "Bullshit. You almost got me killed. Then, when you couldn't kill me, you set a honey trap. Do I get to fuck you again if I lay off? Is that my reward? Because if it is, let me tell you, sweetheart, it just wasn't that great."

"I'm sorry you're so angry."

"You're sorry you screwed up."

"May I have my gun, too?"

Taylor handed Rosenberg her gun.

"And the clip?"

"I'll keep the clip," he said.

"You don't trust me," she said.

"I can't imagine why not," Taylor said.

Later, after Rosenberg had left, Taylor sat in his kitchen, drinking coffee until dawn. He remembered what his grandfather Sam had told him about the Nazis, about how President Eisenhower was a Nazi. Didn't he save the Germans from the Russians? Didn't he help Germany rebuild? Wasn't Eisenhower a German name?

Sam taught Taylor that the Nazis were everywhere. "You think you're an American," Sam had said, "because that's what your parents raised you to believe. But the other Americans, they think you're a Jew. And the only people you can trust are other Jews."

Taylor remembered lying in bed at night, thinking that when he grew up he would organize an army of Jewish storm troopers who would wear Star of David armbands. He imagined them in black leather coats goosestepping down Fifth Avenue, smashing windows and pulling Nazis out of the stores and beating them up. He imagined the whole world cowering in terror before the Star of David.

Now, thought Taylor, his mixed-up adolescent fantasies had come true: there were Jewish storm troopers in the world, Jews who could watch another Jew murdered and do nothing. There were Jews who would murder other Jews. His grandfather had been wrong. There was no one you could trust.

By the time Sarah Kalman called, Taylor was too angry to hear the excitement in her voice.

"But, Dov," she protested, "it's all there in the diaries. You don't know what I had to go through to get it. Please, come to the shop. Hear what I have to tell you. Then decide what you want to do."

For the first time in months, Taylor pictured himself walking into a bar and ordering a drink. The image shocked him.

Keep busy, he told himself. If you don't go to see Sarah, what will you do today? Forget today. What will you do in the next thirty minutes?

"All right," he said, "I'll be right over."

Taylor got his gun from his dresser drawer and slipped it into his coat. He checked to see that his answering machine was on, and then he let himself out of his apartment.

Closing the door, he felt someone behind him. He spun around, reaching for his gun.

"No," said Maria Radziwell. "Don't shoot."

61

JFK International Airport
New York
Tuesday, October 29

"Benny, go check again," said Augusta Lerner, poking her husband in the ribs.

"I just checked a minute ago," said Benjamin Lerner.

"So check again," Augusta said.

"You're making me crazy, Gussie."

"All right. Don't go. I'll go."

"No, it's all right. I'll go."

"Don't do me no favors, Benny. If it's so much trouble for you, I'll go."

"Oh, for chrissakes," said Ben Lerner, standing up to

check again when Flight 1418—carrying Gussie's son Saul, his wife, and their kids—was due to arrive. The last five times he had checked, the plane had been on time, just as it had been on time when he had phoned the airport from their apartment in Brooklyn, which they had left, by Lerner's reckoning, at least two hours early—God forbid Gussie's kid should have to wait two seconds for them to pick him up at the terminal.

"Benny."

"What?"

"For me, take the cigar out of your mouth. It makes you look like a tout."

Ben Lerner chomped down on his unlit cigar and glared at his wife. In truth, Gussie was right. In his tan sans belt slacks, burgundy polo shirt buttoned at the neck, and black-and-white-checked sport jacket, Ben Lerner did look like a race-track tout. And he knew it. But why Gussie should keep harping on it was one of the mysteries of their marriage. After all, upon coming to America after the war, Lerner had gravitated to the track, to Belmont, first sweeping out stalls, and later becoming an expert doper. With his needles and drugs, Lerner could make any broken-down old dray horse run like Kelso or, conversely—and more easily—make Kelso run like a candidate for the glue factory. So what should he look like? A college professor?

"For chrissake, Gussie," said Lerner, "the doctors won't let me smoke it, the airport guys give me dirty looks when they see it, and now you want to take away one of the last pleasures of my life."

"Please, Benny. For me."

Lerner took the chewed cigar out of his mouth and dropped it into his coat pocket. He could never refuse Gus. When he had come to America from Poland, his life utterly obliterated, Gussie had appeared to him like a goddess—a golden American girl, as beautiful as any movie queen. That she would go out with him, a poor greenhorn who spoke broken English, was amazing. That she would marry him—short, stubby, balding Benny with no family and no prospects—was astonishing. Through all her nagging, her bullying, and her complaining, Lerner never stopped feeling grateful, never stopped loving her. And they did all right, he always told himself. His only regret was that she refused to have any more children. He would have liked to start another family, but Gussie had been adamant. Her Saul was to remain unique.

Lerner walked to the desk and looked up at the television screen above it. Flight 1418 had landed.

"Gussie!" he called over his shoulder to his wife. "It's here."

Gussie walked over to Lerner, took his arm, and squeezed.

"You excited, Gussie?" he asked.

In response, Gussie reached up and rearranged the few strands of hair left on her husband's head. Then she fixed her eyes on the gate through which her son would soon emerge, her expression as rapt as a poor immigrant's upon first seeing the Statue of Liberty.

And there he was. Gussie started jumping up and down, waving. "Solly! Solly! Over here."

Lerner saw his stepson walking stiffly toward his mother, his little blond wife and their two blond children bringing up the rear. He saw Saul look left and right, hoping that no one was watching, and he turned away in disgust.

The boy was embarrassed by his mother and, Lerner knew, embarrassed by his stepfather. He thinks we're *prost*, thought Ben. There was no good English word for it. *Prost*. Uneducated. Vulgar. That's what the big shots called him when he was a boy in Poland, and that's what his stepson thought of him now.

"Hello, Ben," Saul said dryly, breaking free of his mother's embrace and extending his hand. Yes, thought Ben, taking it and pumping it once before letting it go, the boy had always been polite to him, always tolerated him, and had always let him know what that tolerance masked.

"So how's England?" Lerner asked.

"Fine, Ben," said Saul.

"Yeah? Okay, so let's go," Lerner called.

"Wait," said Gussie. "I have to kiss my beautiful grandchildren. Come, children, come to Grandma."

People streamed through the gate as Gussie crouched down and opened her arms. Lerner saw Saul's wife push her reluctant children toward their grandmother. Strangers, he thought. This is no real family.

Saul was still looking around, growing more uncomfortable by the second, eager to get this over with, and Lerner felt the urge to hit him. That's what the kid always needed, thought Ben. A good smack. Knock some of the snot out of him. Of course, Gussie had never let him raise a hand to her precious one.

Out of the corner of his eye, Lerner saw a man who looked familiar stepping through the gate. Suddenly riveted, he watched the man walk toward him, passing not two feet away. Couldn't be, thought Ben as he began to follow him, his feet carrying him unthinkingly in the man's wake.

"Benny!" he heard Gus call. "Where're you going?"

Lerner felt his feet moving faster. He passed the man, trotted a few more steps, and then, panting from the exertion, turned around to look at him. Again the man walked past him.

It was him, thought Lerner. Older. Much older. And fatter. Much fatter. But it was him.

Lerner felt as if he were in a free-falling elevator. His stomach felt empty, and his heart rose into his throat. It was coming back. The dark. The cold. He shivered in the darkness, in the cold. He heard the harsh voices. And the crazy screaming that never stopped. He flinched away from the screams. Then he heard the boots on the wooden floors. He heard the sucking sound the boots made in the mud.

"Benny, what is it?"

He saw him standing high above him, looking down into the deep trench, the moon and stars behind him, the torches lighting his face. He felt dizzy. He saw him smiling, laughing, pointing his revolver at him. Then he saw the mouth of the gun, a gaping black hole. Then he saw the eyes, more like a fox's eyes than a person's.

Lerner felt hands pulling at his legs. He looked down and saw rags flapping around his white, spindly legs. He saw the

faces of the dead and dying. He saw their open mouths. He
saw their blackened eyes. He saw bloody hands, reaching for
him, pulling him down.

He was falling.

He saw a flash. He heard the pistol's dry crack.

He screamed.

"Benny! For God's sake, Benny, what's the matter?"

Someone was shaking him. It was Gussie.

"What is it, Benny? What's the matter with you? You
having a stroke? For God's sake, he's having a stroke."

"Masha," whispered Ben, pronouncing the name of his
first wife, the beautiful, solemn-faced child, barely eighteen,
who bore his two sons, the two sons he never saw again after
that night when the Nazis found their hiding place in Lublin.

"Who's Masha?" Saul asked.

"Please stop, Benny, you're scaring me," Gussie said,
stroking her husband's cheek. "Solly, he's going to have an
attack. Come back to me, Benny."

Ben Lerner's eyes focused and he saw his wife, his American wife, staring at him with terrified eyes.

"Oh, my God, Gussie," he said. "I saw him. My God,
my God, I saw him."

"Saw who, Benny? Who did you see?"

"I saw him, Gussie. I saw him. From Belzec. From the
camp. The camp where I was. My God, Gussie. Oh my God.
He's alive. That Nazi bastard Czartoryski is alive."

62

Sullivan Street
SoHo, Manhattan
Tuesday, October 29

Talking in a low, husky voice, touching first a window
shade, then straightening a photograph on the wall, then bend-

ing over to rearrange the cushions on the couch, Maria Radziwell circled Dov Taylor's living room, returning again and again to where Taylor sat looking up at her.

She's dancing, thought Taylor. She's dancing out her anxiety, and she's dancing to seduce me.

And it's working.

As before, when he had visited her in her apartment, he was acutely aware of her body, of her physical presence, even though she was wearing a cotton raincoat belted at the waist and buttoned at the throat. As she spoke, he cataloged: her hands, big as a man's but slender; her long legs, muscular but lithe; her broad shoulders, her deep chest. After a lifetime of imagining himself with tall, powerfully built women, here, standing in his apartment, touching his possessions, was the objective correlative of all his erotic dreams. And when she stood in front of him, and his face was level with her crotch, he could swear he could smell her—pineapple, vanilla, and musk. He forced himself to concentrate on what she was saying.

Her name, she told him, was not Mary Rubel; it was Maria Radziwell. She was sorry she had lied to him, but she feared for her life. The men she had been with were murderers, monsters. The man who had enticed her from her home in Warsaw with promises of riches, this Ladislaw Czartoryski, was a sadist. He had been, and still was, a Nazi. The other man was a madman. He was called the Cutter. They stole the diamond. They murdered that diamond dealer and his secretary. And they also killed that poor Mr. Levin. She had not known what they were planning. She had not known about any of the murders. She hated them.

She sat on the couch beside him and clasped her hands in her lap. She leaned forward, touching her forehead to her knees, and stayed that way for a moment. He could see the nape of her neck and two vertebrae bulging beneath the fine blond down that grew there. She seemed like a child, vulnerable.

Another move in the dance, thought Taylor.

Then she straightened, stood up, and again began circling the room. A few days ago, she continued, she had finally escaped from them. And she had taken the diamond. Now, she wanted to sell it back to the Jews. The Jews, she knew, were rich. The money would be no problem for them. They would be coming for her. They would try to kill her. She needed money, a lot of money, to go far away and hide.

"Let me take you to the police," Taylor said, wondering what form her objection would take. "Let the police catch them and then you won't be afraid."

The police, she said, could not be trusted. And even if they could catch the men, which she doubted, they had friends, many friends, who would come after her and kill her. No, selling the diamond to the Jews was the only way. She did not want much. Only two hundred thousand. The diamond was worth far more than that, but that would be enough for her to get away, to go somewhere and change her name, her life.

"Where is it?" Taylor asked. "The diamond."

She walked behind the couch, and Taylor stood up to face her. His eyes, he noted, were level with hers.

"I want to trust you," she said, now walking around the couch to stand next to him, "but . . . I feel you are a good man, that is why I come to you. But if I tell you where is the diamond, I have nothing. Do you understand? First, I must feel safe."

"What will make you feel safe?" Taylor asked.

"Help me," she said, and Taylor felt her touch his hand lightly with her finger. "Tell the Jews I have the diamond. Help me get the money. Then they will have their diamond back and I will go away."

Taylor tried to read her wide-set brown eyes. He saw desperation there, calculation. Yes, he thought, she's afraid. That's not an act, although just about everything else is. Of course she'd fuck me. That's what she wants. That's what would make her feel safe. That's how she feels safe with men.

I could end it now, he thought. I could call Frank Hill, turn her in, and it would be over for me. Maybe he'd catch Czartoryski and the guy who stabbed me, maybe not. But would the *rebbe* get his diamond back? No. The goddamn

Israelis would grab it. No doubt about that. They might also grab Czartoryski. Take him back to Israel. Disappear him. Their old Nazi pal.

What does the diamond mean to the Israelis? Power? An old debt settled? What does it mean to the Hasidim? A part of their past? A symbol of peace between the Lubavitchers and the Satmarers? A wedding dowry?

Which is more important?

And I'm in a position to decide, Hirsh Leib's great-great-grandson. Well, who better?

Taylor made his decision.

"Where are you staying?" he asked Radziwell.

"I have no place," she said. "I thought, maybe until I sell the diamond, I can stay here, on your sofa."

She touched his hand again. Her eyes seemed to grow larger. Taylor felt his chest grow tight, his stomach knot. He felt something like tears welling up in his throat. Her head tilted slightly back and to the side. Just a kiss, he thought. Just take a kiss.

Her lips parted instantly and molded themselves to his, and her tongue forced itself between his teeth. He felt himself tremble slightly. His arm went around her waist. Her hand grabbed his buttocks, and their groins ground against each other. Her hand left his ass and stroked his erection. She wrapped one leg around him and rubbed his calf with hers. He felt her breasts pressing against his chest as she clung to him. Too fast, he thought, breaking the kiss to look at her.

Her eyes opened wide in surprise, like a dreamer suddenly awakened. Her mouth opened and closed as she gulped for air. He went to stroke her cheek, and she caught his hand and lightly bit the mound beneath his thumb, looking up at him with sly eyes. He jerked his hand away, and then he cuffed her cheek lightly with an open hand. She smiled and arched her back, rubbing her belly against his. A big cat, he thought. She's like a big cat. She caught his hand again and brought it against her face, hard, slapping herself with his hand.

Taylor grabbed her hair and pulled her head back. He saw the muscles and tendons stand out in her neck. He closed his eyes and plunged his tongue into her open mouth, and he felt her nails rake his back through his shirt. She bit his tongue. It hurt. Shocked and angry, he pulled back and slapped her hard. She gasped, and her hand began fumbling with his belt. A strange rage bubbled up from his stomach, filling his chest. He lifted his hand to slap her again. He wanted to hit her as hard as he could. He wanted to close his fist and punch her and then rip her clothes off and make her scream. Out of the corner of his eye, he saw his own fist.

What was he doing? What was happening to him?

This was something he would not do.

"No," said Taylor, stepping backward, releasing her.

Radziwell lost her balance and staggered back against the couch. Her raincoat had come open and had slipped off her shoulders. Taylor could see her breasts rising and falling beneath a loose white sweater. Seeing them, he remembered how they felt against him, and it was almost like feeling them again. She pulled up the raincoat and covered herself.

"What is the matter? I do something wrong?"

"No," said Taylor, repelled by his desire to hurt her, but still in an erotic fog that seemed to fill his head with smoke. A sadistic streak? You get off on hitting women? Where did that come from?

"It's not you," he said. "You didn't do anything. It's just, this isn't the right time for this."

"I am sorry," she said. "I thought . . ."

"Don't be sorry," Taylor said. "It's me. My fault."

"I don't understand."

"I just can't. Not now."

"You have a girlfriend?"

Did he? He had had no problem sleeping with Carol Rosenberg. That hadn't felt like an infidelity. But this was different. This felt like betrayal.

"No, it's not that," he said. What could he say? You frightened me because I wanted to hurt you?

"You don't want me to stay here?" she asked.

"No. I mean, it's not safe here," he said, wondering if he meant not safe for her or not safe for him. Or both. "Can you stay in a hotel?"

"In a hotel," she said after a moment, "too many people see me. And I cannot be alone like that, no."

"I need a glass of water," said Taylor. "Would you like one?"

Radziwell nodded, and Taylor went into the kitchen. He turned on the water, splashed his face, and filled two glasses. He returned and handed her a glass.

"Well," he said, "if you can't stay in a hotel, we'll have to find someplace else."

Taylor thought for a minute, then called Rabbi Kalman at his office in the Mathew Rosenthal Yeshiva. He asked him if he could hide someone, a woman, for a day or two. Kalman said he could and told Taylor to meet him at the *yeshiva*.

"We're going to Brooklyn," Taylor told Radziwell. "We'll find a place to hide you. I'll call a cab. I'll go downstairs and wait until it comes. When it does, I'll ring the bell once, and you come right down. The door will lock behind you. Move quickly, but don't run. Don't look around, and don't stop. When you get in the cab, put your head down. Do you understand?"

"You think people are watching you?" Radziwell asked.

"I know people are watching," said Taylor, picking up the phone. "I just don't know who."

63

El Al
West Forty-ninth Street, New York
Tuesday, October 29

After he had dropped Gussie, Saul's wife, and the kids off in Brooklyn, Ben Lerner had wanted to turn right around and head back to the city. Saul had insisted upon driving him. "You're too upset to drive," he had said. So now Lerner squirmed as they sat stuck in traffic in the Brooklyn-Battery Tunnel.

"I told you to take the bridge," said Lerner. "The tunnel is always like this."

"Ben, the tunnel is much faster. You just didn't want to pay the toll."

"Two and a half bucks is crazy when the bridge is free. And the bridge is faster."

Saul tapped the steering wheel and thought of the old Jack Benny joke: Your money or your life, the mugger says. I'm thinking, I'm thinking, says Benny. That was Ben.

"You don't believe me," Lerner said after a moment. "You think I'm losing my marbles."

"I just think it's been a long time, Ben. Fifty years? How can you be sure?"

"You think I can forget something like that?" asked Lerner. "*Ach*, what do you know?"

They lapsed into silence as they sat in the tunnel, not moving. Saul turned on the radio, got nothing but static, and switched it off.

"I still think you should go to the police," he said. "Or if you don't want to go to the police, go to the Israeli embassy. What's El Al supposed to do?"

"For your information," said Lerner, "they got real soldiers at El Al. At the embassy they got nothing but paper pushers. Do you know that El Al is the safest airline in the world? Do you know why? Because they don't take shit. They got soldiers there, anyone looks suspicious, they stick an Uzi up their ass."

"Okay. So what about the police?"

"I told you already. The cops won't do nothing. What do they care? They got *shvartzers* killing each other all over the city; they got *meshuggeners* running around stabbing each other. You know what they'll do if I tell them I seen a Nazi? *Gornit mit a nit*," Lerner spat. "Nothing. Not a goddamn thing. They'll send me to Bellevue, lock me up with the nuts."

"All right, Ben, all right. Don't get so worked up. You'll have a stroke."

Lerner took a deep breath and felt his heart pounding. Saul was right. Calm down.

The traffic broke. Once out of the tunnel, they made good time up the West Side, then slowed again as they cut across town. Lerner continued to breathe deeply, responding to Saul's occasional questions with grunts.

When they finally pulled up in front of the El Al offices on West Forty-ninth, Lerner told Saul to wait in the car while he went inside.

Lerner shuffled up to the front desk and asked a pretty young woman standing in front of a huge color photo of the Old City of Jerusalem to speak to someone in charge. He was directed to another pretty young woman sitting behind a small desk, who asked him to sit down and then asked him what she could do for him.

Lowering himself onto the chair, Lerner suddenly felt old. These young women, he thought, couldn't help him, couldn't begin to understand him. They were strangers. What had he expected? Old men like himself? These big, healthy Israeli girls didn't even look Jewish.

"Are you all right, sir?" the woman asked.

"Yeah, just give me a minute."

Lerner took in the sparkling El Al office. He looked at the giant photographs of beaches and scuba divers, of orange groves and smiling children wearing colorfully knitted *yarmulkes*, of the gleaming towers of Tel Aviv and the luxury hotels of Haifa. What's this got to do with me? Lerner asked himself, recalling the little *shtetl* of Kotsk where he was born: the muddy streets, the gray, broken-down houses, the children with dirty faces wearing rags. He remembered his father, a wagon driver, coming home in the dark, exhausted, and his mother screaming at him. He remembered being hungry, always hungry, and he felt the aching emptiness in his belly.

What's happening to me? thought Lerner.

"Can I get you a glass of water, sir?" asked the young woman, alarmed by Lerner's pallor.

Lerner pulled himself together. "I want to report a criminal," he said. "I want to speak to someone in charge, an officer. At the airport today, I saw a man, a man I know from the war, from the concentration camp, a Nazi. I want to report him. I want someone to know. I want someone to catch him up, to arrest the son of a bitch. This is a man I know, see? A Nazi bastard from the concentration camp. A murderer.''

"I'll get you a glass of water," the woman said, standing up and walking to the back of the room, where Lerner saw her whispering to a stocky, smiling young man with jet black hair wearing a plaid sport jacket and a white, open-collar shirt. The man nodded and looked over at Lerner. Lerner looked down and saw that his hands were trembling. He put them under his thighs and sat on them, sweating. Like a horse, he thought.

The woman returned with the water. Lerner gulped it, and it felt like lumpy mashed potatoes going down.

"Are you feeling better, sir?" the woman asked.

"Yeah," Lerner lied.

"Would you follow me, sir? There's a couch in the back where you could lie down for a minute."

"I want to speak to someone," said Lerner, standing, holding the back of the chair and feeling dizzy.

"You see that man there?" the woman asked, pointing to the man with whom she had been whispering a moment before. "You tell him what you told me."

The woman took Lerner's elbow and led him to the smiling man, who stuck out his hand. "My name is Gideon Katz," he said. "Call me Giddy."

"Ben Lerner."

"Let's go inside, Mr. Lerner."

Katz led Lerner through a door into a hallway. They turned into a small, dimly lit room containing a desk, a chair, a leather couch, and more picture-postcard scenes of Israel. Ben sat on the couch, and Katz pulled his chair over to him. They sat opposite each other with their knees almost touching.

"So, may I call you Ben? Yes? So, Ben, tell me who you saw."

"You're a soldier?" asked Lerner.

"Captain Katz at your service, Ben, but please call me Giddy.''

Lerner fought the pain beginning to flash across his chest and told Gideon Katz about Belzec and about Czartoryski, the murderer. He described Czartoryski, and Katz took notes. Then, when he finished, he asked Katz if he could lie down and rest a moment.

"Would you like me to call a doctor?" Katz asked.

"Yeah, sure," said Lerner, gritting his teeth against the pain moving down his left arm. "I think I'm having a heart attack. My wife's son, he's in a car outside."

After the ambulance came and Ben Lerner was wheeled out through the El Al office on a stretcher, the smiling children with their colorful *yarmulkes* waving down at him from the walls, Gideon Katz called the embassy and spoke to the Mossad station chief. An hour later Carol Rosenberg was informed that a man answering to Ladislaw Czartoryski's description had been seen deplaning from a London flight at Kennedy Airport that morning. If he did not make contact within twelve hours, he was to be considered renegade and appropriate action taken.

"Unless he's got a goddamn good story," her chief said, "we'll do what we should have done as soon as Horowitz went missing. Get the ad in tomorrow's paper. We'll waken the Cutter."

64

The Mathew Rosenthal Lubavitcher Yeshiva
Crown Heights, Brooklyn
Tuesday, October 29

Walking through the study hall toward Rabbi Kalman's office, Dov Taylor saw the students looking up from their books to stare at Maria Radziwell. They might as well be a different species, thought Taylor—the sickly-looking students, their sallow faces framed by curly black beards and wispy earlocks, and the tall, broad-shouldered Amazon by his side. Taylor smiled as he imagined the students' shock: a six-foot blonde in the *yeshiva*! A *shiksa* in the *yeshiva*!

Taylor had been hypervigilant on the ride from Manhattan to Crown Heights, turning continually to see if they were being followed, and Radziwell had slumped, eyes closed, against the cab's door, a little canvas traveling bag on the floor between her feet. When they'd crossed over the bridge, Radziwell had asked him to point out the Statue of Liberty. He'd leaned over, his shoulder pressing against hers, and found it in the mouth of the harbor.

"I thought it would be bigger," she had said as he'd moved back to his side of the seat, shaking off the feel of her body like a dog shook off water. Had he ever been so alive to another body? he asked himself.

"I've never been there," Taylor had said, turning around again to look out the cab's rear window, again seeing nothing and knowing how little that meant. He knew he was being watched. He knew it.

They had completed the ride in silence.

By some telepathy, Rabbi Kalman opened the door to his office just as Taylor was about to knock.

He introduced Radziwell to the rabbi as Mary Rubel, and Kalman was, it seemed to Taylor, oddly enthusiastic. He was extremely solicitous, asking her if she was hungry, if she was cold, did she need clothing, would she please sit down, rest, nodding and smiling as if she were his long-lost daughter. Was the rabbi affected by her, too? he wondered.

"May I use the phone, Rabbi?" asked Taylor.

Kalman gestured toward the phone on his desk and asked Radziwell if she would like some tea.

"Yes, very much," said Radziwell, and the rabbi left to get some.

Taylor dialed the Satmarer *rebbe*'s office. Pinchus Mayer picked up.

"Mr. Mayer? This is Dov Taylor."

"Hello, Mr. Taylor. You have news for us?"

"Yes," said Taylor. He saw Maria Radziwell watching

him expectantly. "Yes," he repeated, "I have news, and I have to see the *rebbe*. Immediately. Today."

"Tonight, perhaps?" said Mayer. "The *rebbe* is not in right now, he is at the study house, and then, after evening service, he has guests at his table, people who have come from Israel for the wedding. It's only a week away now. But after, about midnight, you could come, yes? The *rebbe* should be finished by then. What can I tell him to expect? What is your news?"

"I'll be there at midnight," said Taylor, hanging up as Rabbi Kalman returned carrying a cup and saucer.

"Here," said Kalman, handing the tea to Radziwell and producing a handful of sugar cubes from his pocket. "I didn't know if you took sugar, so I brought. Also," he said, producing a crumpled plastic bag, "a little lemon. I'm sorry, we have no milk."

"Thank you very much," said Radziwell.

"I'm going to go now, Mary," Taylor said. "The rabbi will take good care of you. I'll call you later."

"Thank you, Mr. Taylor," she said, pressing his hand. Her touch felt intimate, and it made Taylor uncomfortable. He regretted what had happened in his apartment. She let go of his hand. "Thank you for everything," she said. "Perhaps, when this is all over, you can show me the village you spoke of before."

For a moment Taylor did not know what she was talking about, and then he remembered. Months ago, standing in the doorway of her apartment, wondering if she were offering him a kiss, he had offered to take her around Greenwich Village. Now, of course, she had offered much more.

"Sure," he said. He let go of her hand and left the office with Rabbi Kalman.

"A beautiful girl," said Kalman as they walked back through the study hall. This time none of the students looked up from their books. "She is, God forbid, in danger?" Kalman asked.

"I think so," said Taylor.

"She has something to do with the murder, with the diamond?" Kalman asked.

"Yes," said Taylor, "but, please, Rabbi, let's not talk. The less you know, the better. You understand?"

"Of course I understand," said Kalman. "What's so hard to understand? I won't ask."

They reached the doors of the *yeshiva*. "Rubel is a Jewish name, I think," said Rabbi Kalman, smiling. "It's wonderful how Jews come in all sizes and shapes."

What is he so pleased about? Taylor wondered. "I think Rubel is her married name. Her husband was Jewish," he said. "I don't think she is."

Kalman's smile vanished. "She's married? I didn't see a ring."

"She's a widow," said Taylor.

"Oh," said Kalman, his smile returning. "So young to be a widow. So sad. You like her?" he asked, and Taylor realized that Kalman was happy because a woman, any woman, but especially a beautiful one, might mean that Taylor would be seeing less of Sarah.

Annoyed, Taylor shrugged noncommittally. "Where will you put her up, Rabbi?" he asked.

"Don't worry," said Kalman. "I'll keep her safe. As you said, better you shouldn't know. All right?"

"All right. But try not to let the whole neighborhood know. I don't expect it'll be for more than a night or two. I'll call as soon as I know what's happening. I'll call tonight whatever happens. Now"—Taylor watched Kalman closely—"I've got to see Sarah. I promised I'd drop by the shop."

A small frown crossed Kalman's face. "Yes, I know," he said. "She went to the Satmarer *rebbe*'s house with Adam Seligson. I helped to arrange it. She is very fond of you, my daughter."

I'm right, Taylor thought. He doesn't want me for a son-in-law. Can you blame him? An unemployed, divorced alcoholic? Not what every father dreams of. Still, he resented Kalman judging him.

Taylor walked down Kingston Street toward All Things Beautiful. The sun was setting, and he looked at his watch. Only four-thirty, he thought. The days are getting shorter. Winter's coming.

Up and down the block he saw the Hasidim closing their stores, pulling down their shades, locking the iron gates in front of their doors and windows. The women were all inside, preparing dinner; their children were either helping them or doing their homework. Bearded men in overcoats chatted as they hurried toward the temple for evening prayers.

Not so long ago, Taylor thought, this all would have been completely alien to me. Now, it's almost as if I have lived this life.

The door to All Things Beautiful was closed, and the shop was dark. Taylor could see a small light burning in the back, and he knocked. After a moment Sarah Kalman emerged, wearing a burgundy coat with a black fur-lined collar. Her red hair was tucked inside.

"Where have you been?" she asked. "You said you were coming right over. I've been worried."

"I'm sorry," said Taylor. "I should have called. I was over at the *yeshiva* with your father. Something came up."

"Well, my mother's expecting me to help with dinner. She's had the flu."

"I could walk you home."

"All right," said Sarah, locking the door behind her.

"Everybody has security gates," Taylor noted. "I guess Crown Heights isn't as safe as it once was."

They began heading up Kingston Street, walking closer to each other than strangers would have but keeping their hands in their pockets. The street lamps came on, and the sky above had turned a deep purple.

"There have always been gates," said Sarah. "Ever since the blackout in the seventies. The blacks and Puerto Ricans threw rocks through the windows and looted the stores, so everybody got the gates. Now it's even worse with the blacks from the islands. They hate us."

"I know," said Taylor. "Why, do you think?"

"I think it's because we love each other and they don't So they're jealous."

"What do you mean?"

"Well, we have our own schools, our own stores. We buy buildings and make apartments for our people. The mayor and the politicians have to pay attention to us because we vote together. But the blacks, they hate themselves, so they hate each other. They go and rob each other and kill each other, so the politicians don't have to pay attention to them. Then they look at us and they get angry about what we have, so they think we're taking something away from them.''

"But the Hasidim have used their power to grab public housing for themselves. They're pushing the blacks out of their own neighborhood."

"But if they had respect for each other, we could not do it. I'm not prejudiced, Dov, believe me. Sometimes the women come into my shop, and sometimes they buy. They can be very nice. But I wanted to tell you what I discovered in the *rebbe*'s diary."

They turned down President Street. "The Seer's stone," said Sarah Kalman. "The Israelis think it belongs to them, and the Satmarers think it's theirs."

"Is that what the diary says?"

"Yes. It says the Satmarers gave the stone to Adolf Eichmann so that he would let them go. Then, when the Israelis captured Eichmann, he tried to bribe them with it. And one of the Israelis who caught Eichmann gave it back to the Satmarers without telling the others."

"So who do you think it belongs to, Sarah?"

They stopped in front of the Kalmans' brownstone. "Would you like to come in for dinner?" Sarah asked.

"I can't, thank you. I'm pretty tired. I'm just going to go home, get some rest."

"All right. There's more I can tell you later. I should go inside."

"You didn't answer me, Sarah. Who do you think the Seer's stone belongs to?"

Sarah Kalman stepped up onto the first step of the stoop leading to her home, bringing her eyes level with Taylor's. She looked down at her feet, and Taylor—free of her bright, intelligent gaze and feeling unobserved—wished he could touch her cheek, just this once, to feel its softness. Her features were so fine, he thought, so precious.

"You know," she said, looking up after a moment, "the

stone certainly belonged to the Seer, and according to your vision, he gave it to Hirsh Leib. In a way, Dov, I guess the stone belongs to you.''

She turned, went up the stoop, and opened the door. Light poured out of the house, and Taylor squinted, trying to see Sarah Kalman's face.

"Good night, Dov," he heard her say, and then she disappeared, the door closed, and Taylor stood alone in the darkness.

My stone, he thought, summoning up a memory of Lublin. The Seer lay propped against a wall, blood trickling from his mouth. Taylor crouched next to him, and the Seer whispered, "Take the angel's heart, my friend." There was more. What was the Seer saying? Lublin came and went inside Dov Taylor like the waxing and waning of the moon.

He walked back up President Street toward the subway. Once, he thought he heard hoofbeats, and he quickly turned around and stared down the empty street.

Sarah Kalman was met at the door by her mother.

"We have a guest," she said. "Hurry."

Sarah Kalman walked into the dining room, and sitting at the table was a giantess: a beautiful blond woman with wide-set brown eyes.

"Sarah," her mother said, "this is Dov Taylor's friend Mary Rubel. Mary, this is my daughter, Sarah."

65

JFK International Airport
New York
Wednesday, October 30

There had been a family of Hasids sitting close to the Cutter on the flight from London—a man, a woman, and their three sons—and they were met at the airport by about ten more. They embraced and chattered in Yiddish as the Cutter walked around them, hating them.

They were, he had understood from their conversation on the plane, to be guests at the wedding.

The Cutter thought that he would go, too.

On the endless flight, his bowels twisting like some small, furry animal caught in a trap, the Cutter had stared at the Hasidic family, had watched how they looked only at one another, trying to shut out a world they considered unclean. And he recalled how the Hasidim had cleaved to each other even in the concentration camp's democracy of death. They seemed to be saying that they were the only ones who were suffering, that they were the only real Jews, the real martyrs, and all the rest were dying on their time.

Sometimes, as he had pulled the gold from their dead mouths, the Cutter had thought that they were right: he was there on their account. If it were not for the Hasidim flaunting their Jewishness, living up to the worst imaginings of the Christians—clannish, arrogant, secretive, wearing their clothes of perpetual mourning—would all of Europe have turned against them?

Take them, he had wanted to scream. They think they're better than us? Let them die in our place.

And he burned with shame.

Now they were turning Israel into a ghetto, bringing the filthy ways of the *shtetl* to the clean new land. They spoke Yiddish, not Hebrew; their sons would not work, would not serve in the army; they spat on women they deemed immodest, and they threw stones at buses that traveled on the Sabbath. Every year their numbers grew, and every year more of them arrived from New York, their *rebbes*, each one a little Ayatollah, issuing proclamations and running for the Knesset.

The Cutter clenched his fists as the bile rose in his throat. Another lightning bolt of pain shot through his stomach. He imagined himself on the floor of his father's slaughterhouse, standing in the blood-soaked sawdust, a knife in his hand. He imagined Hasidim hanging upside down from the hooks, and he saw himself slitting their throats, splitting their chests, pulling out their entrails, examining their lungs, one after another, his hands wet and warm from the blood. He walked up to another hanging Hasid, spun him around.

It was his father.

The Cutter rubbed his hands together. They were wet with sweat.

He passed through customs. He felt weak, sick, tired unto death, and even the thought of killing that whore Radziwell could not revive him. He knew that no matter how much he made her suffer, no matter what he did to her white flesh, sooner or later he would have to grant her the peace that had eluded him ever since the day the Germans had come for him and his family.

He picked up an early edition of *The New York Times* at a newsstand, and as he always did upon arriving in New York, he turned to the classified ads and looked under "Lost and Found." To his shock, there was a message for him: *"Lost: $1,000 REWARD for return of 1 box containing office documents of Deborah Int'l Corp. Call 212-553-5495."*

He slipped into a phone booth and punched up the number. A man's voice answered on the first ring, and the Cutter identified himself. "The Metro," the voice said, "on Seventh. At three, eight, or twelve. All right?"

"Yes," said the Cutter, hanging up and looking at his watch. It was one A.M. Plenty of time to make the three A.M. meeting.

It had been years since Deborah had given him instructions. It had been years since he had met anyone from the service. Now he had been given three separate times to meet someone at the Metro.

The Cutter looked at his watch again. Too late to call the Hotel Carlyle where the Magician would be staying. He would call in the morning.

The Cutter left the booth. He walked through the empty terminal, his footsteps echoing off the walls. He stepped outside through the glass doors and saw the line of cabs with their drivers dozing behind the wheels. The chill air cut through his thin leather jacket. He looked up into the night sky, but the airport lights hid the stars.

He walked up to the first cab and bent down to look through its window. A bearded face stared back at him, and for a moment the Cutter thought it was a Hasid.

The driver leaned over and rolled down his window. "Manhattan," he said. "I'm only going to Manhattan."

"Yes," said the Cutter, sliding onto the backseat. He looked at the driver's ID. A Greek. "The Metro, on Seventh," the Cutter said, and then leaned back in his seat, wondering what the Mossad could want of him.

The driver asked him where he had come from.

The Cutter studied the dark face in the mirror. "Drive," he said. "Just drive. And for God's sake, watch where you're going."

66

The Satmarer Rebbe's *Home*
South Ninth Street, Williamsburg
Wednesday, October 30

Dov Taylor looked at his watch again. It was two o'clock in the morning. He had been waiting in the parlor for over two hours as men and women rushed up and down the stairs, and from all over the house came the sounds of people arguing, crying, and laughing. Pinchus Mayer had come down to keep him company, but Taylor was growing impatient.

"It's two o'clock already," said Taylor.

"Yes, I know," said Mayer. "From now on, we will all get little sleep. Only six days to go before the wedding, and there's so much to be done. Arrangements"—he waved his hand vaguely in the air—"and negotiations. You will be there, of course."

"At the wedding?"

"Yes. You are coming?"

"Sure."

"Good. It will be something, the biggest *khasseneh* in anyone's memory. Over twenty thousand guests. Can you imagine all the food to feed so many? If I told you how much the caterer—who is taking no profit, let me assure you—is charging, you wouldn't believe it. And who knows how much Rebbe Seligson is paying for liquor and flowers? But for such a momentous occasion, who cares for money? There will be television, also."

"What?"

"Yes. The Lubavitchers put everything on television. They say that over three million Jews all over the world saw Rebbe Seligson last Hannukah. They wanted to make the *khasseneh* broadcast live, as it was going on. But to this the *rebbe* would not agree. So they will record it and show it at some other time.

"And can you imagine? With all that, the *ketubah* is not yet finished. It is making me crazy. Your friend Reb Kalman is very reasonable for a Lubavitcher, but still it is difficult to come to an agreement. You know what is the *ketubah*?"

"Yes. The marriage contract. I had one."

"Of course. But the one you had is not like a real one," said Mayer. "The one you had, for *goyishe Yidn*, is nothing. A real *ketubah* stipulates the *kest*, the period of time the *rebbe* will support the couple while the groom continues his studies. Of course, in this case, it is nominal. Adam Seligson is already a grown man, yes, and rich. Of course, the *rebbe* has bought the couple an apartment, on Seventh Street. Very nice, three bedrooms. Plenty of room for the *kinder*, the Lord willing.

"And you know what the *rebbe* has given the Lubavitcher, the father?" Mayer leaned forward conspiratorially. "A gold watch, very beautiful, very expensive, and a full set of Talmud, printed in Vilna by Akiba Druker, may his memory be blessed.

"The *ketubah* also tells what the groom will provide for his wife in the marriage. As is normal, we have agreed that the *rebbe*'s daughter will receive new clothes for Pesakh—that is Passover," Mayer added helpfully, "and the New Year."

Mayer lowered his voice. "I think a fur coat would be nice, yes? Women love fur coats, and the Seligsons can certainly afford it. They are so wealthy, you wouldn't believe. So, it is not in the document, it just stipulates new clothes, but I think Kalman understands. I gave him the name of a furrier. He will make sure the boy knows what we expect. And I don't think his bride will be shy about letting him know. She is, she will forgive me for saying it, very *Amerikanishe*, like so many of the young women today."

"All that goes in the *ketubah*?" Taylor asked.

"Certainly," said Mayer. "And the alimony if, the Lord forbid, there is a divorce. And the dowry, of course."

"And what's in the dowry?" asked Taylor, wondering how much Mayer knew about the Seer's stone.

Mayer seemed about to answer, and then he coughed. "Many things, many things. A bride, the Lord forbid, cannot go empty-handed to her husband. My mother's family, may their blood be avenged, lost all their wealth and property— in a pogrom, yes—and so my mother, may her memory be blessed, had to come to my father like a beggar woman. The shame followed her all her life. Thank the Holy One, there is no worry about Esther Teitel's dowry.

"And can you believe we don't have yet a *badkhen*?" Mayer said in a rush. "Of course, I'm not worried. With that, time is not a problem. All the best *badkhens* are waiting to hear from us. They all want the honor. We will choose Elijah Zimmerman, I think. He's the best, a brilliant man. Very pious, very learned, and such a voice, so deep you feel it here, in your belly. Your Reb Kalman wants a Lubavitcher *badkhen*, but it is traditional for the bride's family to pick the *badkhen*. We will have Zimmerman."

"What is a *badkhen*?" Taylor asked, willing to let the dowry drop.

Mayer gave him a look that mixed equal parts pity and contempt. "The *badkhen*," he explained as if speaking to a child, "is the one who reminds the bride and bridegroom of their duties to each other and to Israel. He is the one who introduces the honored guests. He is the one who announces the gifts. He is the one who calls the dances, sings the songs, and makes merry and sad in equal parts. He reminds the couple that the world was created for them, they should be joyous, but also that they are ashes and dust, so they should be solemn.''

"He's the emcee, right?" said Taylor.

"What is 'emcee'?" Mayer asked.

"The *badkhen*," said Taylor.

"So you knew what is a *badkhen*. Why did you ask?"

Just then Taylor saw a young woman in tears dash down the hall, trailed by several other women. "Who was that?" he asked.

"The bride," said Mayer, smiling.

"She was crying."

"Of course she cries. Brides cry always. They cry because they are leaving their mother's home. They cry for the hair they will soon lose. Tonight, her friends braided her hair and attached a sugar cube to each braid for a sweet life. The bride empties her heart of tears now so that she will be able to come to her husband with a light heart. Crying is good."

Taylor checked his watch again.

"I'm sorry," said Mayer, noticing, "but it is unavoidable. There are so many people coming from all over the world, old friends of the *rebbe*, and they are, of course, guests—''

Mayer broke off. A young Hasid had appeared in the parlor doorway, announcing himself with a decorous cough. Mayer addressed him in Yiddish, and Taylor heard the word *rebbe* several times. The young man nodded, and Mayer stood up. "You can go in now," he said to Taylor.

Taylor, stiff from having sat so long, climbed the stairs to the *rebbe*'s office. Halfway up, he realized that Mayer was not following him. He turned around, and Mayer waved him on with a flip of his hand.

So I'm one of the household now, Taylor thought. I don't have to be escorted.

The door to the *rebbe*'s office was open. Taylor stepped inside the smoke-filled room. The *rebbe* walked up to meet him and offered his hand. Taylor was surprised.

"I thought one doesn't touch the *rebbe*," he said.

The *rebbe* reached up to take Taylor's hand and gave it

one hearty, unpracticed shake before releasing it. Then he coughed and, producing a soiled handkerchief from his coat pocket, spat into it. He studied the phlegm for a moment before crumpling the handkerchief and stuffing it back in his pocket. "Our son-in-law-to-be's father shakes hands all the time, with anybody, so we should be less modern?" the *rebbe* said. "Sit, sit."

Taylor sat on the leather chair in front of the *rebbe*'s desk, which was in its usual state of disorder with papers and books piled high around its centerpiece: the hubcap-size metal ashtray containing its mountain of cigarette butts. The *rebbe* walked around and sat behind the mountain, lighting another Lucky Strike. He took a deep drag and blew smoke through his nostrils, continuing the process of turning his white beard a musty-colored yellow. He picked a fleck of tobacco off his lower lip and rolled it between his thumb and forefinger.

"So, my friend," the *rebbe* said, "Reb Mayer says you have news for us on the eve of our daughter's wedding. On our instructions, Reb Mayer has left the dowry portion of the *ketubah* blank, and as you know, there are left only six days before the ceremony. I hope that I will be able to tell him to fill it in, and I hope that we will both be able to say the blessing for good news, the *hatov vehametiv*. If you don't know it, I will teach it to you."

"I'm not sure if what I have to tell you is good news or not, *Rebbe*."

"Is that so? Let me decide. What is it that you have to tell us, Dov Taylor?"

"A person who says they have the diamond says they are willing to sell it back to you."

"They have it now? In New York?"

"Yes. That's what they say."

"And you believe they do, in truth, possess it?"

"I do."

"The Lord be praised. And how much do they want?"

"Two hundred thousand."

"That is not a problem, thank the Lord," said the *rebbe*, leaning back in his chair and blowing more smoke. "Make the arrangements. We will have the money before sunset. Congratulations, Dov Taylor,'' he said, stubbing out his cigarette and smiling. ''With the aid of God, you have done well. Your great-great-grandfather is pleased.''

''And that's it? That's all?''

''What do you mean, is that all? What more is there? You have something more to tell me?''

''You don't mind buying back your own diamond?'' Taylor asked, annoyed by the *rebbe*'s easy acquiescence. He had expected him to refuse or at least protest.

''It is what I expected. It is always money. That is what the *goyim* always want. Because they have nothing else, money is what they worship. As it is written, the ransom of captives is the highest *mitzvah*. Once, the stone was used to ransom our people from the Nazi murderer Eichmann, may his soul burn forever. Now it is the stone that is captive, so we ransom it to bring it its freedom.''

''And what about the men who murdered Zalman Gottleib and Shirley Stein? And Ariel Levin and who knows how many more? You don't want to know who they are? What if I were to tell you that one of the men is probably a Jew, maybe even a Hasid?''

''You think to shock me with this?'' asked Rebbe Teitel. ''You must think me a very unworldly man. There are Jews in this world, even Hasids, worse than Nazis. I have met them. As for the rest, these people are murderers. What more do I need to know? Their names? I know their names. Their names are Evil.''

''And what about Gottleib and Stein?''

''Their blood will be avenged. Do you doubt that the Lord will punish these murderers? That He will strike them down with His right hand?''

''Yes, I doubt it,'' said Taylor. ''I don't know anything about right hands or left hands. All I know is that these men are killers. How many people have died for this diamond? Not just Gottleib and Stein. You know what I mean. You should know what I'm talking about. If no one else knows, you should. You were there with me, in Lublin. You can't just buy the diamond, or ransom it, and be finished with it. If nothing else, what kind of marriage can your daughter have with a dowry that has so much blood on it?''

"So what would you have me do, Mr. Policeman?''

"Let me call the police. Let me use the diamond to set a trap for the killers."

"And what if they trap you instead? What if they kill you and make away with the stone? No. I will have no violence on the eve of my daughter's wedding.

"You are hot like Hirsh Leib, my friend," said the *rebbe*. He stood up and walked over to Taylor, placing his hand on Taylor's shoulder. "Let me counsel you as Rebbe Yitzhak, the Seer of Lublin, would have counseled your great-great-grandfather. Put modesty in your heart and thank the Lord for what He has enabled you to do, as we thank Him for returning to us His gift. The Seer's stone has purchased the lives of many of my Hasidim, and now it will crown my daughter as a princess of Israel. Be satisfied with that, and leave the rest to the Holy One, Blessed is He.

"This is a joyful time, Dov Taylor. My daughter is about to become the bride of the future Lubavitcher *rebbe*. Satmar and Lubavitch, so long divided, will be joined in their love, and together we will redeem all of Israel, which is in great need of it. This wedding hastens the coming of the Messiah, I am sure of it.

"Pinchus Mayer will go to the bank and withdraw the money, and you will ransom our diamond. God's gift has returned to His people. Come," said the *rebbe*, "say with me the blessing 'Who is good and dispenseth good to others.' *Barukh ato Adonoi*—"

"I'm sorry, *Rebbe*," said Taylor, standing up. "I'll be your go-between; I'll get the stone for you, for your daughter. But those murderers are out there, their friends are out there, and I can't forget that."

"We asked you to retrieve the stone, Dov Taylor; we did not ask you to redeem the world," said the *rebbe* sternly. "You are not yet on that plane. Do not imagine that you are now a *zaddik*."

"What about you?" asked Taylor. "Aren't you a *zaddik*?

Aren't you supposed to take some responsibility for the world?"

"I do," said the Satmarer *rebbe*. "I take even responsibility for you, who are not one of my followers. But the Evil Impulse is not chasing you, Dov Taylor; you are still chasing him. The *teshuvah*, the turning, is not yet complete, and—"

"Stop it," said Taylor. "I don't want to hear about *teshuvah*, or say any prayers, or sing any songs. I want, I want . . ."

"Yes, Dov Taylor? What is it that you want?"

Taylor looked down at the *rebbe*'s upturned face. It was not like the Seer's, he thought. It was not a gateway to another world.

What was it the Seer had said as he lay dying? What were his words? "The world and the men in it are broken vessels." Is that what he said? There was more. What was it?

"I want to end this, finally," said Taylor, trying to remember what the Seer had said, what he had charged him with. "I want to finish this, and I want to be made whole," he said. "That's what I want."

But, he knew, that wasn't it. It was true, but it wasn't all.

67

Rabbi Kalman's Home
President Street, Crown Heights
Wednesday, October 30

"Would you like another cup of coffee, Mary?" Sarah Kalman asked Maria Radziwell.

"No, thank you," said Radziwell.

Sarah's mother came into the kitchen, wearing her coat. "Did you sleep well, Miss Rubel?" she asked.

"Yes, very well," said Radziwell. "Thank you. Thank you for giving me a bed."

"It's nothing. I only hope you were comfortable. Sarah," said Sophie Kalman, turning to her daughter, "I'm going out to see if my new *sheitl*, the one I ordered for the wedding, is ready yet. All the women have ordered new wigs for the wedding of our *rebbe*'s son," she explained to Radziwell, "and poor Mrs. Walberg is so busy with the fittings, they're driving her crazy. You know how women are. Perhaps you'll take Miss Rubel to your shop today, Sarah? My daughter has a beautiful dress shop. Maybe you need a dress?"

"I'm sure Miss Rubel is not interested in the kinds of clothes in my store," said Sarah Kalman, eyeing Rubel's white silk blouse, open at the throat, and the short beige skirt stretched tightly across her thighs. "Has Poppa gone to the *yeshiva* yet?"

"What's wrong with the clothes in your shop? They're very modern, very *Amerikanishe*. God knows what Esther Teitel will be wearing to the wedding—I'm sure she will look beautiful; all brides look beautiful, even though I'm told she's a little bit cock-eyed. Now what was I saying?" Sophie Kalman paused to collect her thoughts. "Oh, yes," she said, "what I was going to say is that she should have gone to you for her wedding dress. What do the Satmarers know about fashion? So don't listen to my daughter, Miss Rubel. She's always apologizing like she's ashamed for something. She has beautiful dresses."

"Has Poppa gone?"

"Yes, but he's not going to the *yeshiva* today. He was going to Williamsburg," said Sophie Kalman, "to meet with that Pinchus Mayer about the *ketubah*. That's the marriage contract," she said to Radziwell. "My husband is making it."

Maria Radziwell looked down into her coffee cup.

"Have you eaten?" Sophie Kalman asked. "God forgive me, I forgot to ask. I could make some pancakes before I go. Some pancakes with a little honey and fruit."

"We're fine, Mama. Don't keep Mrs. Walberg waiting."

"All right. You young people want to talk. I understand. Who wants your old mother around? You sure I couldn't make you a little something?"

"I'm sure, Mama. Go already."

"I'm going, I'm going. There's a delicious fruit compote sitting in the refrigerator. I bet Miss Rubel has never had a compote like I make. All right, I'm gone," said Sophie Kalman, seeing the look on her daughter's face. "I'm out the door."

When Sarah heard the door shut, she got up and poured herself another cup of coffee. Turning back to the kitchen table, she was struck afresh by Mary Rubel's strangeness. That blond hair. And sitting on the chair, her back to Sarah, you could see how big her shoulders were. Sarah thought that she had never seen a woman with such broad shoulders.

Last night, over supper, Sarah had tried to ask Mary Rubel about herself and about how she knew Dov Taylor, but all the woman would say was that Taylor was an old friend who was helping her through a difficult time. She had turned aside Sarah's other questions, protesting that her English was not very good. Sarah had thought that she was being evasive and even a little rude. Right after eating, Rubel announced that she was very tired and wished to go to sleep. Sarah's mother had taken her upstairs to Moshe's old bedroom, turned down the sheets, watered the old mother-in-law's tongue plant in the glass brick, and turned off the light. Sophie Kalman, who shared her husband's view of Dov Taylor's suitability as a suitor, had done everything but tuck Rubel in and kiss her good night.

After Rubel had left the table, Sarah had asked her father about the woman. Was she involved in what Dov Taylor was doing? Did she know something about the Seer's stone? Rabbi Kalman had responded that he had better things to do than worry about chasing criminals—leave that to men like Dov Taylor and women like this Rubel—and that Sarah also had better things to think about, including helping her mother mend her dress for Reb Adam's wedding.

In bed, Sarah had lain awake thinking about the woman sleeping in the room next to hers, her brother's old bedroom. What would Moshe say if he knew? Sarah thought suddenly, smiling in the dark. He'd die. A giant yellow-haired *shiksa* lying in his old bed.

But Sarah's smile had quickly vanished. The sudden appearance of this strange creature in her home was disturbing. Obviously the woman was in trouble. That was clear. She was visibly exhausted. Her hands, Sarah had noticed at dinner, had been trembling. But she was also hiding something. That, too, was clear. And Sarah did not believe that Taylor was simply an old friend, or a friend of any kind. This, Sarah had thought, was not a woman who had friends, especially not male friends. This, she thought, was the kind of woman she had read about in novels when she was living in her own apartment and going to school. This was a woman who had lovers.

Was Dov Taylor one of them? Sarah had fallen asleep with that question in her mind, and now, staring at the back of Rubel's head, it returned, like an unpleasant guest who kept showing up at your door no matter how much you discouraged her.

Of course, what did it matter? Sarah asked herself. Why shouldn't Dov Taylor have a lover, or many lovers? What business was it of hers, a little old maid who ran a dress shop in Crown Heights?

But this woman? While one part of Sarah's mind knew that Rubel was an *Amerikanishe* ideal—tall, blond, slender with a big bosom—another part could not believe that Taylor, or indeed any man, could find her attractive. Those shoulders. Those hands. She was like a man, thought Sarah, not a woman. What would a man do with such a one as this?

And there was something about her that said she was keeping secrets. Sarah did not trust her, did not like her, and now she was annoyed, not amused, that her father had given her Moshe's old room, the one Dov Taylor had slept in when Sarah had first met him over the *Shabbos* meal.

"How long are you planning to stay here?" Sarah blurted out.

Maria Radziwell, who had not been paying much attention to Sarah, was surprised to hear the hostility in her voice. She turned around on her chair to study her. Could this pretty little red-haired Jewess be the reason the detective had pushed her away yesterday?

"I don't know," Radziwell said in a low voice. "I will go as soon as I can. Mr. Taylor," she said, looking to see if she could observe any change in Sarah's expression, "he said he would come for me as soon as he could."

The doorbell rang. Sarah started and saw that Mary Rubel had also jumped. What is she so afraid of? Sarah wondered, walking down the long hallway from the kitchen to answer the door.

Sarah squinted through the peephole and saw a Hasid looking down at his feet. Probably someone for her father, she thought, lifting the dead bolt and sliding it back. She opened the door halfway. "Can I help you?" she asked in Yiddish. "The rabbi is not home."

In an instant the man was through the door, his left hand clamping down on Sarah's upper arm, pushing her backward into the house, almost lifting her off her feet, kicking the door shut.

"*Shtil*. Do not scream, Miss Kalman," he whispered fiercely in Yiddish. "Please. Don't make a sound. Don't do anything. I don't want to hurt you."

Sarah gasped in pain. Her arm was on fire. His fingers, like the iron hands of some *golem*, dug into her muscles.

"Please tell me where she is," he said, pushing her backward, making her stumble down the hall.

Sarah turned her head to look behind her and saw Mary Rubel standing in the kitchen doorway. Then she disappeared.

The man had obviously seen her, too, for suddenly Sarah was yanked off her feet as the man bolted for the kitchen, dragging her behind him. Her shoulder wrenched, and a wave of nausea shook her. My arm will come off from my body, she thought.

Then she was flying through the air. She landed on her hip on the kitchen floor and slid up against the refrigerator. Raising her head, she saw Mary Rubel throwing silverware out of a drawer, then turn around holding one of Sophie Kalman's meat knives in both hands.

The man began walking slowly toward Rubel. "You do not have to be afraid of me, Maria," he said in English. "I only want to talk."

Rubel slid to her left, her back against the sink, holding the knife in front of her. The man moved with her, slowly closing the distance between them. He stopped at the kitchen table and casually placed a hand on the back of a chair as if he were going to have a pleasant chat. "Put down the knife, Maria," he said. "It will not do you any good. You know that.

"It was very stupid to run," the man continued, his voice smooth and his words unhurried. "You think we would not find you? It was stupid to steal. You think you could steal from us? But we forgive you. We just want what you took. You can go then. You can go where you want. Perhaps we will give you a little money. You see? We want to be reasonable."

Sarah Kalman began inching toward the kitchen door, pulling herself along the floor. When I get to the hallway, she told herself, I'll get up and run.

"I will stick this in your heart, you bastard!" Rubel shrieked.

Sarah heard a crash and turned around. The man had tossed aside the chair and tipped over the kitchen table. Now he was on top of the woman, bending her backward over the sink. Sarah saw the knife high in the air as the man shook Rubel's wrist back and forth. Then he slammed it down on the counter. Sarah heard the knife clatter to the floor as she scrambled to her feet. Before she could take two steps, the man had grabbed her by her hair, snapping her head back. As Sarah started to scream, the man clapped his hand over her mouth and shook her head roughly.

"No," he said, and Sarah, frightened and enraged, bit deeply into his thumb. The man growled and stomped down on her foot. The pain caused Sarah to open her mouth wide, releasing his hand. The man struck her face with the back of his hand. Everything was suddenly fuzzy and dark. Was she dreaming? And then she felt herself spinning.

For a moment Sarah saw a woman on her hands and knees on the kitchen floor, her blond head hanging between her arms. Then the man, his hand still in Sarah's hair, pulled her down the hallway and opened the door to the bathroom. He threw her into the room, and she fell sideways, banging the back of her head against the radiator.

"If you come out, I will have to kill you, Miss Kalman," the man said, shutting the door on her.

Sarah pulled herself up into a sitting position and leaned against the toilet bowl. Her arm and shoulder burned where the man had gripped it, her elbow throbbed. Her foot ached. She touched her mouth and then looked at her fingers. They were bloody.

Sarah heard another crash from the kitchen, heard plates and silverware hitting the floor. And the *rebbetzin* always keeps such a neat kitchen, Sarah thought. She'll be so upset.

Sarah stood up and walked to the bathroom door. She turned the lock. There. She would stay here quietly until that man went away. That horrible man.

She looked at herself in the mirror. Her chin was covered with blood. Her left cheekbone was turning purple. Her hair was tangled.

She bent her head. Her head seemed full of water, as if she had a cold.

She ran the water in the sink.

More sounds were coming from the kitchen. Sarah cupped her hands, filled them with lukewarm water, and then stared into the little pool in her palms. She thought she could see tiny creatures, made of glass, twisting and turning, rising and falling, swimming in the water. Isn't that wonderful, she thought. My eyes have become like microscopes.

Sarah Kalman was still staring at her hands when she heard a knock on the door. "Go away," she said in Yiddish. *Gay avek.*

"We have to go now," said that man. "Open the door."

Sarah slowly shook her head. He must be crazy, she thought. Why should she open the door for him?

The door burst open, the wood splintering, the lock torn from the jamb. Sarah stood where she was, trembling, her head hanging over the sink.

"I'm sorry, Miss Kalman," the man said. He took a white hand towel from the rack and held it under the faucet. Then, putting his hand under Sarah's chin, he turned her head and wiped her face gently, dabbing her lips with the moist towel. He smoothed her hair. Then he took her by the elbow. "Please, Miss Kalman," he said, "come with me."

He led Sarah out of the bathroom. She stopped and turned to look into the kitchen. She saw the table lying on its side. She saw plates and silverware and glasses and cups strewn on the floor.

"I should clean up," she said softly.

"Later," said the man. "When you come back, you can clean. I apologize for the disruption. You will need your coat. Where is it?"

"In the closet," said Sarah.

"The closet by the door?" asked the man.

Sarah nodded, and her face hurt again. There was something she should see, she knew, in the kitchen.

"I'm all right now," she said to the man. "You don't have to worry about me."

The man released her elbow, and Sarah dashed into the kitchen. There, lying on her back beneath the sink, was Maria Radziwell. Her arms were spread out on either side of her, and her legs were open, too. Her skirt was twisted up to her waist, and blood was collecting between her thighs. Sarah could see her panties and felt embarrassed for her. Even a *goy* should not be left so immodestly, she thought.

The front of her blouse, Sarah saw, was dark and wet. There was blood on her neck, blood on her face, blood in her blond hair. There was blood everywhere, on the cupboards and the floor. The room, Sarah thought suddenly, smelled like the shop where Reb Sternberg hung up his freshly slaughtered chickens.

Who was once a beautiful yellow bird is now a plucked chicken, thought Sarah.

She looked down at her feet. Her mouth filled with her morning coffee rushing up from her stomach. She bent over and vomited.

The man put his arm around her shoulder and turned her around.

"She was a bad woman," he said. "She was a thief and a prostitute." He led Sarah down the hallway.

Sarah stepped away from his arm. "Please don't touch me," she said, her eyes filling with tears.

The man nodded, opened the closet door, and stepped back. Sarah picked out her coat and put it on.

"Will you kill me, too?" she asked.

The man stood in front of the door. "You don't remember me, Miss Kalman?" he asked. "You don't know who I am?"

She forced herself to look into the man's cadaverous face. Then she looked away. "No," she said.

"The beard disguises me. When I take it off, you will know. I came to you once on the street," the man said. "I asked for your permission to speak to your father about a match. I said I would come back for you. You do not remember?"

Sarah Kalman shook her head. She had no desire to remember anything, she had no desire to think at all.

"We will go now, Miss Kalman," she heard the man say. "You will walk next to me to my car. It is just across the street. You will smile and look pleasantly, as if you were enjoying the sun, enjoying the day. It is beautiful outside."

The man opened the door and they stepped through it, side by side.

The man was right, Sarah thought. It was a beautiful day.

68

The Carlyle Hotel
Madison Avenue, Manhattan
Wednesday, October 30

The afternoon sun poured through the hotel window. Ladislaw Czartoryski sat on an overstuffed chair, his eyes closed, letting the sun warm his face. He was feeling drowsy. It took him longer to recover from flying these days, which he chalked down to his advancing age. He scolded himself: You are becoming an old man, Ladislaw, sleeping in the sun like a cat. But he could not move; it was too delicious just to sit there dreaming, letting his thoughts come and go.

For some reason, the past was becoming more interesting to him than the present. Right now, for example, he was remembering the feel of the sun on his face as he sat in a cafe in Beirut speaking to the young man he would come to know as the Cutter.

How odd that so much of his life had been taken up by Jews. The Cutter, a Jew, was perhaps his oldest associate. Then there were the Jews of his childhood and the Jews in the camps. And after the war, the Odessa had often found its interests running parallel to Israel's. Sometimes Czartoryski thought that the Israelis should thank men like him. After all, if it had not been for the camps and the work they did, there would be no Israel. For thousands of years the Jews had wandered from country to country, scorned and despised. His father, Czartoryski recalled, used to compare them to fleas on a dog. Then came the war, and its aftermath, and suddenly they had their own nation.

And the Israelis were tough, no doubt about that. Their Mossad had once been the best security outfit in the world. Natural selection, thought Czartoryski, smiling to himself. We eliminated all the weak ones. Another reason they should thank us.

Of course, the new ones, the ones who came of age after the war, were not so strong. They had become bourgeois businessmen, reverting, thought Czartoryski, to Jewish type. His first Israeli would never have trusted him to turn over the diamond. But these new Israelis were greedy and careless. With Jews, thought Czartoryski, it always came back to money, to *shekels*.

His first Israeli, what was his name? Nir? Ben something? It was probably once Hymie Yidstein; they all changed their European names to Hebrew ones. As if they could erase the memory of the ghetto. As if they could cut themselves off from their bearded fathers, nipping the thread of history to which they felt ashamed to be bound. But now the beards were back. The Hasidim. Again the Yids revert to type.

Anyway, one day—was it in Paris? No, it was still Warsaw—they had gotten drunk, and the Israeli had said to him that something secret and intimate had passed between the Jews and the Nazis during the war. He said that in order to survive, the Jews would have to remember what the Nazis had whispered in their ear. They would have to remember how to be brutal.

And they did well, Czartoryski thought, feeling paternal toward the Jews, his Jews. Then he felt a shadow pass across his face. He opened his eyes. The sun had slipped behind a building. He looked at his watch. Three o'clock. In an hour it would be dark.

Where was the Cutter?

He sighed and stood up, his joints stiff. His mood changed. He felt gloomy. He looked out the window and saw the traffic creeping along far below. What was left of the Odessa? he asked himself. After General Gehlen's death, there was really no one to take his place, no one to give us a sense of high purpose. Now that the Soviets had committed suicide, there was not even an enemy. NATO was a relic; its intelligence operations were without funds. The Americans were turning away from Europe, thinking that they had won their contest with the Communists.

Our old friends in Paraguay, El Salvador, and Argentina are dying; their governments are slipping from our control. The blacks are seizing power in South Africa. What's left? Czartoryski asked himself. A handful of old men like myself. A handful of young opportunists with no loyalty. Men like Ukridge who think only of lining their own pockets.

I could retire now, Czartoryski thought. With the diamond, I could retire to, say, Jakarta, and live in comfort. There are still comrades in Indonesia, scattered on the islands. We could sit and watch the sun set and talk about the old times when every day we held life and death in our hands.

I should thank the Jews for that, thought Czartoryski. In Belzec, whenever I looked into the eyes of a Jew and saw there the understanding that he was about to receive death from my hands, I knew what a god must feel like.

Alive. So alive.

Perhaps I should go down to Forty-seventh Street before it closes, he thought. Walk among them again. See them looking at me with their frightened eyes.

Czartoryski slipped on his shoes. Now he had a direction, a goal, but his depression refused to lift. As he rode the elevator down to the lobby, his thoughts returned to the Cutter.

Could he have been detained in London? What could he be doing? Why hadn't he made contact?

I am quite alone, he thought, and for a moment he felt a touch of fear. Then, as he stepped out onto the street, he thought of Ukridge, his face blackening in his own fireplace, and he felt once more alive.

I'm not dead yet, the Magician told himself. Not yet.

69

Rabbi Kalman's Home
President Street, Crown Heights
Wednesday, October 30

It was a scene Dov Taylor knew all too well, in a play he thought he had left behind. But now he had a new role in it.

"Tell me about your relationship to the deceased," Detective Ray Antonelli asked again, the shield in his wallet hanging over his jacket's chest pocket, a notebook and pen in his hands. He pulled his chair closer to the couch in the Kalmans' living room where Taylor was sitting. Their knees almost touched.

A little intimidation, thought Taylor. Well, he'd do the same; in fact, he had done the same, many times.

"I met her twice, for a total of a few hours. That's all," said Taylor. "That was our entire relationship."

"You asked your rabbi to take care of someone you only knew for a few hours?"

"That's right."

"And you say her name was Rubel, or Radziwell? Is one a married name?"

"I told you," said Taylor. "I don't know." Next, he thought, he's going to ask for my assistance.

"You're not being very helpful, Mr. Taylor," said Antonelli. "I'm sure you can do better."

"I'll do anything I can," Taylor said.

Taylor had wanted to speak to Rabbi Kalman, to apologize for bringing death into his home, to reassure him that his daughter would be safe. But Antonelli, going by the book, had spirited the rabbi away. There would be no communication between principals in an Antonelli-run investigation.

"You've got a long night of depositions in front of you, Mr. Taylor," Antonelli was saying now. "A very long night. I'm going to want to take a full statement. You have no objections, right?"

A young uniformed officer came into the living room and whispered in Antonelli's ear. Antonelli nodded, said, "Okay," and the uniform left the room.

Through the living room door, Taylor could see Rabbi Kalman being led down the hall. The rabbi, his eyes red, his hair disheveled, turned and looked at Taylor. What, he asked himself, had he done to this family?

"Don't let him touch anything," Antonelli called out as the young patrolman led the rabbi upstairs. To comfort his wife, thought Taylor.

Then Antonelli turned back to Taylor. "So," he said, "where were we?" He glanced down at his notebook. "So, Rubel and Radziwell. Are there any other names you know about that she might have used?"

"The rabbi doesn't know anything about this," said Taylor. "I didn't tell him anything."

"So tell me," Antonelli said.

There was something a bit show bizzy about Antonelli, Taylor decided. With his slicked-back hair and his Italian suit, Taylor thought he looked like someone bucking for captain. He's going to take me in, Taylor thought. That's what I would do. And if he takes me in, how am I going to find Sarah?

"She once told me her real name was Rubelski," said Taylor. "But that was before she told me it was Radziwell. And maybe she used her husband's name. I think she told me it was Rudenstein. I have it in my notebook back at my apartment. But I'm not sure she was really married."

"I count four names. Not bad. Interesting lady. So let's start again," said Antonelli. "From the top. And slower this time. With feeling."

Taylor sighed. There was no way Antonelli was going to like the story Taylor was telling him. He wasn't even going to like the parts that were true.

I introduce a woman I barely know—I don't even know her real name—to my rabbi, and ask him to hide her. Why? Because she has information about a crime, a murder, and she's afraid for her life.

Do I call the police with this information? No, I do not. I do not call the police.

The next day she's murdered, and the rabbi's daughter disappears.

Does it matter that I didn't know that the rabbi was going to take her into his own home? No, it does not.

And what information did the victim have about this murder?

She said she knew the men who committed it. She said she had taken something from them, something the murder was committed for, something they wanted.

And what was that something?

I don't know, Officer. She wouldn't tell me.

Sure, thought Taylor, he'll take me in. He'll conduct a formal interrogation. Why not? That's what I'd do. I might even throw me in the cage. If not as a suspect or a material witness, then just for being a wiseguy. Anyway, right now, I'm all he's got.

As Taylor repeated his story, not mentioning the diamond that he knew would put him away for withholding evidence from a criminal investigation, he watched men walking up and down the hallway outside the living room, acting out their parts in the crime scene drama.

Some carried plastic bags containing evidence: towels, cups, silverware, maybe the murder weapon. The crime lab people, wearing their plastic gloves and white overalls, were dusting for prints. The photographer was snapping pictures of the kitchen, the bathroom, and the hallway. The men from the morgue were waiting with a body bag, waiting for the medical examiner to finish. His job would be simple tonight. The body was fresh—rigor had not yet set in. Given the time the Kalmans had left the house, and the time they had returned, plus the rate of lividity—blood, pulled by gravity, settling in the backs of the thighs, the buttocks, the back— the time of death would be relatively easy to establish. And the corpse displayed numerous large wounds, obviously from a knife.

It was curious, thought Taylor, how different men reacted in the presence of death. Some whispered, others spoke louder than necessary. Some treated death with respect, others regarded it with contempt. Still others were frozen in anger— how dare death invade their lives, intrude on their watch?— and others kept death at bay with jokes or with the efficiency with which they carried out their tasks.

One thing Taylor knew from his years on the force: no one was untouched, no one was ever truly indifferent. There was no event that changed a man's world as much as violent death, even the death of a stranger.

But there was no stranger here.

After having received Rabbi Kalman's phone call, after having tried, unsuccessfully, to calm him down, and after having told him to call 911, Taylor had left a message for Frank Hill. Then he'd cabbed to Crown Heights. The police were there when he arrived, and Antonelli, after listening to Taylor explain who he was, had led him into the kitchen to identify Maria Radziwell's corpse.

Taylor had seen lots of bodies. Over the years he had trained himself to stop seeing them as people, to see them as people-shaped boxes containing clues, nothing more. He had tried to do that here, but his mind animated the corpse on the kitchen floor.

He saw her walking around his apartment.

He saw her standing, her head thrown back, waiting for his kiss.

He saw her walking through the Lubavitcher study hall with athletic strides, the students' eyes upon her.

He saw her as he had left her, standing in Rabbi Kalman's office in her cotton raincoat, thanking him for protecting her.

He had failed her, and now she was dead. She had come to him for help, and she had ended up dead.

Just the day before, he had been aroused by this body. Now the thought of touching it repelled him—140 pounds of fat, meat, and bone weltering in its own blood. Tissue breaking down; gases building up, making the belly swell. The exsanguination was almost complete, Taylor noted. The corpse was extremely livid; the blood that once warmed it was oxidizing, turning brown on the linoleum floor.

A uniform had cracked a joke about one hell of a period. Another uniform had told him to shut up.

Did it end here? Taylor asked himself. Did it end, as it had in Lublin, in blood, death, and disaster? Was the Seer's stone gone forever? Czartoryski and the Cutter, were they on their way to who knew where? What could he tell Antonelli about them? He couldn't even describe them. Go ask the Israelis, thought Taylor. Find that son of a bitch Phil Horowitz and ask him. And Sarah. What had happened to Sarah?

That was the one ray of hope, Taylor told himself. The fact that Sarah was missing could mean only one thing. Why else would they have taken her?

But trading for her is going to pose a problem, Taylor thought, since I don't know where the stone is.

"Let me get this straight," Antonelli was saying. "You were investigating the murder of this diamond dealer for the Satmarer *rebbe*, but you're not a private investigator. Your last job was as a guard at the First Bank of Williamsburg. You don't have a PI's license. And you accepted money for this? You were paid money for whatever it is you thought you were doing?"

Taylor saw two uniforms carrying the body bag down the hallway. They stopped as the front door opened and Frank Hill, wearing sneakers, jeans, and a blue windbreaker over a blue-and-red New York Knicks sweatshirt, stepped into the apartment.

Hill told the men to put the bag down and open it up. He bent over for a moment and then straightened up. "Hi, Taylor," he called over. "You want to look?"

"I've seen it."

"Schumacher's bombshell, right? The big blonde."

"Schumach," said Taylor.

"Whatever," Hill said, walking into the room. He shook hands with Antonelli and introduced himself.

"He tell you he called me?" Hill asked Antonelli. "You like his story?"

"Love it," said Antonelli. "Can't get enough of it. Want to hear it, oh, say, about ten or twenty times."

"You taking him in?"

"Oh, absolutely."

"Mind if I join in?"

"Be my guest."

"Wait a second, guys," said Taylor. "Detective Antonelli, may I have a word alone with Detective Hill? Just for a moment?"

Hill looked at Antonelli, and Antonelli nodded. He walked out of the room, and Hill sat on the couch next to Taylor.

"They're going to try to get in touch with me, Frank," said Taylor.

Hill laughed mirthlessly. "I just don't know, man. There's so many ways I could respond to that. Like, for instance, who's gonna get in touch with you? That's a good start. Or, why? Or maybe they're going to have a hard time getting hold of you in jail."

"If Antonelli takes me in," said Taylor, "they're just going to wait until I get out to ask me what they want to know."

"Okay. I'll play. Who the fuck are 'they'?"

"I know there are at least two of them. An old guy, a Pole, named Ladislaw Czartoryski. I don't know the other one's name. The girl called him the Cutter. According to the girl, they're the guys who killed Gottleib and Stein, and probably Levin. They're the guys who stabbed me. The girl thought they were in New York. She thought they were going to come after her. I guess she was right."

"You fucking asshole," said Hill, standing up abruptly. "I can't believe you're still jerking me around. You think I'm fucking lame? You think I'm going to ask Antonelli to let you walk away from this, you don't even tell me what it's all about?

"I've had it with you, man. I really have. Do you realize what you've done? You tried to hide a fucking material witness to a fucking felony murder, and now she's dead. You know how bad that is? You fucking ought to. Where were your brains, Taylor? Were you fucking her? Is that it?"

"All right, Frank."

"No, man. It is not all right. She's dead, and as far as I'm concerned it's your fault. Your fault, motherfucker. And let me tell you, you don't stop playing these fucking games, you're not just going to be held, you're going to be charged. You're going to be sitting in a fucking cell waiting for a grand jury, which the Brooklyn DA will call in about two fucking seconds. You understand? I'm tired of sniffing corpses while you play twenty questions with me."

My fault? thought Taylor. No. I did what I could. I did what I had to.

"All right, Frank," said Taylor, "all right. Sit down. Come on." Hill remained standing, his arms folded across his chest. "Okay," said Taylor. "You're right, I'm wrong. Maybe I've been wrong all along. Listen."

Taylor took a deep breath. He looked at Hill, at his belly hanging over his jeans. He thought about Hill's home, the broken toys lying on the filthy rug, the big backyard with its "fuck you" weeds growing high and wild. How could he make Hill see that he was beginning to understand that he was tied to the people who had come before him, and, more important, he was bound to the people who shared the earth with him. And that because of those ties, it might be possible to heal a wound that had been bleeding, uninterrupted, for over one hundred and fifty years.

No, he decided. It was not possible. He knew what Hill

believed in. Like all cops, Hill believed that wounds never healed; they only festered. That's why so many cops ate their guns.

"They took a stone from the dealer, from Gottleib," Taylor began, knowing that he would give Hill all the truth he could—and that that might amount to only half. "Czartoryski, the Cutter, probably the girl, too. A diamond, Frank. A special diamond. That's what this is all about. A diamond that's belonged to the Satmarers for hundreds of years. No one knows anything about it. There's no record of its existence. Nobody but the Hasids have ever seen it. Not recently, anyway. It was a secret. It's tied up to their religion, to their history, in ways I can't explain. Not because I don't want to, Frank. I just can't. I don't have the words. But what's important is that it was going to be the Satmarer *rebbe*'s daughter's dowry.

"It's a big deal, this wedding. A very big deal. It's like, in the Middle Ages, if the king of France's daughter and king of England's son were getting married. It's more than a marriage; it's a political alliance.

"Anyway, the blonde stole the diamond from Czartoryski and the Cutter. I figure that's why they took the rabbi's daughter. Rubel didn't tell them where it was. They figure I know. They figure she told me."

"Did she?"

"No."

Hill made a face.

"Honest to God, Frank," said Taylor, "she didn't tell me, and I got no idea where it might be."

"No idea?"

Taylor shook his head.

"I'm going to search this apartment," said Hill.

"Good, search away. I hope you find it."

"And I should believe you on this because you've been so straight with me all along?" said Hill.

"I couldn't tell you about the diamond before. The *rebbe* made me swear not to."

"Well, maybe the *rebbe* will post your bail when we charge you with obstruction and withholding evidence."

"Come on. You can't get an indictment, Frank. Withholding from what? Obstruction of what? An investigation that didn't have a suspect? The theft of a diamond no one knew existed? Maybe after you make a case, then you get an indictment. But how are you going to make a case? Against who? Ladislaw Czartoryski? No way he's using that name here.

"So you hold me now, for what? Twenty-four hours? Forty-eight hours? They're still going to come after me, Frank. And what about the girl, the rabbi's daughter? The longer they hold her, the worse it'll be for her. You know that."

"Maybe they already got the diamond, Taylor. You think about that? Maybe the blonde had it on her. Maybe they took it when they offed her."

"I don't think so. If they got the diamond, why would they take the rabbi's daughter?"

"Because she witnessed a murder. We'll probably find her body in an alley somewhere, or stuffed in the trunk of a car on the Cross-Bronx."

Taylor repeated Hill's words to himself, but his mind wouldn't accept them. It couldn't be true.

"Why leave one body on the floor and then try to hide another?" he protested. "No, Frank. They want to trade the girl for the diamond. I'm sure of it."

"Even if I go along with that, you got a problem, don't you, Taylor?" said Hill. "You just said you didn't know where it was."

"That's true, but they don't know that."

Hill was silent a moment. "You want me to use you as bait," he said.

"That's right," said Taylor. "Tap my phone. Put a tail on me. Put men in my bedroom. Move in with me. I don't care. When they call, I'll tell them I got the stone. I'll wear a wire. Then, when it's time for the swap, you're ready to pick them up."

Hill sat back down on the couch. "What else do you know?" he asked Taylor.

"What do you mean?"

"I mean what else do you know about the blonde, about the Pole, and the other guy, this Cutter character? You got a description, anything?"

"Nothing, Frank," said Taylor. "Not a thing. That's why you have to go along with me on this."

Hill was silent.

"Frank, I'm not asking you to trust me," said Taylor. "I know, well, there's no reason you should. I'm just asking you to use me. You know it's the right play."

"And when you make the meet and there's no stone, what then?" said Hill. "They don't seem to be the type of guys'll take it so fucking well."

"You'll be there."

"And what if I'm not? Shit happens, you know."

"I know," said Taylor. "Well, if shit happens, shit happens. You haven't lost anything."

"I know you've asked around about these guys. Maybe you didn't get a description, but you got something," said Hill. "Don't shit me, Taylor. You've made a good start, and maybe I'll ask Antonelli to go along with you on this, but what else did you find out?"

"For what it's worth," said Taylor, "the Polack, Czartoryski, seems to have been a Nazi, and he's a known diamond criminal. Big-time. The South African police got him on file. I can give you the name of a guy in Miami, a retired diamond cop, who got the information for me. Or you can go direct to the International Diamond Security Organization. And I think there's Israelis involved. I'm sure of it. The Israelis know about the diamond. And the guy who set me up in the diamond district, the Hasid I told you about, the one nobody can find, Horowitz, I think he works for the Israelis."

Hill stood up again. "You know," he said, "it's very interesting that you should say that. Around five in the morning we found a stiff downtown. In a Dumpster. Throat cut. We found some telephone numbers. One of them was the Israeli embassy."

"What was his name?"

"It wasn't a him," said Hill, "it was a her. And her name was Rosenberg. Carol Rosenberg."

70

East Fourth Street
The Lower East Side, Manhattan
Thursday, October 31

"I could get you something to drink," the Cutter said.

A cockroach skittered along the baseboard. Sarah Kalman, sitting on a mattress, hugging her knees to her chest, watched it.

"I could get you some ice for your face," the Cutter said.

The cockroach began climbing up the gray, water-stained wall.

"I will get you some ice," said the Cutter.

In the kitchen, the Cutter worried a blue plastic ice tray out of the freezer's frozen grasp. He twisted the tray, and the ice cubes popped out and clattered into the sink. He scooped them up, dropped them into a gray, rust-stained washcloth, and brought them back to Sarah Kalman.

"Here," said the Cutter. "Put this on your face. It will make it feel better."

Kalman made no move to accept the cloth. The Cutter set it down on the floor by the edge of the mattress and retreated to his chair by the window.

Kalman bent forward, her hair falling over her face, and picked up the washcloth full of ice. She pressed it against her bruised lips and then against her purpling cheek.

How beautiful she is, thought the Cutter. How strong she is. A true daughter of Israel. A true warrior bride of Israel. Sitting there in silence, her hair a red curtain over her shoulders and arms, it's as if she lives every moment wearing a crimson bridal veil. She doesn't need a veil of linen and lace; she was shaped by the Creator to be a bride.

But not mine, thought the Cutter. There is nothing of that life left for me.

"We have food," said the Cutter. "Would you like something to eat?"

The cockroach fell off the wall onto its back. It waved its legs wildly, righted itself, and headed back toward the baseboard to resume its climb. Sarah thought that if the roach could successfully negotiate the wall, she would live.

"Soon I will take you home," the Cutter said. "Soon we will be finished. Until then, you must eat."

But the Cutter knew that she would not eat, knew that she would not accept food from a murderer's hand. How could he have ever imagined that he would stand with her under some flowery wedding canopy, his heart and soul so full of blood and death? In order to do that, he thought, he would have to create a world so full of horror that his own world would, by comparison, seem innocent and pure. In order to do that, he thought, he would have to slaughter thousands.

I could have married her in the camp, the Cutter thought suddenly. Only in the camp could we have been wed. The commandant could have been our rabbi. Any one of the guards could have served as our *badkhen*. No. Czartoryski. The Magician. He would be the perfect *badkhen*. He would remind us of how the breath of life escapes with every kiss. And then I would break the glass and with its broken edge cut the *badkhen*'s throat. I would toast the wedding party with a glass of his blood, and my father would sit there with the other guests—all of them dead, of course—and shout *Mazl tov!* Good luck, my only son.

The Cutter stood up abruptly, thinking he had heard his father's voice. He looked down at Sarah Kalman, and sadness overwhelmed him. If only we had met then, he thought. We could have been happy then.

But from death can only come more death, the Cutter thought. Has any good come from any of my deeds? Well, it is good that Maria Radziwell is dead. That, certainly, is a great good. And it is good that that Israeli whore, Rosenberg, is dead. Perhaps a few more deaths can set things right. Yes, there is still work to be done. The world can still be improved by removing a few more people from it.

He walked back into the kitchen, where a telephone hung on the wall. He dialed the detective's number.

Dov Taylor picked up.

"You have the stone?" the Cutter asked.

"Yes," said Taylor. "I have it. It's hidden."

"The stone for the rabbi's daughter, Sarah Kalman," the Cutter said. "That is my offer."

"Agreed," said Taylor. "How? Where?"

"I will tell you soon. Do not go away from your telephone," the Cutter said, hanging up before the call could be traced.

Taylor put down the phone and turned to Frank Hill, who was listening in on the extension he had brought to Taylor's apartment. "He's being very cute," said Hill.

"What did the Israelis say about Rosenberg?" Taylor asked, fighting the image that came to him of her in his arms. He was tired of seeing himself making love to dead women.

"They said she was a secretary in some division, cultural interest, I think, promoting Israeli artists. Look, I don't have enough clout to get a straight answer. I took it to the captain. We'll see."

The Cutter left the kitchen and stood over Sarah Kalman. "I'll make soup. If you don't want it, don't eat it, I won't force you. But I'm making it."

The Cutter saw the cockroach on the wall. "I'm sorry," he said to Kalman, and, reaching out, he flicked the bug off the wall. It fell to the floor. He stepped on it.

Sarah Kalman began to rock back and forth. Was it a sin, she wondered, to say the *Shema* for an insect?

71

JFK International Airport
New York
Friday, November 1

They came from Israel, from the old Hasidic communities of Jerusalem and Tel Aviv, and they came from the new settlements on the West Bank. The planes carrying them touched down from Paris and Johannesburg, from London and from Sydney, Australia. They were rabbis, teachers, tailors, and engineers. They were cabdrivers, computer salesmen, and diamond dealers. The men wearing black fedoras or plush fur *shtreimls*, the women wearing new wigs and their best holiday dresses, they came by the thousands to celebrate the *Shabbos* with the *rebbes* of Satmar and Lubavitch. And they came to rejoice in the wedding of their children.

They were met by relatives and friends. The Lubavitchers were picked up by the "*mitzvah* wagons," with "We Want Messiah Now" and "Messiah Is on the Way" lettered on their sides in Hebrew and English. The Satmarers piled into the old yellow schoolbuses that Pinchus Mayer had rented.

The buses and cars and vans crossed the Triboro Bridge. It was a perfect, cloudless day. But while the women pointed out the skyscrapers to their weary children, the men barely gave the city a glance—they were deep in conversation, discussing the miracles that their respective *rebbes* had wrought, not the least of which was this marriage between the two old enemies, Satmar and Lubavitch.

In Williamsburg, the Satmarer merchants on Division Avenue and Lee Avenue prayed that the Sabbath would hold off, that the sun would pause in the sky while the pilgrims shopped for sweets in the bakeries and for souvenirs in the bookstores: *tefillin* and *tallisim*, guaranteed *kosher*, manufactured according to the strictest religious specifications; tapes of the *rebbe*'s talks; books of the *rebbe*'s thoughts; Passover *seder* plates with the *rebbe*'s likeness on them; dollar bills with the *rebbe*'s face laminated over George Washington's. In Crown Heights, on Kingston Street, Lubavitcher merchants manning their cash registers whispered the same prayers as their Satmarer brethren.

Outside Lubavitcher World Headquarters at 770 Eastern Parkway, the crowd of bearded men in black grew as the week inched slowly toward its close. Many pilgrims wore their *tefillin*, and many carried prayer books that they had brought from home in the hope that the *rebbe* would bless them at the gathering that would be held in 770's basement tomorrow night after the *havdolah*, the bittersweet ceremony that divided the holy Sabbath from the profane working week. Others prayed only for a glimpse of their *rebbe*—the man who was more than a man, the only *zaddik* of the age, the one who was, some believed, the Messiah Himself.

The Sabbath siren blew, shredding the air. Men turned and embraced. Many had tears in their eyes. They had come so far; they had endured so much; they had kept hope alive. Many of them went to sleep every night with a suitcase at the foot of their beds. If the Messiah should come, they would be ready, their bags already packed. But now *Shabbos* was upon them, and they were welcoming their beautiful *Shabbos* bride in Brooklyn, the beating heart of the Hasidic world. No longer were they the odd men out, no longer were their clothes and manners the target of *goyishe* ridicule. Now they were surrounded by the soothing sound of Yiddish, the *mama-loshn*, the mother tongue. Perhaps the Lord Himself would look down upon this joyous, pious throng of His chosen people and be unable to resist joining in their celebration. Perhaps He would stretch out His right hand—right now! at this very moment—and sweep them all up to His heavenly bosom, as He had lifted His prophets into the sky in the olden days.

In apartments throughout Crown Heights and Williamsburg, women were setting the *Shabbos* tables with their finest linens, placing the *Shabbos* candles in their best silver holders. Their homes were crowded with guests and children, and large kitchens suddenly seemed small. Arguments broke out over what spices went into the *tsimmes*; whether the gefilte fish should be served warm, as the Litvaks liked, or cold, as the Poles liked; whether the salad dressing should use lemon or vinegar, as women from different lands lobbied for the supremacy of their grandmothers' recipes.

And then the moment came for the lighting of the candles, and the children gathered around the table to watch their mother cover her head and close her eyes and draw the flames to her breast as she murmured the *Shabbos* prayer—adding a wish for the happiness of the soon-to-be married Adam Seligson and Esther Teitel.

In Williamsburg, inside Congregation Yetev Lev, the main Satmarer synagogue on Rodney Street, Pinchus Mayer tried to focus on his prayers. But for the first time in his life, he was finding it hard to put aside this world, *olam hazeh*, to concentrate on *olam habo*, the world to come. His worries were legion.

Would the off-duty police he had engaged to guard the wedding presents show up? Who could trust the *goyim*?

Would there be trouble between the police and the private Lubavitcher guards—those thugs—who the Lubavitcher *rebbe* had insisted be there? Who could trust the Lubavitchers?

Even at so joyous an occasion, who knew for certain what would happen when so many Lubavitchers and Satmarers shared the street?

And what about troublemakers? Certainly there were many who did not want to see this *khasseneh* take place—Nazis and anti-Semites of all kinds. And even some Hasidim. Not to mention those *goyishe* Israelis. Would they make trouble?

And, of course, there was the caterer. Would there be enough to eat, enough to drink? The groom's family was in charge of the liquor, so who knew?

And the *ketubah*! Mayer almost clapped his hand to his forehead in the middle of a prayer. The dowry portion was still blank, which meant the *ketubah* could not be signed, which meant there could be no wedding. Why wouldn't the *rebbe* let him finish? What was missing from Esther Teitel's dowry that could possibly be so important?

In Dov Taylor's apartment, Frank Hill was popping open another beer, a *New York Newsday* spread out on the table in front of him. "Hey," he called out, "there's a story here about the wedding. It says there are thirty thousand invited guests: twenty-five thousand on the groom's side, five thousand on the bride's. Incredible. And it says a lot more are going to show up in the streets. They're going to be closing off Bedford and Rodney for two blocks in every direction. In-fucking-credible. And I thought I had a big mick wedding. Jesus, I can just imagine five thousand of my wife's nutty relatives. It would be hell."

Taylor walked into the kitchen and poured himself a cup of coffee.

"It says printers all over the city were competing for the invitation order," Hill continued. "It says there are over eighty chartered buses to shuttle people between Crown Heights and Williamsburg, one hundred and forty ushers, and fifty attendants.

"It says there are over a hundred thousand Satmarers, with twenty-five thousand in Brooklyn. It says there are four hundred thousand Lubavitchers worldwide, thirty-five thousand in Brooklyn. Did you know that?"

"The Hasids never discuss numbers," said Taylor. "They think it attracts the evil eye. Once they get past thirteen, they never tell you how old they are."

"Just like my wife," said Hill. "The reception's going to be at Pratt, in the gym."

"I know," Taylor said.

"It says there's going to be two entrances to the gym, one for the men, one for the women, and they'll be sitting at separate tables. Wild." The telephone rang. Taylor picked it up and nodded to Hill.

"You will bring the stone to the wedding," the voice said.

"The girl will be there?"

"You will bring the stone."

"Sarah Kalman will be there, at the wedding?" Taylor repeated.

The voice was silent.

"How will I find you? How will I recognize you?" Taylor demanded.

The line went dead.

"I guess he'll find you," said Hill, putting down the extension. "Think again, Taylor. The girl didn't say anything about where she might've hid the diamond?"

Taylor put his hand under his shirt, touching the raised keloid scar that had formed over the wound the Cutter had left him. Frank Hill had searched the Kalman's home from top to bottom without turning up the diamond. It's lost, Taylor thought. Good. Let it stay lost.

The Cutter looked at Sarah Kalman, staring out of the dirty window in the tenement apartment on the Lower East Side, not ten blocks from where Dov Taylor and Frank Hill shared their vigil. For two days she had said nothing, eaten nothing. Her hair still gleamed. The Cutter's love for her grew. It was time to call the Magician. It was time for the last act. He had waited long enough.

But first the Cutter lifted up a handful of Sarah Kalman's hair. Like fire, he thought, so red. Like silk, he thought, so fine.

The scissors sliced through her hair, a sickle through ripe wheat. The Cutter let it fall to the floor, where it fanned out and flickered like a sunset. He lifted up another handful.

"I know it's traditional to cut the *kaleh*'s hair after the *khasseneh*," the Cutter said softly, apologetically, "but then there may be very little time. In any case, it is the final result that matters, yes?"

72

Williamsburg, Brooklyn
Tuesday, November 5

Three men stood behind the sawhorses that blocked off traffic on Rodney Street. They leaned against the doors of the patrol car and spoke into walkie-talkies. Two were dark and husky, and they wore the blue nylon windbreakers of New York City police officers; the third was a young, pale Hasid with a wispy blond beard, a black fedora, and the large, telltale bulge of a gun beneath his coat. Leaning over the sawhorse and shouting, Dov Taylor waved his invitation at the Hasid, as did two other men in suits standing next to him. The Hasid looked at them briefly, contemptuously, and then went back to shouting into his walkie-talkie. He had been ignoring Taylor and the others for the past ten minutes, and Taylor was cold and angry.

Beyond the sawhorses and the patrol car, Taylor could see other police units, ambulances, and fire trucks parked along Rodney Street. On the sidewalks, and spilling into the street, he saw the backs of thousands of Hasidim jostling each other, all moving in the same direction. He looked down the street, over their heads, toward Yetev Lev Synagogue. Stretched between lampposts, Hebrew banners overhung the street, and at the end of the long block, beneath the purpling sky, Taylor could see arc lights illuminating the flatbed trucks that were lined up to form a platform at the intersection of Bedford and Rodney. It's like a night game at Shea Stadium, he thought. He checked his watch. It was seven o'clock, almost time for the first pitch. Then, far away, he caught sight of the top of the *khupa*, the wedding canopy.

"Hey," Taylor called to one of the police officers, waving his invitation in the air, "can you give me a hand here?"

The cop walked over slowly, looked at the invitation,

shrugged, and slowly walked back to the young Hasid. He poked him and said something Taylor couldn't make out. The Hasid lowered his walkie-talkie and trotted over to Taylor.

"What do you want?" he asked gruffly, and Taylor suddenly thought that this Hasid looked extremely familiar. For some reason, despite the fact that he had been treating Taylor rudely, Taylor felt well disposed toward him.

"I'd like to get through," Taylor said, holding up his invitation. The two men standing next to Taylor also thrust their invitations at the Hasid. "I'm invited to the wedding," one of them shouted.

The Hasid grabbed Taylor's invitation and held it up close to his face, studying it as if he were a border guard and it was a suspicious passport. Then he looked back at Taylor. "How did you get this?" he demanded.

"In the ordinary way," Taylor said. "I'm a guest."

At that moment a Hasid came up behind Taylor and shouldered him aside. He called out the young Hasid's name (it was Motl, as Taylor knew it would be) and said a few words to him in Yiddish. Motl pulled the sawhorse back to let the man through. Then he replaced it and began walking away with Taylor's invitation still in his hand.

"Hey!" shouted Taylor. "Come back here! Where are you going? *Vu geyt ir, Motl?*" he yelled, summoning up the little Yiddish Sarah Kalman had taught him. "*Kum tsurik, Motl.*" Come back.

The Hasid turned around and stalked back to Taylor.

"How do you know my name?" Motl asked in English.

"You'd be surprised what I know," said Taylor. "For example, I know you want to protect the bride and bridegroom, and the wedding ceremony. I respect that. And believe me, Motl, that's what I want to do, too. Our interests are the same. Just as before."

"I don't know what you're talking about. You're crazy. Who are you?" Motl demanded.

"I'm a friend of Rabbi Kalman's" said Taylor. "I'm also a friend of Rebbe Teitel's. I'm a friend of both Satmar and Lubvavitch."

The Hasid squinted at Taylor and began twisting his blond beard nervously.

"I'm telling you," Taylor said patiently, remembering how little anger had availed Hirsh Leib with this Motl back at the Seer's *hoyf* in Lublin, "I'm a guest of the *rebbe*'s. I know the *gabbai*, Pinchus Mayer. The *gabbai* invited me personally. *Farshtey*, Motl? Understand?"

"For chrissakes, Motty," said one of the police officers. "Let the guy through. What the hell do you want from him? Blood? He's got a fucking invite."

Motl handed Taylor's invitation back to him and then pulled the sawhorse away, allowing Taylor to pass. *"Gay gezunt,"* he heard Motl say. Taylor turned and looked at Motl, whose face was twisted as if he were working out a difficult problem in Torah.

"I don't understand, either," said Taylor. *"Gay gezunt"*—Go in health—and then he plunged into the crowd, working his way toward the light.

Taylor pushed and shoved. The gun in his shoulder holster bruised his ribs.

It's the same, he thought. The same excited crowd, the same Hasids in black. What difference, after all, did a hundred and seventy-nine years make? It's all the same to these people, and now it's all the same to me. The same smells of onions and cabbage and sweat. The same sense of being buffeted by arms and legs and chests. The same feeling of losing control. The same fear of being swept off my feet, of losing my balance, of falling, of being trampled.

Panic rose in Taylor's chest. Would there be a knife waiting for me? he thought, the same knife that had waited for the Seer in the crowded streets of Lublin on *erev* Simkhas Torah, the same saber that had slashed down on my great-great-grandfather, Hirsh Leib, the *Zaddik* of Orlik? The sense of déjà vu was overwhelming.

Taylor was having trouble breathing. The street seemed more dense with people than the sidewalk, so he worked his way toward the edges of the crowd, moving down the block sideways, his back to the buildings along Rodney Street. That was better. At least his back was protected. He felt his heart slow down. He paused for a moment and felt for the small microphone that Frank Hill had taped to his chest that afternoon. "I'm through. I'm on the street," he said into his chest, knowing that his words would be picked up in the police van parked somewhere nearby. How anybody could get through this crowd to reach him if there was trouble was, however, another matter.

Somewhere, either on the street or in the synagogue, Taylor knew that Frank Hill would be keeping an eye out for him. Somehow that did not make him feel terribly secure. Somewhere in the crowd, Taylor knew, would be the men who were holding Sarah hostage.

He started moving again, with difficulty, through the happy throng.

All he could do was wait for them to approach him.

And ask for the Seer's stone.

Which he did not have.

Up ahead, the sky grew brighter, and Taylor knew he was nearing the flatbed trucks and the wedding canopy. He pushed on. Around him, men were already dancing in groups to the sound of Klezmer music piped through the loudspeakers, either trying out their steps for the wedding feast, already intoxicated, or simply unable to contain their excitement.

They'll be waiting next to the *khupa*, Taylor thought. That's where they'll be. In the heart of the crowd.

But where will Sarah be?

"Nothing yet," he said into his chest.

Taylor recalled his own wedding. He remembered the rabbi he hardly knew mumbling the Hebrew prayers neither he nor Carol could understand; he remembered standing under the *khupa* and stomping on the glass. Actually, now that he thought about it, he wasn't sure that it wasn't a flashbulb.

He remembered thinking that Carol looked terrible: she was wearing too much makeup; her hair was frozen in some awful style; the dress made her ass look fat. It was depressing. Weren't all brides supposed to be beautiful on their wedding day? Why not his?

Of course, he had been no prize. The pictures from the

wedding showed a young drunk and drug addict—slitted eyes and a slack mouth—a face he had seen a few thousand times in a few hundred AA meetings.

He remembered pouring too many drinks on top of the Percodans in his belly and falling asleep in the cab that took them to the airport hotel. He was so tired. And wasn't Carol angry when he couldn't get an erection that night. It was all a mistake. Carol, the wedding, a big mistake.

Were today's bride and groom—who, Taylor knew, had barely met—any stranger to each other than Carol and he had been on their wedding day or even, for that matter, after ten years of marriage?

Taylor fought to steady himself against the swirling crowd. He recalled what he knew about Orthodox weddings. By now, the bride, sitting on a chair piled high with pillows, surrounded by her friends and relatives, would have been veiled. Either the groom or the *badkhen* would have instructed her on her duties as a Jewish wife. Then grain would have been sprinkled on both their heads to promote fertility.

Suddenly Taylor heard a roar. The Klezmer music stopped. A Hasid standing next to him shouted in English, "They're leading the *khossen*!" Everyone around him was shouting in English and Yiddish: "They're leading the *khossen*!"

Taylor lunged through another knot of men and suddenly found himself up against the side of the flatbed truck. The platform brushed his cheek. Looking up, he saw the billowing *khupa*, a huge blue-and-ivory sail with silver embroidery borne aloft on tall wooden poles held by four men.

Across the street, coming out of the synagogue, Taylor could see a procession of bearded men carrying tall, lighted candles, walking beneath strings of lights strung across the street. There looked to be ten—no, twenty of them. Then, between them, leaning against him, looking neither left nor right, Taylor could see a pale young man. That must be Adam Seligson, he thought. He looks sick. Well, Taylor thought, recalling what Rabbi Kalman had told him, he would have been fasting all day.

The procession made its way toward the lights, toward the *khupa*, and then mounted the steps onto the platform. Taylor spotted Rebbe Menachem Seligson, the grand Lubavitcher *rebbe*, being helped up the steps, a tall silk hat balanced on his enormous head, his gray beard flowing halfway down his chest. He looks fierce, Taylor thought, like an ancient king of Israel. He noticed that the *rebbe*'s lips were moving, but he didn't seem to be talking to anyone. He's singing to himself, Taylor decided. He's singing to his God.

My God? wondered Taylor. Perhaps. We'll see.

Rabbi Kalman should be among this group, Taylor thought, but he could not see him.

The men carrying the candles fanned out around the *khupa*, gathering on the left side of the platform, and as Adam Seligson took his place under it, another roar came from the crowd: "They're leading the *kaleh*! They're leading the *kaleh*!"

Taylor felt a hand on his shoulder. He spun around, preparing to drive his elbow into the assassin's throat. A large, burly, black-bearded Hasid stood smiling at him. "I thought it was you," he shouted over the noise of the crowd. "I told myself, It's him. I recognized the back of your head. You remember me?"

Taylor forced a grin as his heart pounded in his chest. Jesus, he thought. "Of course I remember you, Mr. Schumach. How are you?"

"Wonderful, wonderful," shouted Schumach. "Of course. How could anyone not be wonderful tonight? It is beautiful, yes?"

"Yes," said Taylor. "Beautiful."

"So, Mr. Detective. I don't hear that anyone catches the *momzers* who killed Zally, may he rest in peace, and poor Miss Stein."

"I'm still working on it, Mr. Schumach."

"Really? Wait," Morris Schumach said, rising up on his toes. "Here comes the bride."

Taylor turned. He could see, coming down the street from his right, another procession carrying candles, this one made up of young girls. Behind them walked Esther Teitel, dressed in white lace. Just behind her, marching with high steps like a toy soldier on parade, Taylor saw Rebbe Joel Teitel. For a moment Taylor imagined that their eyes met.

I may disappoint you, Taylor thought, and as if Teitel had read his mind, he saw the *zaddik* nod.

The bride's party mounted the steps of the platform. Then Esther Teitel and her friends and relatives began circling the *khupa*. They walked seven times around as the cantor sang, his voice booming through the loudspeakers ringing the platform, echoing down Rodney Street. To Taylor, standing just below a speaker, it sounded like the voice of God himself. He could feel the bass in his belly and chest; he could feel his bones vibrating.

After the seventh round, Esther Teitel stepped forward, joining Adam Seligson under the *khupa*, standing to his right. A rabbi Taylor did not recognize stepped in front of them and lifted the bride's veil for a moment, then let it fall.

The cantor had stopped. The crowd had grown still. Taylor looked around him, hoping to see Sarah Kalman's face somewhere. He stood up on his toes, hoping that someone would see him. Where were they? He turned around to look behind him. Morris Schumach was gone.

Under the *khupa*, Adam Seligson took a sip from a small crystal wineglass and held it out for Esther Teitel. She lifted her veil, bent her head, and drank.

The rabbi held up a document and began reading the wedding contract aloud in Hebrew. Was he talking about the Seer's stone right now? Taylor wondered. After a few minutes the rabbi finished, and the bride and groom bent to sign the paper.

Taylor saw Adam Seligson turn toward Esther Teitel, take her hand, place the ring on her finger, and mumble the prayer: "Behold, thou art consecrated unto me, according to the Law of Moses and Israel."

Now the crowd was absolutely silent. Taylor could hear the wedding party shuffling on the platform. He could hear the faint sound of traffic blocks away, a distant plane overhead, and the heavy breathing of the man pressing against him from behind. Taylor wanted to turn around, to look—was this Czartoryski? the Cutter?—but the crowd was pressed so tightly against the platform that it was impossible for him to move.

He could slip a knife between my ribs right now, he thought. I wouldn't even fall; I'd die standing up.

Where were they?

Up on the platform Taylor heard a stomp, heard the crowd roar *"Mazl tov!"* and knew that the groom had broken the glass.

Suddenly he was spun around and hugged hard by a chunky Hasid burying his head in Taylor's chest. Then he was released, spun around again, and hugged by another. People were pounding his back, pounding his shoulders. All around him men were congratulating each other, embracing, weeping, shouting. The Klezmorim started up, the clarinet wailing, the violins shrieking, the drums and cymbals crashing double time. The wedding was over; the party had begun.

The crowd surged, carrying him away from the platform, back down Rodney Street, toward the Pratt Institute Gymnasium on DeKalb and Willoughby for the wedding dinner. It was futile to resist, so Taylor went with the flow.

Where were they? Where was Czartoryski, the Cutter, Sarah? What was happening?

Taylor ducked into a doorway and felt for the microphone taped to his chest. It was gone. He stuck his hand under his coat, into his shirt, and found it lying above his belt. The wires were torn. Taylor slipped it into his pocket.

Looking out from the doorway, Taylor saw the Hasidim streaming down the block. What could he do? He joined them. The gymnasium was only a few blocks away.

He felt someone come up on his left and catch his left wrist, bending it slightly forward. The ease and fluidity of the move shocked Taylor and shook his confidence. He recognized the hold and knew that whoever had him could break his wrist in an instant, break it before he could come close to getting his gun out of its holster.

"Are you Czartoryski?" Taylor asked the tall, thin Hasid walking next to him.

"Stop walking."

Taylor stopped. Without releasing his wrist, the Cutter stepped in front of Taylor.

"Do not move," the Cutter said. "I am going to take your gun. If you resist me, I will kill you."

Taylor looked at the Cutter's face, at his sorrowful eyes and hollow cheeks. There was no uncertainty in that face, no nervousness, no excitement. It was like looking at a corpse. Taylor allowed him to reach into his coat, take his weapon, and drop it into his pocket.

"Now start walking again, please," the Cutter said. "Do you have the diamond?"

"Do you have Sarah Kalman?" Taylor asked, and as soon as the words were out of his mouth, the pain in his wrist made him gasp. His knees buckled.

The Cutter pulled Taylor by the elbow, keeping him upright and walking. All around them on the dark street Hasids were hurrying toward the wedding feast, hoping to find a place near their *rebbe*'s table.

"I do not have the time to play with you," the Cutter said. "You will have the girl when I have the stone, *farshtay*?"

"No," said Taylor, preparing himself for the pain he knew was coming. "First the girl, then the stone."

Taylor felt the small bones in his wrist shatter. He bit down on his lip to keep from screaming. He thought he might pass out.

"I could kill you right here," the Cutter whispered in Taylor's ear. "There is a gun in my pocket. Feel it?" Taylor felt it in his ribs.

"I could kill you before you could cry out," the Cutter continued. "Believe me. I have done it before. Your wrist is broken now. I could put a bullet in your elbow. Then you will be a cripple for life. That would be lucky for you. Otherwise, I will put one in your eye. Then you will be dead. The stone, please."

Tears ran down Taylor's cheeks as he tried to move his left hand. He felt the Cutter's hand slide up his arm and come up underneath his armpit, finding the pressure point there.

"Fuck you," said Taylor, the rage building in his chest. Who was this man to threaten him, to hurt him? Who was this bastard to sacrifice Zalman Gottleib and Shirley Stein?

Ariel Levin, Maria Radziwell, and Carol Rosenberg? And now Sarah Kalman. This murderer of Jews. This Jewish Nazi.

"Fuck you," Taylor said again. "You Nazi fuck. I don't care what the fuck you do, no stone unless I see the girl. Go ahead, kill me; you'll never get it."

"Then come," said the Cutter, pulling Taylor forward. "You shall see. You shall see I am not a Nazi. Not me. You shall be a witness."

They were moving down the street now, almost running, moving faster even than the Hasidim rushing to the wedding feast. They passed an ambulance, and Taylor saw people being ministered to. They passed the patrol cars, and Taylor saw cops leaning against their units.

He was sweating now, his wrist throbbing, his fingers growing numb. The Cutter's gun dug into his ribs.

They crossed DeKalb Avenue, and Taylor saw the bright entrance of the Pratt Institute. He saw the crowd divide—the women heading for the Willoughby Avenue entrance, the men for DeKalb.

"Your invitation," the Cutter said to him. "Give it to me." Taylor reached into his pocket with his right hand and handed the invitation to the Cutter.

"You think I am a Nazi?" the Cutter said as they pushed their way across the street. They slammed into the crowd in front of the entrance, and the pain in Taylor's wrist took his breath away. His vision grew dark around the edges. He heard a clarinet screeching; it sounded like a lunatic laughing.

"I killed Nazis," the Cutter said. "Thousands of them. You don't believe me? I fought the enemies of Israel. You'll see. I was in the camps," he said, grunting as they bulled their way toward the doors, the Cutter striking out with his left arm, warding people off, pulling Taylor along with his hand on Taylor's elbow; Taylor fighting to keep from passing out from the exquisite agony of his shattered wrist.

"I watched them take my family, my mother and father and brothers and sisters," the Cutter hissed into Taylor's ear. "I stood up to my waist in Jewish blood. My father was a slaughterer. I looked into his mouth for gold when he was dead. It poisoned my stomach forever. The pain, I could die from it. I planted dynamite up the arses of the English for the Jews. I ate their hearts. You call me a Nazi? Who are you? What do you know? You don't deserve the woman."

They were inside the building, entering the gymnasium. The Klezmorim were shrieking away. A white trellis draped with a dark green plastic grapevine ran the length of the room, dividing the men from the women. A long table covered with a white tablecloth was pushed up against the back of the gym. It stretched from one end of the room to the other, while smaller tables were scattered across the floor. Two Hasids were dancing atop the long table. Taylor saw the Satmarer *rebbe* clapping and laughing.

"Where is she?" Taylor asked, his mouth dry, his lips cracked. He felt the mouth of the Cutter's gun pressing against his vertebrae, urging him forward.

"There is a room," the Cutter said from behind him, leaning forward over Taylor's shoulder to be heard above the roar of the Klezmorim. "In this room is the real marriage. What you saw before is just business. Contracts. But after the business is done, the *kaleh* and *khossen* go into this room alone, alone for the first time. No one must go in but them. They go in through one door as strangers, they come out another door married. That is where we go. That is where you'll see."

They left the gymnasium by a side door and headed down a hall. After the mob scene on the street and the crush through the Institute's doors, the hallway seemed almost empty, although Hasids continued pouring into the building.

They stopped in front of a door. The Cutter opened it and motioned for Taylor to step inside.

A small, compact, elderly man with white hair and red cheeks, wearing a beautifully tailored gray pinstripe suit with a black-and-green tie, stood in the center of an ordinary classroom that had had all its seats taken out. There was an automatic pistol in his hand, pointing toward the floor. A woman with short red hair sat on an elaborately carved wooden chair. She stared at the floor. The gun hung by her cheek. Taylor recognized Sarah Kalman.

"You cut her hair? Why did you cut her hair?" Taylor asked the man.

"Ah, you'll have to ask my friend that," the man said, indicating the Cutter. "Some Jewish custom, I imagine. My name is Ladislaw Czartoryski, Mr. Taylor. I believe you have something that belongs to me."

"Sarah," said Taylor.

Sarah Kalman looked up at Taylor, her face drawn, her skin pale. She nodded.

"When you and your friend put down your guns," said Taylor, "and when I am standing outside the door with Miss Kalman, I'll tell you where the stone is."

"You were instructed to have the stone on your person," said Czartoryski. "You were told to bring it with you. You do not have it?"

"No," said Taylor.

"Truthfully?" said Czartoryski. "You are serious?"

"Yes."

"That was foolish, Mr. Taylor," said Czartoryski. "Incredibly foolish. Fatally foolish for Miss Kalman. Even though you do not wear a beard, you run true to type. Even with the young woman at the point of death, you bargain, you bluff, you try to gain an advantage. I see that you do not understand. Well, I must make you understand."

Czartoryski's eyes left Taylor's and turned toward Sarah Kalman. His gun hand moved toward her temple.

"No!" Taylor shouted. Czartoryski turned back to Taylor, and as he did Taylor heard an explosive sigh. A small black hole suddenly appeared just below Czartoryski's left eye, and blood began to seep out of the hole and run down his pink cheek. The gun fell out of his hand. He swayed. Another sigh, and another hole appeared above the eye, toward the center of his forehead.

The Magician saw a surging pool of water open at his feet. Its waters were a deep cerulean, and a thousand diamonds flashed in its ripples. So lovely. So inviting. Was there any reason to tarry here? None.

He threw himself into the dark waters, reaching for the gems. The diamonds fled from his touch. The water was cold.

Cold and dark. Blind, he plunged toward the bottom of the pool. He began to shiver. It is too damn cold, he thought. I shall shiver myself to pieces.

And then, he did.

Sarah Kalman jumped out of her chair and ran toward a dresser piled high with flowers, incongruous in the otherwise empty classroom.

Taylor turned to the Cutter, who stood, his silenced gun in his hand, staring at the fallen Czartoryski. "You see?" said the Cutter, speaking to the air, his voice rising. "You see what a wonderful *badkhen* he makes. Sarah," said the Cutter, "you see? He reminds us that life is short. It can end, just like that. And yet we must laugh. Must we not laugh?

"You know," said the Cutter, turning to Taylor, "we called this one the Magician. But his magic has run out. And you called me a Nazi. There, there is a Nazi. I thought I could always tell a Nazi. I was wrong. You can never tell. I had to be told by that Israeli whore, told how I had been made a fool. Then I had to wait until he could play the *badkhen* at my wedding. It had to be a surprise to him. I think he was surprised.

"Now you," said the Cutter, "you will be the witness."

"I'll be your witness," Taylor said. "But where's the rest? Let's get nine more men to make a *minyan*. How can you get married without a proper *minyan*?"

"You don't see the rest of my witnesses?" the Cutter said. "There are thousands. Look around, all the dead, may God bless them. Now"—he lifted his gun level with Taylor's eyes—"you shall join them."

"But my dowry," said Sarah Kalman, walking toward the Cutter. "I can't get married without my dowry. What kind of beggar woman brings nothing to the *khasseneh*?"

"Your dowry will be the greatest any woman ever had," said the Cutter, and as he turned to look at Sarah, Taylor lunged for him, knocking his gun hand aside with his right hand, wrapping his left arm around the Cutter's neck. Throwing himself backward, Taylor crashed to the floor, pulling the Cutter on top of him.

The Cutter's fingers immediately found Taylor's broken

wrist and clamped down on it. A Roman candle of agony exploded behind his eyes, and at the tip of each fiery comet was a shimmering diamond.

Taylor pulled back and felt the Cutter's Adam's apple trying to wriggle away from the pressure. Just catch it, Taylor screamed at himself, all the while watching a thousand diamonds drifting through space, falling to earth. Catch it and crush it like a nut.

Taylor jerked backward as he felt the Cutter bring the butt of his pistol down on his wrist. He felt the bones sliding and crackling under the skin, and his eyes flew open to see Sarah Kalman, bending over, pulling at the Cutter's gun.

Again the butt of the pistol thudded into Taylor's wrist, and another rocket of pain exploded. He shut his eyes again, and again he saw the diamonds hurtling toward the earth, striking the ground, burying and extinguishing themselves in the rich soil where the Seer of Lublin could find one of them in his garden, a hundred and seventy-nine years before, entwined in the roots of a strange plant.

There is no before or after in the Torah, he heard Hirsh Leib say.

And Dov Taylor knew where the Seer's stone was hidden.

Taylor felt the Cutter's thumb dig into his wrist, and he screamed. But this time, instead of a rocket, instead of fireworks, a red flower bloomed behind his eyes to reveal Rebecca, his grandmother, smiling. And then her smile vanished and she began to cry, tear her hair, and scratch her cheeks. Blood ran down her cheeks.

"No!" screamed Taylor, shaking his head and squeezing harder. The Cutter's body jerked. Taylor heard the Cutter's palms slapping the floor, he heard a gurgling sound. Then the Cutter shuddered and grew still.

Triumph flamed in Taylor's chest and he roared aloud as he pulled back harder, bowing his back, almost lifting them both off the floor, trying to pull his arm right down through the Cutter's neck, trying to squeeze away all the anger and fear.

"Stop."

Taylor heard a voice, not the Cutter's.

"Stop."

Not Rebecca's. Not Hirsh Leib's.

"Stop."

It was his own.

He opened his eyes and saw Sarah Kalman.

He stopped.

He rolled the Cutter—still breathing but unconscious—off of him and stood up, breathless. He heard people shouting, pounding on the door. He looked at Sarah Kalman and opened his arms. She ran into them, her touch feathery, trembling. Like a bird. Like a wounded bird, he thought, stroking the top of her head. It broke his heart. It healed his heart.

When the door was flung open, that's how they were found, and they clung to each other as they were led back through the halls, back through the riotous gymnasium, where a flushed Adam Seligson was being held aloft atop a stool while men threw paper napkins at him.

Rebbe Joel Teitel appeared before Taylor. "So?" he asked. "The stone? Where is it?"

Taylor looked down at the *rebbe*. "I threw it away," he lied.

The *rebbe* stepped back, his hand flew up to his beard, and he began twisting it. He turned his head and saw his daughter sitting on a high stool, laughing, tears running down her face, while her friends danced a maypole dance around her, white ribbons swirling. He looked down at the floor, frowned, and then he looked up into Taylor's eyes and smiled.

"A *zaddik*," the *rebbe* said. "We have a *zaddik*," he said again, clapping his hands.

"God be praised, a *zaddik*!"

Epilogue
Brooklyn
Thursday, November 7

As HE KNEW HE WOULD, DOV TAYLOR HAD FOUND THE Seer's stone hidden in the bottom of the glass brick flower pot sitting on the windowsill in Moshe Kalman's old bedroom, entwined in the plant's roots. It was actually a very good hiding place, he thought. Through the glass, against the dirt, the diamond was utterly invisible. Maria had done a good job.

Now, as he leaned against the railing, the traffic on the Belt Parkway roaring above and behind him, the World Trade Towers looming over the harbor, a mountain of lights, he threw the Seer's stone out into the darkness, down into the dark waters.

He wasn't sure, but he thought he heard it splash.

He put his hands in his coat. Time to get myself to a meeting, he thought.

If anyone would believe that he could toss away a fortune, it would, he knew, be a roomful of drunks.

Afterword

I PROMISE NOT TO KEEP YOU MUCH LONGER, BUT I THOUGHT you might like to know that the *zaddikim* mentioned in Book Two of *Zaddik* are all historical figures, as are Adam Jerzy Czartoryski, Countess Catherine Radziwell, and Napoleon's mistress, Marie Waleska. Hirsh Leib is a composite figure based on several Hasidic masters.

Martin Buber, in his wonderful novel *For the Sake of Heaven*, imagined a "cosmic conspiracy" in which the *zaddikim* of that era joined forces to pray Napoleon Bonaparte on to victory. Napoleon, who in 1799 had called upon the Jews to rally under the French flag to liberate the Holy Land, was considered a friend to Europe's Jews.

As for the Seer of Lublin, it is recorded that he fell from the window of his study on *erev* Simkhas Torah the autumn before Napoleon's final defeat and final exile. The Seer suffered grievous injuries from which he never recovered.

It is also written that the window from which he allegedly fell was too small for any man to squeeze through, so the true circumstances of his death remain a mystery to this day—leaving us free to speculate.

Glossary

Aleinu (Hebrew). The closing prayer of each daily service.

Aleph-bes (Hebrew). The alphabet.

Alte kockers (Yiddish). Old shits.

Alte moyd (Yiddish). Old maid.

Aron kodesh (Hebrew). The Holy Ark containing the Torah.

Baal teshuvah (Hebrew). Literally, "one who has returned." Converts to Orthodox practice.

Balebatim (Hebrew). Literally, "houseowners." In Yiddish can be used positively, describing substantial people, or negatively, describing pompous big shots.

Badkhen (Hebrew). The man who makes merry at weddings.

Bekekher (Yiddish). The long, silken coat worn by Hasids on Sabbath and festival days.

Bes Din (Hebrew). A Jewish civil and religious court.

Bes-oylem (Hebrew). Cemetery.

Biber (Yiddish). Beaver, as in *biber* hat.

Bimah (Hebrew). The stand upon which the Torah rests when it is read in the synagogue.

Bord (Yiddish). Beard.

Briliant (Yiddish). A diamond.

Brukha (Hebrew). A blessing.

Bukher (Hebrew). A young man. Familiarly, a guy.

Bupkis (Yiddish). Literally, "beans." Something worthless.

Daven (Yiddish). To pray.

Dybbuk (Hebrew). An evil spirit, often one that possesses a living person.

Emes (Hebrew). Truth.

Erev (Hebrew). Eve. The day preceding a holiday.

Farbrengen (Yiddish). A Hasidic gathering.

Frum (Yiddish). Pious. As with a *frummer Yid*.

Gabbai (Hebrew). Literally, "treasurer." The manager of a synagogue or a *rebbe*'s household.

Get (Hebrew). A notice of divorce.

Glatt (Yiddish). Literally, "smooth." Used to define the strictest *kosher* foods.

Golem (Hebrew). A man-made figure in the form of a human being, endowed with life; an automaton created by Rabbi Judah Lowe to fight evil in Prague in the seventeenth century.

Gonef (Hebrew). A thief.

Gornit (Yiddish). Nothing.

Goy (Hebrew). A non-Jew.

Halakhah (Hebrew). Jewish religious law.

Hashem (Hebrew). One of the names for God.

Hasid (Hebrew). Literally, "pious." Describes a follower of a *rebbe* who leads a community of Jews practicing an ecstatic and, in modern times, fundamentalist brand of Judaism. Founded in the first half of the eighteenth century by the Baal Shem Tov.

Havdolah (Hebrew). The service ending the Sabbath.

Hazzan (Hebrew). A cantor.

Heymish (Yiddish). Homey.

Hondlen (Yiddish). To trade, to bargain.

Hoyf (Yiddish). A courtyard.

Kabbalah (Hebrew). Both the accumulation and the study of Jewish mystical thought. A highly abstruse and metaphysical system of thoughts and beliefs.

Kaddish (Hebrew). The prayer of sanctification.

Kaleh (Hebrew). The bride.

Kahal (Hebrew). The Jewish ruling body in the towns of Eastern Europe.

Kavanah (Hebrew). One's inner, holy intent.

Kapote (Hebrew). The black coat worn every day by Hasids.

Kashrus (Hebrew). The dietary laws followed by pious Jews.

Ketubah (Hebrew). A marriage contract.

Khasseneh (Hebrew). Wedding.

Khossen (Hebrew). The bridegroom.

Khevreh (Hebrew). A society or guild.

Kinder (Yiddish). Children.

Kishkes (Yiddish). Intestines.

Khupa (Hebrew). The canopy under which the bride and groom are married.

Kohanim (Hebrew). The decendants of the ancient Hebrew priest class.

Kop (Yiddish). Head.

Kosher (Hebrew). That which is fit and proper to eat or do.

Lamedvovniks (Hebrew). In Hasidic folklore, the thirty-six unknown righteous men for whose sake God preserves the world.

Lantsman (Yiddish). One's countryman.

Maggid (Hebrew). A preacher.

Mama-loshen (Hebrew). Literally, "mother tongue." Yiddish.

Mazl (Hebrew). Luck.

Melamed (Hebrew). A teacher of children.

Meshuggener (Hebrew). A crazy person.

Mezuzah (Hebrew). A scroll with two biblical passages rolled up inside a casing, affixed to the door frames of Jewish homes.

Mikvah (Hebrew). The ritual bath, prescribed to purify women after menstruation. Used also by pious men.

Minyan (Hebrew). The ten males necessary for prayers to be heard. A quorum.

Mitzvah (Hebrew). Literally, a commandment. A good deed.

Momzer (Hebrew). A bastard.

Nofke (Yiddish). A whore.

Nar (Yiddish). A fool.

Nareshkayt (Yiddish). Foolishness.

Nigun (Hebrew). A wordless Hasidic tune, often composed by a *rebbe*.

Nudzh (Yiddish). To pester, to nag.

Payes (Yiddish). The sidelocks worn by Hasidic boys.

Pidyan (Hebrew). A gift of money made to a *rebbe* in return for his blessing.

Porets (Hebrew). A lord or nobleman.

Prost (Yiddish). Working class; vulgar.

Rabbi, reb, rebbe, rov (Hebrew). "Rabbi" literally means teacher. A rabbi can be hired to lead any religious congregation. *Reb* is an honorific term, much like "mister." A *rebbe* is the spiritual leader of a Hasidic community. He has often inherited his mantle of leadership from a male relative. A *rov* can be any authority on religious matters.

Rebbetzin (Hebrew). A rabbi's wife.

Sefiros (Hebrew). In *kabbalistic* thought, these are the ten hidden attributes of God.

Shabbos (Hebrew). The Sabbath.

Shammes (Hebrew). Literally, "servant." The caretaker of a synagogue.

Sheitl (Yiddish). The wig worn by married Hasidic women as a sign of modesty.

Shekhita (Hebrew). The ritual slaughtering necessary to make meats *kosher*.

Shema (Hebrew). Literally, "hear." The call to worship; the prayer that expresses the central Jewish beliefs.

Sheyne (Yiddish). Beautiful.

Sheyne meydele (Yiddish). Beautiful, or simply nice girl.

Sheyner Yid (Yiddish). Literally, "beautiful Jew." An observant, educated, important member of the community.

Shidukh (Hebrew). A match for a marriage.

Shiker (Hebrew). A drunkard.

Shikh un zoken (Yiddish). Literally, "shoes and socks." The nineteenth-century-style slippers and stockings worn by extremely pious Hasids.

Shiksa (Hebrew). A non-Jewish woman. Derogatory.

Shmooze (Yiddish). To chat.

Shnor (Yiddish). To borrow or beg habitually and brazenly.

Shoykhet (Hebrew). A ritual slaughterer.

Shtarker (Yiddish). A strong man; a thug, a gangster.

Shtetl (Yiddish). A small Jewish village.

Shtibl (Yiddish). Literally, "little house." A small, neighborhood synagogue.

Shtot (Yiddish). A town, larger than a *shtetl*.

Shtreiml (Yiddish). The round fur hat worn by pious or well-to-do Hasids.

Shul (Yiddish). A synagogue or school.

Shvartzer (Yiddish). Literally, "a black one." An African-American.

Sidur (Hebrew). A prayer book.

Sofer (Hebrew). A scribe.

Sukkah (Hebrew). The makeshift hut in which Jews are commanded to dwell during the Feast of Tabernacles.

Tallis (Hebrew). The prayer shawl worn by men at most prayer services.

Talmud (Hebrew). The massive compendium of all the commentaries upon the Torah.

Takeh (Yiddish). Really.

Tateh (Yiddish). Father.

Tayvl (Yiddish). The devil.

Tefillin (Hebrew). Two leather straps—one for the left arm, the other for the head—each with a small box attached containing biblical passages. Worn by Orthodox Jewish males for the morning prayers.

Tokhter (Yiddish). Daughter.

Torah (Hebrew). Literally, "teaching." The scrolls containing the five books of Moses: Genesis, Exodus, Leviticus, Numbers, and Deuteronomy.

Treyf (Hebrew). That which is un*kosher*.

Tsdokeh (Hebrew). Charity.

Tsimmes (Hebrew). A stew.

Tzitzis (Hebrew). The fringes at the corners of the prayer shawl.

Tsuris (Hebrew). Troubles.

Yahrzeit (Yiddish). The anniversary of a death. Noted by the lighting of a special candle.

Yeshiva (Yiddish). An advanced religious school.

Yid (Yiddish). A Jew.

Yiddish (Yiddish). Literally, "Jewish." The language of Eastern European Jewry. Its vocabulary is about 70 percent

German-derived, 20 percent Hebrew, and 10 percent Slavic and, recently, English. It is written using the Hebrew alphabet.

Yikhus (Hebrew). Literally, "pedigree." What one receives from one's forebears.

Yontif (Yiddish). A holiday.

Zaddik (Hebrew). A righteous man, a saint.